Burr Junior

George Manville Fenn

Illustrated by Harold C. Earnshaw

ESPRIOS DIGITAL PUBLISHING

Chapter One.

"There'll be such a game directly. Just listen to old Dicksee."

I was very low-spirited, but, as the bright, good-looking lad at my side nudged me with his elbow, I turned from casting my eyes round the great bare oak-panelled room, with its long desks, to the kind of pulpit at the lower end, facing a bigger and more important-looking erection at the upper end, standing upon a broad daïs raised a foot above the rest of the room. For this had been the banqueting hall of Meade Place, in the good old times of James the First, when its owner little thought it would ever be the schoolroom of Dr Browne's "Boarding Establishment for Gentlemen's Sons." In fact, there was a broad opening now, with a sliding door, right through the thick wall into the kitchen, so my companion told me, and that I should see the shoulders of mutton slip through there at dinner-time.

So I looked at the lower pulpit, in which sat Mr Rebble, one of the ushers, a lank, pale-faced, haggard man, with a dotting of freckles, light eyebrows, and pale red hair which stood up straight like that upon a clothes-brush.

He was resting his elbows on the desk and wiping his hands one over the other, as if the air was water and he had a piece of soap between his palms. By him was a boy with a book, reading in a highly-pitched voice which did not seem to fit him, being, like his clothes, too small for such a big fellow, with his broad face and forehead all wrinkled up into puckers with the exertion of reading.

"Tchish! tchish! Silence!" said Mr Rebble, giving three stamps on the floor. "Now go on, Dicksee."

"I say, do listen," said the boy by my side. "He isn't well, and I gave him a dose this morning."

"You did?" I said. "You hit him?"

"No, no," said the boy, laughing. "I often do though—a miserable sneak. I gave him a dose of medicine. He had been eating too many of Polly Hopley's cakes. My father is a doctor!" he added importantly.

"Oh!" I said.

"I say, do listen. Did you ever hear such a whine?"

As he spoke, I heard the big, stoutly-built boy give a tremendous sniff, and then go on reading.

"I love Penny Lope—Penny Lope is loved by me."

"Pen-el-o-pe!" cried the usher angrily, as he snatched the book from the boy's hands, closed it, and boxed his ears with it, right and left, over and over again. "You *dumkopf!*" he shouted; "you muddy-brained ass! you'll never learn anything. You're more trouble than all the rest of the boys put together. There, be off to your seat, and write that piece out twenty-five times, and then learn it by heart."

"Ow, ow, ow! sniff, sniff, snork!"

"Silence, sir, or I'll make the imposition fifty times!"

The howl subsided into a series of subdued sniffs as the big fellow went back to his place, amidst the humming noise made by some

2

fifty boys, who, under the pretence of studying their lessons, kept up conversations, played at odd or even for marbles, or flicked peas at each other across the school.

"Old Reb wouldn't dare to hit him like that if the Doctor was here."

"Your father?" I said.

"No, no—old Swish! Doctor Browne."

Flick-tip.

A pea struck my companion on the ear, and dropped on the floor.

"All right, Burr," said my neighbour; "did that with a pea-shooter. I owe you one."

"I didn't do it!" I whispered eagerly.

"Of course you didn't. It was that long, thin boy yonder. His name's Burr too. He'll be Burr major now, and you'll be Burr junior."

"Oh!" I said, feeling much relieved.

"You'll have to lick him. Regular old bully. Your name's Frank, isn't it?"

"Yes."

"His name's Eliezer. We call him Eely, because he's such a lanky, thin, snaky chap. I say, his father's a tailor in Cork Street, he's got such lots of clothes in his box. He has a bob-tail coat and black kersey sit-upon-'ems, and a vesky with glass buttons, and all covered with embroidery. Such a dandy!—What's your father?"

I did not answer for a few moments, and he looked at me sharply.

"Dead," I said in a low voice.

"Oh!" said my companion softly too. "I didn't know."

"He was shot—out in India—Chillianwallah," I said.—"Died of his wounds."

"Oh, I am sorry! I wish my father had been there."

"Why?"

"He'd have cured him. There's nobody like him for wounds. But, I say, Chillian what's its name?"

"Chillianwallah," I said.

"Why, what a game! That's where old Lomax was. I remember now."

"Is Lomax one of the boys," I asked wonderingly.

"Yah! no. You saw him last night, when you came in the fly. That big chap who lives at the lodge, and helped lift down your box. He had a shot through him, and nearly had his head cut off with a tully something. He'll tell you. He has a pension, and is our drill-master, and teaches boys riding."

This was interesting, and I felt a desire to know old Lomax.

"What's your mother?" said my companion, breaking in upon my musing.

"A lady," I said proudly.

"So's mine. She's the nicest and best and—" At that moment I heard a loud, deep-throated cough, which was followed by a shuffling and stamping, as I saw all the boys rise in their places.

"Get up—get up," whispered my neighbour. "The Doctor."

4

I rose in my place, and saw the tall, stout, clerical-looking gentleman I had seen when I reached Meade Place on the previous night, enter by the middle door, and look gravely and smilingly round.

"Good morning, gentlemen," he said. "Good morning, Mr Rebble;" and then he marched solemnly to the pulpit on the daïs, took his place, waved his hand, there was a repetition of the rustling and shuffling as the boys reseated themselves, and then the humming murmur of the school recommenced.

"I say, how old are you?" whispered my companion.

"Sixteen—nearly," I replied.

"Well, that is rum. So am I. So's lots of fellows here. Where did you go to school before?"

"Nowhere. Had a private tutor at home."

"Well, you must be a muff."

"Why?"

"To give up a private tutor all to yourself to come to school here."

"Obliged to. Uncle said I should grow into a—"

I stopped short.

"Well, what?"

"Less talking there," said Mr Rebble.

"Mind your own business," muttered my neighbour. "What did he say you'd grow into?"

"A milksop; and that I must come and rough it among other boys."

"Ha! ha! what a game! You will have to rough it too, here. I say, who's uncle?"

"My uncle, Colonel Seaborough."

"What's he?—a soldier too?"

"Yes; and I'm going to be a soldier by and by."

"Well, you are a lucky one! Wish I had an uncle who said I should be a soldier. I shall have to be a doctor, I suppose."

Just then, the tall, thin boy pointed out to me a few minutes before as Burr major, came across in a bending, undulating way, with an open book in his hand, glanced up and down to see that the Doctor and his lieutenant were both occupied, and then slipped into the seat at our long desk on the other side of my neighbour, who did not give him time to speak, but began rapidly,—

"I say, this new chap says he'll give you such a leathering if you shoot peas at him."

"Eh? Like to see him begin," said the fresh comer, with a contemptuous look at me. "I say, Senna T, you're in for it."

"What for?"

"Old Dicksee says you gave him some stuff last night, and it's made him so bad he can't learn his lessons. He's going to tell the Doctor."

"Gammon! What do you want?"

"Less talking there," said Mr Rebble sharply.

"Hark at old Reb!" whispered the new-comer. "I say, we're going to have a holiday to-day, ain't we?"

"No such luck."

"Oh, but we must! I've written this out. You'll sign, won't you?"

My neighbour snatched a document consisting of about half a dozen lines, and pushed it back.

"He'll keep us in if we do."

"Not he. I know he wants to drive over to Hastings with the girls. Sign, there's a good chap."

"But you haven't signed."

"No. I shall put my name last."

"Yah! Can't catch old birds with chaff, Eely."

"If you call me Eely again, I'll punch your head."

"You sign first, and I'll put my name next."

"Shan't! and if you don't put your name at once, I'll tear up the paper. I don't want a holiday; it was all for you boys."

"Thank-ye," said my neighbour derisively.

"Just you wait till we're out in the field, Jalap, and I'll serve you out for this."

"Burr junior," said a rich, deep, unctuous voice, which seemed to roll through the school, and there was a dead silence.

"Here, you!—get up. Go on."

"Burr junior!" came in a louder, deeper voice.

"He means you," whispered my neighbour.

"Say *Adsum*," whispered the tall, thin boy, and, on the impulse given, I repeated the Latin word feebly.

"Go up to him," whispered my neighbour, and, pulling my legs out from between the form and the desk, I walked up through the centre opening between the two rows of desks, conscious of tittering and whispering, two or three words reaching my ears, such as "cane," "pickle," "catch it certain."

Then, feeling hot and confused, I found myself on the daïs in front of the desk, where the Doctor was looking searchingly at me through his gold-rimmed spectacles. Then, turning himself round, he slowly and ponderously crossed one leg over the other, and waved his hand.

"Come to the side," he said, and feeling more conscious up there on the daïs, I moved round, and he took my hand.

"I am glad to welcome you among us, Frank, to join in our curriculum of study, and I hope you will do us all credit. Er—rum! Let me see. Burr—Frank Burr. We have another Burr here, who has stuck among us for some years."

The Doctor paused and looked round with a very fat smile, in the midst of a peculiar silence, till Mr Rebble at the other end said loudly,—

"Ha! ha! Excellent!" and there was now a loud burst of laughter.

I thought that I should not like Mr Rebble, but I saw that the Doctor liked his appreciation of his joke, for he smiled pleasantly, and continued,—

"Let me see. I think we have a pleasant little custom here, not more honoured in the breach than in the observance. Eh, Mr Rebble?"

"Certainly, sir, certainly," said that gentleman, and the Doctor frowned at his leg, as he smoothed it down. But his face cleared directly.

"Er—rum!" he continued, clearing his voice. "Of having a brief cessation from our studies upon the advent of a new boy. Young gentlemen, you may close your books for to-day."

There was a hearty cheer at this, and the Doctor rose, thrust his hand into his breast beside his white shirt-frill, then, waving the other majestically, he turned to me as the cheering ceased.

"Burr junior," he said, "you can return to your seat."

I stepped back, forgetting all about the daïs, and fell rather heavily, but sprang up again, scarlet with mortification.

"Not hurt? No? That's right," said the Doctor; and amid a chorus of "Thank you, sir! thank you, sir!" he marched slowly out of the great room, closely followed by Mr Rebble, while I stood, shaken by my fall, and half dazed by the uproar.

Chapter Two.

How strange it all seemed! I had ridden down the previous day by
the Hastings coach, which had left me with my big box at the old inn
at Middlehurst. Here the fly had been ordered to take me the
remaining ten miles on to the school, where I had arrived just at
dusk, and, after a supper of bread and milk, I was shown my bed,
one of six in a large room, and made the acquaintance of Mercer,
who, after pretty well peppering me with questions, allowed me to
go to sleep in peace, till the bell rang at six, when I sprang out of bed,
confused and puzzled at finding myself there instead of at home.
Then, as the reality forced itself upon me, and I was scowled at by
five sleepy boys, all in the ill-humoured state caused by being
obliged to get up before they pleased, I hurriedly dressed, thinking
that I could never settle down to such a life as that, and wondering
what my uncle and my mother would say if I started off, went
straight back, and told them I did not mean to stop at school.

Everything looked cheerless and miserable, for there was a thick fog
outside, one which had been wafted over from the sea, so that there
was no temptation to go out, and, in spite of my low spirits, I was
hungry enough to make me long for breakfast.

This was laid for us in the schoolroom, to which the boys flocked, as
the big bell on the top of the building rang out again, and here I
found that there were two long tables, as I supposed, till I was
warned about being careful, when I found that they were not tables,
but the double school-desks with the lids of the boys' lockers
propped up horizontal.

"And if you don't mind, down they come, and your breakfast goes
outside instead of in," said Mercer.

Milk and water and bread and butter, but they were good and
plentiful, and though I was disappointed at first, and began thinking
of the hot coffee at home, I made a better breakfast than I had
expected; and in due course, after a walk round the big building, of

which I could see nothing for the chilly fog, the bell rang again, and I had to hurry back into the schoolroom, taking a seat pointed out for me by Mercer, with the result related in the last chapter.

"Here, come along!" cried my new friend: "What a game! You are a good chap. I wish a new boy would come every day. Hooray! old Rebble's off. Bet sixpence he goes down to the river bottom-fishing. He never catches anything. Goes and sits in his spectacles, blinking at his float, and the roach come and give it a bob and are off again long before he strikes. Hi yi yi yi!" he shouted; "here we are again!" and, jumping on to the form and from there to the desk, he bent down, took lightly hold of the sides, threw up his heels, and stood on his head.

"Here, look at old Mercer!" cried a boy.

"Bravo, Senna T!" cried another.

A dictionary flew across the room, struck the amateur acrobat in the back, and fell on the floor, but not much more quickly than my new friend went over backwards, the blow having made him overbalance so that his feet came with a crash on the desk, the ink flew out of two little leaden wells, and the performer rolled off on to the form, and then to the floor, with a crash.

"Here!" he cried, springing up. "Who did that? Give me that book. Oh, I know!" he cried, snatching the little fat dictionary, and turning over the leaves quickly. "'Eely-hezer Burr.' Thanky, I wanted some paper. I'm all over ink. What a jolly mess!"

As he spoke, he tore out three or four leaves, and began to wipe the ink off his jacket.

"I say, Burr," cried the big boy who had read about Penelope, "Mercer's tearing up your dictionary."

"You mind your own business!" cried Mercer, tearing out some more leaves, and then throwing the book at the tale-teller just as the tall, thin boy, who bore the same name as I, came striding up with his face flushed and fists doubled, to plant three or four vigorous blows in Mercer's chest and back.

"How dare you tear my book?" he cried. "Here, you, fat Dicksee, bring it here."

"Thought you meant me to use it," cried Mercer, taking the blows good-humouredly enough. "Oh, I say, don't! you hurt!"

"Mischievous beggar!" said my senior taking the book and marching off.

"Go on! Ask your father to buy you a new one," cried Mercer derisively, as he applied a piece of blotting-paper to one leg of his trousers. "Hiss! Goose!"

"Do you wish me to come back and thrash you, Tom Mercer," said the tall boy, with a lordly manner.

"No, sir, thank-ye, sir; please don't, and I'll never do so no more, sir."

"Miserable beggar," said Burr major. "Here, Dicksee, come down the field and bowl for me. Bring five or six little uns to field."

"Yah! Tailor!" said Mercer, as his bully marched out.

"I'll tell him what you said," cried Dicksee.

"Hullo, Penny loaf! you there? Yes, you'd better tell him. Just you come to me for some physic, and you'll see how I'll serve you."

"Don't ketch me taking any of your stuff again," cried the big, fat, sneering-looking fellow. "I'll tell him, and you'll see."

"Go and tell him then," said Mercer contemptuously. "So he is a tailor, and his father's a tailor. Why, I saw his name on a brass plate in Cork Street."

"So's your father got his name on a brass plate," sneered Dicksee.

"Well, what of that? My father's a professional gentleman. Here, come on, Burr, and I'll show you round. Hooray! the sun's come through the mist. Where's your cap? All right. You'll have to get a square trencher by next Sunday. This way."

He led me out into the big playground, and turned.

"Ain't a bad house, is it? Some big lord used to live here, and Magglin says his father says it was empty for years, and it was sold cheap at last to the Doctor, who only used to have four boys at first."

"Who's Magglin?"

"Ha, ha!" laughed Mercer; "he calls himself a gardener because he comes here to help dig, but I know: he's a poacher, that's what he is. You ask Hopley."

"But I don't know Hopley," I said, laughing.

"You soon will. He's General Rye's keeper. I buy birds off him to stuff."

"What, geese?" I said, as I recalled that my companion spoke about a goose just before.

"Geese? no. Magpies and jays and hawks. I stuff 'em with tow; I'll show you how. Old Hopley says Magglin's a rank poacher, and first time he catches him on their grounds he'll pull him up before his master, you know. General's a magistrate. But he won't catch him. Magg's too artful. I say, got any money?"

"Yes, I have some," I said.

"That's right. Don't you spend it. You save up same as I am. Magg's got a gun I want to buy of him. He says he won't sell it, but I know better. He will when we offer him enough. I did offer him ten shillings, but he laughed at me. I say!"

"Yes."

"It's such a beauty. Single barrel, with a flint lock, so that it never wants no caps, and it comes out of the stock quite easy, and the barrel unscrews in the middle, and the ramrod too, so that you can put it all in your pocket, and nobody knows that you're carrying a gun."

"But what's the good of a gun here at school?"

"What? Oh, you don't know because it's all new to you. Why, there are hares in the fields, and pheasants in the coppices, and partridges in the hop-gardens, and the rabbits swarm in the hill-sides down toward the sea."

"But you don't shoot!"

"Not much, because I have no gun, only a pistol, and it don't carry straight. I did nearly hit a rabbit, though, with it."

"But can you get away shooting?"

"Can I? Should think I can. We have all sorts of fun down here. Can you fish?"

"I went once," I said, "on the river."

"But you didn't catch anything," said Mercer, grinning.

"No," I said; "I don't think I had a bite."

"Not you. Just you wait a bit, I'll take you fishing. There's the river where old Rebble goes, and the mill-pond where old Martin gives me leave, and a big old hammer pond out in the middle of General Rye's woods where nobody gives me leave, but I go. It's full of great carp and tench and eels big as boa-constrictors."

"Oh, come!" I said.

"I didn't say big boa-constrictors, did I? there's little ones, I daresay. Here we are. That's Magglin—didn't know he was here to-day."

He pointed out a rough, shambling-looking young man down the great kitchen garden into which he had led me. This gentleman was in his coat, and he was apparently busy doing nothing with a hoe, upon which he rested himself, and took off a very ragged fur cap to wipe his brow as we came up, saluting us with a broad grin.

"Hallo, Magg! you here? This is the new boy, Burr."

"Nay," said the man in a harsh, saw-sharpening voice, "think I don't know better than that? That aren't Master Burr."

"No, not that one. This is the new one. This is Burr junior."

"Oh, I see," said the man. "Mornin', Mr Burr juner. Hope I see you well, sir?"

"Oh, he's all right," said Mercer. "Give him a penny to buy a screw of tobacco, Frank."

I gave the required coin, and Mr Magglin spat on it, spun it in the air, caught it, and placed it in his pocket.

"Thank-ye," he said.

"Got any birds for me?"

"Nay, nary one; but I knows of a beauty you'd give your ears to get."

"What is it?" cried Mercer eagerly.

"All bootiful green, with a head as red as carrots."

"Get out! Gammon! Think I don't know better than that? He means a parrot he's seen in its cage."

"Nay, I don't," said the man. "I mean a big woodpecker down in Squire Hawkus Rye's woods."

"Oh, Magg: get it for me!"

"Nay, I dunno as I can. Old Hopley's on the look-out for me, and if I was to shoot that there bird, he'd swear it was a fezzan."

"Perhaps it is," said Mercer, laughing.

"Nay, not it, my lad," said the man, with a sly-looking smile. "If it was a fezzan I shouldn't bring it to you."

"Why not? I should like to stuff it."

"Daresay you would, my lad, but if I did that, somebody would stuff me."

"Ha, ha!" laughed Mercer. "You'd look well in a glass case, Magg."

"Shouldn't look well in prison," said the man, laughing. "Why, what'd become o' the Doctor's taters?"

"Oh, bother the taters. I say, what about that gun, Magg?"

"What about what gun?" said the man softly, as he gave a sharp glance round.

"Get out! You know."

"Whish!" said the man. "Don't you get thinking about no guns. I wouldn't ha' showed it to you if I'd known. Why, if folks knew I had a gun, there'd be no end of bother, so don't you say nothing about it again."

"Well, then, sell it to me. Burr here's going to join me."

The man gave me a quick glance, and shook his head. "I don't sell guns," he said.

"Then will you shoot that woodpecker for me?"

"Nay, I mustn't shoot, they'd say I was a poacher. I'll try and get it for you, though, only it'll be a shilling."

"Can't afford more than ninepence, Magg."

"Ninepence it is then; I don't want to be hard on a young gentleman."

"But if it's all knocked to pieces and covered with blood, I shall only give you sixpence."

"Oh, this'll be all right, sir."

"When shall you shoot it?"

"Ha'n't I told you I aren't going to shoot it?"

"How will you get it, then?"

"Put some salt on its tail," said the man grinning. "Get out! Here, I say, could we catch some tench in the mill-pond to-day?"

"Mebbe yes, mebbe no."

"Well, we're going to try. You have some worms ready for me—a penn'orth."

"Tuppence, sir."

"A penny. Why, you've just had a penny for nothing."

"All right, master. Going?"

"Yes, I'm showing him round," said Mercer. "Come along, Burry, we'll go and see old Lomax now."

He led the way out of the kitchen garden, and round by a field where the Doctor's Alderney cows were grazing, then through a shrubbery to the back of the thatched cottage I had dimly seen as the fly drove by the previous night.

"Left, right! Three quarters half face. As you never were. Left counter-jumper march! Halt stare at pease!"

All this was shouted by Mercer as we approached the cottage door, and had the effect of bringing out a stiff-looking, sturdy, middle-aged man with a short pipe in his mouth, which he removed, carried one hand to his forehead in a salute, and then stood stiff and erect before us, looking sharply at me.

"Mornin', gentlemen," he said.

"Morning," cried Mercer. "'Tention! Parade for introductions. This is Field-Marshal Commander-in-Chief Drill-master and Riding-master Lomax. This is Burr junior, new boy, come to see you. I say, Lom, he's going to be a soldier. His father was a soldier in India. He was killed at what's-its-name?—Chilly winegar."

"Eh?" cried the old soldier. "Glad to see you, sir. Shake hands, and welcome to your new quarters. Come inside."

"No, not now, I'm showing him round. We'll come another time, and bring you some tobacco, and you shall tell us the story about the fight with the Indian rajahs."

"To be sure I will, lads. Where are you going now?"

"Going? Let's see. Oh, I know. We'll go to Polly Hopley's."

"Ah, I suppose so. You boys are always going to Polly Hopley's. Good-bye."

He shook hands with us, then drew himself up and saluted us ceremoniously, and, as I glanced back, I could see him still standing upright in his erect, military fashion.

"You'll like old As-you-were," said Mercer, as we went on, now along the road. "The Doctor got hold of him cheap, and he does all sorts of things. Cuts and nails the trees, and goes messages to the town. He's a splendid chap to get things for you."

"But may we go right away like this?" I said, as I saw we were now far from the grounds.

"Oh yes, to-day. He's very strict at other times, and we have to get leave when we want to go out, but this is free day, and I want to show you everything because you're new. Nobody showed me anything. I had to find it all out, and I was so jolly miserable at first that I made up my mind to run away and go back home."

"But you did not?" I said eagerly, for, though I felt better now in the interest of meeting fresh people and learning something about the place, I could fully appreciate his words.

"No, I didn't," he said thoughtfully. "You see, I knew I must come to school, and if I ran away from this one, if I hadn't been sent back, I should have been sent back to another one, and there would have been whackings at home, and they would have hurt my mother, who always hated to see me have it, though I always deserved it: father said so. Then there would have been whackings here, and they'd have hurt me, so I made up my mind to stay."

"That was wise," I said, laughing.

"Oh, I don't know," he replied, wrinkling up his face; "the cane only hurts you outside, and it soon goes off, but being miserable hurts you inside, and lasts ever so long. I say, don't you be miserable about coming away from home. You'll soon get over it, and there's lots of things to see. Look there," he cried, stopping at the edge of the road, "you can see the sea here. The doctor will give us leave to go some day, and we shall bathe. There it is. Don't look far off, does it? but it's six miles. But we've got a bathing pool, too. See those woods?"

"Yes," I said, as I gazed over the beautiful expanse of hill and dale, with a valley sweeping right away to the glittering sea.

"Those are the General's, where the pheasants are, and if you look between those fir-trees you can just get a peep of the hammer pond where the big eels are."

"Yes, I can see the water shining in the sun," I said eagerly.

"Yes, that's it; and those fields where you see the tall poles dotted over in threes and fours are—I say, did you ever see hops?"

"Yes, often," I said; "great, long, tight, round sacks piled-up on waggons."

"Yes, that's how they go to market. I mean growing?"

"No."

"Those are hops, then, climbing up the poles. That's where the partridges get. Oh, I say, I wish old Magg would sell us that gun. We'd go halves in buying it, and I'd play fair; you should shoot just as often as I did."

"But he will not sell it," I said.

"Oh, he will some day, when he wants some money."

"And what would Doctor Browne do if he knew?"

"Smug it!" said Mercer, with a comical look, "when he knew. Look! see that open ground there with the clump of fir-trees and the long slope of sand going down to that hollow place!"

"Yes."

"Rabbits, and blackberries. Such fine ones when they're ripe! And just beyond there, at the sandy patch at the edge of the wood, snakes!—big ones, too. I'm going to catch one and stuff it."

"But can you?"

"I should think so—badly, you know, but I'm getting better. I had to find all this out that I'm telling you, but perhaps you don't care about it, and want to go back to the cricket-field?"

"No, no," I cried; "I do like it."

"That's right. If we went back we should only have to bowl for old Eely. Everybody has to bowl for him, and he thinks he's such a dabster with the bat, but he's a regular muff. Never carried the bat out in his life. Like hedgehogs?"

"Well, I don't know," I said. "They're so prickly."

"Yes; but they can't help it, poor things. There's lots about here. Wish we could find one now, we'd take it back and hide it in old Eely's bed. I don't know though, it wouldn't be much fun now, because he'd know directly that I did it. I say, you never saw a dog with a hedgehog. Did you?"

"No," I said.

"It's the finest of fun. Piggy rolls himself up tight like a ball, and Nip,—that's Magg's dog, you know,—he tries to open him, and pricks his nose, and dances round him and barks, but it's no good, piggy knows better than to open out. I've had three. Magg gets them for me. He told me for sixpence how he got them."

"And how's that?" I said, eager to become a master in all this woodcraft.

"Why, you catch a hedgehog first."

"Yes," I said, "but how?"

Mercer looked at me, and rubbed his ear.

"Oh, that is only the first one," he said hurriedly.

"But you must know how to catch the first one first."

"Oh, I say, don't argue like that. It is like doing propositions in Euclid. You have to begin with one hedgehog, that's an axiom. Then you take him in your pocket."

"Doesn't it prick?" I said.

"Oh, I don't know. How you keep interrupting! And you go out at night when it's full moon, and then go and sit down on a felled tree right in the middle of an open place in the wood. You get a bit of stick, a rough bit, and take hold of piggy's foot and rub his hind leg with the stick."

"But suppose he curls up," I said.

"Oh, bother! Don't! How am I to tell you? You mustn't let him curl up. You rub his hind leg with the stick, and then he begins to sing."

"Oh, come!" I said, bursting out laughing.

"Well, squeal, then, ever so loud, and the louder he squeals, the harder you must rub."

"But it hurts him."

"Oh, not much. What's a hedgehog that he isn't to be hurt a bit! Boys get hurt pretty tidy here when the Doctor's cross. Well, as soon as he squeals out, all the hedgehogs who hear him come running to see what's the matter, and you get as many as you like, and put 'em in a hutch, but you mustn't keep live things here, only on the sly. I had so many, the Doctor put a stop to all the boys keeping things, rabbits, and white mice, and all. That's why I stuff."

"What is?"

"Because you can keep frogs, and jays, and polecats, and snakes, and anything, and they don't want to be fed."

"What a nice cottage!" I said suddenly, as we came upon a red-brick, red-tiled place, nearly all over ivy.

"Yes, that's Polly Hopley's—and hi! there goes old Hopley."

A man in a closely fitting cap and brown velveteen jacket, who was going down the road, faced round, took a gun from off his shoulder and placed it under his arm.

He was a big, burly, black-whiskered man, with brown face and dark eyes, and he showed his white teeth as he came slowly to meet us.

"Well, Master Mercer?" he said. "Why ain't you joggryfing?"

"Whole holiday. New boy. This is him. Burr junior, this is Bob Hopley, General's keeper. Chuck your cap up in the air, and he'll make it full of shot-holes. He never misses."

"Oh yes, I do," said the keeper, shaking his head; "and don't you do as he says. Charge of powder and shot's too good to be wasted."

"Oh, all right. I say, got anything for me?"

"No, not yet. I did knock over a hawk, but I cut his head off."

"What for? With your knife?"

"No-o-o! Shot. You shall have the next. Don't want a howl, I s'pose?"

"Yes, yes, a white one. Do shoot one for me, there's a good chap."

"Well, p'raps I may. I know where there's a nest."

"Do you? Oh, where?" cried Mercer. "I want to see one, so does he — this chap here."

"Well, it's in the pigeon-cote up agen Dawson's oast-house, only he won't have 'em touched."

"What a shame!"

"Says they kills the young rats and mice. Like to go and see it?"

"Yes."

"Well, I'm going round by Rigg's Spinney, and I'll meet you at the farm gates. Jem Roff'll let you go up if I ask him."

"How long will you be?"

"Hour! Don't forget!"

"Just as if we should!" cried Mercer, as the keeper shouldered his gun again and marched off. "It's rather awkward, though."

"What is?" I said.

"Being friends with Magglin and Bob Hopley too, because they hate each other awfully. But then, you see, it means natural history, don't it?"

He looked at me as if he meant me to say it, so I said, "Yes."

"An hour. What shall we do for an hour? 'Tisn't long enough to go to the hammer pond, nor yet to hunt snakes, because we should get so interested that we should forget to come back. But, I say, would you rather go back to the school field, where the other chaps are, or come back and pick out your garden? We've all got gardens. Or have a game at rounders, or—"

"No, no no," I said. "I like all this. It's all new to me. I was never in the country like this before."

"Then you do like it?"

"Of course."

"That's right. Then you will not mind old Rebble's impositions, and the Doctor being disagreeable, and going at us, nor the boys pitching into you, as they all do—the big ones—when the Doctor's pitched into them. Why, you don't look so miserable now as you did."

"Don't I?"

"No. It's awful coming away from home, I know, and I do get so tired of learning so many things. You do have to try so much to get to know anything at all. Now, let's see what shall we do for an hour?"

"Go for a walk," I suggested.

"Oh, that's no good, without you're going to do something. I know; we'll go back and make Magg lend us his ferret, and then we'll try for a rabbit."

"Very well," I said eagerly.

"No, that wouldn't do, because his ferret's such a beggar."

"Is he?" I said.

"Yes; he goes into a hole in a bank and comes out somewhere else, far enough off, and you can't find him, or else he goes in and finds a rabbit, and eats him, and then curls up for a sleep, and you waiting all the time. That wouldn't do; there isn't time enough. You want all day for that, and we've only got an hour. Wish I hadn't said we'd go and see the owls."

"Shall we sit down and wait?" I suggested.

"No, no. I can't wait. I never could. It's horrid having to wait. Here, I know. It's lunch-time, and we're here. Let's go into Polly Hopley's and eat cakes and drink ginger-beer till it's time to go."

"Very well," I said, willingly enough, for walking had made me thirsty.

"I haven't got any money, but Polly will trust me."

"I've got some," I ventured to observe.

"Ah, but you mustn't spend that. You've got to help pay for the gun. Come on.—Here, Polly, two bottles of ginger-beer, and sixpenn'orth of bis— I say, got any fresh gingerbread?"

This was to a stoutish, dark-eyed woman of about one-and-twenty, as we entered the cottage, in one of whose windows there was a shelf with a row of bottles of sweets and a glass jar of biscuits.

"Yes, sir, quite new—fresh from Hastings," said the girl eagerly. And she produced a box full of brown, shiny-topped squares.

"Was it some of this old Dicksee had yesterday?" said Mercer.

"Yes, sir. I opened the fresh box for him, and he had four tuppenny bits."

26

"Then we will not," said my companion sharply. "Let's have biscuits instead."

The biscuits were placed before us, and the keeper's daughter then took a couple of tied-down stone bottles from a shelf.

"I say," cried Mercer, "I didn't introduce you. Burr junior, this is Polly Hopley. Polly, this is—"

"Yes, sir, I know. I heard you tell father," said the woman quickly, as she cut the string.

Pop!

Out came the opal-looking, bubbling liquid into a grey mug covered with stripes, and then *Pop!* again, and a mug was filled for my companion, ready for us to nod at each other and take a deep draught of the delicious brewing—that carefully home-made ginger-beer of fifty years ago—so mildly effervescent that it could be preserved in a stone bottle, and its cork held with a string. A very different beverage to the steam-engine-made water fireworks, all wind, fizzle, cayenne pepper, and bang, that is sold now under the name.

"Polly makes this herself on purpose for us," said Mercer importantly. "We boys drink it all."

"And don't always pay for it," said Polly sharply.

I saw Mercer's face change, and I recalled what he had said about credit.

"Why—er—" he began.

"Oh, I don't mean you, sir, and I won't mention any names, but I think young gen'lemen as drinks our ginger-beer ought to pay, and father says so too."

I glanced at Mercer, whose face was now scarlet, and, seeing that he was thinking about what he had said respecting credit, I quietly slipped my hand into my pocket and got hold of a shilling.

"It is beautiful ginger-beer," I said, after another draught.

"Beautiful," said Mercer dismally, but he gave quite a start and then his eyes shone brightly as he glanced at me gratefully, for I had handed the shilling to the keeper's daughter, who took it to a jug on the chimney-piece, dropped it in, and then shook out some half-pence from a cracked glass and gave me my change.

"Here, put your biscuits in your pocket, Burr," cried Mercer, "and we'll go on now."

Saying which, he set the example, finished his ginger-beer, and made the keeper's daughter smile by declaring it was better than ever.

"Glad you like it, sir; and of course you know I didn't mean you, as I've trusted before, and will again, because you always pay."

"Thank-ye. I know whom you mean," he replied. "Come on."

As soon as we were out of sight of the cottage, Mercer laid an arm on my shoulder.

"I can't say what I want to," he said quickly, "but I liked that, and I won't ever forget it. If ever old Eely hits you, I'll go at him, see if I don't, and I don't care how hard he knocks me about, and if ever I can do anything for you, to save you from a caning, I will, or from any other trouble. You see if I don't. I like you, Burr junior, that I do, and—and do come along, or we shall be late."

Chapter Three.

"What a fuss about nothing!" I thought to myself, as we went on, down a beautiful lane, with tempting-looking woods on either side, and fox-gloves on the banks, and other wild-flowers full of attractions to me as a town boy. There was a delicious scent, too, in the air, which I had yet to learn was from the young shoots of the fir-trees, growing warm in the sunshine.

I had made no boy friendships up to then, and, as I glanced sideways at the pleasant, frank face of the lad walking quickly by me, just at a time when I had been oppressed by the loneliness of my position, fresh from home and among strangers, a strong feeling of liking for him began to spring up, and with it forgetfulness of the misery I had suffered.

"Hi! look! there he goes," cried Mercer just then, and he pointed up into an oak tree.

"What is it?" I said excitedly.

"He's gone now; wait a minute, and you'll soon see another. There he is—listen."

He held up his hand, and I stood all attention, but there was no sound for a few minutes. Then from out of the woods came plainly.

Chop chop, chop chop.

"I can't see him," I said. "Some one's cutting down a tree."

Mercer burst into a roar of laughter.

"Oh, I say, you are a Cockney!" he cried. "Cutting down a tree! Why, you don't seem to know anything about the country."

"Well," I rejoined rather warmly, "that isn't my fault. I've always lived in London."

"Among the fogs and blacks. Never mind, you'll soon learn it all. I did. Wish I could learn my Latin and mathicks half as fast. That isn't anybody cutting wood; it's a squirrel."

"A squirrel?"

"Yes; there he goes. He's coming this way. You watch him. He's cross, because he sees us. There, what did I say?"

I looked in the direction he pointed out, and saw the leaves moving. Then there was a rustle, and the little brown and white animal leaped from bough to bough, till I saw it plainly on a great grey and green mossy bough of a beech tree, not thirty feet away, where it stood twisting and jerking its beautiful feathery tail from side to side, and then, as if scolding us, it began to make the sounds I had before heard—*Chop, chop, chop, chop,* wonderfully like the blows of an axe falling on wood.

"Wonder whether I could hit him," cried Mercer, picking up a stone.

"No, no, don't! I want to look at him."

"There's lots about here, and they get no end of the nuts in the autumn. But come along."

We soon left the squirrel behind, and Mercer stopped again, in a shady part of the lane.

"Hear that," he said, as a loud *chizz chizz chizz* came from a dry sandy spot, where the sun shone strongly.

"Yes, and I know what it is," I cried triumphantly. "That's a cricket escaped from the kitchen fireplace."

Mercer laughed.

"It's a cricket," he said, "but it's a field one. You don't know what that is, though," he continued, as a queer sound saluted my ears, — a low, dull whirring, rising and falling, sometimes nearer, sometimes distant, till it died right away.

"Now then, what is it?" he cried.

"Knife-grinder," I said; "you'll hear the blade screech on the stone directly."

"Wrong. That's Dame Durden with her spinning-wheel."

"Ah, well, I knew it was a wheel sound. Is there a cottage in there?"

"No," he said, laughing again; "it's a bird."

"Nonsense!"

"It is. It is a night-jar. They make that noise in their throats, and you can see them of a night, flying round and round the trees, like great swallows, catching the moths."

I looked hard at him.

"I say!"

"Yes; what?"

"Don't you begin cramming me, because, if you do, I shall try a few London tales on you."

Mercer laughed.

"There's an old unbeliever for you. I'm not joking you; I never do that sort of thing. It is a bird really."

"Show it to me then."

"I can't. He's sitting somewhere on a big branch, long way up, and you can't find them because they look so like the bark of the tree, and you don't know where the sound comes from. They're just like the corn-crakes."

"I've read about corn-crakes," I said.

"Well, there's plenty here. You wait till night, and I'll open our bedroom window, and you can hear them craking away down in the meadows. You never can tell whereabouts they are, though, and you very seldom see them. They're light brown birds."

We were walking on now, and twice over he stopped, smiling at me, so that I could listen to the night-jars, making their whirring noise in the wood.

"Now, was I cramming you?" he said.

"No, and I will not doubt you again. Why, what a lot you know about country things!"

"Not I. That's nothing. You soon pick up all that. Ever hear a nightingale?"

"No, I don't think so."

"Then you haven't. You'll hear them to-night, if it's fine, singing away in the copses, and answering one another for miles round."

"Why, this must be a beautiful place, then?"

"I should think it is—it's lovely. I don't mean the school; I hate that, and the way they bore you over the lessons, and the more stupid you are, the harder they are upon you. I'm always catching it. 'Tain't my fault I'm so stupid."

I looked at him sharply, for he seemed to me to be crammed full of knowledge.

"The Doctor told me one day I was a miserable young idiot, and that I thought about nothing but birds and butterflies. Can't help it. I like to. I say, we'll go egging as soon as we've seen the owls. Wonder whether I can get an owl's egg for my collection. I've got two night-jars'."

"Out of the nest?"

"They don't make any nest; I found them just as they were laid on some chips, where they were cutting down and trimming young trees for hop-poles. Such beauties! But come along. Yes, he said I was a young idiot, but father don't mind my wanting to collect things. He likes natural history, and mamma collects plants, and names them. She can tell you the names of all the flowers you pass by, and—whisht—snake!"

"Where? Where?"

"Only gone across here," said my companion, pointing to a winding track in the dusty road, showing where the reptile must have crossed from one side to the other.

"Which way did he go?" I said; "let's hunt him."

"No good," said my companion quietly. "He's off down some hole long enough ago. Never mind him; I can show you plenty of snakes in the woods, and adders too."

"They sting, don't they?" I said.

"No."

"They do. Adders or vipers are poisonous."

"Yes, but they don't sting; they bite. They've got poisoned fangs. You can see an adder along here sometimes. Perhaps we shall see one to-day, warming himself in the sun."

But we did not, for a few minutes later we approached a swing gate, just as the keeper came round a curve in the opposite direction.

"Here you are, then," he said, "just right. Farmer Dawson's gone off to market, and so we shan't have to ask leave. Come on, and let's see if we can find Jem Roff."

He pushed open the gate, and we went along a cart track for some distance, and then on through one of the hop-gardens, with its tall poles draped with the climbing rough-leaved vines, some of which had reached over and joined hands with their fellows, to make loops and festoons, all beautiful to my town-bred eyes, as was the glimpse I caught of a long, low old English farmhouse and garden, with a row of bee-hives, as we went round a great yard surrounded by buildings—stables, barns, sheds, and cow-houses, with at one corner four tall towers, looking like blunt steeples with the tops cut off to accommodate as many large wooden cowls.

"What are they?" I asked.

"Oast-houses."

"What?"

"Oast-houses, where they dry the hops over a fire on horse-hair sheets," said Mercer. "Look! that's the pigeon-cote," he continued, pointing to three rows of holes cut in the woodwork which connected the brick towers. "The owl's nest's in one of those."

Just then a middle-aged man, with a very broad smile upon his face, and a fork in his hand, came up.

"Here, Jem," said the keeper, "the young gentlemen want to see the owl's nest."

The smile departed from the man's face, which he wiped all over with one hand, as he frowned and shook his head.

"Nay, nay," he said. "The master's very 'tickler 'bout them howls. Why, if I was to kill one, he'd 'most kill me."

"The young gents won't hurt 'em, Jem."

"Nay, but they'd be wanting to take eggs, or young ones, or suthin'.'"

"Well, I should like one egg," said Mercer.

"Ah, I thowt so! Nay, you mustn't goo."

"Oh yes, let us go," said Mercer. "There, I won't touch an egg."

"An' you won't touch the birds?"

"No."

"Nor him neither."

"Oh, I won't touch them," I said eagerly.

"You see the master says they do no end of good, killing the mice and young rats."

"And I say they do no end of mischief, killing the young partridges and fezzans and hares," said the keeper. "Better not let me get a sight o' one down our woods."

The man wiped his face again with his hand, and looked at us both attentively.

"Young master here said he'd stooff a magpie for me if you shot one, Bob Hopley."

"So I will," said Mercer, "if Mr Hopley shoots one for you."

"That's a bargain then," said the man, rummaging in his pocket, after sticking the fork in the ground. "Here, this way," he continued, as he drew out a bright key. "Coming, Bob?"

"No, I don't want to see owls, 'less they're nailed on my shed door."

He seated himself on the edge of a great hay-rack, and we followed the farmer's man through a door into the dark interior of one of the oast-houses, where we looked up to see the light coming in through the opening at the side of the cowl, and then followed Jem up some steps into a broad loft, at one corner of which was a short ladder leading up to a trap-door in the floor overhead.

"Mind your heads, young gents, ceiling's pretty low."

We had already found that out by having our caps scraped by a rough beam under which we passed.

"Now then, go up the ladder and push the trap-door open gently, so as not to frighten 'em. Turn the door right over, and let it down by the staple so as it lies on the floor. 'Tain't dark; plenty o' light comes through the pigeon-holes."

"Haven't you got any pigeons now, Jem Roff?"

"No, nor don't want none. Up wi' ye, and let me get back to my work."

Mercer needed no further invitation, and, followed closely by me, he crossed to the corner where the ladder stood, climbed up, thrust the trap-door over, and disappeared—head—shoulders—body—legs.

Then I climbed too, and found myself in a dirty, garret-like place, lit by the rays falling through about a score of pigeon-holes.

For a few moments the place was dim, and I could hardly make out anything, but very soon after my eyes grew accustomed to the half light, and I was ready to join in Mercer's admiration as he cried, — "Isn't he a beauty!"

For we were looking where, in one corner, sitting bolt upright, with his eyes half closed, there was a fine young owl, just fully fledged and fit to fly, while nothing could be more beautiful than his snow-white, flossy breast, and the buff colour of his back, all dotted over with grey, and beautifully-formed dots.

"Oh, shouldn't I like him to stuff!" cried Mercer. "He'll never look so clean and beautiful again."

"But what's that?" I cried, pointing at a hideous-looking goblin-like creature, with a great head, whose bare skin was tufted with patches of white down. Its eyes were enormous, but nearly covered by a nasty-looking skin, which seemed to be stretched over them. Projecting beneath was an ugly great beak, and its nearly naked body, beneath the toppling head and weak neck, was swollen and bloated up as if it would crack at a touch. Altogether it was as disgusting a looking object as it was possible to imagine.

"That's his young brother," cried Mercer, laughing.

"Young nonsense! It must be a very, very old owl that has lost all its feathers."

"Not it. That chap's somewhere about a fortnight old; and look there, you can see an egg in the nest, too. Shouldn't I like it!"

"Then it's the nest belonging to three pairs of owls?" I said.

"No. That's the way they do—hatch one egg at a time. They all belong to the same pair."

I felt a little incredulous, but my attention was taken up then by a semicircle of little animals arranged about two feet from the nesting-place.

"Why, they're all big mice," I said.

"No; nearly all young rats," said Mercer, counting. "Twenty-two," he cried, "and all fresh. Why, they must have been caught last night. That's a fine mouse," he cried, taking one up by its tail.

"Why, that must be a young rat," I said. "That little one's a mouse."

"No; this is a field mouse. Look at his long tail and long ears. The rats have got shorter, thicker tails, and look thicker altogether."

"Now then, are you young gents a-coming down?" shouted Jem.

"Yes. All right. Directly. Oh, isn't that fellow a beauty!" he continued, throwing down the mouse he had lifted back into its place in the owls' larder. "I say, don't the old ones keep up a good supply!"

A second summons from the man made us prepare to descend, the full-grown owl making no effort to escape, but blinking at us, and making a soft, hissing noise. The goblin-looking younger one, however, gaped widely, and seemed to tumble over backwards from the weight of its head. It was so deplorable and old-looking a creature that it seemed impossible that it could ever grow into a soft, thickly feathered bird like the other, and I said so.

"Oh, but it will," said Mercer; "all birds that I know of, except ducks and chickens and geese, are horridly ugly till they are fledged. Young thrushes and rooks are nasty-looking, big-eyed, naked things at first. There: you go on down."

I descended through the trap-door, and he followed, the man looking at us searchingly, as if he had not much faith in our honesty when face to face with such temptations as owls' eggs, but his look was only momentary, and he took it for granted that we had kept our word.

"Where are the old birds, Jem?" said my companion.

"Oh, right away somewhere in the woods, asleep. Want to see them?"

"Of course."

"Then you must come at night, and you'll see these young ones sitting at one of the holes giving a hiss now and then for the old birds to come and feed them, and every now and then one of them flies up."

"Yes, I know," said Mercer, "so still and softly that you can't hear the wings. But I should like that egg."

"Then you had better ask the master, and see what he says."

"Well, my lads," cried Hopley, in his bluff, deep voice, "seen the owls?"

"Yes; and now, I say, Bob Hopley, you'll let us go through the big beech-wood, and round by the hammer pond?"

"What for?" said the keeper.

"It's holiday to-day, and I want to show this chap, our new boy, round."

"What! to teach him mischief like you know?"

"Get out. I don't do any mischief. You might let us go."

"Not my wood, it's master's."

"Well, he wouldn't mind."

"And I've got young fezzans in coops all about the place."

"Well, we don't want the pheasants."

"I should think not, indeed; and just you look here: I see you've got that chap Magglin up at work in your garden again; you just tell him from me that if ever I see him in our woods, I'll give him a peppering with small shot."

"You carry your impudent messages yourself, or tell the Doctor," said Mercer sharply.

"What?" cried the keeper, scowling at us.

"I say, you take your impudent messages yourself. You know you daren't shoot at him."

"Oh, daren't I? I'll let him see."

"It's against the law, and your master's a magistrate. You know you daren't. What would he say?"

The keeper raised his gun with both hands, breathed on the mottled walnut-wood stock, and began to polish it with the sleeve of his velveteen jacket. Then he looked furtively at Jem Roff, then at me, and lastly at Mercer, before letting the gun fall in the hollow of his arm, and taking off his cap to give his head a scratch, while a grim smile began to play about his lips.

"You've got me there, youngster," he said slowly, and Jem began to chuckle.

"Of course I have," said Mercer confidently. "Besides, what's that got to do with me?"

"Why, he's a friend of yours."

"That I'm sure he's not. He's a nasty, mean beggar, who makes me pay ever so much for everything he does for me. You ask him," continued Mercer, giving his head a side wag at me, "if only this morning he didn't make me give him twopence for a pen'orth of worms."

"Yes, that he did," I said, coming to my companion's help.

"Humph!" grunted the keeper. "Well, youngsters, never you mind that, you pay him, and keep him at a distance. He's no good to nobody, and I wonder at Doctor Browne, as teaches young gents to be gents, should keep such a bad un about his place. He's a rank poacher, that's what he is, and there ain't nothing worse than a poacher, is there, Jem Roff?"

"Thief," said that gentleman.

"Thief? I don't know so much about that. Thieves don't go thieving with loaded guns to shoot keepers, do they?"

"Well, no," said Jem.

"Of course they don't, so that's what I say—there aren't nothing worse than a poacher, and don't you young gents have anything to do with him, or, as sure as you stand there, he'll get you into some scrape."

"Who's going to have anything to do with him?" cried Mercer pettishly.

"Why, you are, sir."

"I only buy a bird of him, sometimes, to stuff."

"Yes, birds he's shot on our grounds, I'll be bound, or else trapped ones."

"Well, they're no good, and you never shoot anything for me. P'r'aps he is a bad one, but if I pay him, he is civil. He wouldn't refuse to let two fellows go through the big woods."

"Thought you was going fishing."

"Not till this evening, after tea."

"Where are you going?"

"Down by the mill."

"Wouldn't like to try after a big carp, I s'pose, or one of our old perch?"

"Wouldn't like!" cried Mercer excitedly.

"No, I thought you wouldn't," said the keeper. "There, I must be off."

"Oh, I say, Bob Hopley, do give us leave."

"What leave?"

"To have an hour or two in the hammer pond. There's a good chap, do!"

"The master mightn't like it. Not as he ever said I wasn't to let any one fish."

"Then let's go."

"No, my lads, I'm not going to give you leave," said the keeper, with a twinkle in his eyes; "but there's a couple o' rods and lines all right, under the thatch of the boat-house."

"Yes, Bob, but what about bait?"

"Oh, I don't know 'bout bait. P'r'aps there's some big worms in the moss in that old tin pot in the corner."

"Oh, Bob!" cried Mercer excitedly, while I felt my heart beat heavily.

"Yes, now I come to think of it, there is some worms in that tin pot, as I got to try for an eel or two."

"Then we may go?"

"Nay, nay, don't you be in a hurry. It won't do. Why, if I was to let you two go, you might catch some fish, a big carp, or a perch, or one of they big eels."

"Yes, of course we might."

"And if you did, you'd go right back to the school and tell young Magglin, and he'd be setting night lines by the score all over the pond."

"No; honour! We'll never say a word to him!" we cried.

"Then you'll tell all your schoolmates, and that big long hop-pole chap, what's his name?"

"Burr major," said Mercer eagerly.

"And that big fat-faced boy?"

"Dicksee?"

"Yes, that's him, and I'll give him Dicksee if he chucks stones at my Polly's hens. We shall be having 'em lay eggs with the shells broke."

"Oh, nonsense, Bob! We won't tell."

"And them two, and all the others coming and wanting leave to go fishing too."

"No, no, I tell you," cried Mercer, but the keeper, with a malicious twinkle in his eyes, kept on without heeding him.

"And half of 'em'll be falling in, and t'other half tumble after 'em to pull 'em out, and the whole school getting drowned, and then, what would the Doctor say?"

"I say, Jem Roff, just hark at him!" cried Mercer impatiently.

"Oh, if you don't want to hear me talk, I can keep my mouth shut. Good morning."

He nodded shortly, and, shouldering his gun, marched off.

"Oh, I say, isn't he provoking? and he never gave us leave. —Bob!"

No answer.

"Bob Hopley!"

But the keeper strode on without turning his head, and Mercer stood wrinkling up his forehead, the picture of despair.

"And there are such lots of fish in that pond," he cried, "and I did want to show my friend here, Jem Roff."

"Well, why don't you go, then? He's only teasing you."

"Think so," cried my companion, brightening up.

"Why, didn't he tell you where the rods and lines were, and the worms? You go on and fish. I should."

"You would, Jem?"

"Of course."

"But there won't be time before dinner now," said Mercer thoughtfully. "I say, are you hungry?"

"Not very," I said, "and I've got some biscuits left."

"Then come on," cried Mercer. "Don't tell him weave gone, Jem, and I will stuff that mag for you splendidly, see if I don't."

"I shan't see him, my lad. There, off you go."

"Yes: come on!" cried Mercer excitedly; "and—I say, Jem, lend us a basket."

"What for?"

"To put the fish in?"

"You go and ketch 'em first, lad, and by and by I'll come round that way with one under my arm, and you might give a fellow an eel, if you get one."

"You shall have all the eels, Jem."

"Thank-ye. Then look here! you bait one line with the biggest worms you can find, and do you know the penstock?"

"What, down in the deep corner, under the trees?"

"Yes; it's ten foot deep there. You fish right on the bottom, in that corner, and you'll have some sport."

"Hallo!" cried Mercer, laughing. "I say, Burr, junior, hark at him. How does he know? I say, Jem, how many eels have you caught there, eh?"

"You go and begin," said the man, with a dry laugh. "I won't forget about the basket."

"Nor I about the eels. Come on," cried Mercer. "Here, look sharp; let's run!"

He caught hold of my hand, raced me through the hop-garden, and out into the lane.

"Now, down here," he said, as we reached a stile. "We can get across this field, and then into the woods, and—quick, do as I do!"

As he spoke, he dropped down on his knees, and began hunting about at the bottom of the hedge, while I made clumsy efforts to do the same.

"What is it?" I said eagerly.

"Pretend it's a snake. Can't you see?"

"No."

"There's Eely Burr and old Dicksee coming down the lane, and they'll want to come too. Hist! don't look. Lie down; p'r'aps they haven't seen us, and they'll go by."

"But it's all stinging nettles," I said.

"What of that? Here, this way; they won't sting if you go down hard."

And, throwing himself into a great bed of the venomous weeds, he lay perfectly still, and I was obliged to follow suit, but not without suffering two or three stings.

Chapter Four.

Down by the Penstock.

It seemed a long time before we heard anything, but at last there were steps and voices which soon became plain, and, to my surprise, I found that they were talking about me.

"Oh, he can't fight, Dicksy," said one voice, which I recognised as the tall boy's—my namesake. "Those London chaps are all talk and no do. I shall give him a licking first chance, just to tame him down, and then you'd better have a go at him."

"You think he can't fight, then?"

"Tchah! not he. You can lick him with one hand."

"Then I will," said Dicksee. "I wonder where he went."

"Off with that old Senna T-pot," said Burr major scornfully. "He's taken him with him to pick snails and frogs—an idiot! I hate that chap, Dicksy, he's a beast."

"Yes, that he is."

"You can't shake hands with him, because you never know what he's touched last. I think the Doctor ought to be more particular about the sort of boys he—mumble—hum—hum hum hum!"

The buzzing of a humble-bee, and then silence.

"Ck!"

"Eh?"

"Ck!" ejaculated Mercer, uttering a stifled laugh. "Oh, I say, what a game, and us hearing every word. Thinks the Doctor ought to be

48

more particular what sort of boys he has in the school. I suppose that's meant for me. Well, my father is a gentleman, and could set his to make him a pair of trousers if he liked. Can't shake hands with me, can't he? Well, who wants him to? I wish I could fight, I'd make him smell my hands—my fists. He'd know then what they'd touched. But he can fight, and licked me horrid. Lie still yet, or they'll see us get up; I thought they were in the cricket-field. Tired, I suppose. Such a fuss about making your hands a bit dirty. Daresay I keep 'em as clean as he does his. I say, got stung?"

"A little," I said.

"Never mind; dock's the thing to cure that. All right. Gone. Now then, over the stile, and do as I do."

He crept over the stile, and into the field, and began to run down beside the hedge in a stooping position, while I followed suit, and we did not rise up till we gained the shelter of the trees.

"There we are! This is the beginning of the woods. Oh, it's such a place!"

"You've been before, then?" I said, as we began to wind in and out among large beech-trees, whose smooth grey trunks were spotted with creamy and green moss.

"Lots of times. I go everywhere when I can get away. It's a famous place here for moths. There's old Dame Durden again. This way— now down here; we shall soon be there."

I followed him for about a quarter of an hour through the dim, mossy glades of the grand old wood, till all at once it grew lighter, and we stepped out beside a broad sheet of water dotted with lilies and patches of rush and reed, while about fifty yards farther along the bank of the broad pool there was a roughly-thatched boat-house, with a mossy old punt moored to one of the posts by a rusty chain.

"Now, then, what do you think of this, eh?" said Mercer.

I looked round at the smooth sheet of water glistening in the bright sunshine, completely shut in by giant old trees whose great branches hung down over the sides and even dipped their ends and seemed to be repeated in the mirror-like surface. Here I could see silvery lily-blossoms, and there others of gold floating like cups amongst the broad round leaves, and, turning from the beautiful picture to my companion, I could only say two words:

"It's glorious!"

"I should think it is," he cried. "We two are going to have no end of fun together. You don't mind the other boys bullying you, and old Reb snarling and finding fault, and the Doctor boxing your ears with your books, when you've got places like this to come to. Hi! look at the old moorhen, there, with her young ones," and he pointed to a curious-looking bird swimming about and flicking its black and white tail, as it went in and out among the rushes growing in the water, with six little sooty-looking, downy young ones swimming after it. "Ever see one of them before?"

"No," I said. "There's another over there too."

"No, it isn't; that's a bald coot. It's got a white shield on the top of its head, and the moorhen's got a red one like sealing-wax. Hi! look at that!"

For all of a sudden there was a rush and splash close to the reeds, and the moorhen and five young ones went through the water with a dash to hide among the reeds.

"Know what that was?"

"They saw us, and were frightened. Or did some one throw a big stone?"

"There's no one to throw big stones here. That was Mr Jack."

"Well, did he throw stones?" I said wonderingly.

"No! What a fellow you are! A jack—a pike—a big fish—took one of the young moorhens for his dinner."

"Why, I thought pike lived on fish," I cried.

"They live on anything. I've seen them swallow young ducks and water-rats and frogs—anything they can get. We'll come and set a trimmer for that gentleman some day."

"I suppose I'm very stupid," I said; "but I've always lived in London, and have very seldom been in the country. I don't know anything about birds and fish."

"You soon will. There's always something to see here. Herons come sometimes, but they don't stop, because it's too deep for them to wade except in one place; and there's a hawk's nest over yonder in an old fir-tree, but Bob Hopley shot the old birds, and you can see 'em nailed up against his lodge. There was a magpie's nest, too, up in a big elm tree not far off; but never mind them now. Let's catch some—Hist! look there. See 'em?"

"No," I said, looking down into the water where he pointed.

"Come here. Lie down flat, and slowly peep over the bank through that grass. Go softly, or you'll frighten them off. Then look down."

I did as he told me, and as I looked down into the clear, deep water, that looked almost black from its depth, I could see quite a shoal of fish, with their sides barred with dark stripes, sailing slowly about between me and the dead leaves and rotten branches which strewed the bottom of the pool.

"See 'em?"

"Yes," I whispered; "perch, aren't they?"

"Why, I thought you knew nothing about fish."

51

"I've seen pictures of them in books," I said, "of course."

"Yes, perch, all but that black, soft-looking chap close to the bottom. He's a tench. But come on, and let's get the rods."

He led the way to the boat-house, a green strip of coarse grass about five feet wide leading to the rough building, and Mercer looked longingly at the boat, which was half full of water.

"We'll try her some day," he said; "but she seems very leaky. Here we are."

As he spoke, he took a couple of rough-looking, unjointed rods from where they were laid across some pegs driven into the side of the building just below the thatch eaves.

"All right," he said, examining the stout, strong silk lines twisted lightly about them, and the hooks stuck in pieces of cork which were bound on to the butts of the rods. "Now, then, come for the worms."

He leaned the rods up against the roof of the boat-house, and led me into the open-sided building, where, as described by the keeper, we found an old watering-pot half full of moss, and in this damp moss, and below it, an abundance of fresh, lively-looking worms.

"All right. Now for some fish. This way. Take your rod, I'll carry the pot. That's where we're going."

He pointed to where the pool narrowed, and ran up among the trees almost to a point, where I could see some woodwork, and a post standing up in the middle, with a series of holes pierced through it, and as we walked round by the grassy margin which led to the spot,—

"There, that's the place," cried Mercer. "That's the penstock."

"And what's a penstock."

"Don't you see. They pull up that post, and poke a peg in one of those holes, and that keeps it open, so as the water can run out down that gully behind there through the wood. It's to empty the pond. There used to be hundreds of years ago a great forge there, and the water turned a wheel to work the big hammers when they used to dig iron here, and melt it with charcoal. But never mind that, I want to catch some fish. Now, then, walk out along that woodwork. There's just room for us both on the top of the penstock, and we'll fish from there. Mind how you go, for it's precious deep."

It looked ugly, and the old oak beams and piles were moist, and nearly covered with moss; but I stepped out, and reached the little platform through which the upright post ran, and turned round to look for my companion, who was by my side directly after.

"There," he said; "there isn't too much room."

"Shall I go and fish from the bank?" I said.

"Oh no, we'll manage. Don't talk loud, only whisper, and don't move about. I don't believe that fishes can hear all the same. There," he added, as he baited my hook, "that's old Magglin's way. Let's see, are you deep enough. Yes, that will do. Throw in."

I dropped in my line, Mercer followed suit, and then, in the midst of the profound stillness of the lonely place, we stood on our little square platform, leaning against the post, watching the white tops of the cork floats, and waiting.

"As you've been fishing before, you know what to do," whispered Mercer; "only don't be in a hurry, give 'em plenty of time, and don't strike till they take your float right down."

Half an hour passed away, and my attention began to be drawn from my float to watch the birds that sailed over the pool, or the swallows that skimmed it in search of flies.

"Not deep enough," said Mercer suddenly, and, taking out his line, he adjusted the float higher up, and I followed his example.

Then we began to fish again; but with no better result, and I looked round at Mercer.

"Oh, it's no use to be in a hurry," he said. "Sometimes they won't bite, and then you have to wait till they will. But look, something's at mine."

I looked at his float, which had given a slight bob, and then another; but that was all.

"Off again. Didn't want worms," he said; "wants paste."

There was another long pause.

"Not deep enough," said Mercer again. "Ought to have plumbed the depth."

He altered his float, and I did the same, and we compared them to see that they were about alike, and the fishing went on, till my companion decided that we ought to have fresh worms, and selected a fine fresh one for my hook, and one for his own before throwing the old ones out into the water.

"Well, now," he cried, "look at that!"

I was already looking, for before the old baits had gone down many inches, we saw them both seized by largish fish, which seemed to dart out of some lilies a short distance to our left.

"What are you going to do?" I said.

"Wait a minute and I'll show you," he whispered, laughing, and after attaching the bait, he brought down the floats till they were only about a foot away from the hooks. "Now then, do as I do. Throw your line out as near as you can to those floating leaves."

He threw his own very cleverly, so that the bait dropped into the water with hardly a splash, and I followed his example.

"Too far," he said, as my bait dropped on to a lily leaf, but the weight of the shot drew it slowly off the dark green leaf, and it glided into the water.

"I've got a bite," said Mercer, in an excited whisper. "Hi, look out! Strike! strike!" he cried, for at that moment the white top of my float descended suddenly, rose again and then began to glide in a sloping direction along the edge of the lily bed.

I gave the rod a sharp, upward motion, and a thrill ran up my arm, as I felt the line tighten, and a curious tugging commence.

"Hurrah! you've got him. Don't let him go into the weeds, or you'll lose it. Keep your rod up, and you'll have the gentleman."

I heard all his instructions, but in the flurry of holding my first fish I did nothing but what, as the rod and line were both strong, was for the best. That is to say, I held my rod with both hands, and kept it nearly upright, while the fish I had hooked darted here and there, and tried vainly to make a dive down for the bottom.

"It's all right," said Mercer breathlessly. "It's a big one, and you must have him. Don't hurry."

"Is it very big?" I whispered excitedly.

"I think it is—over a pound, I should say. Let him get tired, or he'll break away. Ah, it's of no use, you're caught fast, old gentleman, whatever you are. It's a big carp or a tench. I think it's a carp, it's so strong."

The struggle went on for fully five minutes before the fish gave in.

"Now we've got to land it," said Mercer. "Can't do it here, or he'll break away. I know. Give me your rod to hold. That's it. Now you go back, and I'll pass it to you."

He laid his own tackle down, and I walked carefully along the narrow woodwork, back to the shore, while he drew the fish round, and then reached toward me, till I could catch hold of the rod and feel the fish still feebly struggling.

The next minute Mercer was by my side, the fish was drawn in close up amongst the sedge growing on the bank. My companion went down flat, reached a hand into the water, and scooped out my capture, which lay now flapping feebly in all the glory of its golden scale armour, a short, thick, broad-backed carp.

"There," cried Mercer, "didn't I tell you this was a grand place? Why, it must be a two-pounder;" and I stood gloating over the vividly-bright colour of my capture, while Mercer knelt down, took out the hook, and finally deposited the fish in a hollow, and covered it with fern fronds.

"Look! look!" I cried just then.

"Oh, bother! Why, there's one on," said Mercer. "Here, give me your rod;" and he stepped quickly out on to the penstock, and made a cast with my line, trying to throw it over the top part of his own rod, which was slowly sailing away, floating on the water with a curious motion going on at the end, which kept diving down, as if something was trying to draw it under water.

It was all plain enough: a fish had hooked itself, and at the first tug, the light bamboo rod had glided off the penstock, to act as a big, long float, for the cork was deep down somewhere out of sight.

I followed on to the penstock, and stood by as cast after cast was made, always cleverly over the rod, but the hook glided back on being drawn without taking hold.

It was plain enough that in a few minutes the rod would be drawn out of reach, when Mercer made a more lucky cast, for in drawing back, the hook had caught a part of the other line, and directly after there was a steady tightening.

"Hah!" ejaculated Mercer, and he drew in steadily till his own rod was within reach, and I lay down, leaned out as far as I could, and strained to reach it.

"Take care. Hold tight. It's horrid deep here. Mind, or you'll be in."

But I was holding tightly by part of the woodwork, and, after a few more efforts, I touched the butt of the rod with the tips of my fingers, pushing it away, for it to rise again right into my hand, and I rose with it, safe.

"Give it to me. Take yours," cried Mercer, when the exchange was made, and I saw his face light up as he began to play a good-sized fish, but with my hook still attached to his line.

"It's a big one," he panted, as the struggle went on, with, the fish fighting now to reach the water-lilies, but without success. "That wouldn't do," he cried. "If he once got in there, he'd wind the weeds about the line, and break away."

So, by steady force, the fish was led back, and again I went ashore first, took Mercer's rod, and held it while he scooped out, and threw high our second capture, which proved to be another carp, nearly, but not quite so big as mine.

We were soon fishing again from our old place, but without the slightest success now, the struggles with our golden prisoners having apparently scared away all the other fish.

"This won't do," said Mercer at last; "we shall have to try somewhere else. Here, I forgot all about Jem Roff; and look at 'em."

"Look at what?"

"Why, the eels. Can't you see them?"

"No."

"Why, look at those bubbles coming up. That's eels at work stirring up the mud at the bottom, or coming out of their holes. We'll soon talk to them."

His way of talking to the eels was to raise the floats so high, that, after trying several times, it became evident that he had adjusted the depth so that the bait touched the ground, and the floats lay half over on their sides.

"Now then," he said, after examining the worms, "we ought to catch old Jem's supper pretty soon. Throw in there, near me."

I did as I was told, and the patient waiting began again, with changes of baits and moves in fresh positions, but without result, and I was beginning to get rather tired and hungry, when my companion said dolefully, —

"Don't seem to bite. They won't begin till it's nearly dusk, and we shall have to go back before very long, for we must have some tea. Wonder whether cook'll give us some meat? I know: we'll get some eggs of Polly Hopley; she'll boil 'em for us, and we'll take 'em back."

We fished for another hour.

"It's no good," said Mercer; "I'm very sorry. I wanted you to catch a big eel, and then you'd want to come again, and now you won't care about it."

"Oh yes, I shall," I said. "It was worth coming too, even if we didn't catch any more fish."

"You think so? Look! you've got him!"

For my float was bobbing gently, and moving slowly away.

"No, no, don't strike. Yes—let him have it. That's an eel biting, and he will not leave it. You'll see."

The gentle bob, bob, bob of the float went on as it glided slowly away foot after foot, till I could bear the excitement no longer, and I turned my eyes to my companion as if to say, "Do let me strike now—strike gently."

"Yes," he cried, "he must have got it;" and I struck gently, and felt directly as if the hook was in a stump or a dead branch at the bottom of the pool.

"It isn't a fish," I said, looking at Mercer.

"What is it then?" he replied, laughing. "It's an eel."

"But it don't move or run about."

"You wait a minute. It's an eel, and a big one."

My acquaintance with eels so far had been upon the slabs at the fishmonger's shops, or in pieces browned and garnished with fried parsley, and my line remained so tight and still that I still doubted my companion's words.

"He has got his tail in a hole, or twined about a stump."

"But don't you think the hook's in a stump?"

"I never knew a stump bite at a worm, and run away with your float. There, he's loose now. Keep him up, and don't let him go down low again."

I heard his words, but felt that all I could do was to let the eel go where it liked. For it started the fight by swinging its head rapidly from side to side in a succession of sharp jerks, and then began to make the line and the top of the rod quiver, as it worked its way backward, trying to descend to the bottom, while my efforts were, of course, directed towards pulling it to the top.

"That's right; you've got him fast," said Mercer. "It's of no use to try and play him, he'll keep on like that for long enough. Give me the rod while you get back to the bank. Then you must pull him out quickly, right up on to the grass, and put your foot upon him. Not afraid of eels, are you?"

"I don't know," I said.

"Because the big ones will bite—hard."

I handed the rod, and walked back along the woodwork that was like the isthmus of our tiny wooden peninsula, and as soon as I was ashore, Mercer left his rod again, and handed me mine, following directly after, as I felt the snaky-looking creature writhing and undulating at the end of the line, sending quite a galvanic thrill up my arms the while.

"Now then," said Mercer, "pull steady; and when it is near the top, run it right out on to the grass."

I tried to obey his orders; but when I saw the creature keeping up its rapid serpentine motion, I felt disposed to let it go down again into its watery depths. I did not, however, but gradually swept the point of my rod round, drawing my prisoner nearly to the bank, and then with one good swing drew it right out on to the grass, where, in an instant, it tied itself right up in a knot, with the line twisted about it.

"Oh my, what a mess!" cried Mercer, coming to my help. "Ugh! you nasty, slimy wretch! Mind, or he'll be off back into the— Ah, would you?"

He seized the line, and drew the eel farther from the water's edge, waiting his opportunity, which came directly, for the fish rapidly untwined itself, plunged its head amongst the grass, and began to make its way like a snake when its course was checked by Mercer's foot planted firmly behind its head.

"Ugh! how cruel!" I said.

"Serve him right. He's grown to be as big as this by catching and eating all the poor little fish that went near him. He's good to eat too, and what a big one! Why, he must be over a pound. Oh my, what a mess!" he continued. "He has swallowed the hook right down, and there's no getting it out till he's dead. Here, give me your handkerchief, I'll use mine when I catch one."

I took out my handkerchief, and by his directions spread it upon the grass, when he raised his foot, lifted up the line, and the fish again twisted itself into a knot.

"That's the way," he said. "Now then, I'll drop him gently on to the handkerchief, and you take the cross corners and tie them over him tight, and then the other two. Ready?"

"Yes," I said, feeling no little repugnance to the slimy creature, but getting first one knot and then the other fast over the big round writhing fish, and this done to my companion's satisfaction, he whipped out his knife and cut the line.

"There," he said, "we mustn't lose sight of him, or he'll eat his way out if he don't find another way through the folds. No; I think he's safe. I'll hang him here."

"Here" was the rugged stump of a small branch of one of the nearest trees.

"Now," he said, "I'll try and catch one too before we go, and we shan't have done so very badly."

"But you've cut my hook off," I said. "How am I to fish?"

" 'GOT YOU THIS TIME THEN,' HE SAID GRUFFLY."

"You'll have to watch me, for I haven't another hook. Come along. We mustn't stop much longer, or we shan't be back to tea. Stand your rod up against that tree."

He was already half-way back to the penstock and caught up his rod, but no fish had attacked it this time, and we stood side by side once more, leaning against the post, watching his float, as he tried first in one place, then in another, without success.

"We shall have to give it up and go," he said at last. "We must get back to tea. We'll give the carp to Polly Hopley, she likes fish, and the eel too."

"Look! a bite," I whispered, for I distinctly saw a slight quivering of the top of the float.

"No," he said despondently. "I did that, shaking the top of the rod. I'm not so lucky as you. Yes, it is. Hooray!"

For the faint quiver was repeated, then there were one or two little bobs, then others, and at last the float began to dance slowly away toward the shore.

"He has got it, and is going to take it to his hole," whispered Mercer. "But he don't go here to-night. He's going into the frying-pan, I think. Hah! Got him!"

For he now struck sharply, and the rod bent tremendously. There was no steady, motionless pull here, but a fierce shaking of the head and a hard, vibratory tugging at the line.

"Bigger than yours," he cried. "A thumper! My, how he pulls! Ah, would you? No, you don't, my fine fellow. He wants to get to the bank, I suppose, but he's coming out here into deep water, where there's nothing to twist about, and he's not going ashore till I go first."

Just then the eel made a rush first in one direction, then in another, but with a heavy pressure kept up, and the rod bending nearly double. Then it made a rush for the shore, and Mercer raised the point of his rod and stepped back, while I uttered a cry, for the rod had struck me sharply on the ear.

But it was not at the blow, but at the tremendous splash, for, forgetful in his excitement of where he stood, Mercer's step was off the narrow penstock right into the deep water, and as I clung to the post with one hand, I was looking down into the huge bubbling ring he had made, to see first the rod come up, then Mercer's hand, and then his face, close to his floating cap, but quite a dozen feet away from where I stood.

I was too much startled to move for a few moments, while Mercer beat the water with his hands frantically for a bit, and then went under again, but rose and called to me hoarsely, —

"Help!"

"Swim!" I shouted. "Swim!" But he only gazed at me wildly, and I saw him go down again.

For an instant or two I stood as if turned to stone, then a thought struck me, and I ran along the woodwork to where I had left my rod, and, without thinking of the danger and the narrowness of the path, I ran back again in time to see Mercer rise again, beating the water frantically.

"Here, quick!" I shouted. "Catch hold;" and I held out the thin bamboo pole to him, but it did not reach within a couple of yards of where he was beating the water.

But it had its effect upon him. It was a chance for life, and in a curious laboured way he struck out now to swim, but came on very slowly, being hampered in some way by his own rod.

"Oh, try, try, try!" I shouted, and I saw him set his teeth and swim on desperately till one hand closed upon the thin bamboo, and then the other caught hold.

"Tight! Hold tight," I shouted, and, dropping on my knees, I began to draw the rod through my hands slowly, as if it was a rope, my eyes feeling as if they were starting as I saw his wild pallid face and set teeth, for I was in momentary dread that he would let go.

It seemed long enough before I had drawn him within reach and snatched at one of his wrists, then at the other, drawing myself back so as to get him closer. Then I got tight hold of his jacket collar, and, as I did so, my knees glided away from me back over the other side of the penstock, and a curious sickening sensation came over me. The water and Mercer's white face were blurred and swimming before me, and I was fast losing consciousness, but the faintness was not much more than momentary, and the sickening sensation began to wear away as rapidly as it came, as I fully realised the fact that I was half off the little platform, with my legs in the water, but holding my companion all the time with a desperate clutch, while he clung as tightly to my wrists.

Then I tried to speak, but at first no words came, and it was all like some terrible dream.

At last, though, the power of utterance came, and I cried loudly, in a voice which did not seem like mine, —

"I've got you safe. Now climb out."

He did not move, only gazed wildly in my eyes till he seemed to irritate me.

"Do you hear, you coward?" I half screamed; "climb out on to here. Do you want me to fall right in?"

Still he did not reply, and I shouted at him again in my despairing rage, for a curious sensation of weakness crept through me, and the horrible thought came that sooner or later I must let him go.

"Do you hear? Don't play the fool. Climb out."

"Can't," he said in a husky whisper. "I tried—hard."

"Try again."

In obedience to my fierce order, he made an effort, splashing the water a little, but ceased directly, and gazed at me wildly still.

"Can't. Line—round my legs."

His words sent a flash of light through me, for they explained his miserable attempts to swim, and I realised that the stout silk line had been twisted about him by the eel in its efforts to escape.

"Try again," I said in a voice as husky as his own. "*You must.*"

He struggled feebly, but gave up at once.

"I can't," he groaned. "No strength."

The poor fellow seemed paralysed, save that I could feel his hands grasping me with a clutch that did not relax for a moment, as I lay there on my chest, thinking what I must do. It was evident that I should get no help from him: for the shock of the accident, and his discovery that he was fast bound and helpless, had completely unnerved him, and it was plain to me that before long his desperate clutch would relax, and, when I could hold him no longer, he would sink back and drown before my eyes.

I looked despairingly round, but only to see deep water, and the bank so near and yet so far, for it was out of reach.

At last my mind was made up. I would get my knees on the penstock again, and then by main force drag him out, at all events into a sitting position, where I could hold him against the post while he recovered sufficiently to walk to the shore.

I waited a few moments, and then began, but to my horror found that my feet glided over the slimy, rotten woodwork of the piles beneath the water, and that I could get no hold anywhere. If I could have had my hands free for a few moments, it would have been easy enough, but I dared not let go of him, and, after a brief and weakening struggle, I gave up, and hung over panting, with for the only result the feeling that the water was now farther up my legs than before.

I soon got my breath again, and made a fresh effort, but with a worse result, and this was repeated till a chilly sensation of dread ran through me, and I felt half stunned at the horror of my position.

Then I recovered a little. "Mercer," I said, "do you feel rested now?"

He did not speak, only looked at me in a curious, half vacant way, and I shivered, for this was, I felt sure, the first step toward his losing consciousness and loosening his hold.

"I say," I cried, "don't give up like that. You've got to climb up on to these boards. I'm going to help you, but I can't unless you help me too."

There was no reply, only the same fixed stare in his dilated eyes, and in my horror I looked wildly round at the place I had thought so beautiful, but which was now all terrible to me, and felt how utterly we were away from help.

I began again, twining my legs now about the nearest post, and this enabled me to hold on, but I could get up no farther. I tried, though, to drag Mercer on to the woodwork, but my position crippled me, and I should have required double the muscular power I possessed.

I believe I made other trials, but a curious sensation of weakness and confusion was coming over me, as I uttered one after the other my loud cries for help.

It was horrible, and yet it seemed ridiculous that we two lads could not struggle up there into safety; but though I thought so then, I have often felt since that in my cramped position I was loaded down, as it were, with my companion's weight.

The end seemed to be coming fast. I had no dread for myself, since I felt that, once free of Mercer's tight clutch and the hold I had upon him, I could grasp the far edge of the woodwork, draw myself farther up, and sit and rest. But before I could do this I knew that he would have sunk away from me, and in a confused fashion I began to wonder whether I should hear him scream out as he was drowning, or whether he would sink down gently without a sound.

I shouted again, but my voice sounded weak, and as if it did not penetrate the trees which closed us in, and now it seemed to be all over, for the horrible sense of faintness was returning fast, and I made one more desperate effort before I felt that I too was going to sink back into the black water; and in that wild last fit of energy I uttered what was quite a shriek, and then felt half choked by the spasm of joy that seemed to rise into my throat.

For from quite close at hand there came quite a cheery, —

"Hillo!"

"Here—quick—help!" I gasped; and then I was silent, and hearing a loud ejaculation, as I felt the wood of the penstock tremble.

"All right. Hold tight, lad," said a familiar voice, and a hand grasped my collar. "I've got you, and I've got him too. Here, can you climb out?"

"If—if you can hold him," I said.

"I can hold him, and give you a help too. That's the way—get tight hold of the edge, draw yourself up. Well done. Now sit down, and put your arm round the post."

I had been conscious of a strong hand grasping my waistband and giving me a drag up, and now I was sitting trembling and holding tightly by the post.

"Now then, Master Mercer, don't stare like that, lad. I've got you safe. There, out you come. My word, you're wet! Stop a moment, though; you'd better try and get ashore before I pull him right out. There ain't room for three of us. Can you manage it now?"

"Yes," I said, standing up with my teeth chattering.

"Sure? Don't tumble in."

"I can do it," I said, and, trembling the while as if cold, I walked dripping along the woodwork to the shore, where I sank down on the grass as if my legs had suddenly given way, and crouched there watching, as I saw the man from the farm, Jem Roff, with his arm round Mercer, whom he had lifted right out, bring him streaming with water to the shore, and the fishing-rod behind, while, as he lowered him on to the grass, there was a horrible writhe from something wet close to me, which made me start away.

"What have you two chaps been at?" cried Roff wonderingly. "The line's all twissen round his legs,—and hold hard a minute till I get my knife. I must have that eel."

Chapter Five.

"He's a two and a half pounder, he is," said Jem Roff as, after a bit of a struggle, he got tight hold of the writhing monster. "My word," he continued, holding it down, "he's a strong un! Here, you just slip your hand into my jacket pocket and get out my knife. Open it, will you?"

I followed out his instructions, and handed him the opened knife, when with one clever cut he divided the eel's backbone, and its writhings almost ceased.

"There," continued Jem, taking hold of the line, "let's get you off. What a tangle! why, it's reg'lar twissen all about your ankles. I must break it. Why, it's tough as—look ye here," he continued, tugging at the plaited silk, "it's strong enough to hold a whale. I shall have to cut it. Bob Hopley won't mind."

Snick, and the line was divided, the eel thrown down, and Jem began to untwine the line from about Mercer's legs, as the poor fellow, looking terribly white and scared, now sat up on the grass, looking dolefully from one to the other.

"My heye! you do look like a drownded rat, master," said Jem, chuckling. "Lucky I come, warn't it?"

I looked angrily at the man, for he seemed horribly unfeeling, and then, turning to Mercer,—

"How are you now?" I said.

"Very wet," he replied feebly.

"Raw, haw!" laughed Jem. "There, get up, you're clear now. Couldn't swim a bit like that."

"No," said Mercer, getting up shivering, and shaking the water from his hair.

"Worse disasters at sea, lads. Here, come on along o' me. Let's put the rods back again;" and, taking the one he had dragged ashore with Mercer, he whipped the line round the other and pulled it ashore, swung the lines round both, and trotted with them to the boat-house, where he laid them on the pegs, and then came back to where we stood, so utterly upset that neither of us had spoken a word.

"Now then," cried Jem, taking hold of the scrap of line to which the eel was attached and twisting it round his finger. "This all you caught?"

"No," I said helplessly; "there's an eel in that handkerchief hanging on the tree."

Jem dropped the big eel again and trotted to the tree.

"Big as t'other?" he said. "Raw, haw! Here's the hankerchy, but there's no eel. Look ye here, he's worked a hole through and gone. You didn't kill him first?"

"It must be down there," I said.

"Down here!" said Jem contemptuously; "he's found his way back to the water again. Eels goos through the grass like snakes. Ketch anything else?"

"Two carp," I said. "Here they are."

"Ah, that's better, and all alive, oh! I'll carry 'em. Come along."

He thrust a twig of willow through the gills of the fish, and led the way through the woods, and across some fields to a cottage, where a woman came to the door.

"Here, missus," he said, "pitch some more wood on the fire. Young squire here stepped into the pond."

"Oh, a mercy me!" cried the woman. "Pore dear, he do look bad."

"Not he. All right again direckly. You let him warm himself, and I'll run up to the schoolhouse and fetch him some dry clothes."

"No," cried Mercer, rousing himself now. "We'll both run up, and get in without any one seeing us, and go and change our things."

"Ay, that'll be best," said Jem; "and, if I was you, I'd start at once. Run all the way, and it'll warm you up."

"Yes. Thank you for coming and helping us," said Mercer, who had now quite found his tongue.

"Oh, that's all right," said the man jocularly. "That's a fine eel, but don't fish for 'em that way again. Going in after 'em ain't the best way; you see they're quicker, and more used to the water than you are."

Mercer shuddered.

"Come along, Burr," he said feebly.

"Wait a minute. Here's your eel and the carp. Where's that there rush basket, missus?"

"Oh, we don't want the fish," said Mercer, with a shiver. "Come along, Burr."

He hurried out of the cottage, and into a lane. "Keep listening," he said. "If you hear any one, we'll go across the fields."

"There's some one coming now," I said.

"Oh dear! it's old Rebble. He hasn't seen us. This way."

He stooped down, and ran to a gate, crept through, and then, leading the way, he walked fast along by the side of a hedge till we had crossed one field, and then began to trot, seeming to get stronger every minute, while I followed, with my wet trousers clinging to my legs, and the water going "suck suck" in my boots.

We crossed two or three fields, and then Mercer drew up, panting, and with the natural colour coming back into his face.

"We'll walk now," he said, "and go right round, and slip in through the garden. Perhaps we can get in and up to our room without being seen."

"Yes, do," I said, looking dolefully at my wet legs, and my jacket all covered with green from the penstock. "Feel better now?"

"Yes, I'm getting all right. I say, didn't I seem like a horrid coward?"

"I don't think so," I said. "It was enough to frighten anybody."

Mercer was silent for a few minutes. Then he began again.

"I never felt like that before. I was going to swim, but the eel had gone about my legs, and as soon as I felt the line round them, and that horrid great thing twining it all over me, I tried hard to kick it off; but you haven't got much strength in the water, and then, as I felt that I couldn't get my legs clear, I came over all queer, and so horribly frightened that I couldn't do anything. It was just like having a dream in the night, after eating too much cake."

"It was very horrible," I said, with a shiver at the recollection, though I was beginning to feel warm.

"Yes, wasn't it? I say, don't go and think me a coward, there's a good chap."

"I was not going to think you a coward," I said. "It isn't likely."

"But I must have seemed like one, because I can swim ever so far, but when I found myself like that, all the strength went out of me. —I say!"

"Yes?" I said, for he remained silent, and trudged on, looking hard at the ground.

"I did like you for paying at Polly Hopley's, and I said I'd do anything for you, but I can't tell you what I feel now, for your helping me."

"Don't wish you to tell me," I replied. "Come along. I want to get on some dry things."

"But—"

"Hold your tongue," I said. "There's some one coming."

He looked sharply in the indicated direction, and a shout saluted us.

"It's some of the boys," he whispered. "Come on." He led the way to a hedge, forced his way through, and I followed, and once more he led me along at a trot, with the great house right before us among the trees, and then, striking off to the right, he went through field after field, and then through a gate, and along by the side of a deep ditch, to stop short all at once, as a man started out of the hollow, and tried to hide a small gun.

"Why, Magglin," cried Mercer, "you're after rabbits."

"Nay, nay; rats. They comes after the taters. Been fishing?"

"Come on," whispered Mercer, and he ran along by the hedge, turning once more to the left, and at last pulling up in a clump of fir-trees, on the north side of the big house.

"Now then," he said, "I daresay the Doctor hasn't come back, and the ladies are sure to be with him. We'll creep in by the front door and get up-stairs. Keep close to me."

'A MAN STARTED OUT OF THE HOLLOW'

He paused for a few minutes to get breath, and then started off, through the shrubbery, across the lawn, and in at the front door.

The hall was empty, and he sprang up the well-carpeted staircase, reached the first floor, ran lightly along a passage, and through a baize door, which separated the Doctor's part of the house from the boys' dormitories.

"All right!" he whispered, as he held the baize door for me to pass through; "nobody saw us, and the boys will not be up here."

He led the way down a long passage to another staircase, ran up, and I recognised the floor where our bed room was, when, just as we were making a rush for it, a door opened, and the big fat boy Dicksee came out, stared, and then burst into a roar of laughter.

"Oh, here's a game!" he shouted. "Old Senna's been diving after podnoddles, and giving the new chap lessons."

Mercer rushed at him so savagely that Dicksee stepped back, and the next minute we had reached our room, rushed in, and banged the door.

"Oh, isn't he a beast?" cried my companion, panting, and looking all aglow now. "He'll go and tell the boys, but we mustn't say where we've been."

Half an hour after, we went down, dressed in our other suits, feeling very little the worse for our adventure, and just as we reached the big schoolroom, the big clock up in the turret chimed.

"Why, we're in good time for tea after all," said Mercer. "They always have it late on holidays. Quarter of an hour to wait. Let's go and walk down to the boys' gardens."

He led the way out and across the playground to a gate in the hedge, through which we passed, to come plump on the Doctor, three ladies, and Mr Rebble, who carried a creel by the strap, and had a rod over his shoulder.

"So you've had no sport, Mr Rebble?" the Doctor was saying.

"No, sir, none. The wind was in the wrong quarter again."

"Aha!" said the Doctor, as he caught sight of us; "our new young friend, Burr junior. My dears, this is our new student. Burr junior, my wife and daughters."

We both took off our caps.

"Friends already, eh?" said the Doctor. "History repeats itself, the modern based upon the classic. Quite a young Pylades and Orestes. Well, Burr, have you made acquaintance with all your schoolfellows?"

I turned scarlet, and was at a loss as to what to say. But there was no occasion for me to feel troubled—the Doctor did not want an answer. He nodded pleasantly, the ladies bowed and passed on with him, while Mercer hurried me away.

"What a game!" he said; "and you've only made friends with one. I say, poor old Reb's been fishing all day again for roach, and never caught one. He never does. I wish he'd had the ducking instead of me."

"Nonsense!" I said. "You don't."

"Oh, but I just do," he said. "I say, let's go round and see cook."

"What for?"

"To ask her to dry our clothes for us. This way." He ran off, and I followed him, to pass through a gate into a paved yard, across which was a sloping-roofed building, at the side of the long schoolroom.

Mercer tapped at a door, and a sharp voice shouted,—

"Come in!"

"Mustn't. Forbidden," said Mercer to me, and he knocked again.

"Don't want any!" shouted the same voice, and a big, sour-looking, dark-faced woman came to the door.

"Oh, it's you, is it, Master Mercer? What do you want?"

"I say, Cookie, this is the new boy."

"Nice pair of you, I'll be bound," she said roughly.

"We've been out, and had an accident, and tumbled into a pond."

"Serve you both right. Wonder you weren't both drowned," she said sharply.

"Don't tell anybody," continued Mercer, in no wise alarmed. "We nearly were, only Jem Roff at Dawson's farm came and pulled us out."

"Oh, my dear bairns," cried the woman, with her face and voice changing, "what would your poor mammas have said?"

"It's all right, though," said Mercer, "only our things are soaked. Do have 'em down and dried for us by the morning."

"Why, of course I will, my dears."

"And, Cookie, we haven't had any dinner, and it's only bread and butter and milk and water."

"Yes; coming," cried the woman, as a door was heard to open, and a voice to call.

"Go along," she said. "They're calling for the bread and butter. You look under your pillows when you go to bed."

"It's all right," said Mercer. "Come along. She came from our town, and knows our people. My father set her brother-in-law's leg once, after he'd tumbled off a hay stack. Isn't she a gruff one when she likes! This way. Let's get in our places now."

We went in to tea, which was only tea for Mr Rebble, who had a small black pot to himself, and a tiny jug of cream; but the bread and butter and milk and water were delicious, and I had made so good a meal that I had forgotten all about our visit to the cook till we had been in bed some time. I was just dozing off to sleep, when I was roused up by Mercer's hand laid across my mouth.

"Don't speak," he whispered; "the others are asleep. Boiled beef sandwiches in a paper bag, and two jam puffs."

"What?" I whispered. "Where?"

"Here—in my fist. They were tucked under my pillow. Now, then, pitch in."

I sat up in bed, and Mercer sat up in his. It was so dark that we could hardly see each other, but the darkness was no hindrance to our eating, and the next minute there was a sound which may be best expressed as ruminating, varied by the faint rustle made by a hand gliding into a paper bag, followed after a long interval by a faint sigh, and—

"Good-night."

"Good-night."

"Think we shall catch cold?"

"I hope not."

"If we do, I've got some capital stuff in a bottle to cure colds, and I'll give you some."

"Thank you," I said, and there was a pause.

"Are you asleep?" I said after a time, during which I had lain thinking about our experience of the day.

"No."

"What are you thinking about?"

"I was wondering whether Mr and Mrs Jem Roff ate all that eel."

Mercer did not say any more just then, and I seemed to glide back into the cottage, where Mrs Roff was frying eel in a pan over the fire, and just as they had asked me to supper, and I was taking my place, a big bell began to ring, and Mercer shouted, —

"Now, Burr junior, time to get up."

I started and looked round, to see that the sunshine was flooding the room, and that the occupants of the other beds were sitting up grinding their knuckles into their eyes, and yawning as if in chorus.

Chapter Six.

We were none the worse for our adventure at the pond, and I very soon settled down to my school life, finding it, as life is, a mixture of pleasure and pain, joy and sorrow, all just as intense to the boy fifty or sixty years ago as it is now that schools are conducted upon very different principles, and a much higher grade of education is taught.

Perhaps a great deal of the teaching at Meade Place would be looked upon now as lax; but in those days the Doctor's school bore a very high character for the boys it had turned out, many of whom had gone into the East India Company's Service, and the principal drawing-room was decorated with presents sent to him by old pupils, Indian jars and cabinets, brass lotahs and trays, specimens of weapons from Delhi, and ivory carvings; while from pupils who had gone to China and Japan, came bronzes, porcelain, screens, and lacquer of the most beautiful kind.

Neither were the ladies forgotten, Mrs Browne and her daughters being well furnished with Indian scarves, muslin, and Canton crape shawls.

It was, of course, on account of his connection with so many officers that my uncle had chosen this school as the one most likely to prepare me for my future career.

When I first went down, Mr Rebble was the only assistant the doctor had; but I soon learned that the French master came twice a week from Rye, that the other usher had left to go into partnership with a friend in a school at Lewes, and that another was coming in a few days.

The Doctor was one of my informants, for, after passing me through a general examination as to my capabilities, he told me that I was in a most hopeless state of ignorance, and that as soon as the assistant master, Mr Hasnip, arrived, I should have to go under his special charge.

"For we can't have boys like you, Burr junior," he said smiling. "I don't know what would become of my establishment if many were as backward as you."

"I'm very sorry, sir," I said humbly.

"I am glad you are," he said; "for that means repentance for neglected opportunities, and, of course, a stern determination to make up for lost time."

"Yes, sir, I'll try," I said.

"That's right, and try hard. Your English is very weak; your Latin terribly deficient; your writing execrable; and your mathematics absolutely hopeless. There, go back to your place and work hard, my boy—work hard."

I descended from the daïs, with the eyes of the whole school upon me, and, as I walked between the two rows of forms, I could hear whispered remarks intended for me, and it was with a feeling of despair that I reseated myself, opened my desk and took out my Latin grammar, to begin turning over the leaves, looking hopelessly at the declensions and conjugations, with the exceptions and notes.

"What's the matter?" whispered Mercer, who just then returned from Mr Rebble's end, where he had made one of a class in Euclid.

"Doctor says I'm so terribly behindhand that he is ashamed of me."

"Gammon!"

"What?"

"I said, gammon. You're right enough. Forwarder than I am, and I've been here two years."

"Oh no," I said.

"Yes, you are. Don't contradict; 'tisn't gentlemanly. He said your English was weak?"

"How did you know?"

"Your Latin terribly deficient?"

"I say!" I cried, staring.

"Your writing execrable?"

"Mercer!"

"And your mathematics absolutely hopeless?"

"But you were at the other end of the room when he said that," I cried aghast.

"Of course; I was being wigged by old Rebble because I couldn't go through the forty-seventh of Book One; and I can't, and I feel as if I never shall."

"I think I could," I said.

"Of course you could; nearly every chap in the school can but me. I can learn some things easily enough; but I can't remember all about those angles and squares, and all the rest of them."

"You soon will if you try," I whispered. "But how did you know the doctor said all that to me?"

"Because he says it to every new boy. He said it to me, and made me so miserable that I nearly ran away and if I hadn't had a very big cake in my box, that I brought with me, I believe I should have broken my heart."

"But I am very ignorant," I said, after a pause for thought, during which my companion's words had rather a comforting effect.

"So's everybody. I'm awfully ignorant. What would be the good of coming here if we weren't all behind? Oh, how I wish things could be turned round!"

"Turned round?" I said wonderingly.

"Yes, so that I could know all the books of Euclid by heart, and have old Rebble obliged to come and stand before me, and feel as if all he had learned had run out of his head like water out of a sponge."

"Never mind," I said; "let's work and learn."

"You'll have to, my lad."

"Less talking there," said Mr Rebble.

"Oh, very well," whispered Mercer, and then he went on half aloud, but indistinctly, repeating the problem in Euclid over which he had broken down.

I glanced at Mr Rebble, and saw that he was watching us both intently, and I bent over my Latin grammar, and began learning the feminine nouns which ended in "us," while Mercer half turned his head towards me.

"A little less noise at your end of the school, Mr Rebble, if you please," said the Doctor blandly.

"Yes, sir," said Mr Rebble, and then, in a low, severe voice, "Mercer, Burr junior, come up."

Mercer threw his leg over the form, and I followed his example, involuntarily glancing across at my namesake, who made a grimace, and gave himself a writhe, as if suggesting that I should have a cut from the cane after being reported to the Doctor, and I knew that he was watching us both as we went up to the usher's desk.

"Close up, both of you," said Mr Rebble sternly, but in a low voice, so that his words should not reach the Doctor.

We moved closer.

"Now, sir," he said sternly, "I called for silence twice, and you, Mercer, and you, Burr junior, both kept on speaking. I distinctly saw your lips moving—both of you. Now, sir, I insist upon your repeating the words you said as I caught your eye."

"Subtending the right angle, sir," said Mercer promptly.

"And you, sir?" continued Mr Rebble, turning to me.

"*Idus, quercus, ficus, manus*, sir," I replied innocently.

"That will do. Go back to your places, and if I do catch you talking again in school hours—"

"Please, sir, that wasn't talking," said Mercer in expostulation.

"Silence, sir. I say, if I do catch you talking, I shall report you to the Doctor. That will do."

We went demurely enough back to our places, and this summons had the effect upon me of making me feel more ill-used than before. As I once more went on with my Latin, I was conscious that Mercer was writing something on his slate, and when it was done, he wetted his hand, and gave me a nudge, for me to read what he had written.

"He don't like you, because we're friends. He don't like me. Yah! Who don't know how to fish?"

I had barely read this, when Mercer's hand rapidly obliterated the words, and only just in time, for Mr Rebble left his desk and came slowly by us, glancing over our shoulders as he passed, but Mercer was safe, for he had rapidly formed a right-angled triangle on his slate, and was carefully finishing a capital A, as the usher passed on up to the Doctor's end.

Those mornings glided away, and so slowly that it seemed as if the mid-day bell would never ring, but its sonorous tones rang through the place at last, and, hanging back, so as not to be called upon to form part of those who would have to go and field for Burr major and another of the bigger lads, Mercer and I waited our time, one day when I had been there about a fortnight, and then slipped off to the stable-yard, and then up into one of the lofts, which the boys were allowed to use as a kind of workshop.

"What do you want to come here for?" I said, as we ascended the rough ladder, and stood in the dimly lighted place.

"I'll show you directly," he said. "Don't you know what I've got up here?"

"No."

"My museum."

I looked around, but nothing was visible but some willow chips, and a half-formed cricket bat which Dicksee was making, by the help of a spokeshave he had borrowed at the wheelwright's, and which promised to be as clumsy a stump defender as ever was held in two hands.

"Well," I said, "where is it?"

"Here," said Mercer triumphantly, as he led the way to where an old corn-bin stood beneath one of the windows, the lid securely held down by a padlock whose key my companion brought out of his pocket.

"Never mind the old Latin and Euclid. I'll let you come and help me here sometimes, and if old Burr major or Dicksee interferes, you'll have to help me, for I wouldn't have my things spoiled for ever so much."

"Oh, I'll help you," I said, and I waited with some curiosity while he opened the lock, and, after hanging it on a nail, slowly raised the lid, and I looked in to see a strange assortment of odds and ends. What seemed to be dead birds were mixed up with tow, feathers, wire, a file, a pair of cutting pincers, and a flat pomatum pot, on which was printed the word "poison."

"What's that for?" I said wonderingly.

"Oh, that's soap," he said.

"No, no, that—the poison."

"Soap, I tell you. Take off the lid."

I hesitated for a moment, and then raised the lid, to see that the box was half full of a creamy-looking paste, which exhaled an aromatic odour.

"Is that soap?" I said.

"Yes, to brush over the skins of things I want to preserve. Don't touch it. You have to wash your hands ever so many times when you've been using it. Look, that's a starling I began to stuff, but it don't look much like a bird, does it?"

"Looks more like a pincushion," I said. "What's the cotton for?"

"Oh, that's to keep the wings in their places till they're dry. You wind cotton over them, and that holds their feathers down, but I didn't get this one right."

"He's too big and fat," I said.

"Yes, I stuffed him too much; but I'm going to try and do another."

The starling was laid down, and a jay picked up.

"That's another one I tried," he said sadly, "but it never would look like a bird. They're ever so much handsomer than that out in the woods."

"I suppose," — I said, and then quickly — "Are they?"

"Yes, you know they are," said Mercer dolefully. "These are horrid. I know exactly how I want them to look, but they will not come so."

"They will in time," I said, to cheer him, for his failures seemed to make him despondent.

"No," he said, "I'm afraid not. Birds are beautiful things, — starlings are and jays, — and nobody can say that those are beautiful. Regular old Guy Fawkes's of birds, aren't they?"

"You mustn't ask me," I replied evasively. "I'm no judge. But what's this horrid thing?"

"Frog. Better not touch it. I never could get on with that. It's more like a toad than a frog. It's too full of sand."

"Sand! Why, it's quite light."

"I mean, was too full of sand; it's emptied out now. I told you that's how you stuff reptiles, skin 'em, and fill 'em full of sand till they're dry, and then pour it out."

"Oh yes, I remember; but that one is too stout."

"Yes," said Mercer, "that's the worst of it; they will come so if you don't mind. The skins stretch so, and then they come humpy."

"And what's that?" I asked. "Looks like a fur sausage."

"You get out with your fur sausages. See if you could do it better. That's a stoat."

I burst out laughing now, and he looked at me in a disconsolate way, and then smiled sadly.

"Yes, it is a beast after all," he said. "My father has got a book about anatomy, but I never thought anything about that sort of thing till I tried to stuff little animals. You see they haven't got any feathers to hide their shape, and they've got so much shape. A bird's only like an egg, with a head, and two wings on the side, so that if you make up a ball of tow like an egg, and pull the skin over it, you can't be so very far wrong; but an animal wants curves here and hollows there, and nicely rounded hind legs, and his head lifted up gracefully, and that— Ugh! the wretch! I'll burn it first chance. I won't try any more animals."

"A squirrel looks nice stuffed," I observed, as I recalled one I had seen in a glass case, having a nut in its fore paws, and with its tail curved up over its back.

"Does it?" said Mercer dolefully; "mine don't."

"You have stuffed squirrels?" I said.

He nodded sadly.

"Two," he replied. "I didn't skin the first properly, and it smelt so horrid that I buried it."

"And the second one?"

"Oh, that didn't look anything like a squirrel. It was more like a short, fat puppy when I had finished, only you knew it was a squirrel by its tail.—What say?"

"I didn't speak," I said, as he looked up sharply from where he had been leaning down into the old corn-bin.

"I thought you said something. There, that's all I shall show you to-day," he went on disconsolately. "I never knew they were so bad till I brought you up to see them."

"Oh, they're not so very bad," I said, trying to console him by my interest in his works.

"Yes, they are. Horrible! I did mean to have a glass case for some of them, and ornament them with dried moss and grass, but I'm afraid that the more you tried to ornament these, the worse they'd look."

This sounded so perfectly true that I could not say a word in contradiction; and I stood staring at him, quite at a loss for words, and he was staring at me, when there was a shout and a rush along the loft floor, and I saw Burr major and Dicksee coming toward us fast, and half a dozen more boys crowding up through the trap-door into the place.

"Caught you then!" cried Burr major. "Come along, boys, old Senna's going to show us his museum and his doctor's shop."

Mercer banged down the lid of the corn-bin, and was struggling hard to get the hasp over the staple and the padlock on, when Burr major seized him and dragged him away.

"No, no," roared Mercer. "Here, Burr junior, catch hold." He threw the padlock to me, but the key dropped out, and one of the boys pounced upon it, while Dicksee threw his arms round me and held me tight.

"No, you don't," he cried.

"That's right," said Burr major. "Hold him, boys. The artful beggars had sneaked up here to have a tuck-in. We'll eat it all for them."

"There's nothing in the box—there's nothing there!" cried Mercer, struggling vainly, but only to be dragged down on the floor.

"Here, two of you, come and sit on him," said Burr major. "Hold that other beggar tight, Dicksee. Keep quiet, will you, or I will chuck you down the stairs."

By that time, under our tyrant's orders, two boys had come to Dicksee's help, and had seized me by a wrist each, so that I was helpless.

"Now then," continued Burr major, "we'll just see what my gentleman keeps locked up here. He's always sneaking up after something."

"You let that box alone," shouted Mercer, after an ineffective struggle to get free.

"Shan't. You're not going to do just as you like, Physic," said Burr major, and he threw up the lid, looked in, and then uttered a contemptuous "Pah!"

"What a mess!" he cried. "Look here, Dicksee."

The latter crossed to him eagerly, and I stood there a prisoner, but burning with indignation and an intense desire to hit some one.

"I'll tell the Doctor," cried Mercer. "It's a shame!"

"Oh, is it? You'd better tell tales—do. Oh, I say, boys, lookye here. This is a rumtummikos incomprehensibus. What a beast!"

He had taken hold of the unfortunate stoat by the tail and held it out amidst roars of laughter. "We'll have a fire and burn him. What's next?"

He dived down into the great chest, and brought out the starling.

"Here you are, boys," he cried again. "This is the speckled pecker, or measly short-tail."

92

Another roar of laughter.

"And here's the blue-winged cockatooral-looral-looral."

The boys shouted again, and I saw Mercer heave up in his rage, and nearly send the boys off who were sitting upon him, while I wished I had strength enough to send our tormentors flying.

"Hallo! here we are then," cried Burr major. "I knew it. They were going to have a tuck-out. Look, boys, they meant to have 'toad in the hole' for supper, and here's the toad."

This was as he held out the bloated skin of the unfortunate frog.

"Hooray!" shouted the boys, who were looking on with rapturous delight, and the more we struggled to get free, the greater their enjoyment seemed.

"You coward!—you brute!" panted Mercer. "How would you like your box turned out?"

"Ever so. Come and do it and you'll see.—Oh!"

This last was with quite a shout.

"What is it?" cried the boys who held us. "Let's look, Burr."

"You take it out if you dare," cried Mercer, who, however, as he told me afterwards, had not the least idea what was coming next.

"Oh yes, I'll take it out," said Burr major.

"You coward! you miserable old Eely tailor!"

"Hold your tongue, will you!" cried Burr major, turning sharply round and giving Mercer a savage kick as he lay on his back, with one boy sitting on his chest, another on his legs.

"Brute!" cried Mercer, setting his teeth and trying hard not to let the tears come.

"You great long coward!" I cried; "you wouldn't dare to do that if he were not down."

"You hold your row," he cried, and as I stood thus held, I received a sharp, back-handed blow on the mouth, which made my lip bleed.

"Bring it out, Dicksee."

The latter wanted no second telling, but dived down into poor Mercer's treasure-chest, and brought out the pot of preserving paste.

"There!" cried Burr major, taking up the pot with a face wrinkled up with disgust; "now we've found him out. See this, boys. Poison!"

"Oh!" chorused the little party of his parasites.

"That's the way he does it. He's worse than a witch. This is what he keeps to give to the fellows, and pretends it's physic, same as his nasty old father uses."

"I don't, boys—it isn't true; and my father's a gentleman, not an old snip."

"Do you want me to kick you again?" said Burr major savagely.

"Yes, if you dare," cried Mercer defiantly.

"Just you wait a bit, my lad, till I'm done. Yes, boys, that's it Dicksee, he gave you some of that, and it made you so ill the other day."

"Then we'll show it to the Doctor," cried Dicksee.

"I didn't!" cried Mercer. "That's to preserve with."

"Yes, that's it," cried Burr major—"to preserve with. Do you hear, boys? He keeps that to put in jam."

There was a shout at this, and I saw Mercer writhe in his impotence.

"Tell you what, we'll rout out the whole lot, and take them down in the stable-yard and burn them."

"You let them alone," cried Mercer frantically, as Burr major scraped out a double handful of the hoarded treasures and threw them on the floor.

"Hold him down tight, or I shall hurt him," said Burr major contemptuously.

But his words came too late, for Mercer made a sudden heave, which threw the boy on his chest off sidewise, sprang up into a sitting position, and hit out at the boy on his legs, who howled on receiving a crack on the ear; and this so roused me to action that I too wrested myself free and followed suit. I flew at Dicksee, and struck him full in the breast, sending him in his surprise down in a sitting position, just as Mercer struck our tyrant a sounding smack on the cheek.

Burr major staggered back and held his hand to his face.

"Oh, that's it, is it?" he said with a snarl. "All right, boys, Senna Tea wants me to boil him up again."

"You stand by me, Burr junior, won't you?" cried Mercer, who looked now as if he were a little startled at his daring.

"Yes," I said desperately, though I felt horribly afraid.

"Oh no, you don't," said Burr major, taking off his jacket; "I don't want to knock your silly head off. You wait till I've thrashed Master Physic, and then old Dicksee shall give you your dose."

I saw Dicksee look at him with rather a startled aspect, but Burr major took no notice beyond giving him a contemptuous glance, as he neatly folded up his jacket, and then removed his waistcoat.

"Here, Bill Ducie, go down and shut the stable door, and lock it inside," continued Burr major in a lofty tone; "we don't want to be interrupted before we've polished off these two beggars."

The boy ran down, and it sounded very formidable to hear the door bang and the rusty lock turned.

"Now then, off with that coat, sir," said Burr major, as he began rolling up his shirt over his thin white arms. "I'm not going to wait all day. The bell will ring for dinner directly. Hold my clothes, one of you; I don't want them dirty."

I saw Mercer set his teeth as he pulled off his jacket and vest, and he pitched them both into the big bin, looking very stubborn and determined the while.

"Here, Dicksee, you come and second me, I'll second you afterward. You new boy, you'd better second old Senna. Pah! how physicky he smells!"

I had the vaguest notions of what I had to do, but I imitated Dicksee as well as I could, as the boys stood on one side breathless with excitement, and Burr major and Mercer faced each other with their fists clenched.

Then there was a due amount of sparring, followed by a few blows given and taken, and Burr major drew back and sat down on Dicksee's knee, Mercer taking his place on mine.

"Did he hurt you much?" I whispered.

"Horrid," was whispered back, "and I can't half get to hit at him."

Then some one shouted, and they fought again, with the result that my blood seemed to boil as poor Mercer came staggering back.

"Had enough?" said Burr major in lofty tones.

For answer Mercer flew at him, and there was another long, fierce round, which seemed to consist in Mercer's adversary driving him about the place, knocking him about just as much as he liked, and ending by sending him staggering back, so that he would have fallen all in a heap had I not caught him in my arms.

"Had enough, Doctor?" cried Burr major contemptuously, and as I supported Mercer he uttered a low sob of misery.

"Yes, he's done. Now, Dicksee, I'll second you.—Off with your togs and polish him off till his face shines. Now then, look sharp, Senna, you've got to back your chap."

I heard Mercer grind his teeth, and I felt giddy with excitement as he whispered to me,—

"Don't be afraid of him, he's a coward. Take off your things, and you try hard if you can't lick him."

"Must I fight?" I said.

"Now then, you sir, off with that jacket," cried Burr major, "or he'll give you the coward's blow."

This roused me, and I stripped for the battle, feeling very nervous and uncomfortable, while Mercer drew a long breath, mastered the pain he was in, and, after throwing my jacket and waistcoat in the bin with his own, began to whisper his instructions to me.

"Now then, off you go," said Burr major. "Be smart, Dicksee, the bell will go directly."

Dicksee made a savage run at me as I put up my arms, there were a few blows, all of which came to my share, and there was a roar of laughter as the round ended in a struggle, and I went down, with Dicksee on me, and my head giving a stunning rap on the boards.

"Don't let him wrestle with you," whispered Mercer excitedly, as he helped me up, and I sat upon his knee, feeling very dizzy and half blind with rage.

"There," shouted Burr major, "finish the beggar this time, Dicky!"

I have some recollection of our encountering again, and feeling blow after blow on my face, on my ear, chest, and shoulders; and our going down once more in another wrestling match.

"Never mind," whispered Mercer; "you're doing splendidly."

"Am I?" I gasped.

"Yes; only keep him off more, and hit straight out like he does."

"Now then," cried Burr major again, "I want to go and wash my hands. Come along, new boy, and lay your nose against old Dicksy's left, and your left eye against his right, and then he'll smooth your cheeks over and lay you on the boards, and by that time I think you'll be about cooked."

"Don't let him lick you," whispered Mercer imploringly. "Do give it him this time. Hit him on the nose always, he don't like that."

"There!" roared Burr major, as, giddy and confused, I was swinging my arms about, hitting nothing half the time, and never getting one blow home with any force to signify, and at last, after a few minutes of burning rage and confusion, during which I had received quite a shower of blows, I found myself, giddy and panting, seated upon the floor, listening to Burr major's voice.

"That's enough, Dicky; that'll do the beggars no end of good, and make 'em behave themselves when they meet gentlemen. Come on, boys. Here, you two, go and wash yourselves, and make yourselves right. The bell will ring directly, and if old Reb sees you've been fighting, he'll report you both to the Doctor, and you'll get no end of punishment."

This seemed the unkindest cut of all, and as soon as the boys had gone racing down into the yard, where Dicksee gave vent to a loud "Cock-a-doodle-doo," I slowly rose to my feet and faced Mercer, who was gazing straight before him.

"I say," I panted, for I was breathless still, "did I win?"

"You? No," he cried savagely. "You can't fight any more than I can, and the brutes have beaten us both. Here, let's look at you. Oh, you ain't much marked, only your nose bleeds a bit. That's where you ought to have hit him."

"I did try to," I said despondently; "but he wouldn't let me."

"Never mind, put on your things. I say, are my eyes swollen?"

"One of them's puffed up a bit, and your lip's cut like mine is."

"Never mind. Come and have a wash."

"Shan't you lock up your museum?"

"Not now. I don't care for it after what they've done. Yes, I do; I'll come up afterwards," he continued, rapidly replacing the pot of preserving paste. "Come along, and try and look as if nothing was the matter."

I followed him as soon as we had put on our clothes, and then we hurried to the row of basins and towels, barely completing our ablutions when the bell rang, and not looking so very much the worse.

"Never mind, old chap," whispered Mercer, as we went into the schoolroom to dinner, with the boys all watching us and making remarks; "wait a bit, and we'll have revenge."

"How?" I said, as with a horrifying rapidity the pot of poison came into my mind.

"Never you mind;" he whispered tragically. "Bitter revenge! Only you wait."

There was a tapping on the end table just then, and all the boys rose. Then the Doctor's deep, bland voice uttered the word, —

"Grace!"

Chapter Seven.

I ate that dinner very uneasily. For one thing, I had no appetite, having had enough before I took my place. For another, I was worried by the furtive grins and whispers of the boys near me, the news of the fight having run like lightning through the school. Then I was in a constant state of dread lest my appearance should be noticed by either Mr Rebble, the Doctor, or the new assistant master, who was dining on the principal's left, for the Doctor made our dinner his lunch and of course had his late. I had not had a chance to look in a glass, and, as my face ached and felt tight, I imagined terrible black eyes, a horribly swollen nose, and that my top lip was puffed out to a large size. In fact, I felt that I must be in that state; and as I glanced at Mercer, I was surprised to see that he hardly showed a mark. Lastly, I could not get on with my dinner, because my mouth would not open and shut properly, while every attempt to move my lower jaw sidewise gave me intense pain.

I was in hopes that this was not noticed, and to get over the difficulty of being seen with my plate of meat untouched, I furtively slipped two slices, a potato, and a piece of bread under the table, where I knew that the two cats would be foraging according to their custom.

I thought the act was not noticed, but the boy on my right had been keenly watching me.

"Can't you eat your dinner?" he whispered.

There was no other course open save making a paltry excuse, so I said gruffly,—

"Never mind, old chap," he said, to my surprise. "Lots of us laugh at you, but—. I say, don't tell 'em I said so."

"I don't sneak and tell tales," I said morosely.

"No, of course you wouldn't. I was going to say lots of us laugh at you, but lots of us wish you and Senna Tea had given those two bullies an awful licking."

"Thank-ye," I said, for these words were quite cheering, and I glanced at Mercer, who was fiddling his dinner about, and cutting the pink-looking cold boiled beef up in very small squares.

"Can't you get on?" I whispered.

"No. 'Tain't likely; but just you wait."

"What for?"

"Never mind!"

The dinner went on, with the clattering of knives and forks upon plates, and, the meat being ended, the pudding came along, round, stodgy slices, with glittering bits of yellow suet in it, and here and there a raisin, or plum, as we called it, playing at bo-peep with those on the other side, — "Spotted Dog," we used to call it, — and I got on a little better, for it was nice and warm and sweet, from the facts that the Doctor never stinted us boys in our food, and that, while the cook always said she hated all boys, she contrived to make our dinners tasty and good.

"Try the pudding," I whispered to Mercer.

"Shan't. I should like to shy it bang in old Burr major's face."

"Oh, never mind."

"But I do mind; but just you wait!"

"Well, I am waiting," I said. "Why don't you tell me what you mean?"

Mercer was silent.

"I say!"

"Well?"

"You're not going to give him anything nasty, are you?"

"Yes."

"Oh!"

"You wait and see!"

"But you mustn't; it wouldn't do."

"Wouldn't it? Ah, just you wait. We'll make 'em sorry for this."

"I'm not going to do anything nasty," I said sturdily.

"Yes, you are; you're going to do as I do. We're mates, and you've got to help me as I helped you."

I thought of the pot marked "poison;" of Dicksee being bad through taking something Mercer had given him; and a curious sensation of sickness came over me, and I left half my pudding, just as Mercer took up his fork, chopped his disk up into eight pieces, and began to bolt them fiercely.

"Eat your pudding," he said, noticing that I had left off.

"Can't. I've had enough."

"You must. I want you to grow strong. I shall give you some tonic stuff my father prescribes for people."

I looked at him in horror, but he was glaring at the last piece of pudding on his fork.

"Just you wait!" he said gloomily.

"I will not help him in anything I think wrong," I said to myself; and a few minutes after, Mercer leaned towards me.

"Look!" he whispered; "there's Eely Burr and Fathead grinning at us. Wait a bit! They don't know what a horrible revenge we're going to have on them."

"But if it's *we*," I said, "you ought to tell me what the revenge is going to be."

"I'll tell you some time," he whispered. "Perhaps to-morrow, perhaps to-night.—You wait!"

"Oh, how I do hate being treated like that!" I thought to myself, and I was about to beg of him to tell me then, and to try to persuade him not to, do anything foolish, when the Doctor tapped the table with the handle of his cheese-knife, grace was said, and we all adjourned to the play-field for the half-hour at our disposal before we resumed our studies.

I had no further opportunity for speaking to Mercer that afternoon, for, when we returned to the schoolroom, the Doctor made us a speech, in which he said he, "regretted deeply to find."—Here he stopped to blow his nose, and I turned hot, cold, and then wet, as I felt that we two would be publicly reproved and perhaps punished for fighting.

"That," continued the Doctor, "many of the boys had been going back in minor subjects."

I breathed more freely at this.

Mr Hasnip, whom he now publicly presented to us, was an Oxford gentleman, who would take our weak points in hand, strengthen them, and help him, the Doctor, to maintain the high position his establishment had held for so many years.

Of course we all looked very hard at the new usher, who was a pale, yellowish-looking man, with eyes hidden by smoked glasses, which enabled him to see without being seen, and he now smiled at us as if he were going to bite, and was nicknamed Parsnip by Mercer on the instant.

"He'll be a teaser," whispered Mercer. "Going to strengthen our weak parts, is he? Wish he could strengthen mine in the way I want. I suppose we shall be turned over to him. Can't be worse than old Reb."

Mercer was right; we two were the first boys turned over to the new usher, and this was fortunate for us, for he knew nothing about our personal appearance; and the swellings that did come on, and which would have been noticed directly by Mr Rebble, passed unheeded by him.

I was very glad when tea-time came, for my head was so confused that Mr Hasnip was quite right in telling me I was a very stupid boy, for I was that afternoon—very.

But the meal-time did come, and as soon as tea was over, instead of going into the play-field with the others, I sat down alone, sore, aching, and disconsolate, to try and master some of the things Mr Hasnip had said I was behindhand in.

I had just taken up my book, with my head feeling more hazy than ever, and the shouts of the boys floating in at the open window, when Mercer came in hurriedly.

"Here, put that book away," he said quickly.

"What for? I don't want to come out."

"But you must. I've been and put away my specimens, and that settled it. Come along."

"But why must I come out? I don't want to play, and the other fellows will only laugh at us."

"No, they will not. They're not going to see us. Come along. Revenge!"

I got up and took my cap unwillingly, but, as we got out in the soft evening air, I began to think that perhaps I could keep him back if he were going to do anything wrong, so I walked on by his side with more alacrity.

"Going for a walk?" I said, as I found that he avoided the play-field.

"No. You wait and you'll see."

"Well, you needn't be so disagreeable with me," I said gruffly.

"I'm not, only I ache and burn, and I'm full of it. Come on."

To my surprise, he led me down to the lodge cottage, where the big, soldierly-looking fellow was enjoying his evening pipe in his neatly-kept little garden.

"Evening, young gents," he said, saluting us. "When do you two begin your drill?"

"I don't know, Lomax. When the new master's done thumping Latin and Euclid into us."

"Humph! Well, gentlemen, I hear that the Romans were very fine soldiers, and Euclid's all about angles and squares, isn't it?"

"Yes."

"Well, they're right enough in infantry formation—squares are, and the angles in fortification, which is a thing I don't know much about, having been in the cavalry; but when you are ready, so am I, and I'll set you up and make men of you as your fa—" he glanced at me and pulled himself up short—"as your people shall be proud of."

"That's right, Lom, and I'll bring you some prime tobacco soon as I can. I say, you can fight, can't you?"

"Well," he said, smiling and drawing himself up, "they used to say I could once upon a time. There's my old sword hanging up over the chimney-piece, and if it could speak—"

"Yes, yes, I know, and you've been wounded," cried Mercer hastily; "but I don't mean with swords and pistols, I mean with your fists."

"Oh, I see. Boxing."

"Yes," cried Mercer eagerly.

And I was still so dull and confused by the knocking about I had received, that I had not a glimmer of what he was aiming at.

"Yes; boxing. I want you to teach us."

"Yes, I was a dabster at it when I was in the —th. We had no end of it, and we lads used to have a regular subscription round to buy new gloves. Oh yes, I gave lessons to the officers regularly. Long time since I've had the gloves on, but I could handle my fists as well as ever, I daresay."

"Then you'll teach us?"

"Teach you? No, no, my lads. Infantry drill; clubs and dumb-bells; singlestick and foil; riding with a military seat; but—use of the gloves! Oh dear no! What do you think the Doctor would say?"

"But he won't know, Lom, and we'll pay you, honour bright."

"I know you would, Master Mercer; and if this young gent, whose father was in the cavalry—"

"Yes, at Chilly—" began Mercer.

"Wallah, sir," said Lomax severely. "If he says he'll pay me, of course he would. But no, sir, no. Besides, we've got no gloves, and boxing-gloves—two pairs—cost money."

"Of course. I know they would, but we'd buy them, or you should for us, and then we could come here now and then, and you could teach us in your room, and nobody would know."

"No, sir, no," said the sergeant, shaking his head.

"I say, Lom, look at us both," said Mercer. "See anything?"

"Well, yes, I do, plain, my lads. You two don't want any teaching. You've got swelled lips, and mousy eyes rising, and your noses are a bit puffy. You have both been fighting."

"Yes, Lom, and see how we've been knocked about."

"Well, boys who will fight must take what they get and not grumble."

"But we didn't want to fight. They made us."

"Why, I thought you two were such friends and mates already. Bah! lads, you shouldn't fight without there's good reason."

"But we didn't fight," cried Mercer angrily.

"Why, just look at you both! your faces say it as plain as your lips."

"But I mean not together. Eely Burr and big Dicksee came and thrashed us. They would not leave us alone."

"Oh, come: that's bullying," said Lomax, shaking his head, "and it isn't a fair match; they're a good two years older than you, and used to fighting, and you ain't."

"No," said Mercer excitedly; "and it's cruel and cowardly. I'm not a bit afraid of him, and Burr junior wasn't of his man, and we did the best we could, but they knocked us about just as they liked, and hit us where they pleased, and we couldn't hurt them a bit."

"No, you wouldn't be able of course," said the old sergeant thoughtfully, taking our arms and feeling our muscles. "Well, it was very plucky of you both to stand up and face 'em, that's all I can say. Is that why you want to learn to use your fists?"

"Yes, and as soon as we can both box well, we want to give them both such lickings!" cried Mercer eagerly.

The old sergeant began to laugh in a quiet way, and wiped the tears out of his eyes.

"Then you want to learn on the sly, and astonish 'em some day?"

"Yes, yes," I said eagerly, for I was as excited as my companion, whose idea of revenge, now it was explained, seemed to me to be glorious.

"Well, it is tempting," said the sergeant thoughtfully.

"And you'll teach us?"

"And his father fought at Chillianwallah! Yes, it is tempting. You ought to be able to take your own part if big cowards tackle you."

"Yes, Lom. Then do teach us."

"No. What would the Doctor say?"

"He never should know. We'd never tell, either of us, would we, Burr?"

"Never!" I cried.

"I believe you, boys, that I do," said the old man; "and it was never forbidden. Never even mentioned," he continued thoughtfully. "I should like to oblige an old soldier's son."

"And I mean to be an army surgeon," said Mercer.

"And you couldn't do better, my lad."

"Then you'll teach us?" cried Mercer, and I hung upon his answer, with the spirit of retaliation strong within me now.

"Do you know what it means, my lads? Deal of knocking about."

"We don't care how much, do we, Burr?"

"No," I cried excitedly. "You may knock me down hundreds of times, if you'll teach me how to knock you down."

"But the gloves will cost about a pound."

"A pound!" said Mercer in dismay. Then a happy thought struck him.

"We shall have to give up buying Magglin's gun for the present," he whispered to me. Then aloud—

"All right Lom. If we bring you the money, will you buy the gloves?"

"Yes, my lads, I will; and good ones."

"And you will teach us?"

"I'll teach you," said the sergeant, "for the sake of helping to make a strong man of the son of a brave officer, who died for his country. There!"

"Hooray!" cried Mercer; "and how much will you charge for the lessons, Lom? because you must make it a little more, as we shall have to go tick for a bit, because of paying so much for the gloves."

"How much?" said the sergeant thoughtfully. "Let me see. First and foremost, your words of honour that you'll never tell a soul I taught you how to fight, for it might lead to unpleasantness."

"On my honour, I'll never tell!" cried Mercer.

"And on my honour I never will!" I said excitedly.

"Right, then, so far," said Lomax. "Now about those gloves. If I recollect right, they're eight-and-six a pair, and two pairs are seventeen shillings."

"And the carriage," said Mercer.

"Stop a bit. I think, being an old soldier, and teaching, the makers'll take something off for me. I know they'll send 'em down carriage paid, and Jem Roff'll get 'em for me from the cross when the waggon goes in. Got your money?"

"I've got half a sovereign," said Mercer.

"I've got seven shillings," I said.

"Hand over then," said the sergeant, and we lightened our purses tremendously.

"That's right," said Lomax. "Now about the pay for the lessons. I want that in advance."

"Oh!" we both ejaculated in dismay.

"We can't pay now, Lom," said Mercer, "but we will."

"Yes, you can."

"But how?"

"Give me your fists, both of you, in a hearty soldier's grip, my lads. That's my pay in advance, and if in less than six months you two don't give those two bullies a big dressing down, why, I'm a Dutchman."

"Oh, Lom!"

"Oh, thank you!" I cried.

"Thank you, my lads, and God bless you both. Fighting's generally bad, but it's good sometimes. There, be off, both of you, and I'll write a letter for those gloves to-night."

We left him with our hearts beating high.

"I don't mind my face swelling a bit now," said Mercer.

"I should like to begin learning to-morrow," I said, and then we were both silent for a few minutes, till Mercer turned round with a queer laugh on his swollen face.

"I say," he cried, with a chuckle, "I wonder whether old Dicksee will cry cock-a-doodle-doo next time when we've done."

"Let's wait and see," said I; and that night I dreamed that I was a wind-mill, and that every time my sails, which were just the same as arms, went round, they came down bang on Dicksee's head, and made him yell.

I woke up after that dream, to find it was broad daylight, and crept out of bed to look at my face in the glass, and shrank away aghast, for my lip was more swollen, and there was a nasty dark look under my eye.

Chapter Eight.

I stood gazing into the little looking-glass with my spirits sinking down and down in that dreary way in which they will drop with a boy who wakes up in the morning with some trouble resting upon his shoulders like so much lead.

I was more stiff and sore, too, at first waking, and all this combined to make me feel so miserable, that I began to think about home and my mother, and what would be the consequences if I were to dress quickly, slip out, and go back.

She would be so glad to see me again, I thought, that she would not be cross; and when I told her how miserable I was at the school, she would pity me, and it would be all right again.

I was so elated by the prospect, and—young impostor that I was—so glad of the excuse which the marks upon my face would form to a doting mother, that I began to dress quickly, and had got as far as I could without beginning to splash in the water and rattle the little white jug and basin, when the great obstacle to my evasion came before me with crushing power, and I sat on my bed gazing blankly before me.

For a terrible question had come for an answer, and it was this:

"What will uncle say?"

And as I sat on the edge of my bed, his handsome, clearly-cut face, with the closely-cropped white hair and great grey moustache, was there before me, looking at me with a contemptuous sneer, which seemed to say, "You miserable, despicable young coward! Is this the way you fulfil your promise of trying to be a man, worthy of your poor father, who was a brave soldier and a gentleman? Out upon you for a miserable young sneak!"

That all came up wonderfully real before me, and I felt the skin of my forehead wrinkle up and tighten other parts of my face, while I groaned to myself, as if apologising to my uncle, —

"But I can't stop here, I am so miserable, and I shall be horribly punished for what I could not help. The boys say the Doctor is very severe, sometimes."

There was my uncle's stern face still, just as I had conjured it up, and he was frowning.

He will be horribly angry with me, I thought, and it would make poor mamma so unhappy, and —

"I can't go, and I won't go," I said, half aloud. "I don't care if the Doctor cuts me to pieces; and I won't tell how I got the marks, for, if I do, all the boys will think I am a sneak."

"Fill the tea-cup—fill the tea-cup—fill the tea-cup! High up—high up—high up! Fine morning—fine morning—fine morning!"

The notes of a thrush, sounding exactly like that, with the help of a little imagination; and I rose, went to the window, gazed out, and there was the sun, looking like a great globe of orange, lighting up the mists in the hollows, and making everything look so glorious, that I began to feel a little better.

Turning round to look at my schoolfellows asleep in their little narrow beds, all in exceedingly ungraceful attitudes, and looking towzley and queer, I saw that, as I held the blind on one side, the sunlight shone full on Mercer, and I hurt myself directly by bursting out into a silent fit of laughter, which drew my bruised face into pain-producing puckers. But it was impossible to help it, all the same, for Mercer's phiz looked so comic.

The swelling about his eyes had gone down, and there were only very faint marks beneath them, but his mouth was twisted all on one side, and his nose looked nearly twice as big as usual.

114

He's worse than I am, I thought, as I stood gazing at him, and this brought up our visit to the lodge the previous evening, and a grim feeling of satisfaction began to make me glow, as I dwelt upon Mercer's plans, and in imagination I saw myself about to be possessed of a powerful talisman, which would enable me to retaliate on my enemies, and be always one who could protect the weak from the oppressor. And as I stood thinking all this, I turned again to look out of the window, where the lovely landscape of the Sussex weald lay stretched out before me, and listened to the birds bursting forth into their full morning song, as the sun literally cut up the mists, which rose and dispersed just as the last of the mental mists were rising fast from about me. There was the glorious country, with all its attractions for a town boy, and close by me lay Mercer, who seemed to me quite a profound sage in his knowledge of all around, and I felt that, after all, I had got too much budding manliness in me to give up like a coward, who would run away at the first trouble he had to meet.

I was a natural boy once again, and, going back to Mercer's bedside, I began to think that there was no fun in seeing him sleeping away there while I was wide awake; so, stealing softly to his little wash-stand, I took the towel, dipped one corner carefully in the jug, and then, with a big drop ready to fall, I held it close to his nose, squeezed it a little, and the drop fell.

The effect was instantaneous.

Mercer gave a spring which made his bed creak, and sat up staring at me.

"What are you doing?" he said. "Why can't you be quiet? Has the bell rung?"

"I don't know," I said. "I haven't heard it."

"Why—why, it's ever so early yet, and you're half dressed. Oh, how my nose burns! I say, is it swelled?"

"Horribly!" I said.

He leaped out of bed, ran to the glass, stared in, and looked round again at me.

"Oh my!" he ejaculated, as he gazed at me wildly; "there's no getting out of this. Bathing won't take a nose like that down. It ought to have on a big linseed meal poultice."

"But you couldn't breathe with a thing like that on."

"Oh yes, you could," he said, with the voice of authority. "You get two big swan quills, and cut them, and put one up each nostril, and then put on your plaster. That's how my father does."

"But you couldn't go about like that."

"No, you lie in bed on your back, and whistle every time you breathe."

I laughed.

"Ah, it's all very fine to laugh, but we shall be had up to the Doctor's desk this morning, and he'll want to know about the fighting."

"Well, we must tell him, I suppose," I said. "They began on us."

"No," said Mercer, shaking his head, and looking as depressed as I did when I woke; "that wouldn't do here. The fellows never tell on each other, and we should be sent to Coventry. It's precious hard to be licked, and then punished after, when you couldn't help it, isn't it?"

"Yes," I said. "Then you won't tell about Burr major and Dicksee."

"Oh no. Never do. We shall have to take it and grin and bear it, whether it's the cane or impositions. Worst of it is, it'll mean ever so much keeping in. I wouldn't care if it had been a month or two ago."

"What difference would that have made?"

"Why, it was all wet weather then. Now it's so fine, I want for us to go and collect things, and I'm not going to be beaten over that stuffing. Next time I shall look at a live bird ever so long before I try to stuff one, and then you'll see. We'll be on the watch next time, so that old Eely shan't catch us, and—ha, ha, ha! Oh my! oh my! oh my!" he cried, sitting down on the edge of his bed, rocking himself to and fro, and kicking up his bare feet and working his toes about in the air.

"What are you laughing about?" I said, feeling glad to see that he too was getting rid of the depression.

"Wait a bit," he whispered. "Won't we astonish them! Oh, my nose, how it does hurt!" he added, covering the swollen organ with his hand, and speaking in a snuffling tone. "I shall aim straight at old Eely's snub all the time, so as to make it twice as big as mine is. He will be so mad, for he's as proud of himself as a peacock, and thinks he's handsome. What do you think he does?"

"I don't know," I said.

"Puts scent on his handkerchief every morning—musk. Oh, he is a dandy! But wait a bit! Seventeen shillings! Isn't it a lot for two pairs of gloves? And, I say!"

"Yes."

"He's an awful dandy about his gloves too. By and by, when he's had his licking,—two lickings, for you shall give him one too,—I'll tell you what we'll always say to him."

"Well?"

"We'll say, 'What sized gloves do you take?'"

117

"But he will not know anything about the gloves," I said, interrupting a laugh. "We shan't have gloves on then."

"No more we shall. What a pity! That spoils my joke. Never mind. Let's dress, and go and look at the gardens—perhaps there may be some good butterflies out in the sunshine; and as soon as cook's down, I'll beg some hot water to bathe my nose."

But Mercer did not put in a petition for the hot water. "It's no good," he said, when we were down by the gardens, soon after we were dressed. "It's like physic; we've got to take it, so we may as well face it all out and get it over."

Very good philosophy, of course, but I did not feel hopeful about what was to come.

It all began at breakfast, where we were no sooner seated, than Mr Rebble came by with the new assistant master.

"Bless me! Good gracious! Look, Mr Hasnip. Did you ever see such a nose? No, no, Mercer: sit up, sir."

Poor Mercer had ducked down to hide his bulbous organ, but he had to sit up while Mr Hasnip brought his smoke-tinted spectacles to bear upon it.

"Terrible!" he said. "The boy must have been fighting."

"Yes; and here's the other culprit," cried Mr Rebble. "Look at this boy's eye and mouth. Have you two boys been fighting?"

"Yes, sir," I said in a low voice.

"Disgraceful! Well, the Doctor must know of it, and he will punish you both severely."

The two masters moved off to their table, and a buzz of excitement ran through the nearest boys, while, as I looked up, I could see Burr major standing up in his place and looking over toward us.

"I say," whispered Mercer, "here's a game; they think we two have been fighting together like old Lom did. Let 'em think so. Don't you say a word."

"But it will be so dishonest," I expostulated.

"No, it won't. If they ask you who you fought with, you must say nothing."

"Not tell them?"

"No. The Doctor will say you are stubborn and obstinate, and threaten to expel you; but he don't mean it, and you've got to hold your tongue, as I told you before. We never split on each other here."

"Will the Doctor know, do you think?" I asked, as we went on with our breakfast.

"Sure to. Old Reb's safe to go and tell him directly he comes."

I soon heard that this opinion was shared, for one of the bigger boys came over from his seat near Burr major.

"I say," he said, "Reb's sure to tell the Doctor about you two. Shall you say that you had a round with big Burr and old Fatsee?"

"Did Eely tell you to come and ask?" said Mercer, glancing toward where Burr major was anxiously watching in our direction.

"Never you mind. Are you going to tell?"

"What is it to you?"

"A good deal. You tell, and half a dozen of us mean to wallop you two, and you won't like that."

"Oh, I shouldn't mind, and Burr junior wouldn't. I know old Squirmy sent you to ask because—there, look at him—he's all in a fiddle for fear the Doctor should punish him—a great coward!—for knocking smaller boys about."

"Look here," whispered the ambassador, "don't you be quite so saucy."

"Shall if I like. You go and tell old Eely, old slimy Snip, that I'm not like his chosen friend Dicksee, a miserable, tale-telling sneak. I shan't let out about Burr major being such a coward, and Burr here won't tell about fat-headed Dicksee, so now you can go."

"And you'd better keep to it," said the boy, looking at me fiercely; but I did not feel afraid, for Mercer's project about the gloves had sent a glow through me, and, as he said, our time would come.

But I felt anything but comfortable an hour later, when I was back in school, after the breakfast had been cleared, for I could see that the boys had their eyes upon us, and were whispering, and I knew it related to the punishment to come.

The worst moments were when the Doctor entered and took his place in his pulpit amidst a suppressed rustle, and I set my teeth as I stood up, and shrank down again at the earliest opportunity, feeling as if the Doctor's eye was fixed upon me, and, as it happened, just as I was wishing he would speak, and, as I felt it, put me out of my misery, he uttered one of his tremendous coughs, which had far more effect in producing silence than Mr Rebble's words.

"Thomas Mercer, Burr junior," he said loudly, "come up here."

"I wish I had run away this morning," was my first thought, but it was gone directly, and I was glad I had not, as I walked as firmly as I could, side by side with my brother offender, right up to the front of the Doctor's desk, where he sat frowning upon us like a judge without his wig and gown.

"Hah!" he ejaculated in his most awe-inspiring tones, as he looked at us searchingly. "No doubt about it. Disgraceful marks, like a pair of rough street boys instead of young gentlemen. So you two have been fighting?"

"Yes, sir."

"Yes, sir."

"I am glad that you have frankness enough to own to it. You, Mercer, knew better; but you, sir, had to learn that you have broken one of the most rigid rules of my establishment. I object to fighting,

121

as savage, brutal, and cruel, and I will not allow it here. Mr Rebble, give these boys heavy impositions, and you will both of you stop in and study every day for a fortnight under Mr Hasnip's directions. Some principals would have administered the cane or the birch, but I object to those instruments as being, like fighting, savage, brutal, and cruel, only to be used as a last resource, when ordinary punishments suitable for gentlemen fail. I presume that you make no defence?" He continued rolling out his words in a broad volume of sound. "You own that you have both been fighting? Silence is a full answer. Return to your places."

I heard Mercer utter a low sigh, and my breast felt overcharged as we went back to our desks, where we were no sooner seated than Mercer whispered, —

"Never mind, old chap! we'll help one another; and he never asked who we had been fighting with, so we didn't get extra punishment for being stubborn. Oh dear me, what a rum place school is!"

Poor Mercer, he had yet to learn, as I had, that the school was only the world in miniature, and that we should find our life there almost exactly the same when we grew up to be men.

"I wonder what Mr Hasnip will set us to do," I thought, as the clock at last told that the morning's studies were nearly at an end, and I was still wondering when the boys rose, and Eely Burr, Dicksee, and the other big fellow, Hodson, came round behind us, and the first whispered, —

"Lucky for you two that you didn't tell. My! I shouldn't have liked to be you, if you had."

"Go and scent your handkerchief," said Mercer angrily. "I'd tell if I liked."

"If they weren't here, I'd punch your ugly head," whispered Eely, and they all three went out, leaving us two alone in the great schoolroom, with the ushers at one end, and the Doctor, contrary to his usual custom, still in his desk at the other.

"Stand, Thomas Mercer and Burr junior," he said. "Or no—Mercer can keep his seat."

I rose with Mercer, who resumed his place.

"Burr junior," said the Doctor, rolling out his words slowly, as if they were so precious that they ought to make a proper impression, "I sentenced you to a certain series of punishments, to endure for fourteen days; but you are new, untrained, and have been so unfortunate as to receive such education as you possess by private tuition. Under these circumstances, you are wanting in social knowledge, especially of the kind bearing upon your conduct to your fellow-workers in a school like this. In consequence, I shall make a point of looking over this your first offence, and exonerating you. That will do."

I murmured my thanks, and remained in my place.

"Well," said the Doctor, as Mr Hasnip coughed to take my attention, "why are you waiting?"

"For Mercer, sir."

"But I have not excused him. He is not a new boy; and besides, I am sure you would like him to be punished."

"No, no!" I said eagerly; "and I don't want to be let off if he is not."

"Hum! Hah!" ejaculated the Doctor, looking at me benevolently through his spectacles. "Well—er—er—yes—I like that. Mercer, you are excused too. That will do."

"Thank you, sir; thank you, sir," cried Mercer joyfully; and we both bowed and hurried away to the loft, Mr Rebble shaking his head at us as we passed his desk, and Mr Hasnip, as I thought, looking sadly disappointed as far as I could judge, though I could not see his eyes.

On reaching the loft, Mercer was in such a state of exultation that he relieved his feelings by standing upon his head on the corn-bin; but I did not feel so glad, for I had not spoken out, and the Doctor had been acting under a misconception, and I said so.

"Oh, never mind," cried Mercer, speaking with his heels in the air. "We couldn't explain, and it don't matter. Oh, I say, won't old Eely be pleased that we've got off!"

I did not answer, for I still felt that I should like to go and tell the Doctor frankly everything that had passed.

Chapter Nine.

Mercer was terribly exercised in mind about Magglin's gun, and his having to give that up for the sake of his revenge, but a letter from home containing five shillings revived his hopes, and it was put aside as a nest-egg, so that the amount might be raised at last, though what the amount was we had no idea.

Our injuries soon became better, and were forgotten, as the days went rapidly by, while I grew so much at home that the arrival of a new pupil made me feel quite one of the old boys. I had my patch of garden given me, and took great pride in digging and planting it, and as soon as my interest was noticed by my namesake, he coolly walked across it twice, laughing at me contemptuously the while, as if he knew that I dared not retaliate.

And all this time I worked hard with my lessons, with more or less success, I suppose, for Mr Hasnip, who was a kind of encyclopaedia, and seemed to know everything, did not scold me and box my ears with the book he held every day.

We did not have another fishing trip, for the keeper met us one day and informed us that we owed him two shillings for damage done to his lines, and this debt I undertook to repay as soon as I obtained some more money from home. But we had several afternoons in the woods, and brought back treasures which were safely deposited in Mercer's box, ready for examination at some future time.

Some people would not have called them treasures, though they were looked upon as such by Mercer, who was exceedingly proud of a snake-skin which he found in a patch of dwarf furze, and of a great snail shell that was nearly white, and had belonged to one of the molluscs used by the Romans for their soup.

Among other things was an enormous frog, which was kept alive in some fresh damp moss stuffed into a fig drum, into which a certain number of unfortunate flies were thrust every day through a hole, filled directly after by a peg. Whether those flies were eaten by the frog, or whether they got out again, I never knew, but Mercer had perfect faith in their being consumed.

Just about this time, too, my chosen companion got in debt.

It was in this wise. We went down the garden one day, talking very earnestly about how long it was before the gloves needed for our lessons came down, wondering, too, that we had never been able to catch sight of the old sergeant, when Mercer suddenly became aware of the fact that Magglin, who was hoeing weeds, was also making mysterious signs to us to go round to his side of the garden; and when we reached him he whispered to my companion, after looking cautiously round to see that we were not observed, —

"You don't want to buy a ferret, do you, Master Mercer?"

"Yes," cried the latter eagerly; "I do want a ferret to hunt the rats in the stable. No, I don't," he said sadly; "I haven't got any money."

"You not got no money!" said the gipsy-looking fellow. "Oh, I like that, and you a gentleman."

"How much is it?" said Mercer.

"Oh, only five shillin'. It's like giving it away, only a chap I know wants some money, and he ast me to see if any of the young gents would like to buy it."

"'Tisn't your old ferret, then?"

"Oh no, sir; I got rid o' that long enough ago, because I thought people would say I kep' it to catch rabbids. They are so disagreeable. But this is an out and outer to catch rabbids," he whispered.

"But five shillings is such a lot of money for a ferret, Magg."

"Lot! Well, there! It's giving of it away. Why, if I wanted such a thing, and had the chance to get such a good one as this, I'd give ten shillin' for it."

"But is it a good one, Magg?"

"Splendid. You come and look at it. I've got it in the tool-house in a watering-pot."

"Let's go and see it, Frank," cried Mercer, and we followed the slouching-looking fellow into the tool-shed, where a watering-pot stood, with a piece of slate over the half open top and a piece of brick laid on that.

"There!" cried Magglin, removing the cover and taking out a sandy-coloured snaky-looking animal, with sharp nose and pink eyes, one which writhed about almost like an eel.

"Why, it's your old one, Magg, that you had in the hedge that day."

"Nay, not it. It's something like it, but this is an ever so much better one. Why, don't you recollect? That one used to get in the holes and wouldn't come out again for hours and hours."

"Oh yes, I recollect, and how cold it was. This is it."

"Why, don't I keep telling of you it ain't. This is a hever so much better one as I've got to sell for a chap for five shillin': but if you don't want to buy it, you needn't keep finding fault with it. I dessay Mr Big Burr will buy it. It's a beauty—ain't yer?"

"But I do want to buy it," said Mercer, watching the man as he stroked and caressed the thin creature, "but I haven't got any money to spare."

"That don't matter. If you like to buy the ferret, I dessay the chap'll wait and take a shillin' one time and a shillin' another, till it's all paid off."

"Oh," cried Mercer, "if he'll sell it like that I'll have it; but you're sure it's not your old one?"

"Sartain as sartain. That's a ferret as'll do anybody credit."

"But will it hunt rabbits up into holes, and stop sucking their blood?"

"Oh, I don't know nothing about rabbids," said Magglin. "It won't do so with me; 'tis yours then."

"Will it bite?" I asked.

"Rats, sir. You try him, he's as tame as a kitten. But I must get back to my work. Where'll you have it?"

"I want it up in my box—the old corn-bin up in the loft, Magg. Will you take it and put it in if I give you the key?"

"Course I will, sir."

"And bring me back the key?"

"Course I will, sir."

"I don't like to take it myself, because one of the fellows might see me, and they'd want to know what I'd got."

"All right, sir, I'll take it; and am I to put it in the box?"

"No. I forgot. It would eat the skins and things."

"That he would and no mistake," said Magglin, grinning hugely. "Shall I leave him in the can? There is a stone in the spout so as he can't squeeze his way out, for he'll go through any hole a'most."

"Yes; put it right up in the dark corner at the far end."

"Right, sir. And you owe me five shillin'."

"No, it's to your friend."

"All the same, sir. Thank-ye."

"I'm afraid he has cheated me," said Mercer thoughtfully, as we walked away. "Now I come to recollect, his old ferret had a bit nipped out of the top of its little ear like that has, and Magg said a rat bit it out one day."

"If he has cheated you, I wouldn't pay for it," I said.

"I don't know how it is," continued Mercer thoughtfully, "but it seems to me as if people like to cheat schoolboys. We never did two shillings worth of damage to those fishing lines—and I've got a horrible thought, Burr!"

"What is it?" I said.

"Why, it's all that time since we gave old Lom the money, and for the first week he was always winking and laying his finger up against the side of his nose every time he saw us, and now we can't ever see him at all."

"Oh!" I ejaculated. "No. Impossible! He's an old soldier, and he couldn't cheat us like that."

"Well, if he has, I'll tell the Doctor, and have him punished."

"You couldn't tell," I said dolefully.

"No, I forgot that. Well, let's go and see if he's at home now. Why, he hasn't done any drilling this week! Why's that?"

I shook my head, feeling horrified at the idea of such a fine-looking, frank old soldier being guilty of a piece of trickery, and I said so, but declared that I would not believe it.

"I don't want to, but people do cheat us. Even Polly Hopley charges us double for lots of the things we have."

By this time we had reached the lodge, but the door was shut, and Mercer looked at me very gloomily.

"There's all our money gone," he said; "and I'll never trust anybody again. I wish I hadn't bought that ferret. You see if it don't cheat us too, and run away. This makes eight times we've come to look for old Lom, and he must be— What?"

"Look," I said eagerly. "I knew he couldn't do such a thing. There he is in that cart."

Sure enough, there was the sergeant; and then as the cart drew nearer, it was pulled up, and the old man leaped down, thanked the farmer for giving him a lift, and walked toward his cottage, carrying a big long carpet-bag.

"Ah, Mr Lomax!" I cried, as I hurried towards him, but he laid his finger to the side of his nose, nodded, frowned, unlocked his door and went in.

"There, that's how he always goes on now," said Mercer spitefully. "It was all gammon, and he never meant to teach us, and we shan't be able to serve those two out. Come on."

We were moving off disconsolately, I with quite a feeling of pain in my breast, when a voice said, "Hi!" and, looking round, there was the sergeant beckoning to us.

My heart seemed to leap again, and I hurried back.

"How are you both?" he said, putting his hand in his pocket and taking out a flat steel tobacco-box which opened with a spring. "I had to go up to town more than a week ago to an inspection and about my pension, and while I was up I thought I'd go and see my sisters, and then I thought I'd go and see about those—you know what."

"And did you?" I cried eagerly.

"Wait a moment," he said, taking out four shillings and handing them to us—two to each. "I did write about them, and they asked so much that I wrote to another place, and they were dear too; and then, as I had to go up, I went to a place I remembered, and saw the man, and told him what I wanted, and he brought out two pairs of his best, which had been in the shop three years, and got faded to look at, but he said they were better than ever, and he let me have 'em for thirteen shillings."

"Oh, Lom!" cried Mercer excitedly. "But when are they coming down?"

"They are down. Didn't you see?"

"No, I didn't see."

"They were in the carpet-bag," I cried. "Oh, do let's look!"

"No, not to-day, my lads. They're all right, and if you like to get up to-morrow morning and come to me at five o'clock, I'll give you your first lesson. Now I must go and report myself to the Doctor, or he'll be drumming me out of the regiment for not doing my work."

He saluted us and marched off, while we went round to the back and made our way to the stables and up into the loft, for Mercer to have a peep at the ferret, which tried hard to get out. Then, closing the slate down close, he spun round, cut a caper, struck an attitude, and began sparring and dancing round me in the most absurd manner.

"Oh, only wait!" he cried, pausing to take breath. "I do feel so glad! But, I say, we mustn't have that ferret there. I know. I'll put it in the bin, watering-pot and all, or it'll either get out, or some of the boys'll come and look, and let it go."

"But you haven't got the key."

"I forgot. I didn't get it from old Magg, again. Let's go and find him. No, it's all right. He has put it in the padlock."

The bin was thrown open; but the pot was not placed therein, for Mercer remembered a box with a lid, which, as he expressed it, lived in there, and it was emptied and brought forth.

"Just make him a splendid little hutch!" he cried, "Here, come along, Sandy."

He thrust his hand into the pot, took hold of the ferret, and was about to place it in the box; but it gave a wriggle and writhe, glided out of Mercer's hand, crept under the corn-bin, and, as he tried to reach it, I saw it run out at the back, and creep down a hole in the floor boards, one evidently made by a rat.

"Oh!" ejaculated Mercer dolefully. "There goes five shillings down that hole. What an unlucky beggar I am!"

"Oh, he'll soon come out again," I said.

"Not he; and that's the worst of you, Burr—you will make the best of things so. He won't come out—he'll live down there hunting the rats; and I'm sure now that we shall never get him again, for it is the one Magg used to have, and he has tricked me. I know it by that bit out of its ear. It is his ferret."

"Well, you haven't paid him for it," I said, laughing. "And if he has cheated you, I wouldn't pay."

"But I said I would," replied Mercer, shaking his head; "and one must keep one's promises, even with cheats. But never mind; old Lom's got the gloves, and if Magg gives me any of his nonsense, I'll thrash him, too, eh?"

"Tea!" I cried, for just then the bell began to ring.

Chapter Ten.

That evening after tea, while Mercer and I were down by the gardens, where I found that somebody had been dancing a jig on my newly-raked beds, we heard a good deal of chattering and laughing over in the play-field, and Burr major's voice dominating all the others so queerly that I laughed.

"I say, isn't it rum!" said Mercer, joining in. "I hope we shan't be like that by and by. Hodson is sometimes. There, hark!"

I listened, and Burr major was speaking sharply in a highly-pitched voice, that was all squeak, and then it descended suddenly into a gruff bass like a man's.

"Do you know what old Reb said he was one day?" said Mercer, wiping his eyes, for a chance to laugh at his tyrant always afforded him the most profound satisfaction.

"No. A dandy?"

"A hobbledehoy! and he looks it, don't he? It did make him so savage when he heard, and he said he wasn't half such a hobbledehoy as old Reb was, and Dicksee said he'd go and tell."

"And did he?"

"Did he? You know how my nose was swelled up."

"Of course."

"Well, that was nothing to Dicksee's. His is a nose that a tap will swell up, and when old Eely regularly hammered till it was soft, it looked dreadful, and when he said he'd go straight to the Doctor, Eely hammered him again till he went down on his knees and begged Eely's pardon, and promised to say it was done by a cricket-ball. I say, hark! they've got something over there. Let's go and see."

We went down along the hedge to the gate, and as soon as we passed through we could see Burr major standing up tall and thin in the midst of a group of boys, to whom he was showing something, and, our curiosity being excited, we strolled up to the group, to find that a general inspection was going on of a little bright new silver watch which Burr major had received in a box along with some new clothes that day from his father in London.

The great tall, thin fellow was giving himself the most ridiculous airs, and talking in a haughty condescending way to the boys about him, just as if watches were the commonest things in the world to him.

"Then, you know," he was saying, as we drew nigh, "you press on that little round place very lightly with your nail, and the back flies open—see."

He pressed the spring, the back opened, showing the polished interior of the case, and then shut it with a snap two or three times, the case flashing in the evening light; and as I glanced at Mercer, I quite wondered to see the eager look of interest and longing he directed at that watch.

"I say, how do you wind it up?" cried a small boy.

"Why, you just push the key in that little hole, and turn it a few times so. Oh, I forgot—I did wind it up before."

"Why, you wound it up six times," said Dicksee, with a sneer.

"Well, it's my own watch, isn't it, stupid? I can wind it up a hundred times if I like," cried Burr major contemptuously.

"I say, how much did it cost?" said Hodson.

"How should I know? I'm not going to ask my father how much a thing costs when he gives me a present. Lot of money—ten or fifteen pounds, I daresay."

"Yah! Silver watches don't cost so much as that," sneered Dicksee.

"Look here, Dicky," cried Burr major, "you're getting too cheeky. I shall have to take you down a peg or two."

"Oh, never mind old Fatsides," cried another boy. "Here, Burr, old chap, show us the works."

"Oh, nonsense, boys! I'm going to put it away now," said Burr major, opening and shutting the back, so as to make a loud snapping noise.

"I say, I should have a gold chain if I were you, Burr," said another boy.

"No, I don't think I shall," said the big fellow nonchalantly; "not for school. Silver would be good enough when a fellow's playing cricket or football."

"Oh, I say, do show us the works!" said the boy who had spoken before.

"Oh, very well. What young noodles you are! Any one would think you had never seen a watch before. You see this is one of the best class of watches, and you open the glass by pressing your nail in there. That's it, you see; and then you stick your nail on that little steel thing, and then it comes open—so. Here, keep back, some of you. Breathing on the works spoils a watch."

"Oh, what a beauty!" rose in chorus, and I saw Mercer press forward with his eyes dilated, and an intense look of longing in his countenance, as he gazed at the bright yellow works, and the tiny wheel swinging to and fro upon its hair-spring.

"Yes, it's a good watch," said Burr major, in a voice full of careless indifference. "Not the same make as my father's. His is gold, of course, and when you open it, there's a cap fits right over the top— just over there. His is a repeater, and when you touch a spring, it strikes the quarters and the hours."

Mercer looked on as if fascinated.

"Like a clock," said Hodson.

"Of course it does like a clock," said Burr major contemptuously. "It's jewelled, too, in ever so many holes. It cost a hundred guineas, I think, without the chain."

"Oh!" rose in chorus.

"Is that jewelled in lots of holes?" said one of the boys.

"Of course it is. My father wouldn't send me a watch without it was."

"I can't see any holes," said one.

"And I don't see any jewels," said another.

"Where are they, then?" said Hodson.

"The other side, of course."

"Then what's the good of them?"

"Makes a watch more valuable," said Burr major haughtily. "There, don't crowd in so. I'm going to put it away now."

"What jewels are they?" said a boy. "Pearls?"

"Diamonds," said Mercer, with his eyes fixed on the watch, "to make hard points for the wheels to swing upon, because diamonds won't wear."

"Oh, hark at him!" cried Burr major. "Old Senna knows all about it. Hardly ever saw a watch before in his life."

"Haven't I?" cried Mercer. "Why, my father has a beauty, with second hands—a stop watch."

"Ha, ha, ha!" cried Burr major, closing his new present with a loud snap. "A stop watch! that's an old one that won't go, boys. Poor old Mercer!—poor old Senna Tea! Did your father buy it cheap?"

There was a roar of laughter at this, for the boys always laughed at Burr major's jokes.

"No; I know," said Hodson. "One of old Senna's patients that he killed, left it him in his will."

I saw Mercer turn scarlet.

"Did you ever take it to pieces, and stuff it again, Senna?" and there was another roar of laughter.

"He did, I know, and that's why it won't go."

"Come along," whispered Mercer to me, for, now that the watch had disappeared in its owner's pocket, the attraction which had held my companion there seemed to have gone, and we began to walk away.

"There they go," cried Burr major; "pair of 'em. Burr junior's getting on nicely with his stuffing. I say, young un, how many doses of physic has he made you take?"

"Come away," whispered Mercer; "let's go back to the gardens. If I stop here, I shall fly out at him, and get knocked about again."

"Ah! Oh! Go home!" was shouted, Burr major starting the cry, and his followers taking it up in chorus till we had passed through the gate, when Mercer clenched his fists, and gave both feet a stamp.

"And him to have a watch like that!" he cried; "and I've longed for one ever since I was ten. Oh, I do hate that chap! Shouldn't you have liked to hit him?"

"No," I said. "I felt all the time as if I should have liked to kick him."

"Oh, I felt that too. But, I say, shouldn't you like a watch the same as his?"

"Yes," I said, "of course. Perhaps we shall have watches some day."

"Let's save up and buy one between us, and you have it one week, and me the other."

"But you wanted to save up and buy the gun that takes to pieces, so that we could go shooting."

"Yes, so I did," said Mercer — "so I do. But I should like that watch."

"Perhaps he'll get tired of it soon," I said, "and want to sell it."

"No; he isn't that sort of fellow. He always sticks to his things, and you never know him give anything away. But, I say, it is a beautiful watch, isn't it?"

"Yes; so new and bright. It was going, too."

"Wish he'd lose it when he was jumping or playing cricket, and I could find it."

"But you couldn't keep it, if you did find it. You'd know it was his."

"But perhaps I mightn't know he'd lost it, and it was his. Then I might keep it, mightn't I?"

I burst out laughing at him.

"Why, you've taken quite a fancy to that watch, Tom," I said, and he looked at me with his forehead all puckered up.

"Yes, I suppose so," he said dreamily. "I felt as if I'd give everything I have got to have it."

"Stuffed birds, and the frog, and the ferret, and the boxing-gloves?" I said merrily.

"No, no, no! that I wouldn't. There, I'm not going to think about it any more. I say, the gloves—to-morrow morning. Oh!"

Chapter Eleven.

"I say, isn't it time to get up?"

It was a low whisper in my ear, and I started into full wakefulness, to find it was dark, and that Mercer was sitting on the edge of my bed, while the other boys were snoring.

"What time is it?" was my first and natural question.

"I don't know. If I'd got old Eely's watch, I could have had it under my pillow, and seen directly."

"No, you couldn't," I said grumpily, for I was sleepy and cross; "it's too dark."

"Well, I could have run my finger over the hands, and told by the touch. You see, I should have held the watch perfectly upright, and then the twelve would have been by the handle, and I could have told directly."

"But you haven't got a watch, and so you don't know."

"No," he said, with a sigh, "I haven't got that watch. Old Eely's got it—a nasty, consequential, bully dandy."

"Do go and lie down again," I said. "I am so sleepy!"

"What for? It's time to get up."

"It can't be; see how dark it is."

"Oh, that's only because it's a dark morning. Get up and dress, and don't be so grumpy because I've woke you up."

"But I haven't had sleep enough," I grumbled, "and I don't believe it's twelve o'clock yet. Look at the stars shining."

"Well, they always do shine, don't they? What's that got to do with it?"

"But it isn't daylight, and we were not to go to Lomax till five."

"By the time we're washed and dressed, the sun will be up, and then there won't be any waiting."

"Hark!" I said, for the turret clock, below the big bell, chimed.

One, two—three, four—five, six—seven, eight.

Then a long pause.

"Five o'clock," whispered Mercer.

Chang!

We waited as the stroke of the striking hammer rang out loudly, and we could hear the vibration of the bell quivering in the air.

"Well, go on, stupid," said Mercer at last.

"Go on indeed!" I said angrily. "What's the good of coming and disturbing a fellow like this? It's only one o'clock."

"Don't believe it. That clock's wrong. Now, if I had had a watch—"

"Bother the watch!—bother the clock!—bother you!" I cried. "If you don't be off, I'll give you bolster."

"Oh, very well," he said. "But I couldn't sleep. It must be four, though. I'll go and lie down for a bit longer."

He stole back to his bed, and, with a sigh of relief, I sank back into a delicious nap, from which my tormentor roused me twice more, to declare it must be time to get up; but there was not a faint gleam of light yet at the window, and I resolutely refused to rise, sending my companion back to bed, and going off again, to wake at last with the sun shining brilliantly in by the curtain. This time I jumped up, with the full impression upon me that I had overslept myself; while there lay Mercer on his back, with his mouth wide-open, and giving vent every now and then to a guttural snore.

And now we shall be too late, I thought, as I hurried on my trousers, slipped out of the dormitory door, to run down to the end of the passage, where I could look out and see the sun shining brightly on the gold letters of the clock face, where, to my great delight, the hands pointed to half-past four.

Plenty of time, and I went back and roused up Mercer, who started into wakefulness, looking quite guilty.

"All right!" he said. "I only just shut my eyes. What's o'clock?"

"Time you were dressed," I whispered. "Don't talk loud, or you'll wake the others."

We washed and dressed with wonderful celerity, and then crept out and down-stairs, to open one of the schoolroom windows, jump out, and close it after us. Then, in the delicious fresh morning, with the trees all dewy, we started off to go through the shrubbery, and were half-way to the lodge, when Mercer caught me by the arm.

"Look!" he said. "Magglin!" and there, going across one of the fields beyond the road, was that individual, with the pockets of his jacket seeming to be sticking out; and the same idea struck us both.

"He's been poaching!"

But he passed out of sight directly, and we hurried on down to the lodge, to find Lomax standing at the door smoking his morning pipe.

"Five minutes before your time," he said. "That's a good sign. You both want to learn, so you'll learn quickly. Wait a minute, I've just done my bad habit. I learned that years ago, and it's hard to break oneself of it. There, that'll do," he continued, lifting up one foot, and bending down, so as to knock the ashes out of his pipe by tapping the bowl on his heel. "Come along! I've cleared the decks for you."

In fact, as we entered the room, we found that the table and chairs had been taken out, and the little square of carpet and hearthrug rolled up together and stood in a corner, while on the window sill lay the two pairs of boxing-gloves, like four hugely swollen giants' hands, and they looked so ridiculous that we both laughed.

"'Tention!" cried Lomax, shutting and bolting the door. "Business! You can laugh after. Now then, put them on."

We readily obeyed, and as each glove was put on, Lomax tied them securely in their places by the stout strings at the wrists, and once more our comical aspect was too much for us, and we laughed more uproariously than before.

"'Tention, I say, boys. Silence! Now then, I don't do so in drilling you, but the best way to teach a man anything is by letting him go his own way, and then correcting his mistakes. Now, are you ready, both of you, and done with your nonsense?"

"Yes, we are quite serious now," I said.

"Then, to begin with, you, Master Burr, stand up before me, and hit me hard in the chest."

"But it will hurt you," I said.

"You do as I tell you. Hit me in the chest as hard as you can."

I stood up in front of him, and punched him with the soft glove just below his chin.

"Do you call that hard? Try again."

I struck him again.

"Better," he said; "but it wouldn't have killed a blue-bottle. Now you, Master Mercer."

"I'll hit you hard, then, if you will not mind."

"Tchah! just as if you could hurt me! Go on."

Mercer flew at him and struck with all his might.

"Better," said Lomax; "that might have killed a blue-bottle. But it is just as I thought; you're both wrong."

"Wrong?" we echoed.

"Of course you are. So those two gave you both a good thrashing, eh?"

"Yes," I said bitterly.

"Of course they would if you behaved like that. What are those hanging down by your sides?"

"Arms," I said wonderingly.

"Then why do you treat 'em as if they were wind-mill sails, and swing 'em round that fashion?"

"Then you ought to hit straight out," I said, "and not swing your arms round?"

"Of course," said our instructor; "but that isn't all. You both hit at me with your right glove."

"Of course. The right arm's the stronger."

"Exactly, my lad; so keep it to use as a shield."

"But you want to beat a boy when you fight him," I said.

"To be sure you do, and to beat him you must be strong and able to hold out, and to do this you must be ready to keep him first of all from injuring you. It's self-defence, so you keep your best arm to keep the enemy from making your nose swelled like yours was, Master Mercer, and from sticking his fist in your eye like Master Dicksee did in yours, Master Burr. And that isn't all. If you are keeping him from hurting you, he goes on getting tired and more tired, and then your turn comes, and you can thrash him."

"I see," cried Mercer.

"No, you don't; you're only getting a peep yet."

"But mustn't you ever hit with your right fist?"

"Oh yes, at proper times. Wait: I'll tell you when."

"But shall we begin fighting now?" I said eagerly.

146

"No, not till you know what you're going to do. Now look here, boys; I daresay some people would teach you very differently to what I do, but you've asked me, and I shall teach you my way. Some people let those they teach put the gloves on and begin knocking each other about, but that's all waste of time. I want everything you do with your right or your left to be for some reason. Those two boys can't fight, but they thrashed you two because I can see you swung your arms about anyhow, and while you were coming round with one of your wind-mill swings, they hit straight out and you had it. Do you see?"

"Not quite," I said.

"Then look here. See that round table turned up in the corner?"

"Yes."

"Suppose, then, two flies started from the edge to get to the opposite edge, and one went round and the other right across straight, which would get there first?"

"Oh, I know that," said Mercer, rubbing his nose with the back of his glove; "the one that went across the diameter ever so much sooner than the one that went half round the circumference."

"Yes," I said; "the chord is shorter than the arc."

"Never mind about your fine way of putting it," said Lomax. "I see you understand, and that's what I mean. The enemy would diameter you while you tried to circumference him."

The serjeant laughed at his ready adoption of our words, and we laughed too, but he cried "'Tention!" again, and now made us stand face to face on guard, manipulating us and walking round till he had us exactly to his taste, when he suddenly remembered something, and, taking a piece of chalk from his pocket, he drew a line between us, and then raised our hands with their huge gloves to the pitch he considered correct.

"There you are, boys," he said; "that couldn't be better. Now, bear in mind what I said; self-defence is the thing you've got to aim at, just as a general manages his regiments and fences with them till the proper time comes, and then he lets them go. Now, to begin with, you must be the enemy, Master Mercer, and Master Burr here's got to thrash you."

"Oh!" cried Mercer.

"Well, your turn will come next. Now then. Ready?"

"Yes," we cried.

"Then you, Mercer, hit him in the chest."

"And what shall I do?"

"Don't let him. You've got your right ready, haven't you? Now then, off!"

We were both terribly excited, and I was on my guard as Mercer hit at me with his soft glove, and I caught the blow on my right arm.

"Good!" cried Lomax; "bravo! well stopped. But that's all you did, because you didn't know any better. If you had known better, Master Mercer would be sitting on the floor."

"What ought I to have done, then?" I said.

"You wait and I'll show you. Now, Mercer, hit at him again. Hit this time. That's a boxing-glove you've got on."

"Well, I know it is."

"Oh, I thought you fancied it was a snowball that you were going to throw at him."

I burst out laughing.

"Silence! 'Tention! Now then, again. Wait a minute. Now, look here, Burr: as he hits at you, stop it with your right arm as you did before, and just at the same moment you push your left arm out full length, and lean forward straight at his face. Don't hit at him, only keep your left out straight and lean forward suddenly — like this."

He showed me what he meant, and I balanced myself on my legs, and imitated him as well as I could, to get the swing forward he wished, and we prepared for the next encounter.

"I'm going to hit straight out this time, Frank, so look out."

"Oh yes, he'll look out," cried Lomax. "Now, then, take it on your right arm, my lad. Off with you."

Mercer struck out at me awkwardly, and, as I received the blow at my chest full on my forearm, I bent forward sharply, not striking, but giving what seemed to me to be a push with my stiffened left arm straight at Mercer's face, when, to my great astonishment, he went down on the floor and sat there staring at me holding the soft glove up against his nose.

"What did you do that for?" he cried angrily. "He said I was to hit, not you."

"Because I told him," said Lomax, patting me on the shoulder. "Bravo, bravo! That was science against brute force, my lad; I thought it would astonish you."

"But he hit ever so hard," cried Mercer, "and it took me off my guard, because it was I who was to hit."

"And so you did, my lad, as hard as you could unscientifically, while he only just threw himself forward scientifically, and there you are on the ground."

"But he hit so hard."

"Oh no. He just held his arm right, and threw the weight of his body behind it."

"Here, let's change sides," cried Mercer. "I want to try that."

"Right," said Lomax, and the proceedings were reversed, with the effect that, after I had struck at my adversary, I realised that I had thrown my head forward just as he had thrust out his rigid left arm, backed by the whole weight of his body, and I in my turn went down sitting, almost as much astounded as Mercer had been.

"Oh," he cried excitedly, "that's grand! I wish I had known that when old Eely was giving it to me t'other day. Why, I feel as if I could go and lick him now."

"I daresay you do," cried Lomax laughing. "Now, let's have that over again. I want you both to see that a swing round blow, or even a straight out blow, is nothing to one like that, for you see you've got the weight of the body and the speed at which you are both moving to give it force. Why, in a charge, when the men were at full gallop with swords or lances extended, we had— But never mind about that," he added quickly. "Now do you see what I mean?"

"Yes," we cried, and we went through the attack and defence over and over again, till the blows grew so vigorous that I began to feel as if I should like to hit harder.

"That will do," said Lomax suddenly. "You are both getting warm, and it's half-past six."

"Nonsense!" I cried.

"It is, my lad; there goes the bell. Now then, let me untie those gloves. That's your first lesson. What do you think of it?"

"Think of it?" cried Mercer. "I think old Eely Burr had better mind what he's up to, or he'll find he has made a mistake."

"Hah!" said Lomax, "don't you get too puffed up, my lad. You wait, for you don't know anything at all yet. That's just the thin end of the wedge, but still I think you've learned something. That's it," he continued, drawing off the gloves. "By and by you'll have to fight against me, and I shall show you a few things that will startle you. But are you satisfied?"

"Why, it's glorious!" I cried.

"What? to learn to fight with your fists?" said the old sergeant grimly.

"No, but to feel that you need not let everybody bully you."

"Why, you're getting as swollen up as Master Mercer here," said Lomax, laughing. "There; when is it to be—to-morrow morning?"

"Yes, every morning," said Mercer, and the door was unbolted, and we went out, feeling quite hot enough, with the sun shining brightly on the newly dew-washed leaves.

"You'll spoil everything," I said, "if you begin to show that you can fight before we are quite ready."

"Oh, but I'm not going to," he replied; "I'll be as quiet as can be, and let old Eely say and do what he likes for the present. I feel as if I can bear it now. Don't you? There, come along up into the loft, and let's see if we can find our ferret. It does seem hard to lose that directly. Just, too, as one finds one has been cheated by old Magglin. I wish he'd sell that gun. I say, I'll make him show it to you. It is such a handy little thing."

I felt that it would be very interesting to go out, as Mercer proposed, shooting specimens, which he would afterwards show me how to skin and preserve; but I could not help thinking that it would take a rather large supply of pocket-money to pay for all the things my companion wanted, especially if his wants included guns and watches.

We went right up to the loft, and a search was made, and the floor stamped upon, and the boards tapped. But there was no sign of the ferret, and we gave up the search at last in despair, as it was rapidly approaching the time when the bell would ring for breakfast, and we had our lessons to look up ready for Mr Hasnip, who now had us, as he called it, thoroughly in hand.

We both smiled and looked at one another as we crossed the yard, for Burr major and Dicksee had come past together, the latter listening attentively to his companion's words.

"Oh, I say, Burr, if they only knew!" whispered Mercer, with a chuckle. "They little think that we've been— Oh, I say, look; he's taking out his watch to see if it's right by the big clock. Frank, I say: I do wish I had a watch like that!"

I looked at him wonderingly once more, for that watch had completely fascinated him, and till breakfast-time he could talk of nothing else.

"Think your uncle would give you a watch if you asked him?" he said.

"I shouldn't like to ask him, because—well, I'm rather afraid of him."

"What, isn't he kind to you?"

"Yes, I think so," I said; "but he's a severe-looking sort of man, and very particular, and I don't think he'd consider it right for me to have a watch while I am at school."

"That's what my father said when I was home for last holidays. I wanted a watch then, but not half so bad as I feel to want one now. I say!"

"Well?"

"I wonder how much old Eely's father gave for that one. I don't think it could have cost a very great deal."

I shook my head, for I had not the least idea, and then I found myself watching Burr major, who was still comparing his watch with the great clock.

"I won't think about it any more," said Mercer suddenly.

"Think of what?" I said wonderingly.

"That watch. It worries me. I was dreaming about it all last night, and wishing that I'd got it somehow, and that it was mine. And it isn't, and never can be, can it?"

"No," I said, and we walked into the big room, for the breakfast-bell began to ring, and very welcome it sounded to us, after being up so early, and indulging in such violent exercise.

"Here comes Eely," whispered Mercer, "and old Dicksee too. I say: that punch with the left! Oh my!"

Chapter Twelve.

Those were busy times at Meade Place, for Mr Hasnip worked me hard; Mr Rebble harassed me a little whenever he had a chance; and every now and then the Doctor made a sudden unexpected attack upon me with questions uttered in the severest of tones.

All this meant long hours of what the masters called "private study" and the boys "private worry;" while in addition there were the lessons we inflicted upon ourselves, for we never once failed of being at the lodge by five o'clock on those summer mornings, to be scolded, punched, and generally knocked about by our instructor.

Join to these, other lessons in the art of skinning and preserving birds, given by Mercer up in the loft; compulsory games at cricket, as they were called, but which were really hours of toil, fielding for Burr major, Hodson, and Dicksee; sundry expeditions after specimens, visits to Bob Hopley, bathing, fishing, and excursions and incursions generally, and it will be seen that neither Mercer nor I had much spare time.

A busy life is after all the happiest, and, though my lessons often worried and puzzled me, I was perfectly content, and my friendly relations with Mercer rapidly grew more firm.

"I say," he cried one morning, after Lomax had grumbled at us a little less than usual respecting our execution of several of the bits of guarding and hitting he put us through— "I say, don't you think we are perfect yet?"

The serjeant opened his eyes wide, and then burst into a hearty laugh.

"Well," he said, "you will grow into a man some day, and when you do, I daresay you will be a bit modest, for of all the cocksparrowy chaps I ever did meet, you are about the most impudent."

"Thank-ye," said Mercer, and he went off in dudgeon, while Lomax gave me a comical look.

"That's the way to talk to him," he said. "If you don't, he'll grow up so conceited he'll want extra buttons on his jacket to keep him from swelling out too much."

"Now, Burr, are you coming?" shouted Mercer.

"Yes. Good morning," I said to Lomax, and I hurried out.

"I thought we should have learned long before this," said my companion, as we strolled leisurely back. "I don't seem to get on a bit further, and I certainly don't feel as if I could fight. Do you?"

"No," I said frankly.

"You see, it wants testing or proving, same as you do a sum. Shall we have a fall out with them and try?"

"No," I cried excitedly. "That wouldn't do. They might lick us. We ought to try with some one else first."

"But who is there? If we had a fight with some other boys, Eely and Dicksee would know, and we should have no chance to fight them then. I know. Let you and I fall out and have a set to."

I whistled, and put my hands in my pockets.

"Wouldn't that do?" he said.

"No, not at all. It wouldn't be real, and—"

"Hold your tongue. Here's Magglin."

"Morning, young gents," said the man coming up in his nasty, watchful, furtive way, looking first behind him, and then dodging to right and left to look behind us, to see if any one was coming.

"Morning.—Hi! look out! Keeper!" cried Mercer.

"Eh? Where? where?" whispered Magglin huskily.

"Down in the woods," cried Mercer laughingly. "Look at him, Burr; he has been up to some games, or he wouldn't be so frightened."

"Get out!" growled the gipsy-looking fellow sourly. "Doctor don't teach you to behave like that, I know."

"Nor the gardener don't teach you to try and cheat people with ferrets."

"Well, I like that," cried Magglin in an ill-used tone. "I sells you for a mate of mine—"

"No, you didn't, it was for yourself, Magg."

"As good a farret as ever run along a hole."

"As bad a one as ever stopped in and wouldn't come out again."

"And you turn like that on a fellow."

"You're a cheat, Magg, and you took us in. That was your old ferret you sold me, and I wish I'd never paid you a shilling."

"Nay, not you. It's a good farret, and you've only paid me four shillin' out of them five."

"And I don't think I shall pay you any more."

"Nay, you must. Gents can't break their words."

"But they can break blackguards' heads, Magg."

"I ain't a blackguard, and I sold you the ferret fair and square. It weren't my fault you let it run down a hole in the loft."

"When it proved directly that it was your old one, for there it stops."

"I shouldn't pay him the other shilling till he got it out, Tom," I said.

"I don't mean to. How many times have you been to look for it, Magg?"

"How many times? I didn't count. Every morn when I come to work have I gone down on my chestie in that there loft, watching o' them rat-holes."

"Yes, and you've never caught him. Four shillings did I pay you for that ferret—"

"And a shillin' more to pay," said Magglin, grinning. "And only once have I seen his nasty ugly little pink nose since, when he poked it out of a hole and slipped back again.

"But then see how he must have kept down the rats," said the man.

"Bother the rats. I want my ferret." Mercer turned sharply round to me.

"I say," he whispered, "he's a blackguard and a cheat. We wanted to practise. Let's both pitch into him."

I naturally enough laughed at the idea, and, looking round at the under gardener, I saw that he was watching us with his rat-like eyes.

"I say," he whispered, with an accompaniment of nods and winks, "I was lying wait for you two."

"We're not rabbits, Magg," I said.

"Who said you was?" he cried, with a sharp look round behind him.

"Nor yet hares, Magg," cried Mercer.

"Now look ye here," said the fellow appealingly, "it's too bad on you two chuckin' things in a man's face like that now. Ain't I always getting a honest living? You talk like that, and somebody'll be thinkin' I go porching."

"So you do," said Mercer.

"What, porch?"

"Yes. I know. Bob Hopley says so too."

"Only hark at him," cried Magglin, "talking like that! Why, Bob Hopley's a chap as must do something to show for his wage, and he'd take any man's character away. He hate me, he do."

"Yes, and you hate him, Magg," I said.

The fellow turned on me sharply, but a curiously ugly smile began to make curves like parentheses at the corners of his lips, and he showed his teeth directly after.

"Well, I ain't so very fond of him," he said. "But look here, there ain't no harm in a rabbid, and I was looking out for you two to ast if you'd like to meet me, just by accident like, somewheers down to this side o' High Pines, where the sandhills is. There's a wonderful lot o' rabbids there just now."

"Yes, but when?" cried Mercer. "I want a rabbit or two to skin and stuff."

"And you'd gie me the rabbids to eat."

"Of course. When do you mean?"

"I thowt as to-night'd do, 'bout seven, when they're beginning to lope about."

"And you'd shoot some with that little gun of yours?"

"Whisht! Who's got a gun? Nonsense!"

"Ah, we know," cried Mercer.

"But I mean farreting."

"Wouldn't do," said Mercer decisively. "Bob Hopley would be sure to come."

"Nay, he's going to Hastings to-day, and won't be back till ten o'clock."

"How do you know?"

"Little birds out in the woods tells me."

"Magpies, eh?" I said. "Oh, I know."

"Then we'll come," cried Mercer. "But, I say, let us each have a shot with the little gun."

"Nay, I'm a gardener, and ain't got no guns. I meant farreting."

"But you know I've lost the ferret," cried Mercer. "You can't go ferreting without ferrets."

Magglin was standing before us with a curious, furtive smile on his face, and his hands deep down in his pockets, and as Mercer finished speaking, he slowly raised one hand, so that we saw peering out over the top of his jacket pocket the sharp buff hairy head of a ferret, and we both uttered a cry of joy.

"Why, you've got one!" said Mercer. "Why—yes—it is. It's my ferret."

"Yes," said Magglin. "I nipped him this morning. He was out running about the loft, and I got hold of him at once. He's eaten all the rats he could catch, and he was out smelling about, and trying to get into that old corn-bin, so as to have a feed on your stuffed things."

"Lucky he didn't," cried Mercer. "Oh, you are a good chap, and I'll give you the other shilling as soon as I can."

"Ay, do, master, for that chap I knows wants it badly."

"Come along, and let's shut it up safely," said Mercer.

"S'pose you let me take care of him in the tool-shed. I'll put him where he can't get out, and I shall have him ready when you come."

"Very well then," cried Mercer, "you keep him. At the High Pines, then, at seven o'clock."

"That's it, sir," said Magglin, securing the ferret in his pocket.

"Ah, good morning," said a voice; and we two turned sharply, to find that Mr Rebble and Mr Hasnip, who were out early for a constitutional, had come up behind us quietly.

"Good morning, sir.—Good morning, sir," we said, and Magglin touched his cap and went off down the garden.

"Very good, Mercer. Very good, Burr junior," said Mr Hasnip blandly, as he brought his dark spectacles to bear upon us. "I like to see this, and I wish the other boys would be as industrious, and get up these lovely mornings. Been making plans with the gardener about your little gardens, I see. That's right—that's right. But, as I was saying, Rebble," he continued, turning away, "Galileo's opinion, when combined with that of Kepler and Copernicus, is all buzz-buzz-buzz—"

So the latter part of his speech sounded to us, as they went on toward the bottom of the garden.

"All buzz buzz buzz," whispered Mercer; "and that's what lots of others of those old folks' opinions sound like to me—all buzz buzz buzz in my poor head. I say, wasn't it lucky they didn't see the ferret?"

"They think we were speaking to him about gardening."

"Yes. What a game! We must go down to our gardens now, and pretend we got up early to work."

"I shan't," I said shortly. "I hate being so deceptive, and I wish you wouldn't be, Tom."

"Well, it don't sound nice, does it?" he replied thoughtfully. "But it's so easy."

"Perhaps we had better not go after the rabbits."

"Oh, but we must now. Don't you sneak back. I shall go, and nobody will know."

I felt doubtful, but I ended by promising.

"I say," cried Mercer suddenly, "what time is it? Oh, I do wish I had a watch! You can't see the clock from here, but my clock inside says it's breakfast-time."

"Let's go and see, then," I said, and we went toward the schoolroom.

Chapter Thirteen.

That was a most unfortunate day for me in school, for, as happens sometimes, I was wrong over one of my lessons, and was sent down, and it seemed to upset all the others, so that it was just like setting up a row of dominoes, then you touch one and it sends all the rest over.

Scold, find fault, grumble,—Mr Hasnip was just as if his breakfast had not agreed with him because he got up too early; and at last I was back in my seat, with my face burning, my head aching, and a general feeling of misery troubling me, which was made the worse by the keen enjoyment Burr major and his parasites found in triumphing over me, and coming by my place every now and then to whisper— "Poor fellow, then!—turned back—going to be caned," and the like, till I ground my teeth, clenched my fists, and sat there bent over the exercises before me, seeing nothing but the interior of Lomax's cottage, and listening to his instructions how to stop that blow and retort with another, till in imagination I could fancy myself thrashing my enemies, and making for myself a lasting peace.

"Never mind, old chap," whispered Mercer. "Rabbits to-night, and some day such a licking for old Eely and Dicksee."

The thoughts of the expedition that night were comforting, and I tried to think of the High Pines and the sandy slope with the holes where I had often seen the rabbits pop in and out, but my head ached all the same; and in spite of our half-hour in the play-field before dinner, I had no appetite. During the afternoon, when my time came to go up to Mr Hasnip's desk, I felt more stupid than ever, and on casting my eyes sideways in search of a flying thought, there was Mr Rebble watching me intently.

This made me more confused, and my next answer more blundering, so that I was at last sent back to my desk in greater disgrace than ever, to find Mercer, who was always constructing something, boring the edge of his desk with a penknife, so as to make powder holes for a slate pencil cannon.

"Catching it again?" he said.

"Yes," I replied dolefully.

"Didn't say you were to stop in and study, did he?"

"No, he didn't say that."

"Oh, that's all right, then."

"But it isn't all right. He scolded me horribly."

"Pooh! what of that? Every boy gets scolded. Never mind. I say, I daresay we shall get a whole lot of rabbits. How would it be to ask cook to make us a rabbit pie of two of them."

"Nonsense!"

"Oh, would it be? We could keep it up in the bin, and go and have jolly feeds."

"Keep it up there, along with that poison stuff and nasty-smelling skins! Ugh!"

"Well, it would be queer perhaps. I didn't think of that."

"Mr Rebble's looking at you two," whispered the boy nearest, and we hurriedly went on with our work, but not for long. Mercer was too full of the coming expedition, and soon began whispering again.

"But how are we to get away?" I said. "Some one is sure to see us."

"Oh, that's easy enough," he whispered. "There's going to be a bit of a match to-night."

"But suppose they want us to field?"

"Then they'll want, for they will not be able to find us. You leave it to me."

That was a long, dreary afternoon, and tea-time seemed as if it would never arrive. When it did come round, though, with the cool air of evening my headache began to go off, and as I grew better, the excitement of the coming expedition, and the thoughts of how we were going to elude the notice of the other boys, completed the cure.

We had half an hour's walk before us, to reach the High Pines by seven, so that, as it grew near the time I began to be anxious.

We were in the schoolroom, deep in private study, and as Mercer studied, he kept on turning his eyes to gaze round the room, repeating his lessons all the while, so that he would not have looked particular if any one had been watching us, but no one was visible. Every now and then the voices of the boys in the play-field floated toward us, and we sat in momentary expectation of being seen by one of the bigger fellows, and ordered off into the field by our tyrants; but the moments still glided by, and at last Mercer thrust his book into his desk.

"Now, then," he said in a low voice, "we must make a run for it, or old Magg will think we are not coming."

"Which way are you going?" I asked.

"Right out through the garden, and by the back of the lodge. You follow me, and, whatever you do, don't look back, as if you were afraid of being seen."

It was risky work, I knew, but there was nothing to be gained by hesitating, and it seemed to me that the very boldness of our attempt helped us to a successful issue, for we went on, hearing voices from the field, and once that of the Doctor, as he was walking up and down the lawn with one of the ladies, whose light dress was seen for a few moments through the trees. Then we were out in the road, walking fast towards the General's woods, and soon after we passed into a field, reached a copse, and Mercer uttered a faint "Hurrah!"

"I was expecting to hear some one shout after us every minute," he cried, as we now hurried steadily along. "Oh dear, how you do fancy things at a time like this!"

The evening was now delightful, and the fresh, sweet scent of the grass we crushed beneath our feet was supplemented every now and then by that of the abundant field camomile.

"Look out!" said Mercer; "there he goes. Isn't he early? I say, I wonder whether that's one of old Dawson's owls."

For, as we passed along by the edge of the wood, a great white-breasted bird flew by, and went softly along by the side of the trees, till it disappeared far ahead.

"There's a rabbit," I said, as I caught sight of the white tuft of fur which so often betrays the presence of the little creatures, and directly after a sharp *rap, rap*—the warning given by them of danger—was heard ahead, and a dozen ran rushing out of the field into the shelter of the wood.

"Look at them, how they swarm!" cried Mercer. "Why we might catch a hundred, and no one would be a bit the worse for it. Here, make haste, or I shall be shouting at them, and we ought to be quiet now."

"Close there, aren't we?" I said.

"Yes; just through that next patch, and we shall be there."

"And suppose Magg hasn't come?"

"Why, we'll catch some without him."

"Without the ferret?"

"Oh, how stupid I am!" cried Mercer, and he went on, now in silence, through some stunted firs, in and out by patches of gorse, with the character of the ground quite changed, and then up a hilly slope crowned with spruce trees, round which we skirted, to stop at last, breathless, at the bottom of the slope facing south, with the dark green, straight-stemmed trees above us; and Mercer gave his foot an angry stamp as he looked round at the deserted place, where the pine branches glowed of a ruddy bronze in the sunset light, and cried, —

"Oh, what a jolly shame!"

"Not here?" I said.

"No; and it's a nasty, mean trick to drag us all this way. I wish I had kept the ferret instead of trusting him."

"What's to be done?"

"Oh, nothing," he replied despondently. "It's always the way, when I've made up my mind for a bit of fun, something happens to stop it."

"Let's wait," I said. "He may come yet."

"Wait? Why, it'll be too dark to see to do anything in less than an hour. Oh, won't I pay him out for —"

"There he is," I whispered, for I had just caught sight of a figure lying down by a patch of furze; and we started off at a dog-trot, and soon reached the spot.

"Why, I thought you hadn't come, Magg," cried Mercer excitedly.

"That's what I was thinking," said the man. "There, chuck yourselves down; if you stand up like that, somebody may see you."

I did not like this, for it was going in for more hiding and secretiveness, but all the same it was fascinating, and, dropping on our knees in the short, wiry grass, we waited for our instructor in the art of ferreting rabbits to begin.

"Well," I said, as we stared at him, and he stared back at us, "aren't you going to begin?"

"No," he said coolly.

"Then what's the good of our coming?"

"Oh, do begin, Magg! We shall soon have to run back. Where's old longbody?"

"Yonder," said Magglin coolly, nodding his head at the slope just above us.

"Not loose?"

"Yes, he's loose."

"But—"

"Why, can't you see, lad? and do be quiet, or the rabbits won't bolt. I put him in one of the holes ten minutes ago."

A flush of excitement seemed to run through me now, as I noted that every here and there were places in the turfy bank where the sandy soil had been scraped out, and the next moment I saw what had escaped me before, that every hole I could see was covered with a fine net.

Mercer had seen it too, and I saw him rub his hands softly as if delighted with the promise of sport, but another ten minutes passed, and the rabbits made no sign of being anxious to rush out and be caught, and I began to grow impatient.

"Hadn't you better try another place?" I whispered, but the man held up his hand, drew his knees under him, and crouched in an attitude that was almost doglike in its animal aspect.

Then there was a rushing noise just above us, and Magglin scrambled forward and dashed his hands down upon a rabbit which came bounding out of a hole and rolled down the slope, tangled in the net.

The next minute it had received a chop on the back of the neck, ceased struggling, been transferred to Magglin's pocket, and the net was spread over the hole again.

"That's a bad farret, ain't it, Master Mercer?" said Magglin, showing his teeth. "You'd best sell un back to me; I should be glad on it for five shillings."

"Hush! I thought I heard one, Magg," whispered Mercer, ignoring the remark. "I say, let me catch the next."

"Either of you may if you can," he replied; and we waited again for some time.

"Try some fresh place," whispered Mercer.

"Nay; they all run one into another; the ground under here's like the rat-holes up at the old house. There goes one."

For a rabbit bolted from a hole higher up, turned on seeing us, and darted up toward the pines.

"Farret's working beautifully," said Magglin.

"How many holes have you covered?" I asked.

"'Bout four-and-twenty, and all my nets. You young gents ought to pay me for the use of them."

"Here's one!" cried Mercer, making a leap in a similar fashion to that of the under gardener, and he too caught an unfortunate rabbit, whose rush had been right into one of the little loose nets, in which it was tangled directly.

"Here, let me kill un for you," said Magglin.

"No; I know now. I can do it," said Mercer. Then I sprang to my feet, and my first impulse was to run, my second to stand fast, for how he got up to us so close from behind without being seen was a mystery to me; but there, just in the midst of the confusion and excitement of capturing the second rabbit, was Bob Hopley, the keeper, his big, sturdy form seeming to tower above us, and, caught, as we were in this nefarious act, filling me with dread.

"Got you this time then," he said gruffly.

"There, what did I say?" cried Magglin, in a sharp, acid voice that sounded almost like a woman's. "I told you that you oughtn't to be catching them rabbids, and now you see what trouble you're in."

"Oh, you told 'em so, did you, my lad?" said the keeper in a deep, angry voice, and he seemed like a great mastiff growling at a common-looking cur. "Then I 'spose it's their ferret in yon burrows, eh? there it is!" he continued, as the buff-looking, snaky animal now came out of one of the holes close by us, and Mercer stooped and picked it up as it made for the dead rabbit.

"Oh yes, it's their farret, 'tarn't mine," said Magglin quickly.

"Yes, it's my ferret, Mr Hopley," Mercer said dolefully.

"And their nets, eh? Here, you stand still. You try to run away, and I'll send a charge o' small shot after you, and that can run faster than you can."

"'NOW THEN,' SAID MERCER, 'PULL STEADY,'"

"More'n you dare do, big Bob Hopley," cried Magglin, backing away up the hill; and I thought how cowardly the man's nature must be, for him to propose this expedition and then sneak away from us like that. But almost at the same moment I saw a tall, stern gentleman appear from among the pine trees toward which Magglin was backing, for the keeper had presented his gun, evidently to take the labourer's attention, as I saw that, if matters went on in the way in which they were going, our companion would back right up into the new-comer's arms.

"You stop, will you!" cried the keeper.

"You stop yourself," cried Magglin. "You've got them as belongs to the ferret and was rabbiting. Good-night."

"Will you stop, or am I to shoot?" cried Hopley.

"Yah!" came back; and as the keeper dropped his gun into the hollow of his arm with a grim smile on his face, there was a loud *thwack* and a startled, "Oh!" for the tall gentleman had stood still, Magglin had reached him, and a stick fell heavily across the poacher's shoulders.

"You scoundrel!" he roared, making a snatch at Magglin's collar, but the man was too slippery. He dropped on his knees, rolled down the slope a few yards, sprang up, and dashed off.

"Don't matter, Sir Hawkus!" shouted the keeper. "I know my gentleman, and can send him a summons. Now, young gents, you've got in for it this time. Bad company's done for you."

"Oh, Bob," whispered Mercer, "let us go this time! let's run."

"Nay, here's Sir Hawkus coming; and here's some one else too," he continued, as I saw two figures come trotting up by the way we had reached the slope, to get to us nearly as soon as the tall, stern-looking gentleman.

"Who are these?" he cried. "Boys from the Doctor's school? You young dogs, you!" he shouted, shaking his cane. "Who are you?"

"Two of our pupils, Sir Hawkhurst," said Mr Rebble, panting and out of breath. "You wretched boys, has it come to this?"

Mercer looked at the speaker, then at Mr Hasnip's smoked spectacles, and then at me, as General Sir Hawkhurst Rye from the Hall, a gentleman of whom I had often heard, but whom I had never seen, exclaimed,—

"Well, they are caught red-handed. Rabbits, poaching engines—and what's that?"

"A ferret, sir," said Mercer humbly.

"Humph, yes. Now, Mr Schoolmaster, what's it to be? Do you take these boys now, to bring them up before me and another magistrate to-morrow, or shall I have them marched off by my keeper to the lock-up?"

Chapter Fourteen.

Those were terrible moments, and I remember wishing that it would suddenly turn into darkest night, as we two lads stood there, shrinking from the eyes of those four men, at whom I glanced in turn, and they all impressed me differently. The general's mouth was pursed up, and his walking cane, which, I perfectly recollect was a thick malacca with an ivory head, shook in his hand as if he was eager to lay it across our backs. Bob Hopley stood with his arms crossed over his gun, looking, as I thought, hurt, pained, and as if we had committed a most terrible crime. But there was no pain or trouble, as it seemed to me, in either Mr Rebble's or Mr Hasnip's face. It struck me that they were on the whole pleased and satisfied in having found us out in a deed that would give them an opportunity to punish us with heavy impositions.

All these thoughts had passed rapidly through my mind as I stood waiting to hear Mr Rebble's response to the General's question.

"I will take charge of the boys, sir," he said importantly; "and I shall lay the matter at once before the notice of Doctor Browne."

"Hang Doctor Browne!" said the General fiercely. "I want to know what he meant by bringing his confounded school and setting it up close under my nose. What did he mean? Eh?"

"I am Doctor Browne's assistant master, Sir Hawkhurst," replied Mr Rebble, with dignity, "and I cannot answer for his reasons."

"Humph! You can't, eh? You there in the dark barnacles," cried the General, turning upon Mr Hasnip, "what have you to say?"

"That the boys must be severely punished, sir," said Mr Hasnip, who looked quite startled.

"Punished! I should think so indeed. If I were not a magistrate, I'd give the wretched young poachers a severe trouncing. How dare you, eh?—how dare you, I say, come trespassing on my grounds and poaching my rabbits?"

The only answer that I could find was, "I'm very sorry, sir. I did not think; and I'll never do so any more;" but it seemed so ridiculous as I thought it, that I held my tongue.

"Pretty scoundrels, 'pon my word!" cried the General. "Gentlemen's sons, eh? nice gentlemen's sons. They've both got poacher written in their face, and I can see what the end will be—transportation, or hung for killing a keeper. That's it, eh, Hopley?"

"Well, sir," said Bob, giving us each a pitying look, "I wouldn't go quite so far as that."

"No, because you are an easy-going fool. You let people rob me right and left, and you'd stand still and let the young scoundrels shoot you. There, take them away, the pair of them. You two, I mean—you pedagogues. I'll come and see the Doctor myself to-morrow morning, and I'll have those two fellows flogged—soundly flogged. Do you hear, you boys?—flogged. How many rabbits have you got?"

"Only this one, sir," I said.

"What? You dare to tell me only one?"

"There was another, only Magglin put it in his pocket."

"Got a dozen hid somewhere," cried the General. "Where have you hid them, you dog? Stuffed in some burrow, I suppose. Where are they, sir?"

"I told you," I said sharply, for his doubt of my word made me feel hot and angry. "We only caught those two. I shouldn't tell you a lie, sir."

"Humph! Oh!" cried the old gentleman, looking at me searchingly, "you wouldn't tell a lie about it, wouldn't you?"

"Of course not," I replied; "and we did not mean any harm, sir. We thought it would be good fun to come and catch some rabbits."

"Oh, you did? Then I suppose it would be good fun to bring guns and come and shoot my pheasants. Perhaps you'd like to do that, eh?"

"I should," said Mercer innocently.

"What!" roared the old gentleman. "Here, you two, take 'em both into scholastic custody, and tell Dr Browne I'm coming in the morning to put a stop to this sort of thing once and for all. Hopley, where's that ferret?"

"Pocket, Sir Hawkus," said the keeper bluntly.

"'In—my—pocket,' sir!" cried the old gentleman angrily. "I pay you wages, sir, as my servant, and I've a right to proper answers. Let's see the ferret."

The keeper took it out of the big pocket inside his velveteen jacket, and held it up, twisting and writhing to get free and down into one of the rabbit-holes.

"Throw it down and shoot it," said the General.

"No, sir, please don't do that!" cried Mercer excitedly, "It's such a good ferret—please don't kill the poor thing!"

The General looked at him sharply.

"Not kill it?"

"No, sir. Please let it go."

"To live on my rabbits, eh? There, put it in your pocket. And now, you be off with you, and if I don't have your skins well loosened to-morrow, I'll— You'll see."

He marched off in one direction, while our guard took us in the other, talking at us all the time.

"Disgraceful!" Mr Rebble said. "The Doctor will be nearly heart-broken about such a stigma upon his establishment. I don't know what he'll say."

"They will be expelled, I presume," said Mr Hasnip softly. "It is very sad to see such wickedness in those so young."

"I'm afraid so," replied Mr Rebble; and they kept up a cheerful conversation of this kind till we reached the school, where we were at once ordered up to our dormitory, and dropped down upon the sides of our beds to sit looking at each other.

"I say, you've done it now," said Mercer at last; "and I did think we were going to have such fun."

"Fun!" I said; "it's dreadful!"

"It was capital fun till they all came and spoiled it for us. I wouldn't care about being expelled—at least not so much, only my father will be so disappointed."

This made me think of my mother, and of what my uncle would say if I were dismissed from the school in disgrace; and I shivered, for this was the most terrible part of all.

"I tell you what," said Mercer, "we're in for it, and no mistake; and we didn't do it to steal. We only wanted a bit of sport and some rabbits to stuff. Let's tell the doctor we're very sorry, and ask him to flog us. It would be too bad to expel us in disgrace. What do you say?"

"They may flog me," I said sadly; "but I couldn't go home again in disgrace like that."

"Of course not; and it's too bad to call it poaching. I'm sorry we went, though, now."

"Yes," I said, "I'm sorry enough;" and we sat there, miserable enough, waiting till the other boys came up, and it was time to go to bed.

We had not begun to undress, when the door was opened, and three heads were thrust in, and to our disgust, as we looked up, we saw that they belonged to our three principal tormentors, who began at us in a jeering way.

"Hallo, poachers!" said Burr major; "where are the rabbits?"

"I say," cried Hodson, "you fellows are going to be expelled. Leave us the stuffed guys, Senna."

"He won't," cried Dicksee; "he'll want the skins to make a jacket—a beggar!"

"You're a set of miserable cowards," I said indignantly, "or you wouldn't come and jump upon us now we are down."

"You give me any of your cheek, Burr junior, and I'll make you smell fist for your supper."

"Pst! Some one coming!" whispered Hodson, and the three scuffled away, for there were footsteps on the stairs, and directly after Mr Rebble appeared.

"Mercer, Burr junior," he said harshly, "Doctor Browne requests that you will not come down till he sends for you in the morning. As for you, young gentlemen, you will take no notice of the door being fastened; I shall be up here in time to let you out. Good-night."

He went out, and closed and locked the door, and we heard him take out the key and go down the stairs.

"Well, that's a rum one!" cried Mercer. "I say, Burr, old Rebble made an Irish bull, or something like it. How can we go down if the door's locked?"

"It's because they're afraid we shall run away," I said bitterly. "They needn't have thought that."

And somehow that first part of our punishment seemed to be the most bitter of all. It kept me awake for hours, growing more and more low-spirited; and, to make me worse, as I lay there listening to the loud breathing of the boys, Mercer having gone off like the rest, as if nothing was the matter, I could hear an owl come sailing about the place, now close at hand, and now right away in the distance, evidently in Sir Hawkhurst's old park, where, no doubt, it had a home in one of the great hollow beeches. Every now and then it uttered its mournful *hoi, hoi, hoi, hoi!* sounding exactly like some one calling for help, and at times so real that I was ready to awaken Mercer and ask him if he thought it was a bird; but just as I had determined to do so, he spoke half drowsily from his pillow.

"Hear the old owl," he said. "That's the one I told you about the other night. It isn't the same kind as we saw in old Dawson's oast-house. They screech. Get out, you old mouser! I want to sleep."

The owl kept on with its hooting; but Mercer had what he wanted, for he dropped asleep directly, and I must have followed his example immediately after, for the next thing I remember is feeling something warm on my face, which produced an intense desire to sneeze—so it seemed, till I opened my eyes, to find that the blind had been drawn, and Mercer was tickling my nose with the end of a piece of top string twisted up fine.

"Be quiet. Don't!" I cried angrily, as I sat up. "Hallo! where are the other fellows?"

"Dressed and gone down ever so long ago. Didn't you hear the bell?"

"No; I've been very sound asleep," I said, beginning to dress hurriedly. "Shall we be late? Oh!"

"What's the matter?"

"I'd forgotten," I said; for the whole trouble of the previous evening had now come back with a rush.

"Good job, too," said Mercer. "That's why I didn't wake you. Wish I was asleep now, and could forget all about it. I say, it ain't nice, is it?"

I shook my head mournfully.

"It's always the way," continued my companion, "one never does have a bit of fun without being upset after it somehow. We went fishing, and nearly got drowned; I bought the ferret, and we lost it; we went in for lessons in boxing, and I never grumbled much, but oh, how sore and stiff and bruised I've often been afterwards. And now, when we go for just an hour to try the ferret, we get caught like this. There's no real fun in life without trouble afterwards."

"One always feels so before breakfast," I said, as dolefully as Mercer now, and I hurriedly finished dressing. Then we went to the window, and stood looking out, and thinking how beautiful everything appeared in the morning sunshine.

"I say, Tom," I said at last, "don't you wish you were down-stairs finishing your lessons, ready for after breakfast?"

"Ah, that I do!" he cried; "and I never felt so before."

"That's through being locked up like in prison," I said philosophically.

"Yes, it's horrid. I say, the old Doctor won't expel us, will he?"

"I hope not," I said.

"But he will old Magglin. You see if he don't."

"Well, I'm not sorry for him," I said; "he has behaved like a sneak."

"Yes; trying to put it all on to us."

We relapsed into silence for some time. We had opened the window, and were looking out at the mists floating away over the woods, and the distant sea shining like frosted silver.

"Oh, I do wish it was a wet, cloudy morning!" I said at last.

"Why?"

"Because everything looks so beautiful, and makes you long to be out of doors."

We relapsed into silence again, with our punishment growing more painful every moment, till our thoughts were chased away by the ringing of the breakfast-bell.

"Ah, at last!" cried Mercer, and he turned to listen for footsteps.

"I say," he cried crossly, "ain't they going to let us go down to breakfast?"

"No; we're prisoners," I said bitterly.

"Yes; but they don't starve prisoners to death," cried Mercer; "and I want something to eat."

In spite of my misery, I too felt very hungry, for we had gone through a great deal since our evening meal on the previous day, and I was standing watching my companion as he marched up and down the bedroom like an animal in a cage, when we heard steps on the stairs.

"Here's breakfast," cried Mercer joyfully, but his face changed as the door was opened, and Mr Rebble appeared, followed by one of the maids bearing a tray, which she set down on a little table and went away, leaving Mr Rebble looking at us grimly, but with the suggestion of a sneering laugh at the corners of his cleanly-shaven lips.

We both glanced at the tray, which bore a jug and two mugs and a plate with a couple of big hunches of bread. Then Mercer looked up half reproachfully at Mr Rebble, who was moving toward the door.

"They've forgotten the butter, sir," he said.

"No, my boy, no," replied the usher; "butter is a luxury reserved for the good. The Doctor will send for you both by and by."

He went out and locked the door, while we stood listening till the steps had died away.

"It's a jolly shame!" cried Mercer. "I'm not going to stop here and eat dry bread."

"Never mind," I said; "I don't mind for once;" and, taking one of the pieces of bread, I lifted the jug to fill a mug, but set it down again without pouring any out.

"What's the matter?"

"Look," I said.

Mercer darted to the table, looked into the jug, poured out a little of its contents, and set the vessel down, speechless for the moment with rage.

"Water!" he cried at last, and dashing to the table again, he ran with it to the window, and threw both jug and contents flying out into the shrubbery below.

"Oh!" he ejaculated, directly after; "I didn't know you were there."

I ran to the window now, and looked down to see the cook's red face gazing up at us.

"Eh? what say?" said Mercer, leaning out.

"Hush! be quiet. All at breakfast. Got any string?"

"Yes. Oh, I know," cried Mercer joyfully, and he ran to his box and from the bottom dragged out a stick of kite string, whose end he rapidly lowered down to where cook stood, holding something under her apron.

This proved to be a little basket with a cross handle when she whisked her apron off, and, quickly tying the end of the string to it, she stood watching till the basket had reached our hands, and then hurried away round the end of the house.

"Oh, isn't she a good one!" cried Mercer, tearing open the lid, after snapping the string and pitching the ball quickly into the box. "Look here; four eggs, bread and butter—lots, and a bottle of milk—no," he continued, taking out the cork and smelling, "it's coffee. Hooray!"

"What's that in the bit of curl paper?" and I pointed to something twisted up.

"Salt," cried Mercer, "for the eggs. Come on, eat as fast as you can."

I took a piece of bread and butter, and he another, eating away as he poured out two mugfuls of what proved to be delicious coffee.

"Who says we haven't got any friends?" cried Mercer, with his mouth full. "What lots of butter. 'Tis good. I say, wonder what old Rebble would say if he knew! Have an egg."

"No spoons."

"Bet a penny they're hard ones."

So it proved, and we cracked them well all over, peeled off the shells, which for secrecy we thrust into our pockets, and then, dipping the eggs into the salt, we soon finished one each, with the corresponding proportion of bread and butter. Then the other two followed, the last slice of bread and butter disappeared, and the wine-bottle was drained. It was an abundant supply, but at our age the time consumed over the meal was not lengthy, and we then busied ourselves in rinsing out the bottle, which was hidden in my box, after being carefully wiped on a towel, the basket was placed in Mercer's, and as soon as the last sign of our banquet had disappeared, we looked at the two hunches of bread, of which mine alone had been tasted, and burst into a laugh.

"I don't want any—do you?" said Mercer, and I shook my head. "Oh, I do feel so much better! I can take the Doctor's licking now, and hope it will come soon."

"I don't," I said.

"Why not? It's like nasty physic. Of course you don't like it, but the sooner you've swallowed it down, the sooner it's gone, and you haven't got to think any more about it. That's what I feel about my licking."

"Hist! here's some one coming."

Mercer turned sharply round and listened.

"Old Reb," he whispered, and we went and stood together near the window as the steps came nearer; the key was turned, and Mr Rebble appeared, glanced at the tray with its almost untouched bread, and then smiled maliciously.

"Ho, ho! Proud stomached, eh? Oh, very well, only I warn you both you get nothing more to eat until that bread is finished. Now, then, young gentlemen, this way please."

He held the door open, and then led us into a small room at the end of the passage used for spare boxes and lumber. Here we were locked in and left, and as soon as we were alone Mercer burst into a fit of laughter.

"Oh, what a game!" he panted, wiping the tears from his eyes. "I say, though, he never missed the water-jug. What's the matter?"

"Matter!" I cried; "it's a shame to lock us up here like two prisoners in this old lumber-room."

"Oh, never mind! it's only old Reb's nasty petty way. I don't believe the Doctor knows. He isn't petty; he scolds you and canes you if you've done anything he don't like, but as soon as you've had your punishment, it's all over, and he forgets what's past. I say!"

"Well?"

"He will not expel us; I'm not afraid of that."

In about half an hour, we heard Mr Rebble's steps again.

"Now then, the physic's ready," whispered Mercer. "Don't you cry out. It hurts a good deal, and the Doctor hits precious hard, but the pain soon goes off, and it will only please old Rebble if you seem to mind."

Just then the door was opened, and our gaoler appeared again.

"This way," he said shortly, and we went out into the passage once more, while my heart began to flutter, and I wondered whether I could bear a caning without showing that I suffered, and, to be frank, I very much doubted my power in what would be to me quite a new experience. I set my teeth though, and mentally vowed I would try and bear it manfully.

It was all waste energy, for Mr Rebble threw open the door of our dormitory again, drew back for us to enter, and said, with a nasty malicious laugh, as if he enjoyed punishing us, —

"Not a morsel of anything till that bread is eaten."

Then the door was closed, sharply locked, the key withdrawn, and his steps died away.

"What a take in!" grumbled Mercer, as we looked round the neat, clean bedroom, and realised that we had only been locked up in the other place while the maids came to make the beds. "I was all screwed up tight, and would have taken my caning without so much as a squeak. Couldn't you?"

"I don't know," I said, "but I felt ready to go on with it, and now I suppose we shall have to wait."

To our great disgust, we did have to wait hour after hour. We heard the fellows go out from school, and their voices came ringing through the clear summer air, and then we heard them come in to dinner; but we were not called down, nothing was sent up to us, and, though we kept watch at the window looking down into the shrubbery, there was no sign of the cook, and the kite string remained unused.

"But she's sure to come some time," said Mercer. "She won't let old Reb starve us. Hi! look there. Old Lomax. There he goes."

Sure enough, the old sergeant marched down the road, and we watched till he was out of sight, but he did not see us.

"I wonder what he thought when we did not go for our lesson this morning," I said.

"Oh, he had heard of it, safe," cried Mercer. "Hark, there they go out from dinner. I say, I'm getting tired of this. They must have us down soon."

But quite an hour passed away, and we stood sadly looking out at the beautiful view, which never looked more attractive, and we were trying to make out where the hammer pond lay among the trees, when I suddenly nipped Mercer's arm, and we began to watch a light cart, driven by a grey-haired gentleman, with a groom in livery with a cockade in his hat seated by his side, and a big dark fellow in velveteen behind.

"Is he coming here?" whispered Mercer, as we drew back from the window.

We knew he must be, and, peering from behind the white window-curtains, we saw the great fiery-looking roan horse turn at a rapid trot through the open gates, then the wheels of the light, cart seemed to be pulled up at the front entrance, where we saw the groom spring down, and heard the jangle of the big front door bell.

Then we sat down on our chairs by the heads of our beds and waited, and not long, for we soon heard steps on the stairs.

"It's coming now," said Mercer, drawing a long breath.

"Yes, it's coming now," I echoed softly, as a curious sensation of dread ran through me, and directly after the door was unlocked, and Mr Rebble appeared.

"Now, young gentlemen," he said, with a perfectly satisfied air, "the Doctor will see you both in his room."

Chapter Fifteen.

We followed him, and as we turned through the baize door so as to go down the front staircase, Mercer and I managed to exchange a grip of the hand.

Directly after, we caught sight of the great roan horse at the door champing its bit, and sending flakes of foam flying over its glossy coat, and I noticed even then that one white spot fell on the groom's dark brown coat.

Then, once more drawing a deep breath, we walked in together through the door Mr Rebble threw open, and closed behind us, when, as if through a mist, I saw the Doctor sitting at a writing-table, looking very stern and portly, the General, grey, fierce, and rather red-faced, seated a little way to the Doctor's right, with his malacca cane between his legs, and his hands, in their bright brown gloves, resting on the ivory handle, so that his arms and elbows stood out squarely; while again on his right, about a couple of yards away, stood big, dark, and burly-looking Bob Hopley, in his best brown velveteen jacket.

"Er-rum!" coughed the Doctor as the door was closed, and we looked sharply round at the stern faces before us, Bob Hopley favouring us with a solemn wink, which I interpreted to mean, "I forgive you, my lads." Then the Doctor spoke.

"Stand there, Thomas Mercer and Frank Burr. That will do. Now, Sir Hawkhurst, will you have the goodness to repeat the charge in their presence."

The old officer faced fiercely round on the Doctor.

"Hang it all, sir!" he cried; "am I the magistrate, or are you?"

"You are the magistrate, sir," said the Doctor gravely, "but I am the master. The distinction is slight, but I allow no one to stand between

187

me and my boys. Unless you are going to proceed legally against them to punish I must request you to let me be their judge."

"Beg pardon, beg pardon," said the General sharply, "Old soldier, sir—been much in India, and the climate made me hot. Go on!"

I glanced at him quickly as I heard him mention India, and he caught my eye, and shook his fist at me fiercely.

"You young dog!" he roared; "how dare you come after my rabbits!"

"Excuse me," said the Doctor.

"Yes, yes, of course. Well, Doctor Browne, my keeper and I were out taking a look round at the young pheasants in their coops last evening, when we took these confounded young dogs red-handed, ferreting rabbits with that scoundrelly poaching vagabond you have taken into your service, when nobody else would give him a job."

"Ah, yes," said the Doctor blandly, "you complained of my employing that man, Sir Hawkhurst. The fact is, he came to me, saying that he had been cruelly misjudged, that he was half starved, and begged me to give him a job. I did so, to give him another chance. Of course, after this, and the fact that my gardener gives him a very bad character and seems much dissatisfied, I shall not employ him again."

"And very wisely," said the old officer. "Well, sir, that's all I've got to say. That is my evidence."

"Thank you," said the Doctor magisterially. "And you, my good man, were with your master, and saw the boys—my boys—engaged there?"

"Yes, sir," said Bob Hopley, touching the black curls over his forehead. "Rabbit and ferret produced."

As he spoke, he pulled out of one big pocket the dead rabbit, and out of the other the twining and writhing ferret, at which the Doctor gazed with interest through his gold spectacles.

"Singular animal!" said the Doctor, "specially designed by nature for threading its way through the narrow labyrinthine burrows of the rabbit and the rat."

"Confound it all, sir!" said the General—"I beg pardon, I beg pardon."

During the last few minutes the wheels of a carriage had been heard on the gravel drive, and the dog-cart had been driven aside. Then the big bell had clanged, and all had been silent again. For the moment, I had wondered whether it was a parish constable come for us, but the next I had forgotten all about it, till one of the maids entered, with a couple of cards on a tray, which she went round and handed to the Doctor.

"Bless me!" he exclaimed, flushing, as the General made an impatient gesture, and relieved his feelings by shaking his fist at us both, while Bob Hopley began to smooth the ferret with his great brown, hairy hand.

"Well, sir?" said the General.

"Excuse me," said the Doctor. "A most curious coincidence. Two visitors."

"No, sir, no visitors now; business, if you please. Those two boys—"

"Excuse me," said the Doctor blandly. "The two visitors are the relatives of one of these boys."

Mercer gave quite a start, and I pitied him.

Poor Tom's father and mother, I said mentally, and then I gave a start too, for the General said fiercely,—

"By George! then they couldn't have come better. Show them in, and I'll have a word or two with the boy's father."

The Doctor made a sign; the maid withdrew; and I pressed a little closer to Mercer, and pinched his arm.

"I'll take my share," I whispered quietly, as the door was opened. The Doctor and the General both rose, as there was the rustle of silk, and I uttered quite a sob as I was clasped in my mother's arms.

"My dearest boy," she cried, as she kissed me fondly, while I shrank away, for my stern-looking, military uncle came in with her.

"Why, Charley!" roared the General.

"What, Hawk!" cried my uncle boisterously, and the two old officers grasped each other's hands, and stood shaking them heartily.

"Why, my dear old man," cried the General, "this is a surprise!"

"Surprise! I should think it is," cried my uncle. "I am delighted. Like old times, eh?"

"Hah!" ejaculated the General, chuckling, and looking now transformed into a very genial old gentleman, while the Doctor stood softly stroking his shirt-frill and smiling benignantly.

"But one moment," cried my uncle. "My sister—poor old Frank Burr's wife."

"Dear, dear, bless me!" cried the General, advancing with courtly, chivalric respect to shake hands with my mother. "My dear madam," he said softly, "it is an honour. I knew your poor husband well."

As he dropped my mother's hand, she bent her head, and her veil sank down, while the General's eyes fell upon me, and the transformation was comic.

"Here," he whispered to my uncle, as I looked from one to the other, and saw the Doctor smiling blandly. "This—this boy—not—Frank Burr's—"

"Yes," said my uncle, nodding to me. "Pupil here. Send him into the service by and by."

"Bless my soul!—Oh dear me!—Here—I—that is—" stammered the General, looking from one to the other, till his eyes lit on Bob Hopley, when he flushed up angrily.

"How dare you, sir! How dare you stand there, with that rabbit and that wretched ferret! Don't you see that there are ladies present, sir. 'Tention! Put them away. Dress!"

"Here, stop," said my uncle sharply, as he looked round, "We have interrupted some business."

"No, no, no, no, my dear boy!—nothing, nothing!" cried the General. "Mere trifle."

"Trifle, eh?" said my uncle, drawing himself up, and looking the fierce colonel of dragoons. "Frank!"

"Yes, uncle," I said shrinkingly.

"You are in some scrape."

"Yes, uncle."

"What have you been doing?"

"Oh, Charles, pray—pray—" cried my mother.

"Hush," he said, holding up his hand. "Now, sir, speak out."

"Really, my dear Charley—" cried the General.

"Allow me, please, sir," said my uncle; and I caught sight of the Doctor raising his hand and making a sign to my mother, as he placed a chair for her, an act of politeness needed, for she was turning faint. "Now, sir, speak out—the simple facts, please. What have you been doing?"

"Rabbiting with a ferret, uncle, us two, and this gentleman and Bob Hopley came and caught us."

"Rabbiting—poaching?"

"Yes, yes, yes," cried the General. "A mere nothing, my dear madam. The boys were certainly on my grounds watching a poaching scoundrel, and I—yes, I thought I'd say a word to the Doctor. Bad company for him, a poacher—eh, my dear Charley?"

"Yes, rather," said my uncle dryly.

"And now," said the General, "Doctor Browne here—my neighbour—will tell them not to do so any more—eh, Doctor, eh?"

"Certainly," said the Doctor. "I'm sure it will not occur again."

"No, no, of course not," said the General. "Hopley, you can go. Stop! that ferret belongs to the boys, I think."

"To you, Frank?" said my uncle.

"No, uncle, it's his," I said. "But I was helping to use it."

"Hah! that's better," said my uncle sharply.

"I bought the ferret," said Mercer, speaking for the first time, "but I don't want it. I'll give it to you, Bob."

"Yes, yes, very wise of you, my lad. There, go now, Hopley," said the General.

The keeper touched his forehead, and gave a look all round, then winked solemnly at Mercer and me, and left the room.

"Hah!" said the General; "then that little bit of business is settled, Doctor, eh? Just a word or two."

"A few admonitions, my dear sir," said the Doctor blandly. "And now, if you will excuse me for a while, I will retire with Mercer here."

Tom gave me a look so full of appeal, that I ran across to the Doctor.

"Don't punish him, sir!" I said imploringly. "We were both alike."

"What's that, Frank?" said my uncle.

"I asked the Doctor not to punish Tom Mercer, uncle."

"No, no, no: of course not!" cried the General; "I endorse that appeal. Here, you sir, come to me. Gentlemen don't do such things as that; and now we all know better, I've got some capital fishing in my ponds and lakes, and I shall be happy to see you two at any time. There, shake hands."

Tom jumped at him, and it was pleasant to see how delighted he looked as he turned and shot a grateful glance at the General before the door closed on him and the Doctor.

Then the two old officers began chatting eagerly together about past times, while I sat by my mother as she held my hand, and I told her the history of my escapade, which was hardly finished when my uncle said,—

"I'm sorry to come down and find you in disgrace, Frank. Not the conduct of one who means to be an officer and a gentleman by and by."

"No, no: don't say any more," said the General. "The boy behaved very well. Liked a bit of sport; all boys do. He shall have a bit of rabbiting now and then."

"Then I shall say no more," said my uncle. "Try and be like your name, my boy, and you will find me ready to forgive your scrapes; but you must always be a gentleman."

"Amen to that," said the General, rising. "And now, my dear Mrs Burr, I will not say good-bye, but *au revoir*. Seaborough here tells me you are both going to stay in Hastings for a few days. I shall drive over and see you. Good-bye."

He showed the same courtly respect to her again, and was rising to go when the Doctor re-entered, and they parted the best of friends.

"No, no, no," cried the General, as the Doctor was coming out with him, "stay with your visitors. Odd meeting, wasn't it? Here, you, Frank Burr, come and see me off. Good-day, Doctor, good-day. You and I must be better neighbours."

"I shall be proud," said the Doctor, and then I went to the cart with the General, who stood holding my hand at the step, and I could feel a coin therein.

"For you two boys," he said. "There, good-bye, Frank Burr. You must grow up into a brave gentleman like your father. A thorough soldier, sir. God bless you, my boy! Good-bye."

He took the reins and got in, the groom left the horse's head and mounted beside him, and as the cart was driven off, and I stood there with a sovereign in my hand, Bob Hopley, who was in his place behind, gave me another solemn wink, while, after noticing the hired carriage in which my mother and my uncle had driven over from Hastings, I went back into the room and stayed with them, and afterwards went to show them the building and grounds.

An hour after, they were gone, while I hurried off to find Mercer and show him the sovereign.

"Well," he said, "that's all right. But, I say, don't some things turn out rum! What are you going to do with all that money?"

"Half's yours," I said.

"Oh, is it? Well, let's make a bank. It'll do to pay old Lomax and lots of things."

Chapter Sixteen.

My mother and my uncle came over to see me twice during their stay at Hastings, and during one of the visits my uncle spoke to the Doctor about the drill-master, and, after expressing a wish that I should pay attention to that part of my studies, with fencing, asked if this instructor had been in the foot or horse.

"Oh, he was in the cavalry, uncle," I said.

"Good; then, if Doctor Browne does not object, I should like him to give you a few preliminary lessons in riding, so as to get a military seat while you are young, boy."

The Doctor expressed his willingness, but he said with a slight cough,—

"Would not a horse be necessary, or a pony?"

"Well, yes," said my uncle dryly, "I think it would, sir; but that difficulty will be got over. Sir Hawkhurst Rye has offered the boy the use of a stout cob. One of the grooms will bring it over two or three times a week; and, if you would allow me, I should like to have a few words with the old sergeant."

The Doctor was perfectly agreeable; and when they were going, I had the pleasure—for it was a pleasure—of taking them down to Lomax's little, neatly-kept place, where the old sergeant stood ready to draw himself up and salute, with his eyes lighting up, and a proud look of satisfaction in his hard face.

My uncle took him aside, and they remained talking together, while my mother walked up and down with me, holding my hand through her arm, and eagerly whispering her hopes—that I would be very careful, that I would not run into any danger with the riding, and, above all, mind not to do anything my uncle would not like.

Of course I promised with the full intention of performing, and soon after my uncle marched back with Lomax—they did not seem to walk. Everything had apparently gone off satisfactorily, and after plenty of advice from my uncle, he handed my mother into the carriage, followed and they were driven off.

I stood watching the carriage till it was out of sight, and then turned to Lomax, who was standing as upright as if he were on parade, till he caught my eye, and then he gave himself a jerk, thrust one hand into his pocket, and gave the place a slap.

"You're a lucky one," he said, "to have an uncle like that, sir. Hah! there's nothing like a soldier."

"How am I lucky?" I said rather sourly, for I was low-spirited from the parting I had just gone through.

"Lucky to have a fine old officer like that to want me to make a man of you, and teach you everything you ought to know to become an officer and a gentleman."

"Oh, bother!" I said. "Look here, Lomax; you're to teach me riding. Can you?"

"Can I?" he said, with a little laugh; "wait till the horse comes round, and I'll show you, my boy."

"I can ride, you know," I said; "but not military fashion."

"You? you ride, sir?" said the old soldier scornfully. "Rubbish! Don't talk to me. I know how you ride—like a sack of wool with two legs. Knees up to your chin and your nose parting the horse's mane all down his neck."

"Oh, nonsense, Lom!"

"Fact, sir, fact. Think I don't know? A civilian rides, sir, like a monkey, bumping himself up and down, and waggling his elbows

197

out like a young chicken learning to fly. There, you be easy, and I'll teach you how to ride same as I did how to fight."

"But I don't know that you have taught me how to fight. I haven't tried yet."

Lomax chuckled.

"Wait a bit," he said. "You don't want to fight. It's like being a soldier—a British soldier, sir. He don't want to fight, and he will not if he can help it. He always hangs back because he knows that he can fight. But when he does—well, I'm sorry for the other side."

"Then you think I could lick Eely if he knocked me about, or big Dicksee?"

"No, I don't think anything about it, my boy. You wait. Don't fight if you can help it, but if you're obliged to, recollect all I've shown you, and let him have it."

I did not feel in any hurry, and when I talked to Tom Mercer about what I had said to Lomax, he agreed with me that he felt a little nervous about his powers, and said that he should like to try a small boy or two first; but I said no, that would not do; it would be cowardly.

"So it would," said Mercer; "besides, it would let the cat out of the bag, wouldn't it? Look here, I know: we ought to have a quiet set to up in the loft some day."

"But that would only be boxing," I said.

"Why not make a fight of it?" suggested Mercer.

"But we couldn't fight without there was a genuine quarrel."

"Let's quarrel, then."

"What about?"

"Oh, I don't know. Anything. You call me a fool, and I'll hit you, and then you go at me again, and we should know then what we could do."

"Get out!" I said. "I shan't call you a fool; but if I did, you wouldn't be such a beast as to hit me, and if you did, I should be so sorry that I shouldn't hit you again. That wouldn't do."

Tom Mercer scratched his head.

"No," he said dryly, "that wouldn't do. It seems precious rum, though."

"What does?"

"That I shouldn't care to hit you. I feel as if I couldn't hit a fellow who saved my life."

"Look here," I said angrily, "you're always trying to bring up that stupid nonsense about the holding you up on the penstock. If you do it again, I will hit you."

"Boo! Not you. You're afraid," cried Mercer derisively. "Who pulled the chap out of the water when he was half drowned, and saved him? Who—"

I clapped my hand over his mouth.

"Won't do, Tom," I said. "It's all sham. We can't fight. I daresay old Lom's right, though."

"What do you mean?"

"That we shall be able to knock Eely and Dicksee into the middle of next week."

"But it seems to me as if they must feel that we have been learning, or else they would have been sure to have done something before now."

"Never mind," I said, "let's wait. We don't want to fight, as Lom says, but if we're obliged to, we've got to do it well."

The occasion for trying our ability did not come off, though it was very near it several times; but as I grew more confident, the less I felt disposed to try, and Mercer always confessed it was the same with him, though the cock of the school and his miserable toady, Dicksee often led us a sad life.

One morning, soon after the last visit of Uncle Seaborough, Lomax came to the schoolroom door, just as Mr Hasnip was giving me a terrible bullying about the results of a problem in algebra, on to which he had hurried me before I had more than the faintest idea of the meaning of the rules I had been struggling through.

I suppose I was very stupid, but it was terribly confusing to me for the most part. I grasped very well the fact that a plus quantity killed a minus quantity if they were of equal value, and that a little figure two by the side of a letter meant its square, and I somehow blundered through some simple equations, but when Mr Hasnip lit a scholastic fire under me, and began to force on bigger mathematical flowers from my unhappy soil in the Doctor's scholastic hothouse, I began to feel as if I were blighted, and as if quadratic equations were instruments of torture to destroy boys' brains.

On that particular morning, I was, what fat Dicksee called, "catching it," and I was listening gloomily to my teacher's attempts at being witty at my expense.

"How a boy can be so stupid," he said, "is more than I can grasp. It is perfect child's play, and yet you have gone on getting the problem into a hopeless tangle—a ridiculous tangle. You have made a surd perfectly absurd, and—"

"Mr Hasnip!" came from the other end of the great room. Mr Hasnip looked up.

"The drill-master is here. The horse has arrived for Burr junior's riding lesson. Can you excuse him?"

"Certainly, sir," and Mr Hasnip looked at me, showing his teeth in a hungry kind of smile, as if a nice morsel were being snatched from him, and I stood with my heart beating, and the warm blood tingling in my cheeks, conscious that all the boys were looking at me.

"Here, take your book, Burr junior," said my tutor. "Very glad to go, I daresay. Now aren't you?"

I looked up at him, but made no reply.

"Do you hear me, sir?"

"Yes, sir."

"I said, 'Aren't you glad to go?'"

"Yes, sir."

"Of course. There, be off. You'll never learn anything. You are the stupidest boy I ever taught."

My cheeks burned, and as I turned to go, there was fat Dicksee grinning at me in so provoking a way, that if we had been alone, I should in my vexation have tried one of Lomax's blows upon his round, smooth face. But as it was, I went back to my place, where Mercer was seated, with his hands clasped and thrust down between his knees, his back up, and his head down over his book, apparently grinding up his Euclid, upon which he kept his eyes fixed.

"Oh ho!" he whispered; "here you are. Without exception, sir, the stupidest boy I ever taught."

"I'll punch your head by and by, Tom, if you're not quiet," I said.

"Who made the surd absurd?"

"Did you hear what I said?"

"Yes. Oh, you lucky beggar! Who are you, I should like to know, to be having your riding lessons?"

"Less talking there, Burr junior."

This from Mr Rebble, and I went out, passing close to Burr major, who looked me up and down contemptuously, as he took out his watch, and said to the nearest boy, —

"Rank favouritism! if there's much more of it, I shall leave the school."

But I forgot all this directly, as I stepped out, where I found Lomax standing up as stiff as a ramrod, and with a walking cane thrust under his arms and behind his back, trussing him like a chicken, so as to throw out his chest.

He saluted me in military fashion.

"Mornin', sir. Your trooper's waiting. Looks a nice, clever little fellow."

"Trooper?" I faltered in a disappointed tone. "What do you mean? I thought it was the horse come."

"So it is."

"But trooper?"

"Of course. Well, charger, then. Officers' horses are chargers; men's horses, troopers."

"Oh!" I cried, brightening up, but with a feeling of nervousness and excitement making my heart beat more heavily still. "Where is it?"

"Paddock!" said Lomax shortly, and without the slightest disposition to be conversational. In fact, he became more military every moment, and marched along by me, delivering cuts at nothing with his cane, as if he were angry with the air.

Then all at once he glanced at me, looking me up and down.

"Humph! No straps to your overalls," he said snappishly.

"Overalls?"

"Well, trousers, sir. They'll be crawling all up your legs. Get some buttons put on by next time."

He turned into the field devoted to the Doctor's cows and to the junior boys' football, and there I saw the General's groom holding a fiery, untamed-looking steed, as it seemed to me, arching its neck and snorting, as it stood champing its bit till the white foam flew from its mouth.

The groom touched his hat to me as we came up.

"Master's compliments, sir, and as he wants me," he said, "would you mind riding the cob back to the house?"

"Oh yes, of course," I said, glancing at the fierce-looking animal, and mentally asking myself whether he would allow me to ride him home. "Is—is he quiet?"

"Quiet, sir! why, he's like a lamb. Bit playful sometimes, but no more vice in him than there is in an oyster. Mornin', sir."

The man touched his hat and went off, leaving Lomax and me with the horse, which looked enormous then.

Lomax strode round the animal, examining it, and making remarks as he went on.

"Very well groomed," he said. "Saw your old friend Magglin before breakfast. Good legs. Like to get taken on again, he says. Tail wants topping—too long. Lucky for him he didn't get before the magistrates. Doctor won't have him again. Very nice little nag, but too small for service. I told him that all he was fit for was to enlist; some sharp drill-sergeant might knock him into shape in time. He's no use as he is. Now, then, ready?"

"Yes," I said shrinkingly, "I suppose so."

"That's right," cried Lomax, and, lifting up the flap of the saddle, he busied himself, as I supposed, tightening the girths, but all at once they dropped to the ground, and, with the rein over his arm, Lomax lifted off the saddle and placed it upon the hedge.

"Now then," he cried, "come along and I'll give you a leg up."

"But you've taken the saddle off."

"Of course I have. I'm going to teach you how to ride."

"Without a saddle or stirrups?"

"Of course. A man wants to feel at home on a horses, so does a boy. Now then, I'll give you a leg up."

I was like wax in his hands. On lifting one leg as he bade me, the next moment I was sent flying, to come down on the horse's back astride, but so much over to the right that I had to fling myself forward and clutch the mane.

"Bravo! Well done!" cried Lomax sarcastically.

"I'm all right now," I cried.

"All right! Here, come down, sir. Do you know what would have happened if that had been some horses?"

"No," I said, dismounting clumsily.

"Well, then, I'll tell you. They'd either have sent you flying over their heads, or bolted."

"I'm very sorry," I faltered.

"Sorry! I should think you are. Got up like a tailor, sir, and you've come down like one. Bah! It's horrible."

"Well, but you've got to teach me better," I cried.

"True. Good lad. So I have. Now then, give me your leg. That's it. Steady. Up you go."

"That's better," I cried, settling myself into my place.

"Better! No, it isn't. It's not so bad only, sir. Now, then, sit up so that a line dropped from your temple would go down by your heel. Better. Get your fork well open."

"What?"

"Sit close down on the horse's back, then. No, no, you don't want to scratch your ear."

"Well, I know, that," I said, laughing.

"Then what did you cock up your knee that way for? Let your legs hang down. That's better. Toes up and heels well down."

"What for, Lomax?"

"Don't ask questions. Do as I tell you. Well, there you're right. Toes up so that they just rest in the stirrups."

"But I haven't got any stirrups."

"Then act as if you had."

"But why don't you let me have some?"

"Silence in the ranks, sir. Now then, keep your balance. Advance at a walk."

The horse started.

"Halt!" shouted Lomax, and the horse pulled up so short that I went forward.

"What are you doing, sir? You don't want to look into the horse's ears."

"I wasn't trying to," I said sharply.

"What were you going to do, then?—whisper to him to stop?"

"I say, don't tease me, Lom," I said appealingly; "you know I couldn't help it."

"Right, my lad, I know. But 'tention; this won't do. I've got to teach you to ride with a good military seat, and we're not friends now. You're a private, and I'm your riding-master."

"Yes, but one minute, Lom—"

"Sergeant Lomax, sir."

"Yes, Sergeant Lomax. I say, do let me have a saddle."

"What for, sir?"

"It's so much more comfortable."

"A soldier, sir, is a man who scorns comfort and takes things as they come. You've got to learn to ride."

"Of course. Then where's the saddle?"

"When you can ride well without a saddle, you shall have one. Now: no more talking. 'Tention! By your right—March!"

The horse started off without my influencing him in the slightest degree, but before we had got ten yards, the sergeant's stern "Halt!" rang out again, and the horse stopped as suddenly as before, but I was aware of it this time, and gripped him hard with my knees.

"Good. Well done. But you went too far forward. Take a good hold with your knees. And that's not the way to hold your reins. Look here, one rein—no, no, not the curb—the snaffle—that's it now—one rein outside your little finger and one in, and the rest of the rein through your hand, between your forefinger and thumb. Good. Now pick up the curb rein off your horse's neck and let it rest lightly in your hand."

"What for?"

"Don't ask questions. Because it's right. Ready for use if the horse pulls too much or bolts."

"Is he likely to pull too much or bolt?"

"Don't ask questions. No, he isn't. Soldiers generally ride on the curb, but a horse like this don't want it. He has been ridden with cavalry, too. Now then, once more at a walk—March!"

The horse started again, with his soft, warm back feeling terribly slippery, but I sat quite stiffly upright, and he walked straight up the paddock, and seemed as if he were going to leap the hedge, making me wonder which side I should fall; but just as we were close up, the sergeant's voice rang out,—

"Right wheel!"

The horse turned to the right instantly, and had gone a dozen yards when the sergeant shouted again, "Right wheel!" and directly after, "Forward!" with the result that we were now facing him, and went slowly down the paddock, till the sergeant shouted, "Halt!" just as I was beginning to feel a little more comfortable, and not as if I must slide off right or left at any moment.

"Well, that's pretty fair, sir," cried Lomax, as the horse stopped short. "Chest out more, back hollow. Keep your knees well in. Capital horse for you to learn on. Knows all his work. Well, we won't waste time walking. You shall do that now at a trot."

"Without a sad—"

"'Tention. No talking in the ranks."

The horse didn't want to be turned, but came round quickly, almost on a pivot, very much disturbing my equilibrium again; but by gripping tightly with my legs I managed to hold on, and looked anxiously at Lomax.

"Ah," he shouted, "eyes straight for the horse's ears! Now then, you will sit firm, elbows close to your sides. 'Tention! The squadron will advance at a walk. Forward—tr–r–r–ot!"

The horse had only walked a few paces when the second order came, and he broke directly into a trot, which sent me bumping up and down, now a little inclined to the right, then more to the left, then my balance was gone. I made a desperate effort to save myself, and then, perfectly certain that the horse would trample me to death beneath his feet, down I went on my back, and began to scramble up, with my mount stock still beside me.

"Not hurt a bit!" cried Lomax, running up and handing me my cap, which had come off.

"No," I said, beginning to feel myself all over; "I don't think anything is broken."

"And I'm sure there isn't," cried Lomax. "Now then, I'll give you a leg up."

"Am I to get up again—now?" I faltered.

"Without you want to say you haven't pluck enough to learn to ride."

"No," I said; "I haven't pluck enough to say that."

"Not you. Up you go. There. Now that is better. Stick on this time."

"I could if I had stirrups," I said, "and a saddle."

"No, you couldn't, sir, so don't talk nonsense. You've just learnt the finest thing a lad who wants to ride can learn—the thing that gives him plenty of confidence."

"What's that?" I asked; "that it's very hard to keep on?"

"No; that it's very easy to come off and roll on the ground without hurting yourself a bit. Off you go again. Forward—trot!"

The horse snorted and went on, shaking me almost to pieces, and sometimes I was nearly off on one side, sometimes nearly off on the other, but I kept on.

"Right wheel!" came from the other end of the field, then, "Right wheel!" again. "Forward!" and the horse was taking me—for I had nothing whatever to do with him—back toward where the sergeant stood.

I kept my balance pretty well, but my trousers were running up my legs, and I felt as if everything belonging to me was shaken up. Then once more my balance was gone, and off I went on to my back, and over and over a few yards from the sergeant, who ran up, the horse once more stopping short by my side.

"Bravo!" cried Lomax, as I sat up. "You're getting on."

"I thought I was getting off," I said dolefully.

"Rubbish, sir; improving fast. Here, up with you again. It's all strange to you at first, but you've got to grow to that horse's back, till it's like one animal—horse and man. You've got to learn to grip him till you feel as if you can't tumble off."

"But I never shall," I cried.

"Don't tell me. I'll make you. Now then; there you are. Now you just trot down to the bottom and back without coming off like a sack of shavings. Never mind the reins. Let him have his head, and you put all your sperrit into your knees. Keep your position and preserve your balance."

"I know I shall fall again soon."

"Very well, then, fall. But I don't believe you will. Now then, once more."

He gave the order, the horse walked a few steps, then at the second order broke into a trot, and, to my utter astonishment, as I drove my knees into the warm soft sides, away we went, wheeled to the right, then to the right again, and trotted back to the sergeant, who shouted,—

"Halt! Bravo! There, what did I say? Make much of your horse."

The lesson was kept on for fully two hours, and then, to make up, I suppose, for a good deal of bullying, my instructor was loud in his praise, and, opening the gate after replacing the saddle, he signed to me to mount, but I tried and could not, for my legs felt stiff and stretched, my back ached, and there was a peculiar sensation of soreness about the knees.

"Shall I trot him back?" said Lomax.

"If you would, please," I said. "I do feel so stiff."

"I will, my lad. To-morrow morning same time; and I'll get some of that stiffness out of you."

"Thank you," I said rather dolefully; and then I could not help watching the old dragoon with a feeling of envy as he placed one foot in the stirrup, drew himself up till he stood upright, then deliberately threw the right leg over the horse's back, slowly dropped into his place as upright as a dart, and trotted steadily out into the road and away out of sight, while, after closing the gate, I began to retrace my steps in the direction of the school, just as the boys came trooping out for their regular run till the room was ventilated, and the cloth laid for dinner.

"Oh, I say, it's rank favouritism!" came from the middle of a group. "I shall speak to the Doctor about it."

Some one answered this, but I did not hear the words, and I hobbled to the door, and went up to my room, wondering how any one could be envious of the sensations I was experiencing then.

Chapter Seventeen.

"How are your sore knees?" said Mercer one morning soon after my long first lesson in riding.

"Oh, dreadful!" I cried. "They get a little better, and then the riding makes them bad again."

"But why don't he let you have a saddle?"

"He does now," I said—"that is, he did yesterday; but it's worse riding on a saddle, it's so slippery, and he will not let me have any stirrups."

"When are you going again?"

"To-day, I suppose. The Doctor says I'm to get on as fast as possible, and make up with my other studies afterwards."

"Wish I was going to learn to ride."

"You wouldn't much like it if you had to," I replied. "Oh, I don't know. It looks very nice to see you going along. But, I say, it does make Burr major so wild. I heard him tell Dicksee he should make his father send him a horse, and Dicksee said he ought to, and I laughed."

"Did he hear you?"

"Yes, and gave me such a clip on the head with a cricket stump. Feel here."

I placed my hand where he suggested, and there was a good-sized lump.

"What a shame!" I cried indignantly. "Didn't you hit him again?"

"No; I only put it down. We're going to pay it all back some day."

"Yes; but when?" I cried.

Mercer shook his head.

"I say," he continued, "I saw old Magglin this morning before breakfast."

"What was he doing here?"

"Dunno. Wanted to see me, I suppose, and borrow a shilling."

"Did you lend him one?"

"Yes; I felt obliged to."

Just then Burr major came by us, and looked us both over sharply.

"Haven't you two got any lessons to get ready?" he said.

"Yes," I replied.

"Then go in and get them ready before I report you both to Mr Hasnip. Do you hear?"

"Yes," I said; "but I'm going to have my riding lesson."

"Your riding lesson!" he sneered; "you're always going to have your riding lesson. I never saw such a school as it's getting to be. It's shameful! I shall go and ask Mr Hasnip if we boys are to be kept always at work, while you and Tom Mercer are idling about and enjoying yourselves."

"All right," said Mercer oracularly, in a whisper to me, as Burr major walked off importantly for a few yards, attended by his satellites, and then stopped, drew out his watch with a flourish, looked at it, and put it back with an air that he intended to be graceful.

"Look here, you, Tom Mercer—do you hear, Jollop? You're not going to have riding lessons. I give you five minutes to get back to your work, and if you are not there then—you'll see."

"All right," said Mercer again; and then, as Burr major was out of hearing, "Any one would think he was the Doctor. Oh, I should like to—" he continued, grinding his teeth. "Think we could, Frank?"

"I don't know," I said hesitatingly; "but when he talks like that, it makes me feel horribly mad, and as if I should like to try."

"Never mind. Wait a bit; the revolution isn't ripe yet," said Mercer darkly. "Wish I'd got a watch like that."

I was very angry, but my companion's sudden change from thoughts of revenge to covetousness seemed exceedingly droll.

"What are you laughing at?" he said.

"At you about the watch."

"Well, I can't help it, Frank. That watch seems always staring at me with its round white face, and holding out its hands to me. I dream of it of a night, and I'm always longing for it of a day. You can't tell how bad it makes me feel sometimes."

"You shouldn't think about it, Tom."

"I can't help it. I don't want to, but the thoughts will come, dreadfully. I say," he whispered darkly, "I don't wonder at chaps stealing sometimes, if they feel like I do."

"What nonsense!" I cried: "I say, here's Eely coming back."

"Is he?" said Mercer sharply. "Then I'm off in."

"Why, you're never going to be such a coward as to be bullied into obeying his orders."

"Oh yes, I am," replied my companion. "Time isn't ripe yet. But when it is—oh!"

He gave vent to that exclamation with peculiar force, though it was only a low hiss, and I followed him with my eyes, half disposed to think that Tom Mercer would prove a rotten reed to lean upon if I wanted his support in a struggle against our tyrant; though, truth to tell, as Burr came rolling along with half a dozen boys about, all ready at a word from him to rush at me, I did not feel at all confident of being able to resist his authority, and I began to move off.

"Hullo!" he cried. "Here's the gallant horseman, boys. Let's go and see him ride."

"Yah! he can't ride," cried Dicksee; "he'll tumble off."

"Not he," said Burr major. "Old Lom ties his ankles together under the horse. But he does look an awful fool when he's on board. I say, Burr junior, you don't think you can ride, do you?"

"No," I said quietly.

"And you never will. I say, boys, what an ugly beggar he grows! I know why he's learning riding."

"Do you? Why?" cried Dicksee.

"They're going to make a groom of him."

The blood flushed up in my face, and I began to feel as if the time must be getting ripe.

"Why, he was bragging about going to be a soldier!" cried another boy.

"Him! A soldier! Ha, ha, ha!" cried Burr major. "They wouldn't even have a big-eared-looking fellow like that for a parchment-whopper."

"He said a horse soldier."

"Horse sneak," said Burr major scornfully. "A soldier! Ho, ho, ho! Ha, ha, ha! I say, boys—a soldier!"

He burst into a yell of laughter, all forced, of course, and his satellites roared too, some of them, to curry favour, beginning to dance about him, and look eagerly in his face, as if for orders.

Of course it was very absurd to mind, but I could not help it, and tingled all over.

"Oh, I wish Mercer was here!" I thought to myself.

"The time must be ripe;" and I suppose my face showed something of what I felt, for Burr major cried,—

"Look at the puppy, boys; he looks as if he wanted to bite. Did you ever see such an impudent beggar? I don't believe his name's Burr at all. It's only a bit of a show-off."

At that moment there was a hail from the paddock, and the school bell rang for the first lesson.

"There, groom, you're wanted," said Burr major sneeringly. "Go on and learn to ride, and mind you don't hurt yourself."

"Yah! Go on, ugly!" cried Dicksee, and the boys roared.

"Do you hear, sham sodger? Be off, and don't stand staring like that," cried Burr major again. "I told you to go."

"Go yourself," I retorted, now thoroughly roused, and feeling reckless. "Go in to school and learn your lessons, and mind the Doctor don't cane you."

"What?" cried the tall, thin fellow, flushing up, as he advanced upon me menacingly, while the bell was rapidly getting toward its last strokes,—"what's that you say?"

"Go in and get to your lessons, and take that fat-faced booby with you."

"Well!" cried Burr, "of all!" and he looked astounded.

"That's it, is it? Cheeking me because you know I can't stop now. But all right, I shan't forget it. If I do, Dicksee, you remind me after lessons that I've got to warm Jollop and this groom boy. The Doctor's been spoiling them both lately, and they want taking down."

"All in, all in, to begin!" was shouted from the doors.

"Oh yes, we're coming soon," said Burr major, throwing up his head. "Wait a bit, you, sir, and I'll teach you to insult your seniors."

"All in, all in!"

"Here, Dicksee, go and hit that fellow on the mouth for shouting."

"All in, all in!" came again, directed at our group.

"Coming," cried Burr major. Then to me: "After morning studies, you sir. I don't suppose I shall forget."

"If you do, I shan't, bully," I said, and he turned upon me more astonished than ever, and then burst into a fit of derisive laughter.

"He's mad," he cried. "Here, boys, Senna's been gammoning him into taking some of his physic, and he don't know what he's saying."

"Dicksee—Burr major. Come, boys."

Mr Rebble was standing in the schoolhouse doorway, and all but Burr major ran off. He took out his watch, and walked away importantly after the others, while I felt a peculiar nervous thrill run through me, and began wondering whether I had been too bold, as I went off hurriedly now to where Lomax was waiting with the horse.

"I don't care," I said; "he may thrash me, but I won't be bullied like that, and insulted, without a try."

"Come, young gentleman," cried the sergeant. "I began to think you were going to shirk it."

"Not I, Lom," I cried, and, feeling peculiarly excited, I went up to the horse's head and patted him, while the sergeant removed the stirrups. Then he gave me a leg up, and I was hoisted into my seat, and went through my lesson—walk, trot, and gallop, with the saddle seeming less slippery, and without coming off once.

The sergeant, I noticed, was very severe, and barked and shouted at me and the horse, keeping us doing the same things over and over again, and growing more exacting as we went on. But I hardly noticed him, for my head was all in a whirl, and I was thinking about after lessons, and what would happen then. So occupied was I with my thoughts that I never once felt nervous, but as if all I had to do was to sit still and let the horse obey the orders.

Lomax finished me off with a canter round the paddock, which was taken at a pretty good pace, and very easy the horse's pace was, but I was thinking of Burr major's sneering face all the time, and his long arms and bony white hands. Then about Mercer, and what he would say—what he would do.

"Are we both to have a good thrashing?" I asked myself, as the horse cantered on, and "Right wheel—left wheel—forward!" rang in my ears. "Are we to be made more uncomfortable than ever?" I thought; "and shall we forget all about what old Lom taught us?"

My arms did not move, my left hand held the reins on a level with my imaginary waist-belt, about which the sergeant talked, and my right hand hung steadily down just by my leg, but all the time I was on guard, and keenly on the watch for blows from those white bony hands that seemed to be flourished before me. Then I fancied concussions and dizziness, and felt blows, and rolled over upon the grass, but not off the horse, for it was all fancy; and I was just seeing in my mind's eye poor Tom Mercer going down before a heavy blow from Dicksee's fat fist, when there rang out the word, "Halt!" and the horse stopped short.

Lomax strode up in his stiff military fashion, and patted the cob on the neck.

"Well?" he said sharply. "What am I to say to you now?"

"I—I don't know," I faltered. "Shall we go through it again."

"No, no let the trooper breathe a bit. He has been kept at it pretty tightly. Well, how do you feel—stiff?"

"No," I said, flushing a little, full of a feeling of regret for my neglect in my lesson.

"Bit sore about the knees, eh?"

"Oh yes, my knees keep very sore," I faltered.

"Of course they do. Never so hard worked before. Soon get better. Let me see, this makes just a month you've been at it, eh?"

"Yes, this is the end of the fourth week."

"Then don't you think I deserve a bit of credit?"

"Oh yes!" I cried eagerly. "You have taken great pains over me, Lom. I wish I had not been so stupid."

"So do I," he said drily. "Saddle feel very slippery this morning?"

"Oh no, I didn't notice it," I replied.

"Didn't long for the stirrups?"

"I didn't think about them."

"Felt as if you belonged to the horse now, eh, and could let yourself go with him?"

"Oh yes," I said.

"Well, then, all I've got to say, my boy, is, 'Brayvo!' You went through it all wonderfully this morning, and quite astonished me. Seemed as if you and the horse were one, and you never showed the white feather once. Why, in another two or three months your uncle shall be proud of you."

"Then I went through my lesson well?" I said.

"Splendidly, boy, splendidly. Couldn't have done better. Now, trot the nag down home. Stop, you shall have the stirrups."

"No, not to-day, Lomax," I said. "I've got an—an engagement to keep. Please take him down yourself."

"Right. I will. Hah! we've been longer than I thought, for the boys are coming out of school. Then down you come, and good morning."

I leaped off the horse, not feeling a bit stiff. Lomax replaced the stirrups, mounted, and went off again in the upright, steady way I had before admired, while I stood there listening to the shouting of the boys, and thinking of the thrashing I was bound to receive.

Chapter Eighteen.

I had not been standing in the field many minutes, shut in by the hedge, and trying to rouse myself to go, before I heard a familiar voice calling me, and I answered with a feeling of relief, for anything was better than that sensation of shrinking expectancy, and, drawing a deep breath, I prepared myself for the plunge.

"Oh, here you are!" cried Mercer, running up to me excitedly. "I say, here's a go! You've got to come up into the loft directly."

"The loft!" I said, feeling that here was something fresh. "What for?"

"Eely wants us. He sent Dicksee to me to say that we were to go to him directly."

"Do you know what for?" I said huskily.

"Yes, Dicksee told me. He said he was going to punch our heads for being cheeky. But I say, Frank, we're not obliged to go, are we?"

I was silent for a few moments, and then said, with an effort, —

"Yes, I suppose we must."

"But he isn't everybody."

"If we don't go, they'll come and fetch us."

"But you're not going to let him punch your head, are you?"

"I suppose so," I said dismally, for my anger had faded away, and I was quite cool.

"But I'm sick of being knocked about."

"So am I."

"Then don't let's have it. The time isn't anything like ripe, I know, and I don't believe a bit in being able to fight, but—"

"But what?" I said, after a pause.

"I don't know. I hate fighting."

"So do I, Tom," I said dismally. "I wish they'd leave us alone."

"I wish they only would."

"But why does Burr major want us to go into the loft? Why couldn't he come here?"

"Because he thinks he can lick us quietly up there, with only a few of his chaps with him, and two to be scouts. Oh dear me, school ain't nice!"

"Come on, Tom," I said, "and let's get it over."

"What? do you mean to go?"

"Yes," I said gloomily, "I suppose so."

"And do you mean to fight?"

"If I'm obliged. You may just as well have a few cracks at him as take it all for nothing. You'll come?"

"Oh, all right, but we shall get an awful licking," said Tom huskily. "I can't fight a bit. It's all gammon—that poking out your left arm and fending with your right. I like to hit out with my right arm."

"I don't like hitting out at all," I said gloomily.

"But shall you try?"

"I don't know, Tom," I replied in a desponding tone. "Oh, I do wish boys wouldn't be such beasts! Come on."

"All boys ain't," said Mercer, as we moved off toward the yard. "Oh, don't I wish the time had been quite ripe, and we could have astonished 'em! It's always the way. I make such jolly plans, and think they're going to turn out all right, but they don't. Never mind. I never told you what I've got saved up in my box ready in case of accidents."

"No," I said; "what is it?"

"Some of the stuff my father uses for bruises. I bought some — leastwise I got Lom to buy some for me at the chemist's when he went into the town."

"What is it?" I said carelessly, for I did not feel eager to know.

"Arnica. It's in a bottle, and you soak rags in it, and —"

"Here they are," greeted us in chorus, and we were literally taken into custody by about a dozen boys, who hurried us round to the back, where Burr major, Dicksee, Hodson, Stewart, and three more were waiting like so many conspirators.

I may as well own to it; my heart sank, and I felt as if I were going out to execution, or at the least to be severely punished, for Burr major was laughing and chatting to the boys about him, and turned sneeringly to us as we came up.

"Oh, here they are, then," he cried contemptuously. "Bring them up, boys;" and he turned off, entered the old stable, and went up the worn steps into the loft, while we were dragged and pushed unnecessarily till we were up at the top, to find Burr major seated on the big bin, swinging one leg about carelessly—acting as if he were judge and we were two criminals brought up before him.

"Two of you keep the lower door and give notice if any one's coming," said Burr major sharply.

"Oh," cried one of the boys, "don't send us down, please. We shan't see none of the fun."

Nice fun for us, I thought, and then wondered whether it would hurt much.

"All right, then," cried Burr major. "I don't want to be hard. You can keep a look-out from the window." Then, turning sharply, —

"Now, you two," he cried, "what have you got to say for yourselves?"

"Nothing," I said.

"More have I," cried Mercer defiantly.

"Oh, very well," said Burr major. "More cheeky than ever. What shall I do, boys? give 'em stick or let 'em stand up and take it?"

"A fight, a fight!" rose in chorus.

"All right. I'll dress the groom boy, and Dicksee shall give the other chap his dose."

A curious sensation of trouble and bewilderment came over me, as I gave a quick glance round at the bare loft, with its cob-webbed windows and eager little crowd of boys, all expectant and flushed with desire for the scene.

"Ah, look out! he's going to bolt," shouted Hodson.

"I wasn't," I cried indignantly.

"He'd better," said Burr major, coolly taking off his jacket and beginning to fold it up and lay it on the bin. "Now then, major-general of cavalry, off with your duds. I won't keep you long. Just time before dinner."

"But I say," cried Dicksee, "we ain't going to fight both together?"

"No," said Burr major; "you shall dress Jollop down first, and I'll second you."

"No; you do yours first."

"Do as I tell you," cried Burr sharply, "and don't waste time. I shall have to wash after thrashing that dirty groom."

I gave him an angry glance in return for his insult, and then turned to Tom Mercer, who was standing with his brow all wrinkled up, slowly taking off his jacket, which he threw over a beam, and turning up his shirt sleeves above his sharp elbows.

"I'm going to get such a licking," he whispered.

"No, no; do win!" I whispered back.

"Can't. He's so soft you can't hurt him. He's just like a big football that you mustn't kick."

"His head isn't soft," I whispered; "hit that."

"Now then, ready!" cried Burr, and we faced round, to find Dicksee with his sleeves rolled up, and Burr patting him on the shoulder and giving him instructions.

"Now, then, young Mercer, come up to the scratch," cried Burr. "Stand back, you boys, and make a better ring."

Then a shuffling of feet, a few suppressed sounds of excitement, and the boys who were to look out turned from the windows.

"Remember old Lom," I said, feeling very nervous and doubtful as I whispered to my principal. Then the boys were opposite to each other, Dicksee throwing his head about, dancing from leg to leg, and feinting a rush in, while Mercer stood well balanced on his legs, his brow wrinkled, and his fists up in the attitude we had been taught.

"Now, Dicksy, give it up. Go in at him. Look sharp!"

"All right; wait a moment," cried the boy, dancing and dodging about as if to avoid blows that had not been struck at him.

"Go it, Fatty, go it!" shouted the boys.

"Hush! not so much row," cried Burr. "Go on, Fatty. Now then."

"All right; wait—"

But Burr would not wait, for he gave his principal a heavy thrust, sending him forward right on to Tom, who contented himself with thrusting his antagonist back.

"Oh, I say, that ain't fair," cried Dicksee. "You wouldn't like it yourself. You spoiled my plans."

"Go on, then, and finish him off; I want my turn." Then there was a burst of eager incitements, and, unable to defer the attack any longer, seeing, too, that Mercer did not mean to begin, Dicksee gave a final dance, which included a dodge to right and left, and then he rushed in at Mercer, who seemed just to shoot his left shoulder forward with his arm extended, when there was a dull sound, and Dicksee seated himself very suddenly on the floor.

"Hallo! slip?" cried Burr, helping him up,—rather a heavy job,—while a look of perfect astonishment was in the fat face.

"Yes—boards—awkward," he babbled. "Ca–ca–can't we go on the grass?"

"No, no. Go in again."

"Eh?" said Dicksee, with his hand to his face.

"Well done, Tom!" I whispered; "that's it."

"It was right, wasn't it?" he said.

There was no time for more. Incited, almost driven by his second, Dicksee came on again, aimed a blow or two wildly, and was sent down again by Mercer almost without an effort.

And now the wind of favour began to change, so that in the next round boys shouted encouragement to Mercer.

"Hold that row!" cried Burr savagely; "do you want the Doctor to hear? Now, Dicksee, give it him this time."

I must do the fat fellow the credit of saying that he now came on fiercely, swinging his arms wildly, and striking out with all his might, but not one blow took effect, and I had the satisfaction of seeing the triumph of Lomax's instructions, gaining confidence all the while, as Tom delivered a blow here and a blow there, and then one which sent his antagonist down to bump his head upon the boards.

There was quite a little burst of cheers now.

"Will you stop that row!" cried Burr fiercely. "Silence! You, Dicksee," he whispered, as he helped his principal up, "if you don't go in and lick him, I'll lick you."

"Tom," I was whispering, "you're sure to win."

"Am I?" he said stolidly; "but I don't like knocking him about—he can't fight at all."

"Serve him right; he'll remember it in future. Now then. Ready!"

The pair were facing each other again, and the encounter which followed was a little longer, but it ended in Mercer giving his adversary a sharp blow on the cheek, and directly after another on the nose, and Dicksee again seemed to sit down suddenly as if to wipe it, a duty which had certainly become necessary.

"Silence!" cried Burr major, as a burst of cheers followed this last round, for it was seen that the fat lad did not intend to get up again. "Dicksee isn't well to-day; I believe old Jollop has given him something." Then in a whisper, as he half-dragged his principal back, "You beggar!" he said; "I'll serve you out for this."

"Hooray!" cried a small boy at the window; "old Senna has licked —"

"Will you mind and watch that window," cried Burr. "It's all right, boys; I shall have to dress Jollop down as soon as I've done the groom. Here, Hodson, you must second me."

"Oh, Tom," I whispered, with my heart beating, "I wish I could fight like you!"

"So you can," he replied; "better. Look out, he's ready. Take it coolly; never mind his show. I wish I was going at him instead of you. I'm nice and warm now."

"I wish you were," I said.

"No, you don't."

The next minute I was facing my tall adversary, who looked down at me contemptuously, after a smiling glance round at the boys, which seemed to say, — "Now you shall see."

There was a faint cheer at this, followed by a smothered howl, which drew attention to Dicksee, who was now rocking himself to and fro as if in pain.

Then there was what seemed to me a peculiarly ominous kind of silence, and I felt shocked and frightened, not so much of my adversary as at myself. The feeling was mingled with shame, for I began to think that I must be a terrible coward, and I found myself wondering what my uncle would say if he knew how unfit I was to be trained to become a soldier.

These thoughts were momentary, long as they take to describe, and I began to wonder whether it would be best to apologise to Burr major, and ask him to let me off, but as I thought that, I felt that I could not, and that I would sooner he half killed me. This brought up thoughts of my mother's sweet, gentle face, and how she would suffer if she knew what was going on.

Lastly, I began to think I must fight, and that I had better prepare to take care of myself, for Burr major deliberately threw himself into a graceful attitude and addressed me.

"Now, you young sniveller," he said haughtily, "you have brought this on yourself. I am going to give you a lesson that will teach you to behave yourself in future, and you too, Senna Tea. You're fond of physic; you shall have such a dose. Mind, you boys, that old Jollop doesn't sneak off."

"All right!" rose in chorus; "he shan't go."

"Mind he don't lick you, Eely," cried one of the boys at the window.

"Mind Tommy Wilson don't sneak off either," said Burr major. "All right, Tommy, I can't fight you, but I can stretch those ugly great ears for you."

"Ow how! ow how!" cried the little fellow, sparring a peculiar yelling noise, but indulging in a broad grin to his nearest companion. "Oh, my poor ears! I say, Burr junior, you lick him, and then you can take care of me."

I did not speak, for my antagonist had begun sparring at me, making feints and trying to throw me off my guard, but, as if by instinct now, I dropped into the positions and practice Mercer and I had been learning so long, and, as I thought, without avail; but I did begin to find out that it had been good advice to stand on my guard and to let my adversary show-off and tire himself.

I felt very cool, and not so much alarmed now, when the first blow came, intended for my lips, but which I easily stopped, and so I did another and another, the round ending by Burr major making a fierce dash at me, over-reaching himself, and going down without my having delivered one blow.

"How slippery these boards are!" said Burr, jumping up.

"That's right!" whispered Mercer; "keep on as quiet as that, and wait your time."

Then we began again, and I felt very much disinclined to hit out hard, as I felt that I could have done, for fear of hurting my antagonist—for the feeling of animosity and the memory of the insults, blows, and annoyance from which I had suffered had faded away. But all at once, as we stood eyeing each other, Burr's fist came sharply in contact with my lips, there was a dull pain, a sensation of a tooth being loosened, a nasty faint salt taste in my mouth, followed by a short struggle, and I was thrown heavily.

Burr major walked back and sat down on his second's knee, smiling round at the cheering boys, who began to crowd round him, while, as I rose, feeling painful throbbings in one elbow and arm, I was drawn down on Mercer's knee, and he whispered,—

"Never mind. Don't get excited over it. Be quite cool. Now then, he's ready again."

So was I, for there was a buzzing in my temples and a hot feeling in my throat as I once more stood up before my adversary, who was still smiling contemptuously as he began sparring and then dashed forward, but stopped suddenly, and stood back, shaking his head, while I tightened my hand and saw the blood start from one of my knuckles.

"Go on, Burr. Give it him. He's nearly done. Go on, go on!" was chorused on all sides; and, looking very vicious now, Burr came at me with his fists wide apart, and then he rushed at me as if he meant mischief, but to his great surprise as much as to mine, he seemed to run his nose right on to my left fist, and dropped down on the floor.

He was up again, though, directly, amid a buzz of excitement, and I felt that now he was going to avenge himself thoroughly, but, as I struck out with my left exactly as Lomax had instructed me, somehow Burr major went down again.

It almost puzzled me. I could hardly believe it, but it was forced upon me, and the blows which I seemed to deliver at the right time in the most effortless of ways, had a terrible effect, my antagonist going down three times to my once.

And now some of the tide began to set in my direction — the tide of popularity. First of all, little Wilson took heart and gave me a cheer, then he began to grow excited, and to cry in an eager whisper, —

"Well done, Burr junior! Hooray! That's it. Give it him. Hooray! down again."

Burr major got up, looking fierce as well as confused, and sat panting on his second's knee; and as I sat on mine, Tom Mercer gave me a hug.

"Splendid!" he whispered. "Hooray for old Lom! You'll beat him if you keep quiet. You boys, hold that row."

There was a hush directly, and we two faced each other once more.

The confident contempt for me had gone now, and there was no laughing looking round at the boys for their approval, but, pale, excited, and with marks beginning to show in an ugly way, Burr major seemed to be prepared to do his best to crush me by a fierce attack.

For my part, I had been so much hurt that it was as if the shrinking was all knocked out of me, and I was no less eager to begin than he. But we stood facing each other now, with the hum of excitement that greeted our coming forward hushed once more to silence.

I could feel that I might now commence the attack, but my master's lessons all came clear and vivid before me, and knowing that, as the weaker, it was my duty to act on the defensive, I waited, while we watched each other cautiously, my adversary evidently expecting that I should begin.

But, as I did not, he attacked again, and, though I managed to give him several telling blows, he closed with me before I could avoid him, and in the tussle which followed I went down heavily, my head coming in violent contact with the floor.

Everything passed away then for a few moments except sparks dancing before my eyes, but I was conscious directly of Mercer's voice, as he whispered to me excitedly, —

"Oh, don't let him lick you, Frank! — don't let him lick you, pray!"

"No," I panted, with my breath coming rather short, "he isn't going to, but I'm so giddy."

"Had enough of it?" cried Burr major, and the giddiness passed away directly as I rose and faced him.

Satisfied by the result of his last manoeuvre, he tried it again, but this time I was prepared, and, stepping on one side, I gave him, or rather my fist of itself seemed to give him, a stinging blow on the ear, which had so staggering an effect that, as he swung round and came on again, I was able to follow up my blow with three or four more, and the poor fellow went down crash.

It was his turn to look dazed and heavy now, and quite half the boys crowded round, giving me advice, bidding me "go it," and working themselves up to a tremendous pitch of excitement.

Then we were facing each other again, with all pity and compunction gone, and, after receiving one or two blows, I forgot everything but the fact that there was something before me that I must hit, and hit it I did, my deliveries, as it happened, being quite in accordance with Lomax's teaching, which somehow came natural to me; and then I found myself standing over Burr major who was seated on the floor, and with half a dozen boys all wanting to shake hands with me at once.

"Here, I say, Burr major," cried one of his chief parasites, "ain't you going to lick old Senna now?"

I felt sorry for him, for he looked around dazed and despairing, but my blood was up again directly, as I saw the miserable cur of a fellow who had spoken go closer, double his fist, and shake it so close to Burr major's face that he tapped his nose.

"Serve you right!" he cried. "Always knocking other people about. How do you like it now?"

"You let him alone," I cried hotly.

"I shan't. Mind your own—"

"Business," I suppose he meant to say, but my fists had grown so excited by the fight that one of them flew out, and sent the miserable cur staggering against Mercer's chest.

Then I stood upon my guard, but the boy only held his hand to his face, while the others set up a cheer, and I turned to Burr major, who was still seated on the floor.

"I'm very sorry, Burr," I said apologetically. "I didn't want to knock you about so much. You'll shake hands, won't you?"

He looked up at me with rather an ugly expression upon his face, but he made no movement to take my hand, only turned away.

"Help me up, Stewart," he said huskily. "I want to go to my room and wash, and —"

"What is the meaning of all this, pray?" said a cold, harsh voice, and we all looked round to see Mr Rebble's white face just above the trap-door.

"Burr Major and Burr Junior been having it out, sir," cried half a dozen voices at once, and the colour began to burn in my cheeks as I met the usher's eye.

Chapter Nineteen.

Mr Rebble stepped up into the loft, closely followed by Mr Hasnip, who stared from one to the other with a peculiar smile upon his lip.

"Fighting, eh?" said Mr Rebble. "Disgraceful! Why, Dicksee and Dean have been fighting too, and—yes—Mercer."

"Yes, sir," cried little Wilson. "Mercer and Dicksee had theirs first, then Burr major and Burr junior. Bill Dean hasn't been fighting. It was only that Burr junior gave him a wipe."

I felt as if I were the chief offender, and as I heard these words, I longed not to deliver wipes, but to have a good wash.

"Disgraceful!" exclaimed Mr Rebble. "Who began it? You, I suppose, Burr."

My first instinct was to disclaim this excitedly, but I thought it would be cowardly, so I held my tongue, leaving it to Burr major to answer.

To my surprise, though, he remained silent, and little Wilson squeaked out,—

"No, sir, please, sir, it wasn't Burr junior, sir. Eely Burr sent for Burr and Mercer to come and be licked; but," added the boy, with a malicious grin, "he hasn't licked them yet."

"Disgraceful! disgraceful!" cried Mr Rebble. "Well, the Doctor will decide what is to be done. Quick, boys, the dinner bell will.—Ah, there it goes!"

There was a hurried rush off at this, the boys being only too glad to get beyond hearing of the usher's scolding, and we who were left hurriedly scrambled on our jackets in a shamefaced way.

"This matter will have to be thoroughly investigated," said Mr Rebble; "but be quick now and make yourselves presentable. I shudder at what the Doctor would say if he saw you all in this condition. Come, Hasnip."

They both descended like pantomime demons through the trap, and we followed, Burr major going first, with his brow knit and his bruised face looking sulky and sour, while Dicksee turned to give Tom Mercer a savagely vindictive look which was not pleasant to see.

"Won't you shake hands?" I said, as my adversary was about to descend.

He gave me a quick look, but made no answer. Hodson however, spoke as we reached the stable.

"Why, Burr," he said, "I didn't know that you could fight like that."

"No," I said, "and I did not know either."

Then we hurried in and ran up to our room, where I was glad to get soap and towel to my bruised face.

"Oh, you are lucky, Tom!" I panted, as I hurriedly bent over the basin, fully expecting to be reported for coming up to the dormitory out of hours. "Why, you don't show a bit."

"Nor you neither," he replied.

"Oh!" I gasped, as I looked in the glass.

"Well, not so very much," he said.

"But—but I don't hardly know myself," I said despondently. "What a face!"

"Well, it does look rather like a muffin," he cried.

"Ah, you may laugh," I said. "My eyes are just like they were when I was stung by a bee, and my lip's cut inside, and this tooth is loose, and—Oh dear, it's all growing worse!"

"Yes, it's sure to go on getting worse for a day or two, and then it will begin to get better. Ready?"

"Ready! No," I cried, as I listened to his poor consolation. "I'm getting horrid. I daren't go down."

"You must—you must. Come and face it out before you get worse."

"But I don't seem to have got a face," I cried, glaring out of two slits at my reflection in the glass. "It's just as if some one had been sitting on it for a week. Oh, you ugly brute!"

"So are you."

"I meant myself, of course, Tom."

"Never mind, never mind. Hooray! hooray!" he cried, dancing round the room and snapping his fingers; "we've licked 'em—we've licked 'em! and you're cock of the school. Hooray! hooray!"

"But I half wish I hadn't won now," I said.

"You will not to-morrow. Oh dear! poor old Eely! didn't he squirm! Oh, I say! I wish I had given it to old Dicksee ten times as much."

I couldn't help laughing, but it hurt horribly, and I was serious again directly.

"I say," I said painfully, "old Lom did teach us well!"

"Teach us! It was splendid. I feel as if I could go down and fight the Doctor."

"Do you?" I said dolefully. "I feel as if he is going to fight us."

"Not he; come on. You can't afford to be afraid of anything now."

"Hadn't I better stop?" I suggested, with another look in the glass.

"No; you must come. If you don't, the Doctor is sure to send for you, and that will make it worse. I say!"

"Well?"

"People who fight used to take the spoils of the vanquished. I wish I could have taken old Dicksee's four-bladed knife, with the lancet and corkscrew to it, and you could have taken old Eely's watch."

"I don't want his watch," I said snappishly.

"I do, and I'd have changed with you. Come on."

We ran down-stairs, and, feeling very nervous, hurried to the schoolroom, from whose open windows came the clatter of knives and forks.

Fortunately for us, we had to enter at the opposite end to where the Doctor would be seated, nominally taking his meal with us, and of course the ushers knew that we must be late, so with heads bent down we hurried in, conscious that every eye was upon us, and that the temporary cessation of the rattle on the plates was due to the boys leaving off eating to stare at our injuries.

I saw both Mr Rebble and Mr Hasnip look up and frown as they caught sight of my damaged face, and I was congratulating myself on escaping the Doctor's eye, when he looked up, frowned, and went on with his lunch.

"It's all right," whispered Mercer, scuffling into his place beside me, the boys around, to my great surprise, seeming to look at my marks with quite respectful eyes, and evidently as a conqueror's honours or laurels, when there was a sharp tapping on the table from the Doctor's knife-handle.

Profound silence ensued, Mercer just gripping my knee and whispering, —

"Oh, crikey!"

"Mr Rebble," said the doctor in deep tones.

"Sir?"

"To the commercial man punctuality is the soul of business; to the gentleman it is the soul of honour; and to the scholastic pupil it is the soul of er—er—the soul of er—er—er—duty. Be good enough to see that Mercer and Burr junior have impositions. Er—rum! Er—rum!" The Doctor finished by coughing in a peculiar way, and the clatter of knives and forks began again.

"He don't know yet about the fights," I whispered; "and, I say, look!"

"What's the matter?"

"Eely hasn't come down yet."

"Fatty has. I say, just look at his eyes."

"Horrid!" I whispered. "He looks fatter than ever. But Eely—oh, I hope he isn't very bad!"

"I hope he is," said Mercer maliciously. "He's been fagging me these three years. I know he's twice as bad as you, and serve him right."

We began our dinners, but Mercer's appetite was as bad as mine. The salt made my mouth smart, and every bite hurt my loose tooth. But there were congratulatory smiles from all round whenever I looked up, and every boy who could reach me with his foot gave me a friendly kick under the table, Mercer coming in for his share. In fact, I found that I had suddenly become the most popular boy in the school, though I did not at all appreciate the honour then.

"Look: there's Eely," whispered Mercer, as a tall thin figure now appeared at the door, then suddenly grew shorter by the lad bending down as low as possible, and creeping toward his place by Stewart and Dicksee.

But it was all in vain, the clatter of the knives and forks ceased, and the boys watched him, and whispered, drawing the Doctor's attention to the bent figure; and once more, after fixing his gold eyeglasses on the bridge of his nose by the hinge, and watching till my late adversary had crept into his place, he tapped the table with his knife-handle loudly.

"Young gentlemen," he rolled out in sonorous tones, "have the goodness to button up your pockets, and to be on the *qui vive*. I just saw the door darkened by a sinister-looking figure, which crept in as if to commit a burglary, a petty larceny, a scholastic form of shop-lifting, or some crime of that kind, so be upon your guard. Did any one else see the figure?"

There was a pause, then Dicksee spoke with a malicious grin upon his fat face.

"Please, sir, I did. It was Burr major."

"Dear me! Indeed? Mr Burr, have the goodness to stand up and explain this extraordinary conduct."

Oh, poor old Eely! I thought sympathetically, as poor Burr major stood up, hanging his head, and looking much shorter than usual, and I heartily wished that Mercer had punished Dicksee more.

"Dear me! Burr major, what is the er—er—eh? I beg your pardon, Mr Rebble."

The Doctor bent toward his first lieutenant with great dignity, and the latter said a few words in a low tone.

"Dear me! Indeed? Oh, I see!" said the Doctor. "Burr major, you can sit down. You will come to my room directly after dinner, and —er— er—what names did you say Mr Rebble?"

"Oh dear! It's coming, Frank," whispered Mercer.

"Exactly!" said the Doctor, after a conference in a low tone with Mr Rebble. "I see. Er—rum! Dicksee, Hodson."

"Please, sir, I wasn't fighting," cried Hodson excitedly.

Mr Rebble whispered to the Doctor.

"An accessory, it seems, Hodson," said the Doctor. "You will come to my room directly after dinner, with Mercer and Burr junior. I have not heard the names of the other boys who were present," continued the Doctor.

"Please, sir, Wilson was one," cried Dicksee.

"Thank you, Dicksee," said the Doctor drily, as he fixed him with his glittering glasses; "I am obliged to you. History repeats itself. There has always been one in every confederation ready to betray his fellows to save his own skin. I am afraid, Dicksee, that your skin will not be safe. Were you present, Wilson?"

"Yes, sir," said the little fellow.

"Fighting?"

"No, sir, I wasn't fighting; but—"

"But?" said the Doctor; "well, what?"

"Please, sir, I couldn't help liking it."

"Humph!" ejaculated the Doctor. "Well, you need not come this time. To resume, I do not know the names of the boys who were present, and I do not want to know. Dicksee was in too great a hurry. Now proceed with your dinner."

The meal went on, but my face felt more stiff, and my appetite was decidedly worse.

I was longing to go and do as a dog would under the circumstances,—go and curl up somewhere out of sight till I got better, for my head ached, so did my heart; my face throbbed and felt stiff; and altogether I was, like Mercer, as "miserable as mizzer,"—so he put it,—when the Doctor tapped the table again, we all rose, grace was said, and the words of doom came rolling through the place:

"In a quarter of an hour's time, young gentlemen."

Then the Doctor marched sedately out of the room, the masters followed, and the boys trooped into the ground, and we had to go too, feeling doleful in the extreme, but that did give way to a sense of pride, for there was a rush made for us directly; and as I was surrounded by a crowd, all eagerly congratulating me on my conquest, there was poor Burr major almost alone on the other side of the ground, dejected, deposed. Not quite alone, for Hodson and Wilson both went and stood by his side.

It may appear strange, but, of course excepting Mercer, I felt as if I liked those two boys at that moment better than any one in the school, for, young as I was, I could not help thinking that if ever Burr major and I had another encounter, and I were to be beaten, they would all turn from me as quickly as they came over to my side.

I was soon tired of hearing the same praise over and over again, and being asked to show this one and that one how I managed to hit out so well. But Mercer and I had a quiet understanding that we would keep our own counsel about the matter, and let any one who wanted to learn how to box think it out for himself.

I was not kept waiting long to muse over my position, and be stared at by all the boys, who took the greatest interest in my swellings, cuts, and marks, for Mr Rebble came to the door, and shouted, —

"Now, young gentlemen, the Doctor is waiting." I felt a curious shiver run through me, as I glanced round for Tom Mercer.

He was close at hand, ready to whisper, —

"It don't matter what he says, Frank; he can't undo what we have done, and old Eely will never dare to tackle you again."

"Or you."

"Oh, I didn't say that. Come on."

We went up to where Mr Rebble was standing, and found that Mr Hasnip was there too.

As we went in, Mr Hasnip came close to my side. "Nice object you look for a gentleman's son, sir! Going to be a soldier, eh?"

"Yes, sir!"

"Then keep your fighting for the enemy, not for your schoolfellows." Then in a lower voice—"Gave him a thorough good thrashing, didn't you?" he said.

"Yes, sir: I suppose so."

"Humph! serve him right. He wanted his comb cut. Getting insufferable with his conceit!—By the way, you needn't tell any of your schoolfellows I said that, for, of course, you had no business to fight."

"I didn't want to, sir, but Burr major made us fight. He sent a lot of the boys to bring us into the loft, 'to take the conceit out of us,' he said."

"And you took the conceit out of him instead, eh? Well, I daresay he wishes he had not sent for you now."

"I'm afraid he does."

"Yes. Well, here we are. I'm a terrible tartar to you over your lessons, but I'm not angry with you. Had some fights too, when I was your age. Now then, speak up like a man."

The door was thrown open, and we had to walk in, the two ushers standing on either side of the door, like policemen dealing with culprits, and then ranging us before the Doctor's table, behind which he sat, leaning back in his great leather-covered chair.

"Er—rum!" he coughed. "Sit down, Mr Rebble—take a chair, Mr Hasnip. Let me see," he continued, adjusting his gold-rimmed eyeglasses. "Burr major, Burr junior,—humph! ought to be Burr minor,—Natural History Mercer who loves poaching the General's rabbits, Dicksee, and Hodson."

The Doctor looked severe, but not very, as he inspected us all.

"Hah!" he ejaculated at last; "four as disreputable-looking fellows as it would be possible to find in the lowest town in Sussex. Aren't you ashamed of yourselves?"

"No answer, eh?" said the Doctor, after a pause. "Well, Hodson, you are not like these four. You did not fight, I suppose."

"No, sir. I was Burr major's second."

"That's almost as bad as the fighting. Come, you shall speak out. Who was in the wrong?"

"Please, sir, I'd rather not give an opinion."

"Please, sir, I know!" cried Dicksee.

"Thank you. I would rather take some other boy's opinion," cried the Doctor sarcastically. "Your eyes don't look as if you can see clearly. There, it is plain enough to me that you were all in the wrong, and I feel greatly annoyed to find my young gentlemen conducting themselves like the disreputable low boys who frequent the fairs and racecourses of the county. Look at yourselves. Did you ever see such a ghastly sight? Burr major, your face is horrible. As for you, Dicksee, I am ashamed of you. Suppose any of your relatives presented themselves at this moment, and wanted to see you. What could I say? There, actually, as I speak, I can hear wheels coming up the road, and, as they are light wheels, they must either be those of visitors, or of the butcher's cart—I—er—mean some trade-person's cart, which is not likely at this time of day. Fighting, young gentlemen, is a brutal practice, dating back to the very earliest ages of mankind, and no doubt imitated from the wild beasts whom they saw around them. Whereas you live in these later days, in the midst of civilisation in its highest, most cultivated forms, so that there is no excuse whatever for your acts."

The Doctor coughed, and the two ushers looked at each other and nodded their approval.

"Look at yourselves," continued the Doctor; and we all turned sharply to gaze in a small circular mirror at the end of the library.

"No, no," said the Doctor blandly, "I did not mean at your bodily disfigurations in the glass, but at the mental blurs in your natures. I— There, boys!" he cried suddenly; "I am not in the vein to moralise in this way, so I must speak plainly. I am ashamed of you, and, occupying as I do toward you the temporary position of parent, I honestly declare that if I did my duty by you, I should get a cane or a rod, and flog you all severely, but—"

"May I come in?" said a pleasant voice, and the door was slightly opened.

"Yes, my dear. No! engaged. What is it?"

"That lady and gentleman have driven over from Rye about their sons," said Mrs Doctor, coming right in; "and — Oh, my dears! what have you been doing?"

"There, there, Matilda!" cried the Doctor hastily. "Go back! I'll come in a few minutes;" and he hurried the pleasant old lady out of the room, before turning to us.

"There! you see," he cried, — "you see the effect your appearance has upon one who always takes the greatest of interest in you, and, er — Mr Rebble, I feel disposed to be lenient this time, as the boys have pretty well punished themselves. I leave it to you. Moderate impositions. There, go at once and shut yourselves up in your dormitories. No, more fighting, mind, or I shall be as severe as the sternest tyrant you read of in your classic studies."

He hurried out of the library, and the ushers took us all into custody again, and led us out into the playground.

"There!" said Mr Rebble; "you heard the Doctor's orders. Go to your rooms. Not you, Hodson. Come to my desk, and I'll set your imposition at once. Nice and easily you have got off. You can come down to-morrow morning, I suppose."

The two masters went off with Hodson, and we four made our way to the back staircase so hurriedly, that we nearly wedged ourselves at the foot, with the result that we were once more face to face, Mercer and I against Burr major and Dicksee, as in the fight.

I felt shocked now and more sorry than ever for Burr major, as I fully realised how terribly I had knocked him about. My hand twitched, and I was about to raise it, and offer to shake hands, or say something about being sorry; but he checked it at once by giving me a virulent look, and saying, —

"Wait a bit; I'll pay you out for all this," and, thrusting me aside, he sent me staggering against the wall, and rushed up-stairs, but only to trip and fall sprawling.

"Serve you right," cried Dicksee. "Yah!" Then, turning to us, he held out his hand. "Here, I'll be friends with you both."

TURNING TO US, HE HELD OUT HIS HAND

Chapter Twenty.

Nearly a week had gone by before I saw Lomax, and of course there had been no more riding lessons. Mr Rebble had given us our impositions, and we had taken our punishment patiently enough, for, as the smarting and pain went off, we could not help feeling proud and satisfied. The boys had all turned wonderfully friendly, and I was evidently a great authority. In fact, I had completely succeeded to Burr major's throne in the boys' estimation, while he went about the place almost alone, Hodson being the only fellow who tried to associate with him.

As for the Doctor, he never alluded to the encounter again.

The week, then, had passed, and Mercer and I had nearly grown respectable again, when one night, as we were going to bed, my companion turned to me.

"I say," he whispered, "let's get up early to-morrow morning, and go and see old Lom."

I shook my head.

"I've had lessons enough in boxing," I said; "I don't want to fight any more."

"I didn't mean a lesson," said Mercer. "I want to go and tell him all about how we got on."

I agreed that I should like to do that; and I awoke at sunrise, roused Mercer, and, leaving the other boys sleeping, we started for the lodge.

"Oh, I say, what a lovely morning!" cried Mercer. "Look at the dew on the leaves; it's all colours like a rainbow. When are we going fishing again? and I want some birds to stuff; and to go rabbiting, and collecting, and all sorts, and we seem to have done nothing lately."

"Hallo, Magglin!" I cried, as we turned a corner, and came suddenly upon that individual, looking as if he had just come from the big yard.

"Why, what are you doing here?" said Mercer.

"No sir; on'y wish I was. Just came up to see if the gardener's about, and he'd give me a job."

"You know he wouldn't," I said. "The Doctor will not have you about the place again."

"And it's very hard," he whined. "Everybody's agen me, and takes 'vantage of me, even young gents as owes me money and won't pay."

"Why, who owes you money, Magg?"

"You do, sir; four shillin', which I wouldn't ask you for, but—"

"I don't, Magg; I paid you everything I owed you," cried Mercer.

"Oh no, sir; don't you go for to say that which you know aren't true. It's four shillin', and I wouldn't have asked you, only I'm that hungry as never was."

"But I don't owe you anything; do I, Frank?"

"No; he paid you," I said.

"Oh, sir! Master Burr junior knows as it's wicked to tell a lie. I likes mates to stick up for one another, but it ain't right to get a trampling down of the pore. Do pay me, Master Tom Mercer. It's four shillin'."

"I don't owe you a penny, Magg; and you're a cheat."

"Nay, sir, that I aren't. Well, pay me two on it, and I'll go on trusting you the rest."

"But I'm sure I paid you everything I owed you, Magg."

"Oh no, sir. That's the way with you young gents. You forgets, that's what you does. I've lost lots o' money through the Doctor's boys; and it's very hard on a pore fellow who's trying his best to get a honest living, but as every one's agen."

"Ah, that's all gammon, Magg!" cried Mercer. "See how you left us in the lurch over our ferreting."

"I was obliged to, sir; every one's agen me so. Nobody believes in me. Do pay me the two shillin', sir."

"I won't. It's all humbug, and you don't deserve it," cried Mercer.

"There, hark at him, Master Burr junior! Aren't he hard on a pore fellow, who was always doing him kindnesses? Look at the times I've sat up o' nights to ketch him rats and mice or mouldy-warps. Didn't I climb and get you two squirls, and dig out the snake from the big bank for you?"

"Yes; and cut his tail off with the spade," cried Mercer. "You spoiled him."

"Well, I couldn't help that, sir; and I must go now, 'fore the gardener comes along."

"Why, you said you wanted to see him."

"So I did, sir; but I don't think I will. Everybody's so agen me now. Pay me the two shillin' you owe me."

"I won't. I don't owe you a penny."

"Then pay a shilling of it now, sir. I wouldn't ask you, sir, but I am so hungry, sir."

"Let's give him a shilling, Tom," I said; "I'll be half."

"Oh, very well," cried Mercer; and as I was banker that time, I placed a shilling in the man's very dirty hand.

"Thank-ye, sir," he said. "Then that makes three left, but I won't ask you for them to-day."

"That's the worst of getting in debt," said Mercer, "and not keeping account of it. I know I've bought things of him, and he has made me pay for 'em over and over again. I wonder what he was doing about here so soon."

We watched Magglin go off in a furtive way, with his head down and his back bent, so that people should not see him above the hedge, and then turned along down the path, with the gilt hands and figures of the clock looking quite orange in the morning sun. In a few minutes after, we could smell tobacco smoke, and found Lomax bending his stiff back over one of the beds in his garden, which he was busily digging.

"Ah! Mornin', young gentlemen," he shouted. "Come for a quiet lesson?"

"Not this morning, Lomax," cried Mercer.

"Going for a walk, then?"

"Only as far as here," I replied, looking at him merrily.

"Eh? What? Why, hallo!" he cried. "I didn't know. They said you were under punishment for something, but I didn't know what. Why, yes: both of you. Look at your eyes. You've been fighting!"

I nodded, and Mercer laughed.

"We've come to tell you all about it."

Lomax drove his spade down into the ground and left it standing in the bed.

"Here, come along," he cried excitedly, and he led the way into the lodge, placed chairs for us, and re-lit his pipe, before standing smoking with his back to the fire. "Now then," he cried, "let's have it."

We described our encounter, and the old soldier laughed and chuckled with satisfaction.

"Yes, that's it," he cried, as we came to an end, first one and then the other carrying on the thread of the narration to the conclusion. "That's science; that is just the same as with a well-drilled regiment, which can beat a mob of fifty times its size. Well, I'm glad you won, and were such good pupils. Shows you remembered all I taught you. Now take my advice, both of you. Don't you fight again till you are regularly obliged."

"Not going to," I said.

"That's right, boy. You'll be like a man now who has got a blunderbuss in his house. Thieves all about know that he has got one, and so they leave him alone. Well when are you going to have another riding lesson?"

"Let's begin again at once," I said; and he promised to send or go down to the General's, to ask the groom to bring up the horse in the morning.

"I'll go myself if I can," said Lomax, "and ride him up pretty quickly. He'll have had such a rest that he'll be quite skittish."

All this being settled, and it being yet early, we had time for a walk, and the discovery of sundry objects, which Mercer looked upon as treasures, and carefully placed in boxes and pieces of paper.

The first was an unhappy-looking stag beetle which seemed to have been in the wars, for one of its horns was gone, while not a dozen yards farther on we came upon a dissipated cockchafer, with a dent in his horny case, and upon both of these Mercer pounced with delight, transferring them to a flat tin paste-blacking box, inside which we could hear them scratching to get out.

The next thing to attract his attention was a fat worm, which, after a crawl in the cool, dewy night, had lost his way back to his hole, and was now crawling slowly by the roadside, with more sand sticking to him than could have been comfortable.

"Oh, what a big one!" cried Mercer. "I say, I must have him."

"For a bait for an eel or carp?" I said.

"No. To preserve."

"Let the poor thing be," I cried, and, thrusting a piece of stick under the worm, I sent it flying amongst the wet grass.

"Ugh! you cruel wretch!" cried Mercer.

"Come, that's nice," I said. "Better than letting you put it in a box, and carrying it in your hot pocket to kill."

"I shouldn't kill it, I should keep it in a pot of earth."

"Which would dry up, and the poor thing would crawl out and be trodden upon. Come along."

But he would not come along, for Tom Mercer was a true naturalist at heart, and found interest in hundreds of things I should have passed over. For instance, that morning, as we strolled a little way along the lane, we stopped to peer over the gate into a newly ploughed field at some round-looking birds which rose directly with a loud whirr, and then went skimming along, to glide over the hedge at the bottom and disappear.

"Partridges," cried Mercer. "Daresay they've got a nest somewhere not far from here. Oh, I do wish we had bought Magglin's gun. It is such a handy one. You see we could keep it up in the loft, and take it to pieces and bring it out without any one knowing, and shoot our own birds to stuff."

"Mustn't shoot partridges. They're game," I said.

"Oh, I don't know," he replied. "We shouldn't want them to eat, only to stuff, and— Hallo, look there! I haven't found one of those for ever so long."

He climbed over the gate, and picked up something cream-coloured from the hollow between two furrows.

"What is it?" I said, as he came back.

"Worm-eater," and he opened his hand.

"Why, it's a slug," I said. "Throw the nasty slimy thing away."

"'Tisn't slimy," he said, as I looked on with disgust at him poking the long-shaped creamy creature with one finger, as it lay in the palm of his left hand. "You feel it. Quite cool and dry."

"I'm not going to touch the nasty thing," I cried. "And what do you mean by a worm-eater?"

"Mean he's one. See how long and thin he is. That's so that he can creep down the worm-holes and catch the worms and eat 'em."

"Nonsense! Slugs live on lettuces and cabbages, and other green things."

"These don't," said Mercer quietly; "they live on worms."

"How do you know?"

"Because my father told me, and I've kept 'em in boxes and fed 'em with worms."

"Well, throw it away, and come along; we ought to be getting back now."

"Yes, so as to have time to go up to the museum first," he replied, but he did not throw away his last find. That was tucked into a pill-box, with the promise that I should see it eat a live worm that night.

We turned back and took the side lane which would lead us round by the keeper's cottage.

"Let's see what Bob has got stuck up on the barn side," said Mercer. "I daresay there'll be something fresh. He always says he'll save me all the good things he shoots, but he forgets and nails them on. Come on through the wood."

"But we shall get our feet so wet," I said, as Mercer jumped the ditch.

"That we won't. It will be drier here."

I followed him, and, knowing his way well, Mercer took me by a short cut among the trees, which brought us just to the back of the keeper's cottage, where dozens of the supposed enemies of the game were gibbeted. Jays, hawks, owls, little falcons, shrikes, weasels, stoats, and polecats.

"There," said Mercer, pointing, "look at that beautiful fresh jay. He might have let me—"

Mercer stopped short, for we heard Polly Hopley's voice speaking loudly, evidently at the front of the cottage.

"I don't want it, and I won't have it. Give it to some one else."

"No, I shan't," said a harsh voice, which we knew at once as Magglin's. "I bought it o' porpos for you, and you've got to wear it."

"Then I shan't, and if you come talking to me again like that, I shall tell father."

"No, you won't."

"Indeed and I shall, and the sooner you go the better. He isn't far off."

"Yes, he is," said Magglin, "and won't be back for hours."

"How do you know?"

"Because I watched him."

"Yes, that's what you poaching chaps always do, watch the keeper till he's out of the way," said Polly sharply.

"Don't call me a poacher, Polly."

"Yes, I shall; and that's what you are."

"Come away," I whispered; "don't let's stop listening."

"We can't help it, without going all the way back."

"Poachers always make the best keepers, Polly, and I'm going to be a keeper now, and marry you."

"Are you, indeed?" said the girl indignantly. "That you just aren't, and if you ever dare to call me Polly again, I'll throw a bucket o' water over you."

"Not you," said Magglin. "I say, do have it. It's real gold."

"I don't care if it's real silver!" cried Polly. "I've got brooches of my own, thank you, and I'll trouble you to go."

'DON'T CALL ME A POACHER, POLLY'

"'Tarn't good enough for you, I suppose. Well, I'll bring you something better."

Bang.

The cottage door was closed violently. Then we heard footsteps, which ceased after a minute, and we went on out toward the lane.

"Make haste!" I said; "it must be getting late."

"Ah," said Mercer, "if I'd got a watch like old Eely's, we could tell the time."

"And as you haven't, we must guess it," I said. "Look!"

Mercer turned at my words, for he was looking back to see if Polly Hopley was visible at the cottage door, the news we had heard of her father being away robbing us of any desire to call.

There, about fifty yards away, with his back to us, was Magglin, rubbing something on his sleeve. Then he breathed upon it, and gave it another rub, before holding it up in the sunshine, and we could see that it was bright and yellow, possibly a brooch.

The next minute the poacher had leaped into the wood and passed among the trees.

"Oh, what a game!" said Mercer, as we walked away. "If Bob Hopley knows, he'll lick old Magglin with a ramrod. There, come on."

We reached the school in good time, only two or three of the boys being about, and spent the next half-hour turning over Mercer's melancholy-looking specimens of the taxidermist's art, one of the most wretched being a half finished rabbit, all skin and tow.

"Well, I would burn that," I said. "It does look a brute."

"Burn it? I should think not," he cried indignantly. "It looks queer, because it isn't finished. I'm going to make a natural history scene of that in a glass case. That's to be a rabbit just caught by a weasel, and I shall have the weasel holding on by the back of its neck, and the rabbit squealing."

"Where's your weasel?"

"Oh, I shall get Magglin or Bob Hopley to shoot me one some day. Wish I'd got a gun of my own!"

"You're always wishing for guns and watches, or something else you haven't got," I said, laughing.

"Well, that's quite natural, isn't it?" cried Mercer good-humouredly. "I always feel like that, and it does seem a shame that old Eely should have tail coats and white waistcoats and watches, and I shouldn't. But, I say, Frank, he can't fight, can he?"

"No," I said, "but don't talk about it. I hate thinking of it now."

"I don't," said Mercer. "I shall always think about it when I come up here, and feel as I did then, punching poor old Dicksee's big fat head. I say, won't it do him good and make him civil? Look here," he continued, making a bound and pointing to a knot on the rough floor boards, "that's the exact spot where his head came down whop."

Chapter Twenty One.

We boys used to think the days at old Browne's very long and tedious, and often enough feel a mortal hatred of Euclid as a tyrant who had invented geometry for the sake of driving boys mad. What distaste, too, we had for all the old Romans who had bequeathed their language to us; just as if English wasn't ten times better, Mercer used to say.

"Bother their old declensions and conjugations!" he would cry. "What's the good of them all? I call it a stupid language to have no proper prepositions and articles and the rest of it: tucking i's, a's, and e's at the end of words instead."

But what days they were after all—days that never more return! The Doctor was pretty stern at times, and gave us little rest. Mr Rebble seemed to be always lying in wait to puzzle us with questions, and Mr Hasnip appeared to think that we never had enough to learn; while the German and French masters, who came over twice a week from Hastings, both seemed to have been born with the idea that there was nothing of the slightest consequence in the way of our studies but the tongues they taught. And oh, the scoldings we received for what they called our neglect and stupidity!

"*Ach, dumkopf!*" the German master would cry wrathfully; while the French master had a way of screwing up his eyes, wrinkling his face, and grinding his teeth at our pronunciation.

I'm afraid we hated them all, in complete ignorance of the other side of the case, and the constant unwearying application they gave to a set of reckless young rascals, who construed Latin with their lips and the game that was to be played that afternoon with their brains.

I confess it. I must have been very stupid in some things, sharp as I was in others, and I have often thought since that Mr Rebble's irritability was due to the constant trouble we gave him; that Mr Hasnip was at heart a thorough gentleman; and as for "Old

Browne," as we called him, he was a ripe scholar and a genuine loveable old Englishman, with the health and welfare of his boys thoroughly at heart.

We thought nothing of it. A boy's nature does not grasp all these things. To us it was a matter of course that, if we were ill, Mrs Doctor should have us shut up in another part of the house, and, with her two daughters, risk infection, and nurse us back to health. I could not see then, but I can now, what patient devotion was given to us. Of course I could not see it, for I was a happy, thoughtless boy, living my golden days, when to breathe and move was a genuine pleasure, and the clouds and troubles that shut off a bit of life's sunshine only made the light the brighter when it came again!

Ah! it's a grand thing to be a boy, with all your life before you, and if any young sceptic who reads these words, and does not skip them because he thinks they are prosy preaching, doubts what I say, let him wait. It is the simple truth, and I am satisfied, for I know that he will alter his tune later on.

In spite, then, of the many troubles I had to go through, with the weariness of much of the learning, it was a delightful life I led, and though a little dumpy at leaving home after the holidays, I had forgotten my low spirits long before I got back to the Doctor's, and was looking forward longingly to seeing old faces, wondering what the new ones would be like, and eager to renew my friendly relations with Tom Mercer, Lomax, Bob Hopley, and Cook, and to give them the little presents I was taking back.

These were mere trifles, but they went a long way with the recipients. Tom Mercer declared that the blade of the knife I gave him was the best bit of steel he ever saw. It wasn't: for, unless the edge was constantly renewed, there never was such a knife to cut.

Lomax's gift was more satisfactory, for my uncle got it for me with a grim smile, as he thought, I know, of his old soldiering days. It was a quarter of a pound of very choice Virginia tobacco, and it delighted the old sergeant so, that I thought he would have hugged me. I don't know how long that lasted, but I am sure he hoarded some of it up for nearly a year, and he would call my attention to its "glorious scent," as he called it, though to me it was very nasty indeed.

Bob Hopley's present was a red and orange silk kerchief, which he wore proudly on Sundays, and Cook's was in a small box prepared by my mother—a cap with wonderful flowers and ribbons, which obtained for Tom Mercer and me endless little supper snacks as tokens of the woman's delight and gratitude.

So, as time sped on, I had grown so accustomed to the life at "Old Browne's," that I felt little objection, as I have said, to returning after the Christmas holidays; though the weather was bad and there was a long while to wait before there could be much pleasure in out-door sports. But the spring came at last with its pear and apple blossom, the hops began to run up the poles, May and June succeeded, and glided on so that I could hardly believe it when the midsummer holidays came without my feeling that I had advanced much in the past six months.

I suppose I had, for I had worked hard, and the letter I bore home from the Doctor quite satisfied my mother who afterwards informed me in confidence that my uncle was greatly pleased.

Six weeks' holidays were before me, but, before they were at an end, I was beginning to get weary, and longing for the day to come when my new things were brought home ready to try on, pack up, and return to school.

To my studies and interviews with the masters?

Oh, no! nothing of the kind; but to where there were woods and ponds, and the General's cob for my riding lessons, and the cricket-field.

I'm afraid my mother must have thought me careless and unloving. I hope I was not, in my eagerness to get back to Tom Mercer, who made my school life most interesting by his quaintness. For I was always ready to enter into his projects, some of which were as amusing as they were new.

I had seen little of my uncle when I was home last, but he wrote to me twice—stern, military-toned letters, each of which was quite a despatch in itself. In these he laid down the law to me, giving me the best of advice, but it was all very Spartan-like. He insisted above all things upon my recollecting that I was to be a soldier, and that a soldier was always a gentleman and a man of honour, and each time he finished his letter in these words, —

"Never tell a lie, Frank; never do a dirty action; keep yourself smart and clean; and, by the way, I send you a sovereign to spend in trash."

"Only wish I had such an uncle," Tom Mercer used to say. "My father would send me money if he could spare it, but he says his patients won't pay. They're civil enough when they're ill, but when he has wound up their clocks, and set them going again, they're as disagreeable as can be if he wants his bill."

This was after I had gone back from the midsummer holidays.

"Did you ask him for money, then?"

"Yes, and he said that if he wrote at midsummer and asked for payment, the farmers told him they'd pay after harvest, and if he wanted it after harvest, they said they'd pay at. Christmas, and when Christmas came, they told him to wait till midsummer. Oh, won't I serve 'em out if ever I'm a doctor!"

"What would you do?" I said.

"Give 'em such a dose!"

"Not you, Tom."

"Oh, won't I! I don't care, though; father gave me a crown and mamma half a one."

"And enough too. What a fellow you are to grumble!"

"That I'm not. I wanted 'em to buy me a watch."

"Get out! What a fellow you are! Next time the chaps want a nickname for you, I shall call you Watchman."

"All right! I don't mind; but I shan't be happy till I have a watch."

"That's what you used to say about Magglin's take-to-pieces gun, but you never got it, and you've been happy enough without."

"Oh, have I?" said Mercer. "You don't know. I used to long for that gun."

Two or three days afterwards, in one of our strolls, when we were both coming back laden with odds and ends for the museum up in the loft, Mercer proposed that we should cross a field and get into the lower lane, so as to call at Polly Hopley's to get something to eat.

I was nothing loth, and we struck off across country, got into the lane about a couple of hundred yards from the keeper's lodge, and then suddenly stopped short.

"Hush!" I said, as shouts and cries reached our ears.

"There's something the matter," cried Mercer. "Come on."

We set off at a run, and as we passed a bend in the lane, we came full in sight of the keeper's cottage, and saw him in the middle of the road, holding a rough-looking figure by the collar, keeping it down upon its knees, while he vigorously used a stick upon the object's back, in spite of cries and protestations, till there was a sudden wrench, and whoever it was dragged himself away and ran down the lane, Polly Hopley standing at the cottage door laughing, while her father wiped his brow with the sleeve of his coat.

"Hullo, young gents!" he cried. "You were just too late to see the fun."

"Saw some of it, Bob," I said. "But who was it?"

"Didn't you see, sir?"

"I did," cried Mercer. "It was old Magglin."

"Yes, and I'll Magglin him!" cried Bob wrathfully.

"What's he been doing?" I said. "Poaching?"

"Eh? Yes, sir, poaching, that's what he's been up to," said Bob, with a side glance at Polly, who threw her apron over her face, burst out laughing, and ran into the cottage. "He've been told over and over again to keep away, but it's no good, so I've started this here hazel saplin' for him and I've been beating his carpet for him nicely. I don't think he'll come any more."

"What does he come poaching after, Bob—the sweets?" said Mercer.

"Um! Yes, the sweets," said Bob drily; "and he ain't going to have 'em. A lazy, poaching, dishonest scoundrel, that's what he is. I did think we'd got rid of him lots o' times, but he's like a bad shilling, he always comes back. Well, never mind him, sir. When are you coming to have a day's fishing? Sir Orkus told me only t'other day you was to be looked after if you come."

"Oh, some day soon," I said. "We've got a big cricket match coming on first."

"Ay? Well, I must come and see that, young gents. I used to be fond of bowling myself."

We shook hands with the keeper, and then went into the cottage to buy a couple of Polly's turnovers, and found her looking very red-faced and shy, but she was businesslike enough over taking the money, and we went off browsing down the lane upon Polly's pastry and blackberry jam.

"Magg wants to marry Polly," I said oracularly. "Don't you remember that day when we went round by the back, and heard her ordering him off?"

"Yes, I remember," said Mercer, with his mouth full. "I was thinking about it. I don't wonder at Bob whacking him. Polly's too good for such a miserable, shuffling, cheating fellow as he is. I hate him now. I used to like him, though I didn't like him. I liked him because he was so clever at getting snakes and hedgehogs and weasels. He always knew where to find lizards. But he's a cheat. You pay him, and then he says you didn't, and keeps on worrying you for more money. I'll never buy anything of him again."

"That's what you always say, Tom," I replied, "and next time he has a good bird or anything, you buy it."

"Well, I've done with him this time. Look: there he is."

For about fifty yards away there was Magglin, long-haired and dirty-looking, seated on the bank, with his elbows on his knees and his face buried in his hands.

But he was so quick of ear, that, though we were walking along the grassy margin of the road, he heard us coming, and started up fierce and excited of aspect, but only to soften down and touch his cap, with a servile grin upon his face.

"Hullo, Mr Mercer, sir," he whined; "looking for me?"

"No," said my companion. "Why should I look for you?"

"Thought you wanted to pay me that shilling you owe me, sir."

"'HE'D BETTER TOUCH ME AGAIN,' HE CRIED."

"I don't owe you a shilling."

"Oh yes, you do, sir. Don't he, Mr Burr junior?"

"No," I said; "and if you ever have the impudence to say so again, I'll tell Bob Hopley to give you another thrashing."

The gipsy-looking fellow's dark eyes flashed.

"He'd better touch me again," he cried fiercely. "He'd better touch me again. Did you two see?"

"Yes, we saw," said Mercer. "I say, he did make you cry chy-ike."

"He'd better touch me again."

"He will," I said, "if you go hanging about after Polly Hopley."

"What, did he tell you that?"

"No," I said, "we knew well enough. Bob Hopley didn't say a word. Only called it poaching."

Magglin's manner changed directly, and in a snivelling, whining way he began, —

"Well, I can't help it, young gen'lemen. I'm 'bliged to go there, and nothing I can do's good enough for her. If I give her anything, she chucks it at me, because it aren't good enough."

"I should think not, indeed," said Mercer. "What decent girl's going to listen to such a ragged scaramouche as you are?"

"Well, I can't help it, young gen'lemen."

"Yes, you can. Go to work like a man, and grow respectable," I said. "I should be ashamed to idle about as you do."

"Why, aren't you two always idling about?"

"No. We do our work first," I said.

"I say, Magg, here comes Bob Hopley!" cried Mercer mischievously.

The poacher gave a quick glance up the lane in the direction from which we had come, caught sight of the keeper's velveteen coat, and shot into the copse and was gone.

"I don't wonder at Bob thrashing him," I said.

"No," replied Mercer, as we went on. "I shall never deal with him again. If I want a bird or anything, I shall ask Bob Hopley. He's a man, he is. If you give him anything, he says, 'Thank-ye,' and if you don't, he never seems to mind. He knows boys haven't always got any money. I wish Magglin would go right away."

The conversation turned then upon the coming cricket match; after which we dropped in upon Lomax, and talked to him about boxing, and I pleased him very much by telling him how satisfied my uncle had been at the way I had learned to ride a horse; when, with his eyes twinkling, the old soldier took a letter from his chimney-piece, and opened it to show me my uncle's words, thanking him for the way he, an old soldier, had trained the son of a soldier, and enclosing a five-pound note.

"For a rainy day, Master Burr," he said. "I've clapped that in the bank."

Chapter Twenty Two.

If there was any one thing I dearly loved, it was a good game—a regular well-fought struggle—at cricket. Oddly enough, I used to like to be on the losing side, with the eleven who were so far behind that their fight was becoming desperate, and every effort had to be made to steal a run here and another there, slowly building up the score, with the excitement gradually increasing, and the weaker side growing stronger and more hopeful hour by hour, till, perhaps, by the clever batting of one boy, who has got well to work, and who, full of confidence, sets at defiance the best efforts in every change of bowler, the score is lifted right up to the winning-point, and he comes back to the tent with the bat over his shoulder, amidst the cheers of all the lookers-on.

I suppose I got on well with my education at Doctor Browne's. I know I got on well at cricket, for whenever a match was made up for some holiday, I was in so much request that both sides were eager to have me.

The Doctor had promised us a holiday to play the boys of a school at Hastings. They were to come over on an omnibus, and a tent was to be set up in our field, where, after the game, a high tea was to be provided for the visitors before they returned to Hastings in the evening.

I need hardly say that the day was looked forward to with the greatest eagerness, and that plans were made to give our visitors a thorough good thrashing.

Burr major, as captain of the eleven, rather unwillingly, I'm afraid, but for the sake of the credit of the school, selected Mercer and me for the match. I was to be wicket-keeper, and Mercer, from his clever and enduring running, and power to cover so much ground, was made long field off.

Burr major and Stewart were to bowl, with Dicksee as a change when necessary, for he had a peculiar knack and twist in handling a ball, and could puzzle good players by sending in an innocent-looking, slowly-pitched ball, which looked as if it was going wide, and, when it had put the batsman off his guard, and induced him to change his position, so as to send the ball flying out of the field, it would suddenly curl round and go right into the wicket.

All went well. We practised every evening, and again for an hour before breakfast each morning, and, as I warmed up to my task, I easily stopped all Stewart's or Burr major's swiftest balls, and got to know how to deal with what Mercer called "old Dicksee's jerry sneaks." The tent came from Hastings the day before, and was set up ready, and the next day was to be the match.

But, as Burns says, "The best-laid schemes o' mice an' men gang aft a-gley." So it was here; our plans went very much "a-gley," for I awoke on the morning of the match with a headache, which I knew would completely upset me for the day.

I did not know then, but I know now, that it was Polly Hopley's fault, and that her turnovers and cake were far too rich to be eaten in quantity by two boys sitting up in bed, and going to sleep directly after, in spite of the crumbs and scales of crust. I just remember that I had a bad night, full of unpleasant dreams, all connected with the cricket match in some way. Now I was being horribly beaten; now I was running after the ball, which went on and on, far away into space, and would not be overtaken, and it was still bounding away when I awoke with a start. Then I fell asleep again, and lay bound and helpless, as it seemed to me, with Burr major taking advantage of my position to come and triumph over me, which he did at first by sitting on my chest, and then springing up to go through a kind of war-dance upon me, while I stared up at him helplessly.

Then Dicksee came with his face all swollen up, as it was after the fight, but he was grinning derisively at me, and while Burr major seemed to hold me down by keeping one foot pressed on my chest,

Dicksee knelt by my side, and began to beat my head with a cricket bat.

Bang, bang! bang, bang! Blows that fell with the regularity of the beats of a pendulum, and it seemed to me that he beat me into a state of insensibility, for both Burr major and he faded from my eyesight, though the blows of the bat were still falling upon my head when I awoke in the morning; that is to say, they seemed to be falling, and it was some minutes before I fully understood that I was suffering from a bad bilious headache.

"Now then, why don't you jump up?" said Mercer, as I lay with my eyes shut, and at this I got up slowly, began to dress, and then, feeling too giddy to stand, sat down by my bed.

"What's the matter?" cried Mercer.

"So ill. Head's so bad."

"Oh, that will be all right when you've had your breakfast. Mine aches too. Look sharp. It's ever so late."

I tried to look sharp, but I'm afraid I looked very blunt, and it took me a long time to get dressed and down-stairs, and out in the fresh morning air, where I walked up and down a bit, and then suffered myself to be led into the play-field to see what a splendid tent had been raised, with its canvas back close up to the hedge which separated the Doctor's grounds from the farm, with the intervening dry ditch, which always seemed to be full of the biggest stinging nettles I ever saw.

It was a glorious morning, the turf was short and beautifully level, the boys having joined hands the previous night to drag the great roller well over it. But the sunshine, the blue sky, and the delicious green of the hedges and trees were all nothing to me then, and I let Mercer chatter on about the chances of the other side, which, as far as I was concerned, promised to be excellent.

The breakfast-bell rang, and we went in, but that morning meal did not fulfil Mercer's prophecy and carry off my ailment, for I could not touch a bit.

"Oh, you are a fellow!" cried my comrade. "Well; perhaps you are right. My father says it's best not to eat and drink when you have a bad headache. But look sharp and get well; the chaps will be over in good time."

By and by the news reached the captain of our eleven, and he came to me all smiles and civility, for all Burr major's ideas of revenge seemed to have died out, as I thought, because I never presumed upon my victory.

"Oh, I say, Burr junior," he cried, "this won't do! You must look sharp and get well."

"I want to," I replied dolefully; "but I'm afraid I shan't be able to play."

"But you must. If you don't, they'll be sure to beat us, and that would be horrid."

"You mustn't let them beat you," I said, wishing all the while that he would go, for my head throbbed more than ever, and varied it with a sensation as of hot molten lead running round inside my forehead in a way that was agonising.

"But what are we to do for a wicket-keeper?"

"You must take my place," I said feebly. "You are the best wicket-keeper we have."

"No," he cried frankly, "you are; but I think I'm the best bowler."

"Well, you will be obliged to keep wicket to-day," I said, with a groan. "I shall never be able to stir, I'm sure."

"Well, you do look precious mouldy," he cried. "It's a nuisance, and no mistake. I suppose we must make shift, then?"

"Yes; let Dicksee and Hodson bowl all the time."

"And I can put Senna on now and then for an over or two."

"I can't bowl well enough," said Mercer.

"Oh yes, you can when you like," said Burr major. "And, I say," he cried, taking out his watch, "it's getting close to the time."

Mercer's eyes glistened as the watch was examined, and it seemed to me that my companion sighed as the watch was replaced.

Just then Hodson came up.

"How is he?"

"Too bad to play, he says. Isn't it beastly?"

"Do you mean it, Burr junior?"

"Yes," I said. "I'm very, very queer. I couldn't play."

"You ain't shamming, are you?"

"Look at me and see," I replied faintly, and directly after I felt a cool hand laid on my burning forehead.

"There's no gammon about it," said Hodson. "We must do the best we can. Look sharp, Senna."

"Yes," said Burr major; "he'll have to take a turn at the bowling."

"I shan't play if Frank Burr don't," said Mercer stoutly.

"What?" cried the two boys together.

"You must put some one else on instead of me; I've got a headache too."

"Oh, I say," cried Hodson, and he and Burr both tried hard to shake Mercer's sudden resolution. I too tried, but it was of no use; he grew more stubborn every minute; and after Burr major had again referred to his watch, the two lads went off together, disappointed and vexed.

"You might have gone and played with them, Tom," I said.

"I know that," he replied; "but I wasn't going without you. I'm going to stop and talk."

"No, no, don't," I said. "I only want to be quiet till— Oh, my head, my head!"

"Why, Burr junior, what's this?" cried Mr Hasnip, coming up and speaking cheerily. "Bad headache? not going to play?"

"No, sir, I feel too ill."

"Oh, come, this is a bad job. Hi, Rebble!"

The latter gentleman came up.

"Here's Burr junior queer. Does he want a doctor, do you think?"

Mr Rebble looked at me attentively for a few moments, and then said quietly,—

"No; only a bilious headache, I should say. Go and lie down for an hour or two, my lad, and perhaps it will pass off."

I gladly crawled up to our dormitory, took off my jacket and boots, and lay down on the bed, when I seemed to drop at once into a doze, from which I started to find Mercer seated by the window looking out.

"Better?" he said, as I stirred.

"Better! No; I feel very ill. But what are you doing here?"

"Come to sit with you," he said stolidly.

Just then there was a burst of cheering, and the crunching noise made by wheels.

"Here they are," cried Mercer excitedly. "Oh, I say, I do wish you were better! I should like to lick those Hastings chaps."

"Then why don't you go?" I said pettishly. "Go and bowl."

"Shan't, without you," was the only reply I could get, and I lay turning my head from side to side, trying to find a cool spot on the pillow, to hear every now and then a shout from the field, and then a burst of plaudits, or cries of, "Well run!"

"Bravo!"

"Well fielded!" and more hand-clapping, all borne faintly in at the window, where Mercer sat with his arms folded, gazing out, but unable to see the field from where he was.

After a time I once more dropped off into a doze and woke again with a start, under the impression that I had been asleep all day.

My head was not quite so bad, and, after lying still, thinking, and listening to the shouts from the cricket-field, I said weakly, —

"Have they nearly done, Tom?"

"Done! No, of course not."

"What time is it?"

"Don't know. Haven't got a watch."

"Well, what time do you think it is?"

"'Bout two. They've just gone to the wickets again after lunch."

"Why don't you go and join them now?"

"You know. How's your head?"

"A little better, I think."

"Well enough to come down and look on?"

"Oh no," I said, with a shudder; "I feel too sick and ill for that."

"Have another snooze, then, and you'll be better still."

"But it's too bad to keep you out of the fun," I said.

"I didn't grumble. Go to sleep."

I determined that I would not, but I did, and woke again, to repeat my question about the time, and receive the answer that my companion had not got a watch.

"How long have I been asleep, then?" I asked.

"'Bout an hour. Here! hi! what are you going to do?"

"Get up, and go down in the field," I said.

"Hooray! Then it's all right again?"

"No," I replied; "but it's a little better, and I should like to go and lie down under the big hedge, and see our fellows win."

"Come, I do like that," cried Mercer eagerly, as I went to the wash-stand, well bathed my temples, and then, feeling very sick and faint, but not in such pain, I put on my jacket and boots, and we went slowly down-stairs, and out into the field, where every one was too intent to take much notice of us, as Tom led me up to the big hedge, where I lay down on the grass about fifty yards from where the tent stood close up; and from time to time I saw the boys who were about to go in to bat, go to the tent to take off their jackets and vests, and come out ready for the fight.

Our boys were in, and I saw Dicksee change and go to the wicket to come back with a "duck's egg," as we called it. Then Hodson went in and made a stand, but a quarter of an hour later, the boy who faced him was caught, and Burr major walked up to the tent, disappeared, and came out again all in white, with a brand-new bat over his shoulder.

Just then Mercer, who had been round to the scorers, came back, and stood watching Burr major as he marched off.

"Oh, I say," he said, "don't you wish you were in it, Frank?"

"Yes," I said, with a sigh. Then— "How's the game now?"

"We're a hundred behind 'em, and our fellows can't stand their bowling. If Eely and Hodson don't make a big stand, we shall have a horrid licking. Better?"

"Yes, a little," I said faintly, and then I lay watching the game, while Mercer walked about—now going up to the empty tent where the boys' clothes were, now coming back to me to talk about the game. Once he went and lay down near the tent. Another time he went by it out of sight, but he was soon back to see how I was, and off in the other direction, this time to go right round the field and come back by the tent, and throw himself down by my side.

"What do you think of it now? Oh, look! Hooray! hooray! Run! run! run!" he roared, and then joined in the hand-clapping, for Hodson had made a splendid leg hit, which brought us in four, and two more from an overthrow.

This excited Tom Mercer to such an extent that he could not lie still, but went off again in the direction of the tent, while I began to know that I was better, from the interest I was able to take in the game.

Then, after seeing Burr major and Hodson make hit after hit, for they were now well in, and punishing the bowling to a tremendous extent, I began to think about how good-companion-like it had been of Mercer to spoil his own pleasure so as to stay with me, and I lay there resting on my elbow, watching him for a few minutes, as he stood close up to the tent.

"Well, Burr junior, how's the head?" cried Mr Hasnip, strolling up with Mr Rebble.

"A good deal better, sir," I replied, "but very far from well."

"You'll have to take a long night's rest before it will be quite right," said Mr Rebble. "By the way, Mrs Browne said I was to report how you were, so that she could send you something to take if you did not seem better."

"Oh, I'm ever so much better, sir!" I cried hastily, for I had a keen recollection of one of the good lady's doses which she had prescribed, and whose taste I seemed to distinguish then.

"Oh yes, you'll be all right in the morning," said Mr Hasnip. "Well, Mercer, how are we getting on?"

"I haven't been to the scorers' table, sir," said Mercer, who had just come back from a spot near the tent, where he could get a better view of the field than from where I lay under the big oak tree.

"Run and ask, my lad," said Mr Rebble, and he and Mr Hasnip sat down near me, and chatted so pleasantly that I forgot all about the way in which they tortured me sometimes with questions.

In due time Mercer came back to announce that Hodson and Burr major had put on sixty-one between them, and that there were hopes that the game might be pulled out of the fire even then.

Mercer sat down now beside me, and, the ground in front clearing a little, we had a good view of the game, which grew more and more interesting as the strangers fought their best to separate our two strongest men, and stop them from steadily piling up the score; the loud bursts of shouting stirring them on to new efforts, which resulted in the ball being sent here, there, and everywhere, for twos, threes, and fours, till the excitement seemed to have no bounds.

Then came a check, just as the servants had been busy carrying urns, teapots, and piled-up plates into the tent, for it was getting late in the afternoon.

The check was caused by a ball sent skying by Hodson and cleverly caught, with the result that one of our best cricketers shouldered his bat and marched off the ground, but proudly, for he had had a splendid innings, and quite a jubilation of clapping hands ran round the field.

Another took his place, and helped Burr major to make a little longer stand, but the spirit had gone out of his play, which became more and more cautious. He stole one here and sent the ball for one there, but made no more brilliant hits for threes and fours.

At last after a good innings the fresh man was clean bowled, and another took his place.

"Last of 'em," said Mercer. "Oh, if they can only do it! We only want five to win."

But during the next quarter of an hour these five were not made. The new-comer contented himself with playing on the defensive, and with the knowledge to trouble him of the game resting entirely on his shoulders, Burr major grew more and more nervous, missing excellent chances that he would have jumped at earlier in his innings.

"Four to win." Then the fresh boy got a chance, and made one which sent our lads nearly frantic.

"Three only to win," and there seemed to be not a doubt of our success now,—for it was "our" success, though I had had nothing to do with the result.

And now Burr major had a splendid chance, but he was too nervous to take it, and the over proved blank, as did the next. But in the one which followed, the fresh boy sent a ball just by mid-wicket, a run was stolen, and I, too, grew so excited that I forgot my headache and rose to my knees.

It was a fresh over, a change had been made in the bowling, and the first ball was delivered and stopped.

The second ball went rushing by the wicket, but it was not wide; and now the third ball was bowled. It seemed to be an easy one, and in the midst of the most profound excitement, Burr major gathered himself together for a big hit, struck out, and — the ball went flying out of the field?

No; Burr major just missed it, the off-bail was bowled clean and fell a dozen yards away.

We were beaten.

Chapter Twenty Three.

There was a tremendous burst of cheering and a rush for the tent by the boys who had left their jackets within, and among them Burr major, disappointed, but at the same time justly proud of the splendid score he had made, walked up to the door, disappeared amongst plenty of clapping, and soon after came out again in his jacket and vest.

We had all clustered up round about the players, and two masters shook hands with the champion, who directly after caught sight of me.

"Hallo! How's the head?" he cried.

"Getting better now."

"I saw you watching the match," he continued. "Nice time you had of it lying about under that tree, while we fellows did all the work."

"I should have liked to be in it," I said rather drearily; "but I really was very bad."

His attention was called off soon after, and then there was a summons to the tent for the festive high tea, which was to come off directly, as the Hastings boys had a long drive back.

I was much better, but the thought of food in that crowded tent was nauseating, and, watching my opportunity, I slipped away, seeing Tom Mercer looking about as if in search of me before going into the tent.

"I know what I'll do," I thought. "I'll walk gently down along the lane to Bob Hopley's place, and ask Polly to make me a cup of tea and cut me some bread and butter."

The plan was simple enough, and I strolled out and along the road, and then entered a gate, to make a short cut along the hedge side of the fields.

The evening was glorious, and after a broiling day the soft moist odours that came from the copses dotted here and there seemed delightfully refreshing, and so I strolled on and on till I was only a short distance from the cottage, which was separated from me by a couple of fields, when I turned slowly toward a corner of the enclosure I was in, where there was a pond and a patch of moist land where weeds never noticed towered up in abundance, and, to my surprise, I caught sight of Magglin seated on the bank of the pond, with his feet hanging close to the water, and apparently engaged in his evening toilet. It seemed to me that he must have been washing his face, and that he was now wiping it upon some great leaves which he plucked from time to time.

"No, he isn't," I said to myself the next moment. "He has been poaching, and saw me coming. It's all a pretence to throw me off the scent;" and I went on, my way being close by him, and there he was rubbing away at his face with the leaves, while I glanced here and there in search of a wire set for rabbit or hare, though I shrewdly suspected that the wire he had been setting would be over in the copse beyond the pond, in the expectation of getting a pheasant.

He was so quick of hearing that he could detect a footstep some distance off, but this time he turned round sharply when I exclaimed, —

"Hallo, Magglin!"

"Eh—I— Oh, how de do, sir?"

"Better than you do," I said sharply. "What have you been doing to your face?"

"Face? Oh, rubbing it a bit, sir, that's all. Good as washing."

"Dock leaves," I said. "What, have you stung yourself?"

"Oh yes, I forgot that, sir. Just a little bit, sir. I was coming through the hedge down below there, and a 'ormous old nettle flew back and hit me acrost the cheek. But it aren't nothing."

More than I should like to have, I thought to myself, as I went on, for his face was spotted with white patches, and I knew how they must tingle.

Ten minutes after, I was in the lane, in time to meet Polly Hopley, in her best bonnet and with a key in her hand, going up to the cottage door.

She smiled as she saw me, hurried to the cottage, unlocked the door, and stood back for me to enter.

"Been out, Polly?" I said.

"Yes, sir, of course. Father took me to see the cricket match. Doctor Browne told father we might come into the field, and it were lovely. But why didn't you play?"

I told her, and she expressed her sympathy. Then, in a very decided way,—

"Sweets and puffs aren't good for you, sir, and I won't sell you one to-day."

"I don't want any, Polly," I replied. "I was going to ask you to sell me a cup of tea."

"And I won't do that neither, sir; but I'm going to make myself some directly, and if you'll condescend to sit down in father's big chair and have some, I should be glad."

To the girl's great delight, I accepted her offer. The kettle hanging over the smouldering fire of wood ashes was soon boiling, and I partook of a delicious tea, with fresh water-cresses from the spring, and cream in my tea from the General's dairy, while Polly cut bread and butter, and chatted about "father's" troubles with the poachers, and about the baits he had been getting ready for our next fishing visit to the ponds. Then again about the cricket match, and we were carrying on an animated conversation when the door was thrown quickly open, and Bob Hopley appeared.

"Oh, dad, how you startled me!" cried Polly, jumping up.

"Startled you, my lass? I heerd loud talking and I'd been told young Magglin had come down this way, and I thought it was him."

"I saw him just before I came in, over by the pond there by the copse," I said.

"He wasn't likely to be in here, father," said Polly primly. "I should like to catch him trying to come in."

"So should I," said the keeper grimly. "I'd try oak that time 'stead o' hazel."

"Hush, dad! do adone," whispered Polly. Then aloud —

"Master Burr's been poorly all day, and as they were all feasting and junketing at the school, he come down here to ask me to make him some tea, and he's very welcome, aren't he, father?"

"I should just think he is, my lass. But fill up his cup again, and he's got no fresh butter."

"I've done," I said; "and oh, I do feel so much better now! Do you know what a bad sick headache is?"

"No, my lad, no. I aren't had one since —"

"Oh, father!"

"Come, Polly, don't be hard on a man. That was only the club feast."

"I haven't patience with such feasts," said Polly sharply. "I never go to feasts, and come back—"

"Poorly, my lass, poorly," said Bob hastily.

"Yes, very poorly," said Polly sarcastically, "and say, 'My head's fit to split,' next day. Seems to me that's all such heads are fit for then—to split and burn."

"Nay, nay, my lass, they burn quite enough, I can tell 'ee. Man does do stoopid things sometimes."

Bob was very apologetic about sitting down to tea, with me there. Then of course I apologised, and sat watching him drinking great draughts out of a basin and devouring huge slices of bread and butter.

"Rare stuff kettle broth, sir," he said. "Don't give you no headaches; do it, Polly?"

"No, father."

"She don't make it strong enough for that, Mr Burr, sir," he continued, giving me a wink.

"Quite as strong as is good for you, father."

"Right, my lass," said Bob, helping himself to some more cream, "and not so strong as is good for you."

I rose to go soon after, and the keeper joined with his daughter in absolutely refusing to let me pay for my meal.

"Glad to have seen you, sir; and now mind that as soon as ever your young friend Mas' Mercer—Mas' Bri'sh Museum, as I call him—is ready, and you can get a day, I'll take you to our stock pond, where the carps and tenches are so thick, they're asking to be caught. You shall have a day."

"Good-bye, Polly," I said, shaking hands. "You've quite cured my head."

"I am so glad, sir!" she cried; and I went back to the school, Bob seeing me part of the way, and saying to me confidentially as we walked,—

"You see me leathering that poaching vagabond Magglin, sir. It's like this. The reason for it was— No, sir. Good-night. You're too young to talk about that sort o' thing. Don't forget about the fish."

He hurried away without another word, while I went on, and found Tom Mercer looking for me, and eager to hear where I had been.

"What a shame!" he cried. "The high tea was very jolly, but I missed you. I wish I'd gone too. I say, we were licked, but it was a splendid match after all. Hallo! here's Hodson. The chaps all went off on their 'bus cheering and— Hooray, Hodson! what a day!"

"Yes; but I say," said the lad, "Burr major's lost his watch."

"His watch!" cried Mercer, giving quite a jump. "Oh!"

"Yes; he left it in his waistcoat in the tent when he stripped for his innings, and when he felt for it some time after, it was gone."

"Then he didn't miss it directly?" I said.

"No, not till a little while ago. A lot of the fellows are up in the field searching for it. Haven't either of you seen it, have you?"

"No," I said, and Mercer shook his head.

"Come on and help look for it," cried Hodson; and we went up to the field, where the tent was still standing, it being understood that the men were to come and take it down in the morning.

"Lucky they were not here," I said, "or some of them might have been suspected of taking it."

"Yes, it would be ugly for them," assented Hodson. "You see, nobody but our boys and the Hastings chaps went into the tent, except the servants to lay the tables, and of course they wouldn't have taken it."

"But they may have found it," I said. "He is sure to have dropped it somewhere in the grass."

"Of course," cried Mercer; "and some one has put his foot on it and smashed the glass."

"Get out, Senna! you always make the worst of every thing," cried Hodson merrily; and soon after, we reached the field, where the boys were spread about, looking in all kinds of possible and impossible places—impossible because Burr major had never been near them after he had put on his things.

"Are you sure that you brought your watch out in the field," said Mr Hasnip, who was one of the group standing by Burr major.

"Oh yes, sir, certain."

"But it does not do to be too certain, my lad. Have you been up in your bedroom, and looked there?"

"No, sir, because I was so sure I brought it out."

"Why were you so sure?"

"Because—because I thought I would wear it, as we had strangers coming."

"Never mind, you may have altered your mind. Go and look. You see we have thoroughly searched every place where you could have been."

"I'll go and look, sir," said Burr major, "but it's of no use."

He went off toward the schoolhouse, and Mr Rebble then coming up, the two masters began to talk about the missing watch.

"It is so awkward," said Mr Rebble. "We can't write and ask the party if either of them took a watch by mistake. Stop! I have it."

"The watch?" cried Mr Hasnip eagerly.

"No. Wait till he comes back, and I think I can explain it all."

We had not long to wait before Burr major came back to us.

"No, sir," he said. "I've looked everywhere; it isn't in my room."

"Then I think I can help you," said Mr Rebble. "What jacket and vest are those you have on?"

"My third best, sir."

"Are you sure?"

"Yes, sir," said Burr major wonderingly.

"Look at them," continued Mr Rebble. "Are they really your own things, and not the clothes of one of our visitors taken by mistake, and he has taken yours."

Burr major slipped off his jacket and held it up in the dusk to point out a label inside the collar, where, worked in blue silk upon white satin, was the name of the maker, his own father.

"Yes, that's yours," said Mr Rebble in a disappointed tone. "I thought that the mistake might have been made. But the vest—are you sure of that?"

"Oh yes," said Burr major, who then looked inside the collar and found the same maker's name.

"I thought that, sir," said Burr major; "but I could feel that they were my things as soon as I put them on. I say, has any fellow taken my watch for a game?"

There was silence at first, then a murmur of, "No, no, no;" and, as it was getting too dark now to resume the search, we all trooped back to the schoolroom to sit and talk over the one event which had spoiled what would otherwise have been a most enjoyable day, for, as Tom Mercer said when we went up to bed, —

"It's nicer for those Hastings chaps to have won. They've gone back jollier. By and by we shall be going over to play them, and then we shall be in the eleven, and must win."

A pause.

"I said, 'And then we must win.'"

"Yes, I heard you."

"Then why didn't you speak?"

"Because I was thinking about Burr major's watch."

"Oh, bother his watch!" said Mercer hastily. "I'm beginning to be glad that he has lost it. Now he won't be always flourishing it in your face and seeming to say, 'Poor fellow, I'm sorry you haven't got a watch too.'"

"Well, you needn't be so cross about it," I said.

"Why needn't I? One gets sick of his watch. There's always been a fuss about it ever since he came back with it. It's lost now, and a jolly good job too. Now we've heard the end of it. Old Eely's watch is regularly wound up."

Chapter Twenty Four.

But we had not heard the end of it, for the Doctor was so much annoyed that he sent Mr Hasnip on a private diplomatic visit to his brother schoolmaster at Hastings, to speak of the trouble we were in, and to ask if it were possible that the watch had been taken by mistake.

Mr Hasnip's mission was as useless as the search made by the boys, who all stood round while the men took down the tent, so as to make sure that no strangers should be more successful than we were.

But the tent was carted away, poles, flags, and all, and then we resumed our search over the space where the erection had stood, even up to the hedge, and boys were sent over it to peer about in the ditch beyond.

Every minute out of school hours was devoted to the search for Burr major's watch, but there was no result; and when Mr Hasnip returned, soon after the boys had again given up the hunt, and told the Doctor what he had done, he came away, and saw Mr Rebble, who told Burr major, and Burr major told Hodson who was the medium that conveyed to the boys generally the fact that the Doctor had shaken his head.

The next day came, and the next, and another day passed, with the memories of the cricket match growing more faint. Burr major's watch was not found, and, after the first two days, the boys had ceased to look suspiciously at one another, and charge a school-fellow with having hid the watch "for a game." Lessons went on as usual, and my riding was kept up, but the cob was only brought over once a week.

I had a pretty good time at the drilling though, but that was only in company with the other boys.

Then the days grew to weeks, and we had our trip to Hastings; that is to say, our eleven; and, being free from headache this time, both Mercer and I played, all coming back in triumph, and nearly sending the private omnibus horses off at a wild gallop as we neared the school: for we came back to announce that we had beaten our adversaries in one innings, they having scored so badly that they had to follow on.

This trip revived the talk about Burr major's watch, but only for a day or two, and then once more the topic died out, though I heard incidentally from Mr Hasnip that the Doctor was bitterly grieved at such a loss taking place in his school.

I worked hard in those days, and made rapid progress, I afterwards found, though I did not grasp it at the time, and I had now grown to like my school life intensely.

Now and then a letter came from the General, asking leave for Mercer and me to go over to early dinner, the old gentleman welcoming us warmly, and making me give proofs of my progress in all parts of my education that had a military bearing. Then we were sent back in the dog-cart, generally with a crown a piece, and a big basket of fruit—a present, this latter, which made us very popular with the other boys, who envied our luck, as they called it, greatly, particularly our expeditions to the General's ponds, from which we brought creels full of trophies in triumph. But only to have our pride lowered by the cook, to whom we took our prizes, that lady declaring them all to be rubbish except the eels, and those, she said, were too muddy to be worth the trouble of taking off their skins.

Then, too, we had natural history excursions to make additions to the museum in the bin.

I thoroughly enjoyed these trips, and became the most enthusiastic of collectors, but I regret to say that with possession my interest ceased.

Mercer bullied me sharply, but it was of no good. If lizards were to be plunged in spirits and suspended by a silken thread or fine wire to the cork of the bottle, he had to do it; and though he showed me how, at least a dozen times, to skin a snake through its mouth, so as to strip off the covering whole and ready to fill up with sand, so as to preserve its shape, he never could get me to undertake the task.

Certainly I began to pin out a few butterflies on cork, but I never ended them, nor became an adept at skinning and mounting quadrupeds and birds.

"It's all sheer laziness," Mercer used to say pettishly.

"Not it," I said. "I like the birds and things best unstuffed. They look a hundred times better than when you've done them your way."

"But they won't keep, stupid," he cried.

"Good thing too. I'd rather look at them for two days as they are, than for two years at your guys of things."

"What!" he cried indignantly. "Guys!"

"Well, so they are," I said. "Look at that owl; look at the squirrel, with one hind leg fat and the other lean, and his body so full that he seems to have eaten too many nuts."

"But those were some of the first stuffings," he pleaded.

"But the last are worse," I cried, laughing. "Then look at the rabbit. Who'd ever know that was a rabbit, if it wasn't for his ears and the colour of his skin? He looks more like a bladder made of fur."

"But he isn't finished yet."

"Nor never will be," I cried merrily.

"Ah, you're getting tired of natural history," said Mercer, seating himself on the edge of the bin, and looking lovingly down at its contents, for this conversation took place up in the loft.

"Wrong!" I cried. "I get fonder of it every day; but I'm not going to skin and stuff things to please anybody, not even you."

"I'm sorry for you," said Mercer. "You're going to be a soldier. My father says I'm to be a doctor. You're going to destroy, and I'm going to preserve."

I burst out laughing.

"I say, Tom," I cried, as he looked up at me innocently, in surprise at my mirth, and I went and sat at the other end of the bin; "had one better kill poor people out of their misery than preserve them to look like that?" and I pointed down at the half-stuffed rabbit.

"Go on," he said quietly. "Scientific people always get laughed at. I don't mind."

"More do I."

"I've had lots of fun out of all these things, and it's better than racing all over a field, kicking a bag of wind about, and knocking one another down in a charge, and then playing more sacks on the mill, till a fellow's most squeezed flat. I hate football, and so do you."

"No, you don't," I said; "you love a game sometimes as much as I do. What I don't like in it is, that when I'm hurt, I always want to hit somebody."

"Yes, that is the worst of it," he said quietly; "and since I've found out that I can fight, I'm ever so much readier to punch anybody's head."

"But you don't."

"No; I don't, because it don't seem fair. I don't care, though, how you laugh. I shall go on with my natural history even when I grow a man, and have to drive round like father does, giving people stuff. It gives you something to think about."

"Yes, it gives you something to think about," I said merrily. "I always get thinking about these."

"I say: don't," cried Mercer; "you've upset my owl on to that blackbird. I wish you wouldn't be so fond of larking."

"All right, Tom; I won't tease you," I said. "It's all right, and I'll always go with you collecting. I never knew there were half so many things to see out of doors, till I went out with you. When shall we have a regular good walk through the General's woods?"

"Any time we can get away," he cried, brightening up. "I'm ready."

"All right," I said; "then we will go first chance."

"We must tell Bob Hopley we're going, or he may hear us in the wood, and pepper us, thinking it's old Magglin."

"What?"

"He said he would, if ever he caught him there."

"Seen him lately?" I said.

"No; have you?"

"Not since the cricket match day, when I was going to Bob Hopley's."

"One of the boys said he saw him hanging about, twice over, and I suppose he was trying to see me, and get a shilling out of me. I'm sure he's had nearly a pound out of me, that I didn't owe him. I wish I wasn't so soft."

"So do I."

"Ah, now you're laughing at me. Never mind, I've done with him now. Never a penny does he ever get out of me again."

"Till next time, Tom," I said.

"No, nor next time neither. I don't suppose we shall see much more of him here, for Bob Hopley says that so sure as he catches him poaching, he shall speak out pretty plainly, so as to get him sent away. He says that many a time he has let him off with a good licking, sooner than get him sent to prison, for he don't think prison's good for young men like him."

"I suppose it isn't," I said thoughtfully, as I watched my companion, and saw how lovingly he arranged and rearranged his grotesque-looking creatures at the bottom and on the rough shelves of the bin that he had put up from time to time.

And as I watched him, an idea entered my brain which tickled me so, that I had hard work to keep from laughing aloud, and being noticed.

The idea came as he glanced at me, and moved the rabbit to the corner nearest to him—the absurd-looking object being carefully covered over, as if he was afraid I should begin joking him again about its unfinished state.

All at once, moved by the impulse which had set me laughing, I leaned over and stretched out my hand toward the corner where he had placed the rabbit.

"What are you going to do?" he cried excitedly, and he caught my wrist.

"Only going to take out bunny, and see how he's getting on."

"No, no, don't."

"Why not?" I cried merrily. "Because—

because I don't want it touched." "But I can

improve it so."

"No, no: be quiet. Oh, I say, Frank, pray don't touch it."

"Oh, all right," I said, after a good-humoured struggle with him, in which I did not use much force, and I let him shut the bin, and sit on the lid.

Dinner!

For the bell began to ring, and I dashed down, to run out of the stable and across the yard, expecting that he would follow me, and running so blindly that I came right upon Dicksee, just leaving the stable door, and sent him down upon his hands and knees.

"Hallo!" I shouted; "what were you doing there?—listening?"

"What's that to you?" grumbled the boy, as he rose slowly and carefully, examining his hands to see if the skin was off. "You did that on purpose."

"No, I didn't," I replied; "but I would have done it, if I had known you were sneaking and eavesdropping there."

"Who was sneaking and eavesdropping? What was there to listen to?" he retorted. "'Tain't your stable. I've as good a right there as you have. Tom Mercer and you ain't going to have it all to yourselves for your old slugs and snails and dead cats."

"You mind Tom Mercer doesn't catch you," I said. "You don't want him to lick you again, I know."

"Yah!" he shouted, and he ran off just as my companion came down.

"Who was that?" he said.

"Fatty Dicksee. I told him you'd give him another dressing down if he came sneaking about here."

"And so I will," cried Tom. "He has never forgiven me, though, for the last. I know he hates me. So does Eely hate you."

"Let 'em," I said, as we went on.

"But they'll serve us out some day if they can."

"Dinner—dinner!" I cried. "Come on!" and we set off at a trot, for the prospect of hot roast mutton and potatoes just then was of far more consequence to me than my school-fellow's prophecies of evil.

Chapter Twenty Five.

I thought of my little plan that night when I went to bed, and I had it in my mind when I woke next morning, and laughed over it merrily as I dressed.

It was the merest trifle, but it amused me; and I have often thought since of what big things grow sometimes out of the merest trifles. School-days are often so monotonous that boys jump at little things for their entertainment, and as there was some good-humoured mischief in this which would do no one any harm, only create a laugh, in which Tom Mercer would no doubt join after he had got over the first feeling of vexation, I had no hesitation about putting it in force.

I had to wait for my opportunity, and it came that afternoon, when most of the boys were together cricketing and playing rounders. I glanced round the field, and then slipped away unobserved, made my way round by the back, and crossed the open space toward the yard.

It was absolutely necessary for me to meet no one, so as to avoid suspicion when Mercer found out what had been done, and I intended, as soon as I had executed my little plan, to slip back by the same way into the play-field, so as to be able to prove where I was on that afternoon.

But, as a matter of course, just because I did not wish to meet any one, I must meet the cook just returning from the kitchen garden with a bundle of thyme in her hand.

Everybody spoke of Cook as being disagreeable and ready to snap and snarl if she were asked for anything extra because a boy was sick; but they say, "Speak well of the bridge that carries you well over," and I always found her the most kindly of women; and she nodded and smiled.

"What boys you and Master Mercer are!" she said. "Why, you are always going and moping up in that loft instead of being in the fields at play."

She went on toward the house, and I stood hesitating about carrying out my plan.

"She knows I've come," I said, "and if there is a row, and questions asked, she may say that she saw me."

"Nonsense! she'll never hear about it," I said, and, running into the dark stable, I stopped short, for I fancied there was a sound overhead; but I heard no more, and, thinking it was fancy, I ran to the steps, climbed up, and was crossing the floor when I heard a faint rustling in a heap of straw at the far end, in the darkest corner of the loft.

"Rats," I said to myself, as I went on to the place where the big bin stood under a little window, passed it, and reached up to take the key from the beam upon which it was always laid, the simplicity of the hiding-place making it all the more secure.

To my utter astonishment, the key was not there, but a second glance showed me that it was in the padlock.

"Been up here and forgot to lock it," I said to myself. "All the better for me. Some one else may have been up, and done it through his leaving the key there."

I laughed to myself as I took the padlock out and threw open the bin, with the intention of having what I called a game.

This was to consist in my arranging the various stuffed creatures in as comical a way as I could; and my first thought was to take the rabbit, alter its position a little, and lay it upon an extemporised bed, with the doctor—the owl—holding one paw to feel its pulse, while all the other creatures looked on.

"What shall be the matter with him?" I thought. Then directly — "I know: all his stuffing come out."

I seized the owl, and found that I could easily twist the wire down its leg, so that the claw would appear to be grasping the rabbit's wrist, while the sage-looking bird stood on one leg; and, satisfied in this, I was about to arrange the jay and other birds, but thought I would do the rabbit first, and, taking it up, I thrust my hand in the orifice made in the skin when taking it off, and pulled out a good piece of tow, meaning to leave it hanging down. Then I thrust my hand in again, and drew it out in astonishment, for I had taken hold of something hard and flat and round. What it was I could not see; it was too much surrounded by the tow. Then I laughed.

"Why, it's a big leaden nicker!" I said to myself. "Why did he put that in? I know. There are holes in it to fix wire to, and—" I turned cold and queer the next instant, as I divided the soft tow, and stood staring down, with the light from the little window falling full upon that which I held in my hand. Then I felt puzzled and confused; but the next minute I uttered quite a sob, for light flashed into my brain: memories of what I had so often heard my chosen companion say, the envy he had displayed, and the way in which all at once Burr major's watch had disappeared from his jacket in the cricket-field,— all came back with a force that seemed to cause a singing noise in my ears, for here before me was the end of it all,—the explanation of the disappearance of the watch, which was now lying in my hand, with the hands close together and pointing to twelve. At last uttering a sound that was almost a groan, I muttered,—

"Oh, Tom, Tom, how could you do such a thing as this?"

The feeling of confusion came back like a thick mist floating over me, and I turned the watch over in my hand two or three times, asking myself what I should do.

Should I take it to Burr major, and say I had picked it up? Should I go and confide in Mr Hasnip? Should I go straight to Tom Mercer and accuse him of taking it?

No, no, no: I felt that I could do none of these things, and in a dreary, slow, helpless way, I thrust the watch back in amongst the tow, rammed more in after it, and then stood, after laying the rabbit down, asking myself what I should do next, while a poignant sense of misery and wretchedness seemed to make my position unbearable.

It all came back now: how, ever since Burr major had that watch, Mercer had been envious, and longed for it. Scarcely a day had passed that he had not said something about his longings; and now here it was plainly enough before me: he had gone on coveting that wretched toy till the desire had been too strong for him, and it had ended in my manly, quaint, good-tempered school-fellow descending to become a contemptible pickpocket and thief.

The blood flushed up into my cheeks and made them burn, while my fists clenched hard, and I thought to myself that I had learned boxing for some purpose.

"I can't go and tell tales of him," I said. "I can't betray him, for it would disgrace him for ever. He would be expelled from the school, and, shamefaced and miserable, go home to his father and mother, who would be nearly broken-hearted. No. I can't tell."

Then I felt that, painful as it would be to confess all, and speak against the boy I had grown to care for as if he had been my brother, I ought to go straight to the Doctor and tell him. It was my duty, and it might act beneficially for Tom Mercer. The severe punishment might be such a lesson to him that it would check what otherwise might prove to be a downward course. If I were silent, he might do such a thing again, as this had been so easy; and get worse and worse. I must—I ought to tell, I said to myself; and then, as I dropped on my knees by the old bin, and rested my head on the edge, the hot tears came to my eyes, and my misery seemed greater than I could bear, for I felt it as bitterly as if I myself had been led into this disgraceful crime.

I rose again with a clearer view of what I should do under the circumstances, for I had been having a terrible fight with bewildering thoughts; now thinking I would lock up the bin and go away as if I had not found the watch, and do nothing but separate myself from my school-fellow, now going in the opposite direction, in which I felt quite determined.

"That's it," I said to myself. "I shall break with Tom Mercer for ever, but I'll tell him why. We've learned to box for something, and perhaps he'll be best man. No, he won't. I shall have right on my side, and as he is guilty he will feel cowardly. I will thrash him till he can hardly crawl, and then, when he is weak and miserable, I'll tell him all I have found out, and make him go and put the watch back where Eely can find it, and then it will never be known who took it, and Mercer will not be expelled in disgrace as a common thief. Why, it would break his mother's heart!"

"Yes, that will be the way," I thought, feeling clearer and more relieved now. "It shall be a secret, but I will punish him as severely as I can, and though we shall never be friends again, I'll try hard to check him from going downward like that, and though he will hate me for what I have done, he will thank me some day when he has grown up to be a man."

I closed the lid of the bin and thrust the top of the padlock through the staple and locked it; withdrew the key, and had raised my hand mechanically to put it in its old hiding-place on the beam, but I altered my mind.

"No," I thought; "I'll bring him up here, and give him the key then, and make him open the bin and take out the watch before I thrash him. It shall be a lesson for him from beginning to end. He must have some shame in him, and I want him to feel it, so that he can never forget it again."

I thrust the key into my pocket and went down into the yard. It was a glorious sunny afternoon when I went up into the loft, and the weather had not changed; but everything seemed to be overclouded and wretched now, as I started off for the play-field, determined to waste no time, but take the culprit to task at once.

I looked about, and could see Burr major, but Mercer was not there, and I crossed to where I could see little Wilson, and asked if he had seen him.

"Senna!" he cried; "yes, I saw him a little while ago. Perhaps he's by the gardens, digging up grubs and things to make physic."

I could not smile then, but went to the gardens. He was not there, and, thinking he might have gone up to our room, I went into the house, and up to the dormitories; but my journey was vain, and I went down again, and once more sought the field, to look all over at the little parties playing cricket, dotted here and there, but no Mercer. To my great surprise, though, I saw Dicksee talking earnestly to Burr major.

"They've made it up," I thought, and it seemed to me very contemptible and small of Burr major to take up again with a boy who had behaved so despicably to him.

I passed pretty near them as I went on across the field, and they both looked at me rather curiously—in a way, in fact, which made me think that they were plotting something against me. Perhaps a fresh fight.

"Well, I don't mind now," I said to myself. "Nothing seems of any consequence but Tom Mercer's act. Where can he be?"

I had another look round, and then saw that Burr major, Hodson, and Dicksee had gone up to the house together, and directly after they disappeared, while I went on again, asking after Mercer, to find that every one nearly had seen him only a little while before, but they could not tell me where he was gone.

I kept on looking about, though I half suspected that he must have gone off on some little expedition of his own, as it was half holiday;

and, at the end of another half-hour, I was about to stand near the gate, to watch for his return, when I caught sight of him, apparently coming from the direction of the yard, as if he had been to the loft.

"Oh, here you are then!" he cried, as, after catching sight of me, he ran to meet me, and began vehemently. "I've been hunting everywhere for you."

"I have been hunting everywhere for you," I said coldly.

"Have you? Well, look here, Frank, I was up in the loft last night, and I forgot to lock up the bin."

It was just as I thought.

"I forgot it once or twice before, thinking about something else; and now some one has been and locked it up, and taken the key away."

"Indeed?" I said coldly.

"Yes. Don't look at a fellow that way. I didn't say you'd taken it, because, of course, if you had, you would have put it up on the beam. I say, who could it have been?"

"Ah! who could it have been?" I said.

"What's the matter with you? How queer you are! I tell you, I don't think it was you, but old fatty Dicksee; I've seen him sneaking about the yard a good deal lately, watching me, and he must have found out where we kept the key, and he has nailed it for some lark, or to tease me. Yes, that's it. You see if, next time we go, we don't find a dead dog, or a dead cat, or something nasty, tucked in the bin. Some of 'em served me that way before, when Bob Hopley's old donkey died, and they put in its head. What shall we do?"

"Nothing," I said. "I have the key."

"You have? Oh, I am glad!"

"I went up and found the key there, so I locked it and put it in my pocket."

"Why didn't you put it in the old place, and not give me all this fright?"

"You know," I said solemnly.

"I—er—er—know—er—er—" he drawled tragically. "Dear me, how grand we are!" he added, with a forced laugh. "No, I don't know."

"Then come up there with me, and I'll show you," I said fiercely.

"Oh, sir—no, sir—please, sir—don't, sir—I, sir— Oh, sir—I won't do so any more, sir. Don't take me up there, sir, and punch my head, sir."

"Don't play the fool, but come along with me."

"Why, Frank, old chap, you aren't serious, are you? What's the matter?"

"Come up into the loft and see," I replied, as sternly as I could, but feeling so miserable that I could hardly keep my voice from quivering.

"Oh, all right! I'm ready," he said rather stiffly now. "I've done nothing to offend you that I know of. Come on."

We moved toward the yard, but before we reached the gateway, without speaking now, our names were shouted, and, stopping and looking round, I saw Mr Hasnip and Mr Rebble coming after us, the former beckoning.

We turned and walked toward him, with a cold sensation of dread running through me; for what I knew made me shiver with dread, lest the real cause of the disappearance of the watch should have been discovered; and I remembered now about my headache on the cricket match day, and how Mercer had hung about near me, going and coming between me and the tent.

The next moment we were facing the two masters, and Mr Rebble spoke, looking at me very severely.

"Burr junior," he said, "the Doctor wishes to see you in his room directly."

I felt as if I had turned white, and I saw Mr Hasnip looking at me in a horrified way, as Mr Rebble continued:

"And, Mercer, you are to come as well."

"Poor Tom!" I thought, as my hot anger against him died away. "It is all found out. What will we do? I shall have to tell the whole truth."

Chapter Twenty Six.

Everything seemed to me as if we were in a dream, and I grew more and more troubled as we were marched in separately to the Doctor's library, where to my astonishment I found Burr major and Dicksee standing, while the Doctor sat back in his big chair, with one hand over his eyes.

I glanced once at Mercer, but he did not meet my eyes, and we took our places as pointed out by Mr Rebble, who then stood waiting, and at last coughed softly.

"Yes, Mr Rebble," said the Doctor huskily, as he dropped his hand, and I saw that there was a look of pain on his plump face that I had not seen before. "Yes, Mr Rebble, I see. I was trying to arrange my thoughts, so as to meet this painful case calmly. Pray sit down, Mr Rebble—Mr Hasnip."

The two ushers took chairs, and we boys alone remained standing, while the Doctor cleared his throat, and spoke in a way which drew me toward him as I had never felt drawn before, since, boy-like, I had been rather too apt to look upon my instructor as one of the enemies of my life.

"Gentlemen," he said, "I look upon what I have learned as a catastrophe to my school, a trouble more painful than I can express, but, for all our sakes, I hope that the dark cloud will prove to be a mist of error, which by calm investigation we shall be able to disperse, for, be it understood, I make no accusation."

Mr Rebble and Mr Hasnip both coughed, the Doctor sighed, glanced at me, and then went on.

"Burr major, you have already told me that you had a presentation silver watch from your father."

I had been hoping that I was in error, and that we were called in for reproof about some trivial matter, but now my spirits sank.

"Yes, sir."

"And that, on the day of the cricket match, you left that watch in your vest on the form at the back of the cricket tent?"

"Yes, sir."

"That, when you returned to the tent, and resumed your garments, you afterwards found the watch gone?"

"Yes, sir."

"That every search was made, and that, though, as you say, you had suspicions, about which we will talk by and by, that watch was never found?"

"Yes, sir."

I glanced at Mercer, but he was staring hard at Burr major.

"Now, Dicksee," said the Doctor, "have the goodness to repeat what you told me a short time back."

"Yes, sir," said Dicksee eagerly. "I went up into the big loft over the stable this afternoon, to see if I could find some nice stout pieces of straw in one of the old trusses to make jackstraws with, when I heard somebody coming."

I started as I remembered fancying I heard some one in the loft.

"Yes; go on."

"I looked out of the window, and saw it was Burr junior, so I went and hid myself in the straw."

The rustling I thought was rats.

"Why?" said the Doctor sharply.

"Because Burr junior and Mercer are so jealous about any other boy going up there, and they would have knocked me about, as you know, sir, they did once before, for being up there."

"It isn't true!" I cried.

"Silence, sir," said the Doctor. "You shall be heard afterwards. Go on, Dicksee."

"Yes, sir, please, sir. So I hid under the straw, and then I saw Burr junior come up into the loft, and look round, and out of the window, and everywhere but in the straw."

"State what you saw simply, sir," said the Doctor sternly; "and recollect that you do not stand upon a very good pedestal, for you were playing one of the meanest parts a human being can take, that of a spy."

"Hear! hear!" said the two masters together.

"Please, sir, I was afraid," pleaded Dicksee.

"Go on," said the Doctor.

"And I saw Burr junior open the big bin where he and Mercer keep their rubbish."

"It may not be rubbish to them," said the Doctor, "Go on, sir."

"And after fiddling about a bit, and looking round to see if he was watched, Burr junior took up a stuffed rabbit, put his hand inside, and pulled out some tow, and then he opened that, and took out Burr major's silver watch."

"HE TOOK OUT BURR MAJOR'S SILVER WATCH."

"How do you know it was?" said the Doctor sharply.

"Because we saw it such lots of times, sir, and I knew it again directly."

"It might have been any watch," said the Doctor. "Go on."

"Yes, sir. And he looked at it, and played with it ever so long, and then wrapped it up in tow again, and stuffed it inside the rabbit, and then locked up the bin, put the key in his pocket, and went down."

"And you?"

"I waited till he had gone, sir, and then I ran and told Burr major, sir."

"That will do. Now, Burr major, add what you told me this afternoon; but bear in mind, sir, that it is your duty to be very careful, for this is a charge of theft—of a crime sufficient almost to ruin a school-fellow's career."

Burr major spoke out quickly and eagerly, while I stood with my head down, feeling as if I were being involved in a tangle, out of which it seemed impossible to extricate myself.

"On the day I lost my watch, sir, Burr junior and Mercer were a good deal about near the tent. Burr junior would not play, because he said he had a bad headache, and Tom Mercer wouldn't play either."

"Well, sir?"

"I am very sorry to say it, sir," continued Burr major hesitatingly. "It's a very painful charge to make, and I never said anything before to-day, but I always suspected Burr junior of taking the watch."

"Oh!" I ejaculated indignantly, as I faced round, but he did not meet my eye.

"And, pray, why?" said the Doctor.

"Because, please, sir, he seemed to be hanging about so near the tent."

I began to feel more confused, especially as the Doctor said then, —

"Then now we will adjourn—to the loft." I made a gesture as if to speak, but the Doctor raised his hand.

"After a while, Burr," he said, "after a while. Your turn will come."

I felt in a whirl of emotion, for I was half stunned at the turn matters had taken, and I tried again to catch Mercer's eye, but he did not even glance at me, but stood opening and shutting his hands as he glared at Dicksee, who looked horribly alarmed, and as if he would like to run away.

The Doctor signed to us to go, and we were taken through the house and servants' offices, so as not to attract the attention of the boys, reaching the yard at last, and entering the stable.

My ears seemed to have bells ringing in them as we stood there, and I heard the Doctor say, —

"Rather an awkward place for me to get up, Mr Rebble; but I suppose I must try."

He made the effort after we had all gone before, and reached the top no worse off than by the addition of a little dust upon his glossy black coat. Then, clearing his voice, as we all stood near the bin, in much the same positions as in the library, he began, —

"Ah, that is the straw, I suppose. Burr junior and Mercer have used this place a good deal, I believe, as a kind of atelier or workshop?"

"Yes, sir," said Burr major promptly.

"Then that is the bin, is it, Dicksee?"

"Yes, sir."

"And you say you saw Burr junior lock it up. Have you the key, Burr?"

I stood gazing at him wildly without answering, and then I glanced at Mercer, who met my eye with a look of terror and misery that was piteous to see. For now it was all to come out, and the theft would be brought home to him, for the poor lad to be expelled in disgrace and go home despairingly to those who loved him, and all because he could not restrain that horrible feeling of covetousness.

"I said, 'Have you the key, Burr junior?'" continued the Doctor more sternly, and I shuddered as the thought struck me now that I was becoming mixed up with the trouble, that they would not believe me if I told the truth—that truth which would be so difficult to tell for Mercer's sake.

"Burr junior," cried the Doctor very sharply now, "have you the key of that padlock?"

"Yes; sir," I faltered, giving quite a start now, as his words roused me as from a dream, and I felt horrified as I fully saw how guilty all this made me appear.

"Take the key, Mr Rebble, if you please," continued the Doctor, looking more and more pained, as I withdrew the rusty little instrument from my pocket. "Open the bin, please, and see if Dicksee's statement is made out."

Mr Hasnip was, I found, looking at me, and I felt a choking sensation as he shook his head at me sadly.

Then I glanced at Mercer, and found he was looking at me in a horrified way, and I let my eyes drop as I said to myself,—

"Poor fellow! I shall not have to speak; he'll confess it all. I wish I could save him."

And all the while the usher was unlocking the padlock, taking it from the staple, and throwing open the great lid back against the whitewashed wall, every click and grate of the iron and the creak of the old hinges sounding clear and loud amidst the painful silence.

"Will you come and look, sir?" said Mr Rebble.

"No," said the Doctor sternly. "Is there a rabbit-skin there, as this boy described?"

"Yes, sir."

"Take it out."

Mr Rebble obeyed, and once more I met Mercer's eyes gazing at me wildly, and, as I interpreted the look, imploring me not to speak.

The miserable stuffed distortion was brought out, and I felt half disposed to laugh at it, as I thought of my school-fellow's queer ideas for a group in natural history. But that was only a flying thought, succeeded by a mental pang that was most keen, as the rabbit was laid on the floor, and, acting on the Doctor's instructions, Mr Rebble went down on one knee, held the stuffed animal with one hand, and began to draw out the tow with the other.

A great patch came out, and Mr Rebble pressed it together and then opened it out, and I fancied I heard the Doctor sigh with satisfaction at nothing being found.

"It's further in, sir," cried Dicksee eagerly.

"Ah! you seem to know a great deal about it, Dicksee," said the Doctor.

"Yes, sir; I saw him put it in."

Mr Rebble thrust in his hand again, and my spirits sank lower as he drew out another tuft of tow, compressed it, and then, frowning heavily, began to tear it open.

"There is nothing there, then, Mr Rebble?" cried the Doctor eagerly.

"I am sorry to say, sir, there is," said the usher, as he laid open the tow till it was like a nest, with the little silver watch lying glistening in the middle; and the Doctor drew a long breath, his forehead now full of deeply-cut lines.

"Burr major," said the Doctor huskily. "Have the goodness to look at that watch. Is it yours?"

My school-fellow stepped to the Doctor's side and looked.

"Yes, sir," he said eagerly. "That's the watch I lost."

"How do you know, sir?"

"My father had my initials cut in the little round spot on the case, sir. There they are."

The Doctor took the watch, glanced at the letters, and laid it down.

"Yes," he said sadly, "that is quite right.—Mercer!" Tom started as if he had received a blow, and looked wildly from one to the other.

"Come here."

"Oh, poor, poor Tom!" I sighed to myself, and I looked at him pityingly, while he glanced at me.

"Hah!" ejaculated the Doctor; "there seems to be some understanding between you. Now, sir, that bin has been used by you for some time, has it not, for your collection?"

"Yes, sir," faltered Mercer.

"You and Burr junior have, I noticed, always been companions."

"Yes, sir."

"He joined you in collecting natural history objects?"

"Yes, sir; a little."

"Could he obtain access to that bin when he wished? Had he a key?"

"He could always get the key, sir, when he liked." The Doctor sighed, and there was silence once more, while I glanced at Mercer wildly, and if he could have read my eyes, he would have known that they said, "Speak out now. Confess, and ask the Doctor to forgive you for giving way to this terrible piece of covetousness."

"Now," said the Doctor, and we both started at the firm, sonorous tones, "speak out frankly, sir. This is no time for trying to conceal the truth so as to screen your friend, for I tell you that it would be an unkind act, and you would be injuring his future by such a mistaken policy. Tell me, did you know that the watch was hidden there?"

Mercer was silent.

"Speak, sir," cried the Doctor. "I insist!"

"No, sir," faltered Mercer, after another appealing look at me; and in my agony, as I heard his words, I started forward.

"Burr junior!" roared the Doctor; and I stopped as if fascinated.

"Now, Mercer," he continued, "tell me. Did you know that your school-fellow had that watch in his possession?"

"Oh no, sir!" cried Mercer eagerly. "I'm sure he hadn't."

"Humph!" ejaculated the Doctor. "That will do.—I wish, gentlemen," he continued, turning to the two masters, "to make this painful business as short as possible."

I turned to him quickly, and as I met his eyes, I thought at first that he was looking at me sadly and pityingly, but his face was very stern next moment.

"You are sure, Thomas Mercer," he said, "that you did not know the watch was in that bin—hidden away?"

Tom looked at me again wildly, and then, with his brow all wrinkled up, he said in a hopeless tone full of sadness,—

"No, sir—no, sir; I didn't know it was there."

My hands clenched, and a burst of rage made me turn giddy for the moment. For I felt as if I could have dashed at him, dragged him to his knees, and made him speak the truth.

But that passed off as quickly as it came, and a feeling of pity came for the boy who, in his horror of detection, had felt himself bound to save himself at another's expense, and I found myself wondering whether under the circumstances I should not have done the same.

These thoughts darted through my mind like lightning, and so did those which followed.

"I want to save him," I said to myself, in the midst of the painful silence during which the Doctor stood thinking and softly wiping his forehead and then the palms of his hands upon his white pocket handkerchief; "but I can't take the credit of it all. It is too horrible. But if I tell all I know, he will be expelled, and it will ruin him. Oh, why don't he confess?—why don't he confess?"

It was as if the Doctor had heard these last words as I thought them, for he said now in a deep, grave voice, as he turned to me, just as I was feeling that it would be too cruel to denounce my companion,—

"This is a sad—a painful affair, Burr junior. I wanted to disbelieve in your guilt, I wanted to feel that there was no young gentleman in my establishment who could stoop to such a piece of base pilfering; but the truth is so circumstantially brought home through the despicable meanness of a boy of whose actions I feel the utmost abhorrence, that I am bound to say to you that there is nothing left but for you to own frankly that you have been led into temptation—to say that you bitterly repent of what you have done, and throw yourself upon my mercy. Do this at once, boy, for the sake of those at home who love you."

I felt my face twitch at these words and the picture they evoked, and then, numbed as it were, I stood listening, slightly buoyed up by the feeling that Mercer would speak directly and clear me.

"You were entrusted to my care, Burr junior," continued the Doctor, "as a youth who was in future to enter upon one of the most honourable of careers, that of a soldier; but now that you have disgraced yourself like this—"

"No, no, sir!" I cried. "Don't—pray don't think I took the wretched watch!"

There was so much passionate agony in my voice that the Doctor paused for a few moments, before, in the midst of the solemn silence which ensued, he said coldly,—

"Do you deny that you took the watch?"

"Yes, yes. Indeed, indeed I did not take it, sir!" The Doctor sighed.

"Do you deny that you were seen by Dicksee this morning with the watch in your hands?"

"No, sir; that is true," I said, with a look at Mercer, who hung down his head.

"Then I am bound by the statements that have been made, painful as it is to me, to consider that in a moment of weak impulse you did this base thing. If I am wrong, Heaven forgive me, for *humanum est errare*. The truth, however, seems too clear."

"I—I found it there," I panted.

The Doctor shook his head.

"It is like charging your school-fellow with stealing the watch. Do you do this?"

I was silent.

"Mr Rebble," said the Doctor, "you came here as a gentleman to aid me in the training of these youths. Can you do anything to help me here?"

"I—I," said Mr Rebble huskily, "would gladly do so, sir, if I could. I wouldn't trust Dicksee's word in anything. He is as pitiful and contemptible a boy as ever came under my charge, but I am afraid he has spoken the truth here."

"I fear so," said the Doctor. "Mr Hasnip, you have—been but a short time among us, still you have learned the disposition of the pupils. Can you help me—help us?—for it is terrible to me to have to pass judgment in such a case."

"Doctor Browne," cried Mr Hasnip warmly, and I saw the tears start to his eyes, "I would give anything to be able to say it is all a mistake."

"But you feel that you can not?"

Mr Hasnip shook his head, and turned away to hide the working of his face, while I stood wondering at the feeling he displayed.

There was again a painful silence, and I stood there, shrinking, but with a hot feeling of anger swelling within me, waiting for Tom Mercer to speak out and save me from disgrace. And with this hot tide of bitterness and rage that I should be so doubted and suspected, came a feeling of obstinacy that was maddening, while something within me seemed to say, "They would not believe you if you spoke."

"No," said the Doctor at last, "I am afraid that you cannot; and I now address myself to you, Burr junior. Do you confess that you are guilty?"

"No, sir," I cried angrily, "I am not!" and again there was silence.

"I think I will give you time for reflection," said the Doctor. "Mr Rebble, I place Burr junior in your charge. Of course he must be secluded. I, too, want time for reflection before sending word to the unhappy lad's friends—a most painful task—a most painful task."

He walked slowly toward the steps, and a fresh feeling of excitement surged up within me. I wanted to speak now—to say something in my own defence, as I thought of the Doctor's letter going to my mother, and of her agony, then of my uncle learning this, and coming over. It seemed too terrible, and I tried to call the Doctor back, but no words would come. I saw him descend slowly, and Mr Hasnip sign to the boys to follow, after which, giving me a sad look, he too descended, leaving me alone with Mr Rebble, whose first words were so stern and harsh that I could not turn to him and confide and ask his sympathy and help.

"This way, sir," he said sharply, and without a word I followed him down and across the stable-yard, passing cook at the door ready to give me a pitying glance for being in disgrace.

Then, as if it was all a dream, I was led into the house, and up-stairs to a small room containing only one bed—a room whose window looked out away toward the General's estates.

The door was closed behind me without a word, and as I stood there I heard it locked and the key withdrawn, followed by Mr Rebble's footsteps along the passage, and then I threw myself down on the bed in a passion of rage against Mercer.

"You coward!" I cried, and as I ground my teeth I indulged in a wish that I could have him there.

"Oh!" I cried, "only for half an hour, and then—" I did not finish my sentence, but bounded off the bed to stand up there alone, unconsciously enough in the position Lomax had taught me, and with my left hand raised to strike.

Chapter Twenty Seven.

It was very different to be a prisoner now alone. I longed for Mercer's companionship, but it was so that I might punish him for what I again and again called his miserable cowardice, which seemed to me to make his crime ten times worse. And so I walked up and down the little room restlessly, thinking over the times when my school-fellow had talked about the watch, and his intense longing to possess it, or such a one.

Nothing could be plainer. He had given way at last, and taken it on that unlucky day when he was hanging about talking to me as I lay on the grass with my head throbbing, and then walking away toward the tent or to where he could get a good look at the cricketers.

"Too much for him," I said, — "too much for him, and I am to take the credit of his theft. But I will not. If he is such a mean coward as to let me take his stealing on my shoulders, he is not worth sparing, and he shall take the credit for himself—upon his own shoulders and not mine."

"Oh, what an ass I have been ever to make friends with such a fellow!" I cried, after a pause. "I ought to have known better. Never mind, I do know better now, and to-morrow morning I'll ask to see the Doctor, and I'll tell him everything, and—get him expelled!"

That set me thinking once more about his people at home, and as I did, I began to waver, and call to mind how terrible it would be, and that I liked him too well in spite of all.

For I did like him. I had never had a brother, and he had seemed to fill his place, so that now, for the first time, I fully understood how we two lads had become knit together, and how terribly hard it would be to speak out.

I sat down by the window at last, to let the cool breeze play upon my aching temples, and as I leaned my head against the side, the cheery voices of the boys in the field floated up to me, to make me more wretched still.

"It's nothing to them," I said to myself. "Nobody there cares, and Eely and Dicksee were only too glad to have their revenge upon me. I don't know, though," I said; "they both thought I took the watch, and believed all they said. But it was a triumph for them."

I sat thinking.

"I wonder what Lomax will say? Will he believe that I am a common thief?

"What is Tom doing now? Out at play, I suppose, and glorying in his escape. He knows I would not be such a sneak as to tell, and thinks I shall bear it all patiently—too ready to spare him, or too cowardly to say a word."

I was interrupted by steps, and in my misery I hoped that they would pass the door, but a key was thrust in, and I caught a glimpse of Mr Rebble, who waited outside while one of the maids brought in my tea on a tray,—a plain mug, and a plate of bread and butter; then she gave me a look of commiseration, making my cheeks burn, as I wondered whether she knew that I was shut up because people thought I was a thief, and unfit to associate with the other boys. But no word was spoken; she passed out, the door was shut and locked, and I rested my aching head once more against the side of the window, the very sight of food making me feel disgust; and there I stayed for how long I cannot say, but at last I started up, puzzled and wondering, to find that I must have dropped asleep, regularly wearied out, and that it was growing dusk, and the moon, like a thin curved streak, was sailing down in the faint glow of the heavens, not far from where the sun had gone.

I shivered a little, for I was cold, but my head was better, and I began to go over the events of the afternoon again, wondering whether the

Doctor would send for me in the morning, to say that Mercer had confessed, and that he was glad to be able once more to take me by the hand.

Just then I heard a faint sigh, apparently coming up from the garden, and I involuntarily looked down, but could see nothing.

The sigh rose again, and now I was able to locate it in a clump of evergreens at the edge of the lawn. But I could see nothing save green leaves; and started again and drew back a little a few minutes later, as the sigh was again repeated, this time followed by a faint whisper, and I heard my name.

"Frank—Frank Burr. Hist!"

"Yes; who called?" I said.

"Me. Can't you hear? Tom—Tom Mercer."

I was silent, and stood, feeling hot and angry, gazing down into the grounds.

"Frank!" came up again. "I say!"

I remained silent.

"Have you got any string? Let a piece down."

I knew what that meant. He had been to the kitchens and was going to send me up some supper. In other words, he was going to try and smooth over his despicable behaviour.

"A coward! A sneak! I hate him!" I muttered, as I stood there close to the window, as if unable to drag myself away, but listening greedily all the while, as Mercer went on in an excited whisper, insulting me, as I called it.

"Oh, I say, do speak, Frank," he said. "I can't stop long, and there'd be a row if any one knew I came to you. I am so sorry, Frank. I've been down to Polly Hopley's, and bought a lot of her turnovers and some sweet tuck. I want to send it up to you. Haven't you any string?"

I made no reply.

"Frank! I say: I know: tear up your handkerchiefs. I'll give you some of mine to make up. Tie the bits together so as to make a long string, and let it down. Frank!"

"Go away, you miserable, cowardly sneak!" I cried passionately; "and never dare to speak to me again."

He was silent for a few minutes, as if stunned by my fierce words. Then he began again.

"Oh, I say," he whispered, "don't turn on a chap like that when he was going to stick to you. I couldn't help it."

I knew that the temptation had been too strong for him, but I was none the less bitter against him, and my wrath reached its climax soon after, when he said eagerly, —

"I say, Frank, I am indeed so sorry! and I'd have said it was I did it, if it would have got you off; but they wouldn't have believed me."

Bang!

That was the window, which, in my passion at his coolness, I shut down with all my might, and then went and threw myself on the bed, with my head aching violently, and the sensation of misery increasing, so that at times I felt as if I must try and break open the door, creep down in the night, and run away somewhere — anywhere, so as to end the trouble I was in.

I never knew when, but I suppose the throbbing in my head must have lulled a little, and I once more dropped off to sleep, to wake up with a start in the darkness, wondering where I was, and whether I had been having a confused dream about a watch being stolen, and some one getting into trouble. Who it was I could not quite tell, for my head ached, I felt sick, and everything was confused and strange.

While I was trying hard to collect myself, I suppose I must have dropped to sleep again, for when I next opened my eyes, the sun was shining brightly, and, light-hearted and eager, I jumped off the bed to run and open the window, but, as my feet touched the floor, memory began to come back with its heavy load of misery.

Why was I dressed even to my boots? Why was I in a fresh room? Where was Tom Mercer?

The answers to my questions came, and I stood there with a sinking sensation of misery, increasing moment by moment, till with a sigh I roused myself a little and went toward the window.

"Where is Tom Mercer?" I said to myself again, with a bitter laugh. "Safe, and I am to take the blame for his miserable acts. Where's Tom Mercer?"

I was opening the window as I spoke, and there he was hiding behind a clump of Portugal laurel, where he had been watching, quite ready to spring up eagerly now, and begin to make signs, as he showed me a school bag with something heavy inside.

I knew what it meant, of course, but the bitter feeling against him was too intense for me to accept aid in any form, and I drew back without noticing him further; and, as I did so, my head felt clearer for my night's rest, and I began to see the course that was open to me.

I could not turn upon Tom and become his accuser, for, if the crime was brought home to him, it would be terrible, and I knew I should never forgive myself for saving my own credit by denouncing my companion. No; I had fully made up my mind, in those few minutes since rising, to deny firmly and defiantly the charge of taking the watch. Even if they expelled me, and I was sent away, they might call it in disgrace, but it would not be. And even if Doctor Browne and the masters believed me guilty, I knew there was some one at home who would take my word at once, indignant at such a charge being brought against me.

Yes, that was my course, plain enough: to maintain my innocence firmly, but to say no more. They might find out about Tom Mercer. I would not betray him.

A stubborn feeling of determination came over me now, and all seemed to be as plain as could be. I was actually beginning to wonder that I should have taken it all so much to heart. "She will believe me," I said; "and they will have to at last."

I had just arrived at this point in reasoning out my position, when I was brought to a sudden check by a fresh thought—one which made me turn cold. It was, "What will uncle say?"

I was thrown back into a state of the greatest misery again directly by this. For my uncle was so stern a disciplinarian that in advance I saw with horror the impression such a charge hanging over me would make upon one who had so often impressed upon me the duties of him who would grow up to be a gentleman, and who was to occupy the position of an officer in a gallant service.

"Shall I dare to hold out?" I asked myself; "shall I be able to clear myself without accusing Tom?"

I started, for there was a thud at my window, as if something moderately soft had struck the frame.

But I could see nothing, and I was sinking back into my musing fit again, when something struck me on the back, and then fell with a dull sound upon the floor and rolled under the wash-stand.

I stooped and picked it up, to find that it was one of the solid indiarubber balls we used for our games at rounders, and tightly fastened around it was a piece of thin twine, the strong, light string we used for kites. The twine hung out of the window, and I knew that Mercer had thrown it up, and the second time sent it right in at the open sash,—no difficult task for him, as he was one of the most skilful throwers we had in the school, and he could generally hit a boy running fast when we were engaged in a game, while at cricket, the way in which he could field a ball, and send it up to the wicket-keeper, made him a special acquisition in a game.

"I'm not going to be bribed into silence!" I cried; "I'd sooner starve;" and, going quickly to the window, I hurled the ball down, before drawing back, and then approaching the opening again to peer down from behind one of the white dimity curtains, where, unseen myself, I could watch Mercer slowly winding up the string till the indiarubber ball reached his hands, when, after a doleful look up, he ducked down behind the bushes with the school bag and walked cautiously away.

Chapter Twenty Eight.

Human nature is a curious thing, and the older one grows the more strange and wonderful it seems. There was I watching Tom Mercer from the window, and the minute before I felt as if I would have given anything to have him there alone with our jackets off, to put in force the old sergeant's teaching, knowing that I could in my passion nearly knock his head off. The next minute, as I saw him walk dejectedly away with his head down, evidently bitterly hurt and disappointed, I found myself sorry for him, and wanting to call him back.

And this was from no desire to partake of the good things he had, I was perfectly sure, in the bag, for in my misery I had no appetite or desire to eat anything, but from honest liking for the boy who had been my companion from the first.

But I was too proud to call him back, and in my anger I mentally called him a contemptible, cowardly thief, and vowed that I would never speak to him again.

Boys always keep those vows, of course—for an hour or two, and then break them, and a good thing too. They would be horrible young misanthropes if they did not.

So Tom Mercer was gone, with his bagful, string, and indiarubber ball, and I plumped myself down on a chair by the window, rested my crossed arms on the inner ledge, and, placing my chin upon them, sat staring out over the beautiful Sussex landscape, thinking about what was to come.

But, mingled with those thoughts, there came plenty of memories of the past; as my eyes lit on the woods and fields, with a glint of one of the General's ponds where we boys had fished.

Oh, how lovely it all looked that sunny morning, with the rays flashing from the dewy grass and leaves, and how impossible it seemed that I could be so unhappy, shut up there like a prisoner, and looked upon by every one as a thief!

What should I do? Wait for the truth to come out, or behave like any high-spirited boy would,—high-spirited and gallant from my point of view,—set them all at defiance, wait for my opportunity, and escape—go right away and seek my fortune?

No, I did not want any fortune. My uncle wished me to be a soldier, as my father had been, and that meant study for years, then training perhaps at Woolwich, and at last a commission.

"I will not wait for that," I said to myself; "I'll be a soldier at once. I'll go and enlist, and rise from the ranks, and in years to come, when I am a captain or a major, I will go back home, and tell them that I was perfectly innocent, and they'll be sorry they believed that I was a thief."

These romantic thoughts put me in better spirits, and I began to plan what I would do, and how I could get away, for I could not see in my excitement what a young donkey I was to fill my head with such nonsense, and what a mean, cowardly thing it would be to go off, and make my supposed guilt a certainty with my uncle, break my mother's heart, and generally throw all my future to the winds— always supposing it possible that I could have found any recruiting sergeant who would have taken such a slip of a boy, as, of course, I could not; for to a certainty I should have been laughed at, and come away like a frightened cur, with my tail between my legs.

I was mentally blind then, puffed up with vanity, and as bitter and angry as it is possible for a boy to be, and all I can say in extenuation is that I had had good cause to be upset by the trouble I had gone through.

"I'll go," I said excitedly. "To-night as soon as it is dark, and—"

I stopped short, for I saw a familiar figure going along the road in front of the great house. It was Lomax, having his morning pipe and walk before going back to his garden, and the sight of the old sergeant made me feel sorry for my determination. He had been so friendly, and under his stiff military ways there had been so much kindliness. He had been so proud of the way in which I had acquired the things he taught; and as he went on, tall, upright, and manly-looking, I began to wonder what he would say, and I exclaimed eagerly,—

"He'll know that I have gone off to join the army, and say I have done well."

Down came a wet blanket.

"No," I said dolefully; "he will think I have run away because I was a thief."

"I can't go. It is impossible for me to go," I said passionately, as I began to pace the room, and sheets torn up and tied together with counterpane and blankets, to make out the rope down which I was to slide to liberty, fell away as if they were so much tinder; while the other plan I had of unscrewing the lock of the door, and taking it off with my pocket-knife, so as to steal down the stairs, tumbled to nothing, as soon as I thought that I must steal away.

Just then I started, for there was a tap at the door—a very soft, gentle tap, and then a hoarse whisper.

"Master Burr! Master Burr!"

"Yes," I said sourly. "Who is it? What do you want?"

"It's me, my dear. Cook. I'm just going down. Are you dressed yet?"

"Yes."

"I heard last night that you were shut up. Whatever is the matter?"

I was silent.

"Master Mercer came and told me, and asked me for something to eat for you, because he said he knew they'd only give you bread and water."

"Master Mercer!" I muttered to myself angrily; "and I'm to suffer for him!"

"There, I won't bother you, my dear, but I'm very sorry, and I don't suppose it's anything much. Have you broken a window?"

"No, Cook."

"Now don't say you've been stealing apples, because I'd have given you lots if you'd asked."

"No," I said softly, for the woman's voice sounded so pleasant and sympathetic that I wanted her to stay.

"Then I know: you've been breaking bounds. Oh dear, boys will be boys, and it's quite natural, my dear, for you to want to get away, and run where you like. I don't wonder, shut up as you all are, like being in a cage. There, don't you fret, and it'll all come right. I'll see that you have something beside bread and water. Bread and water, indeed! Such stuff as is only to cook with. Why, they might just as well feed you on flour."

"What time is it, Cook?" I asked.

"Just gone six, my dear; and there: I mustn't stop gossiping, for I've my fire to light, my kitchen to do; but I hate people to be miserable. I can't abide it. There's plenty of worries with one's work, as I told missus only yesterday. There, good-bye, and don't you fret."

I heard the rustling of her dress as she went along the passage, and I stood by the door till it died away, feeling sad but pleased, for it was satisfactory to know that there were people about the place who cared for me. But I felt more low-spirited directly as I thought of what she might say as soon as she knew the real cause of why I was a prisoner.

The bell rang for rising, and I heard some of the boys soon after out in their gardens; then, as I stood back from the window, I caught sight of one or two, and after a while heard the increasing hum and buzz of voices, and knew that some of them must be getting up lessons that had been neglected over-night. And as I listened, I thought of the times when I had murmured and felt dissatisfied at being obliged to give so much time to such work, whereas now I was envying the happy boys who were seated at study, with no greater care upon their minds.

Perhaps I was learning a great lesson then, one that I did not know.

The time went on very slowly, and it seemed many hours since I awoke, when the breakfast-bell rang, and I sat picturing the scene, and fancying I could hear the boys talking and the mugs and spoons clattering, as the great piles of bread and butter disappeared.

I was just thinking this when there were steps in the passage, and soon after the key was rattled in the lock, Mr Rebble appeared, and with him one of the maids, with a tray on which was a mug and a plate of bread and butter.

He did not look at me, only admitted the maid to set down the tray, saw her out, and I was locked in again.

It was very much like the old time, but Tom Mercer was not there to lighten my loneliness.

As the door closed, I noticed that the mug was steaming, and found that I was not to have prison fare though I was a prisoner, for my breakfast was precisely the same as that of the other boys.

"I can't touch it," I said, "It is impossible to eat."

But I was feverishly thirsty, and I took up the mug of milk, just made warm by the addition of some boiling water. It was pleasantly sweet, too, and I half fancied that Cook had put in an extra quantity of sugar.

More from habit than anything else, for I felt sick and full of distaste for food, I broke off a piece of bread and butter and began to eat it mechanically, and now knew that I was right, for, instead of the salt butter we generally had, this was fresh and sweet. Cook had certainly been favouring me, and that scrap led to the finishing of the slice, and finally to the disappearance of all that was on the plate, while the last drop of milk and water was drained from the big mug.

As soon as the breakfast was finished, a morbid feeling of vexation came over me. I was angry because I had touched it, and wished that I had sulked, and shown myself too much injured to go on as if nothing had happened. But it was too late then.

After a while, Mr Rebble came back, looking very severe. He watched the maid as she took the tray, but the girl gave me a sympathetic look, and then I was once more left alone.

Hard people think they do not,—they say, "Oh, he's only a boy; he'll soon forget,"—but boys suffer mentally as keenly, or more keenly, than grown people. Of course they do, for everything about them is young, tender, and easily wounded. I know that they soon recover from some mental injury. Naturally. They are young and elastic, and the sapling, if bent down, springs up again, but for the time they suffer cruelly.

I know I did, shut up there in disgrace, and, as I sat or walked about my prison, it made no difference to me that it was a plainly furnished, neat bedroom, for it was as prison-like to me in my vein as if the floor had been stone, the door of iron-clamped oak with rusty hinges. And as I moved about the place, I began to understand how prisoners gladly made friends with spiders, mice, and rats, or employed themselves cutting their names on the walls, carving pieces of wood, or writing long histories.

But I had no insects or animals to amuse me, no wood to carve, no stone walls upon which to chisel my name.

I had only been a prisoner for a few hours, you may say.

Quite true, but, oh, what hours they were, and what agony I suffered from my thoughts!

I spent most of my time at the window, forcing myself to think of how things were going on in school, and I pictured the boys at their lessons—at the Doctor's desk at Mr Rebble's, and Mr Hasnip's. It was German day, too, and I thought about our quaint foreign master, and about Lomax drilling the boys in the afternoon. He would be asking them where I was; and the question arose in my mind, would the boys tell him, or would they have had orders, as we did once before, about a year back, when a pupil disgraced himself, not to mention the affair outside the school walls.

My spirits rose a little at this, for it would be horrible for Lomax to know, and go and think it over. And I seemed to know that he would take it more to heart about me than if it were any other boy, for I was to be a soldier, and, as he would have expressed it, "One of ours."

Dinner-time at last—the bell ringing, and the shouts and cries of the boys, "All in! all in!" though we used to want very little calling for meals.

After a time, my dinner was brought up, as my breakfast had been, in silence, and I felt then that I should have liked Mr Rebble to speak, if it had only been to bully. But he did not so much as look at me, only stalked into the room and out again.

Who was going to eat and enjoy a dinner, brought like that?

"It's like an animal in a cage being fed," I said angrily; and I was quite angry because the roast beef, potatoes, and greens smelt so nice that I was obliged to sit down and eat and enjoy the meal, for I was very hungry.

After the tray had been fetched, I made up my mind that at any minute now the Doctor might send for me, to give me a severe examination, and I shivered at the idea of being forced to speak out, and say everything I knew. I wished now that it was dark, so that I might have attempted to escape, if only to avoid that meeting. But it was impossible. Even if I could get off the lock, I should be seen, for certain, and brought back in an ignominious fashion, that would be terrible.

But the afternoon wore away, as I sat listening to the shouts of the boys at play, thinking bitterly of how little they thought of me shut up there; and I began wondering where Mercer was, little thinking that he was watching me; but he was, sure enough, for, just close upon tea-time, I caught sight of him, lying down upon his chest, where he had crawled unseen among the shrubs, and there he was, with his elbows on the ground and his chin in his hands, watching me, just as a faithful dog might his master.

I shrank away from the window, as soon as I saw him, and then waited till the bell rang for tea, when I peeped out again, to see that he was gone, but I could trace him by the movement of the laurels, bays, and lilacs, whose branches were thrust aside as he crept through.

"He'll come back again after tea," I thought, and I was right. I had only just finished my own, brought up as before, when, glancing from the window, there I saw him, gazing up at me like a whipped dog, asking to be taken into favour once again.

"Why hasn't the Doctor sent for me?" I asked myself; but I could find only one reason,—he meant me to come to his study quite late in the evening.

But he did not, and that dreary time passed slowly away, as I watched the darkness come on, and the stars peer out one by one.

Then I saw the moon rise far away over the sea, shining brightly, till the sky grew cloudy, as my life seemed now to be.

But no footstep—no summons to go down to the Doctor's room, and, though I kept on fancying that I heard steps on the stairs, I was always deceived, and it was not until I heard the bell ring for prayers and bed, that I knew I should not have to meet the Doctor that night.

There were steps enough now in the corridors and on the stairs, and I sat near the door, for the sake of the company, naming the boys to myself, as I recognised the voices. But I shrank away once, as two boys stopped by my door, and I heard them say,—

"Wonder how old Burr junior's getting on?"

"Ah! he's in for it now. Don't talk, or he'll hear us."

They passed on, and I heard their door close, after which there was a loud scuffling and bumping from the other sides accompanied by smothered laughter and dull blows.

I knew directly what was going on, and sighed, as I recalled how many times I had engaged in the forbidden joys of a bolstering match.

Their merriment only made me feel the pain the more bitterly, and I was glad when I heard a familiar cough at the end of the passage, and the tapping of a stick on the floor.

All was silent in an instant, and by degrees every murmur died away, and I lay down and slept heavily, for mine was weary trouble. There was no guilty conscience to keep me awake.

Chapter Twenty Nine.

I was up in good time next morning, to find that Tom Mercer was beforehand with me, waiting in the shrubbery, and making signs now as soon as he saw me; but I turned away, and with a disconsolate look, he dropped down among the bushes, and crouched where he would be screened.

He disappeared at breakfast-time, but he was back there before dinner, and for a time after, but he suddenly rushed away, and I supposed that some of the boys were coming round to that side of the great house.

Then came another weary time of waiting, and I was beginning to think that I should escape again, when there were steps on the stairs—the decided, heavy steps of Mr Rebble, who always stamped when he came up by the boys' bedrooms—to give him importance, we used to say.

It was not a meal-time, so I felt that at last I was to be taken down to the Doctor's library. Then the door was unlocked, thrown open, and the master said loudly, "Burr junior, the Doctor wishes to see you in his room."

My heart began to beat heavily as I followed him down-stairs, and then through the door on to the front staircase with its thick carpet. The hall was reached, and Mr Rebble crossed to the library, waited till I was on the mat, threw the door wide-open and seemed to scoop me in.

A low murmur of voices fell on my ear as the door was opened, and I knew that I was not to see the Doctor alone, but I did not anticipate facing such a gathering as I gazed at wildly, with my heart throbbing, my cheeks hot, and a film coming over my eyes.

For there before me were the Doctor and his lady, Mr Hasnip, and Mercer, Burr major, and Dicksee. I saw them at a glance, my eyes hardly resting upon them, for there were three strangers in the room, and I divined now why it was that I had not been fetched before.

I was to meet those who had placed me at the school; while beside my mother and my uncle there stood the old General, gazing at me with a very severe scowl.

For a few moments no one spoke, and I felt giddy. A mist was before my eyes, and everything looked blurred and strange, but through it all I could see my mother's eyes gazing yearningly at me, and she half rose from her seat to take me to her heart, but my uncle laid his hand upon her arm and said firmly, —

"Wait, dear. Let us know the whole business first."

And then, as my mother sank back into her seat, I saw Mrs Doctor take a seat by her side, whisper something, and my mother took her hand.

"Now, Doctor Browne, if you please," said my uncle in his sharp, quick, military way, "we are all attention, and want to hear the truth of this miserable business before the boy himself."

"Certainly, Colonel Seaborough," said the Doctor rather nervously, but he spoke firmly directly after. "I thought it my duty first to ask you to come, as I naturally was most loth to proceed to extremities."

"Naturally, sir, naturally," said my uncle sharply. "A prisoner's allowed a fair court-martial, eh, Rye?"

"Yes, yes, of course," said the General, and he opened a gold box and took snuff loudly.

As soon as I could tear my eyes from my mother's, I looked across at the three boys defiantly: at Burr major, who turned his eyes away uneasily; at Dicksee, who was looking at me with a sneering grin upon his countenance, a grin which faded directly into a very uncomfortable look, and he too turned away, and whispered something to Burr major; but by this time my eyes were fixed fiercely upon Mercer, who met my gaze with a pitiful expression, which I read directly to mean, "Don't, pray don't say I did it. They'd never forgive me. They will you. Pray, pray, don't tell!"

I turned from him with a choking sensation of anger rising in my throat, and then stood listening, as all the old business was gone through, much as it had been up in the loft, but with this exception, that in the midst of Burr major's statement the General gazed at him so fiercely that my school-fellow faltered, and quite blundered through his answers.

"One moment, Doctor Browne," said the General. "Here, you, sir; you don't like Frank Burr, do you?"

"Well, sir, I—"

"Answer my question, sir. You don't like him, do you?"

"N–no, sir."

"Thrashed you well, didn't he, for bullying?"

"I had an encounter with Burr junior, sir."

"Yes, and he thrashed you well, I know."

"I beg your pardon, Sir Hawkhurst," said the Doctor warmly. "My pupil here, Burr major, has, I am well aware, been exceedingly tyrannical to his schoolfellows, and when it reached my ears by a side wind that he had been soundly thrashed by his fellow pupil here, I must own to having been glad; but as his tutor it behoves me to say that he is a boy of strictly honourable feelings, and I do not believe he would speak as he has done if he did not believe the truth of all he has said."

"Humph!" said the General. "Quite right, Doctor, quite right. I'm afraid I was unjust."

Then Dicksee, who looked green, made his statement, and before he had done, the General thumped his stick down on the floor loudly.

"Here, Doctor: this fellow won't do at all. He's a sneak and a miserable, malicious scoundrel. You can see it all over his face. You're not going to take up the cudgels for him, are you?"

"I am sorry to say I cannot," replied the Doctor gravely; "and if this sad business rested upon his word alone, I should not have acted as I have; but, as you have heard and will hear, Sir Hawkhurst, we have terribly strong evidence. I wish it were otherwise."

And again the weary business went on, with my mental agony increasing as I saw my mother's eyes fixed upon me. At first imploringly, then they seemed to be full of pain, and later on it seemed to me as if she, were suffering from a sorrow that was too hard for her to bear.

Then she would flush up angrily, and turn a reproachful look upon my uncle, as he questioned the boys and the masters, entered into what seemed to be angry controversies with the Doctor, and generally went against me all through, until I began to look at him with horror, as the greatest enemy I had in the room.

That I was not alone in my opinion was soon evident, for I heard the Doctor sigh, and look reproachfully at him, while twice over Sir Hawkhurst uttered a gruff,—

"No, no, sir. Oh, come, come, Seaborough, be just."

"I am trying to be just," said my uncle sternly, after the General had said this last again. "Recollect, sir, I stand in the position of this boy's father. He is my dear sister's only child, and it has been my great desire to have him brought up as a worthy successor to his brave father,—as a soldier and a gentleman,—and because I speak firmly and feel warmly upon the subject, you say, 'Be just.'"

"Well, well," cried the General, "you have struck me several times as being hard."

"Yes, Sir Hawkhurst," assented the Doctor; "perhaps too hard."

"Absurd, gentlemen!" cried my uncle. "I'm not the boy's mother, to forgive him after a few tears, and tell him he must be a good boy, and never do so again."

"Colonel Seaborough," cried Mrs Doctor reproachfully, "and pray who is to forgive, if it is not a mother?"

"A beautiful sentiment, madam," cried my uncle; "but you forget that, after building up my hopes on this boy's success in life, I am suddenly summoned, not to come ready to defend him from the foul charge, but to have it literally forced upon me that my nephew — No, I'll discard him. If this really is true, and he is proved to be a pitiful, unmanly, contemptible thief, I have done with him for ever."

"No, no, sir," said the Doctor. "You shall not say that. You are a Christian, and you belie your own belief."

"Belie it or no, sir, I cannot bear this!" cried my uncle fiercely. "Now, Frank, speak out. Did you take that contemptible toy?"

"No, uncle," I said firmly.

"Come: that's something. That's the truth or a lie. That wretched fellow says he saw you with the watch in your hand: is that true?"

"Yes, uncle."

"That he saw you hide it in the box?"

"Yes, uncle."

"You locked it up there?"

"Yes, uncle."

"Another question: did you know whose watch it was?"

"Yes, uncle."

"And that it was stolen?"

"Yes, uncle."

"And you were not going to speak about it being in your possession?"

"No, uncle."

There was a terrible pause, and in the midst of the silence, my uncle went on.

"One word or two more, sir. On the day the watch was missed, you refused to play?"

"Yes, uncle."

"And you went and lay down near the tent?"

"Yes, uncle; I had been very ill."

There was another pause, followed by a low murmur among those present, and then, in a fierce voice full of contemptuous rage, my uncle thundered, —

"Now, sir, have you any more to say?" and my mother sank back in her seat with a low moan.

Chapter Thirty.

"Now, sir, have you any more to say?"

A simple enough question, but when spoken to me sternly before those present, in my uncle's fierce, military voice, and accompanied by looks that seemed crushing in their contempt, they were very hard to bear in that strange silence which followed.

There they all stood and sat about me, while I felt like a prisoner at the bar before my judge. It was terrible, and I wavered.

Should I speak, and accuse poor, weak, amiable Tom Mercer, and send him away in disgrace, or should I suffer now, and wait till the truth came out by and by?

I was deciding on the latter, when I heard a sob which seemed to echo in my throat, and I looked up quickly from where my eyes had rested on a particular spot in the pattern of the library carpet, to see my mother's convulsed face and yearning eyes fixed upon me, as Mrs Doctor stood by her side, holding her hand quite affectionately.

That look decided me.

"Poor Tom," I said to myself, "I must throw you over for her sake;" and my lips parted to speak, when my uncle checked me by his stern, harsh voice.

"Silent! The silence of guilt!" he cried bitterly. "I have —"

"Stop a moment, Seaborough," cried the General. "Let me have a word, for poor dead Burr's sake. Frank, boy, I've always liked you, and believed in you, as the bright, manly son of a dear dead friend. Don't let me go away feeling that I can never trust any one again. I won't believe it—I can't believe it—that the blood and breed in your young veins would let you stoop to be a miserable, contemptible thief, and for the sake of a paltry silver watch. Why, my dear boy, you must have known that, as soon as you were old enough to want a watch, you could have had a gold one of the very best. Why, hang it all, sir, for your father's and mother's sake, I'd have hung you all over watches. Come now, speak out before us all like a man, and tell us what all this mystery means. Tell us that you did not steal this watch."

"Why, of course he didn't!" cried a familiar voice, and as I started round at these hopeful words, which seemed to give me life, I saw Cook busily tying the strings of her best cap, the one my mother had sent her, before untying and snatching off her apron, as if she had come to the library in such a hurry that she had not had time to prepare.

"Cook!" exclaimed Mrs Doctor sternly.

"Oh, yes, ma'am, I know," cried Cook defiantly, as she reached back and caught somebody's arm just outside the door. "Here, you come in, Polly 'Opley; there's nothing to be ashamed of, my dear. You come in."

Polly Hopley, dressed in her best, suffered herself to be dragged in, and then, after whispering, "Do adone, do, Cook," began to make bobs and courtesies to everybody in turn.

"Er—rum!" coughed the Doctor. "My good woman," he cried severely, "what is the meaning of this intrusion?"

"You may call it what you like, sir," cried Cook sharply; "and you too, mum," she continued, turning to Mrs Doctor, "and give me my month, or distant ismissal if you like."

Cook meant to say, "instant dismissal," but she was excited, and, giving a defiant look round, she went on, —

"I don't care, and I says it's a shame, not alone to keep the poor boy locked up like a prisoner, and badly fed, as does a growing boy no end of harm; and I will say it, mum," she continued, turning to my mother, "as dear and good a boy as ever came into this school, but to go and say he was a thief, as he couldn't be, sir. You look in his eyes and see."

This to the Doctor, who coughed again.

"My good woman, I must insist upon you leaving the room."

"A moment, Doctor," cried my uncle eagerly; "this person seems to know something. Stop!"

"I wasn't a-going, sir," said Cook sharply, "not till I've spoke out what I've come to say."

"Then, for goodness' sake, speak, woman, and go," cried the Doctor angrily. "We are engaged."

"Which well I know it, sir, and I'm going to speak," said Cook, with dignity; "and if I'd known before Polly 'Opley—your keeper's wife's daughter, Sir Orkus," she continued, turning to the General.

"Oh yes, yes, yes, I knew Polly when she was a baby," said the old gentleman, nodding at the girl, who courtesied to him; "but if you know anything about this—this terrible affair, speak out."

"Which I will, sir, and if I lose my place, and you do happen to want a good plain—"

"Cook, Cook, pray speak out," cried Mrs Doctor.

"Which I'm trying to, ma'am, only you all flurry me so. You see I knowed as Master Burr was shut up, something about some trouble or scrape—as boys will be boys, and always was, but being busy in my kidgen, and plenty to do, and the young gentlemen all forbid to say what it was about, so as I never knowed till this morning, when Polly 'Opley comes and tells me all about it, as Mr Lomax goes and tells her father—your keeper, sir—and Polly only this morning, and she never knowed it before, and then came on and told me something as'll make you all ashamed of treating a poor boy like that."

"Yes, yes, yes," said my uncle impatiently; "but do you know anything about the watch?"

"Which I'm telling you, sir," cried Cook, "though not a word did I know till Polly 'Opley comes just now, when I see it all as plain as pie-crust, and I says to her, 'Polly,' I says, 'they're all in the libery now, and you shall come and tell 'em the whole truth.'"

"Then you know, Polly, my child?" said the General eagerly.

"Yes, Sir Orkus, please, Sir Orkus," said Polly, blushing.

"Then, then, tell us all at once, there's a good girl."

"Yes, Sir Orkus. Not as I ever encouraged him a bit to come to our cottage."

"Humph!" said the Doctor; "you always bait your trap with sweets to get the boys to come, girl."

"Please, sir, I didn't mean the young gentlemen, I meant Dick Magglin."

"Eh, what?" cried the General.

"Please, Sir Orkus, if I've ordered him away once, I've done it fifty times, and father's threatened him and beat him, but he would come."

"What! did he want to marry you?"

"Yes, Sir Orkus, but I wouldn't demean myself to listen to him."

"Of course not! a poaching vagabond. Go on, go on." Every eye was fixed on Polly, whose cheeks were scarlet, as she gave me a sharp look, full of encouragement.

"Yes, Sir Orkus, and he was always bringing me his rubbish, and wanting me to have it, hankychies, and ribbings, and a gilt brooch, as you could see wasn't gold."

"And you wouldn't take them?"

"No, Sir Orkus, never nothing, and then he said it was because I was too proud, and thought they wasn't good enough for me, and then he didn't come any more till one day when he brought me a silver watch."

A curious murmur ran through the room, and my mother ran to my side and threw her arms about my neck.

"Yes, go on, Polly," said the General, rubbing his hands. "What sort of a watch was it?"

"A little one, sir, with a fancy face and two letters cut in a round spot on the back."

"What letters were they?" said the General.

"A Hee and a B, sir."

"Eliezer Burr," said the Doctor loudly. "Hah!" and he took off his gold-rimmed spectacles, rubbed them, and began to beam.

"Should you—" began my uncle.

"No, no, no, Seaborough; allow me," said the General. "My turn. I was coming to that. Now, Polly, be careful, and don't say anything rash, because this is very serious."

"Oh yes, Sir Orkus."

"Dear me, Doctor," said the General apologetically, "I am sorry we have no h's here."

"Pray go on, Sir Hawkhurst," said the Doctor, smiling, and aspirating both in the name forcibly.

"Now, Polly, should you know that watch?"

"Oh yes, Sir Orkus; both the hands were together at twelve o'clock, and the glass was a bit scratched, and I told him I didn't believe he came by the watch honest, and that if ever he dared to come near the place again to want me to accept his rubbish, I'd take father's gun down out of the slings and give him a charge of shot in his legs."

"Then, Polly, you didn't take the watch?"

"Me, Sir Orkus!" cried Polly indignantly; "I should think not, indeed. I told him to be off, and he went away in a huff."

"In a what?"

"A huff, Sir Orkus, a huff—a passion."

"Oh, I see. And now tell me—be careful. Give me the—the—thank you. Now, Polly, is that anything like the watch?"

"Oh yes, Sir Orkus, that's the very one. If you open it, you'll hear it shuts with a very loud snap."

"So it does," said the General, putting it to the test. "And now, tell me, when was this? You don't recollect?"

"Oh yes, I do, Sir Orkus. It was nex' day after the cricket match, because I was cleaning my best shoes, as I wore at the match, when he come."

"Very good, Polly," said the General, rubbing his hands.

"Excellent!" said my uncle; "but that does not prove the man stole it."

"Why, he must have crept along the ditch behind the tent," I cried involuntarily, "and pushed his arm through. Yes, I know," I said, getting more excited, as my mother's arm tightened about me. "I saw him that evening with his face all stung by nettles."

"That ditch is full of nettles," cried Mr Hasnip.

"Good! good!" cried the General.

"But how came the watch hidden in that bin?" cried my uncle sternly.

"I know," said Cook. "Why, of course, he was afraid to keep it; and it's just like him."

"I do not follow you," said my uncle.

"Why, when he was at work in our garden, my smelling-bottle o' salts was stolen, and when I made a fuss about it, some one found it hid away behind the scullery door, where he put it."

"Then you think this man hid it there?" said my uncle.

"I'm sure of it, sir. Why, didn't I catch him one morning early coming out of the stable, and, 'What are you doing there?' I says. 'Looking for the top of my hoe,' he says, 'as I left here when I was at work. Ain't seen it, have you?' he says. 'No,' I says, 'but I see the gardener just now coming to work, and I'll call him.' 'Never mind, mum,' he says, and he went off, and nobody's seen him about here since. Oh, look there! Poor dear!"

I just saved my mother from falling, and she was helped into a chair, clinging to my hand, though, all the time, as she burst into a hysterical fit of sobbing. But she calmed down after a few minutes, and the gentlemen, who had been talking in a low voice earnestly together, now resumed their places, the Doctor clearing his voice loudly.

"Burr junior," he said in his most magisterial tones, and then he stopped short, coughed again, blew his nose, and was silent.

"Forgive me, gentlemen," he said at last. "This has been a great trouble to me—I feel moved—I have painfully hurt the feelings of a dear, sweet lady, to whom I humbly apologise, and I—I make no favourites here, but I have wrongfully suspected—but on very strong evidence, gentlemen," he said, with an appealing look round; "and you agreed with me, Mr Rebble—Mr Hasnip?"

"Yes, sir. Yes, sir," they murmured.

"Wrongfully suspected a boy to whom my wife and I were warmly attached. Burr junior—I—er—Frank, my boy, come here!"

I went up to him, flushed now and trembling.

"Shake hands, my boy," said the old man, "and thank God with me that the truth has at last prevailed. But tell me, Burr, we do not know all yet. You have been very reticent. You denied the charge stoutly, but your manner always impressed us with the belief that you knew more. Now let us clear up this sad business once for all. You will speak out now, will you not?"

"Yes, sir," I said huskily, and my cheeks burned with shame as I glanced at Mercer, who was now making horrible grimaces at me to indicate his joy.

"Then there was something?"

"Yes, sir," I said, and I glanced at my mother, whose face was now pale with fresh alarm. "Dicksee did see me find the watch there and hide it again."

"Yes; go on."

"Ever since Burr major had that watch, Mercer longed for it, and he was always talking about it, and wishing he had one."

"Well, I couldn't help that, Frank," cried Mercer; "but of course I wouldn't have taken it."

"No, Tom," I said, with a gulp, and my voice changing in spite of my efforts to be firm, and, a thorough schoolboy and companion once more, I blundered out, "but I was such a beast, I thought you had stolen it, and I wouldn't speak to save myself for fear you should be expelled."

"Oh!" cried Mercer in the midst of the silence which now fell.

Then, drawing a long breath, he went on, —

"You thought I took it and hid it?"

"Yes, Tom."

"Oh, I say, Frank, when it was all at the worst, and you were locked up, I never thought a word against you; but—" He paused for a moment, and then, forgetting that we were not alone, he rushed at me and caught my hands.

"Then you forgive me?" I said.

"Why, of course," he cried. "Oh, Frank, I am glad!"

The Doctor coughed loudly, and our action seemed to have given the gentlemen present colds. Then the Doctor signed to his wife, whispered to her, and she left the room with Cook and Polly Hopley. Next he signed to Mr Rebble and Mr Hasnip, who both came and shook hands with me, bowed to the General and my uncle, and they too left the room, with Burr major and Dicksee.

"Mercer," said the Doctor then.

"No, no," cried the General; "let him stop. Come here, sir: over here."

The General spoke in so severe a voice, and frowned so much, that Mercer looked at him shrinkingly, and the harder as the old man brought his hand down heavily upon his shoulder—Tom's face seeming to say, "What have I done now?"

"So, sir, you have been longing for a watch all this time, have you, eh?"

"Yes, Sir Hawkhurst," said Tom slowly. Then, with animation, "But I did always try very hard not to want one."

"Then you shall have one, as good a one as money can buy."

Mercer's face was a picture of astonishment, changing to doubt and then to delight as he fully realised that the General meant it.

"Do you hear, Frank? Oh, I say!" Then, catching the old man's hand in both of his; he cried, "May I have a hunter?"

"You shall, my boy. And Frank Burr, you shall have one too."

"No," said my uncle, "that's my present. Frank, my lad, we've all been wrong; but I can't apologise, for you led us astray."

"Oh, that's enough, Seaborough," cried the General. "The boys don't want to hear another word. Eh?—you were going to speak, Doctor."

"Only a few words, sir. Colonel Seaborough, Mrs Burr, I cannot tell you how grieved I am for this painful episode—believe me."

My mother went to the Doctor and placed her hand in his.

"Pray say no more," she said gently.

"I will not, my dear madam, for your looks tell me that I am forgiven for my share of the mental agony I have caused you.—Of course, you will take your son away and place him in another school?"

"Eh? What for?" said the General sharply. "You don't want him to go, do you, stuffy boy?"

"Oh no, sir," cried Mercer.

"Do you want to go, Frank?"

"No, sir," I said eagerly; "I should like to stay."

"Of course," cried the General. "He's to stop, eh, Seaborough?"

"I should regret it, if he left," said my uncle.

"To be sure you would, and I should miss him. Don't expel him, Doctor."

"I? I should only be too glad if he stays."

"Then that's all right," said the General. "Ah, here is Mrs Brown."

He crossed to place a chair for her, and then stood looking from one to the other.

"Yes," he said, "that's it. Ladies, will you honour a solitary old man with your company to dinner at my place this evening? Doctor, will you bring your wife? Seaborough and Mrs Burr, pray come over with me now, and, if the Doctor does not mind, I should like to take these two boys back with us."

Consent was given directly, and the rest of that day was spent in a manner which made me pretty well forget the troubles which had gone before.

Chapter Thirty One.

The General pressed so hard that my mother and my uncle remained at his place for a couple of days longer, driving over in the General's carriage on the third day to say good-bye to me before returning home, and, to Mercer's great delight, a packet was placed in his hand after he had been fetched, with strict orders not to look at it till the carriage had gone. I already had one in my pocket, and in addition a smaller one that I was charged to deliver elsewhere.

Then the farewell was said, and, as soon as the carriage was out of sight, I looked at Mercer, he at me, and with a unity of purpose that was not surprising, we rushed off to the yard and up the rough steps to the loft, where we laid our packets down, and hesitated to cut the strings.

Again we looked at each other, and Mercer at last said huskily, —

"Hadn't we better open 'em? I *am* hungry, but they're rather small and square for cakes."

"Get out!" I said. "Cakes indeed! Here, let's see."

"Whose shall we open first?" whispered Mercer.

"Yours."

"No, yours."

"Both together then."

"Right. Draw knives—Open knives—Cut!"

The strings were divided to the moment, and then the sealing-wax which fastened the brown paper further was broken, and two white paper packets were revealed, also carefully sealed up. This wax was broken in turn, and with trembling hands we removed the white paper, to find within something hard and square wrapped in a quantity of tissue paper.

We paused again, feeling breathless with excitement, and looked at each other.

"Ready?" I said, and we tore off the tissue till a couple of little morocco cases were revealed, and again we paused before unhooking the fastenings, and opening little lids lined with white satin, while below, in crimson velvet, tightly-fitting beds, lay a couple of bright silver watches.

Oh, the delight of that first watch! It fixed itself so in my memory that I shall never forget it. The bright, dazzling look of the engine turning, showing different lights and seeming to be in motion as the position of the watch is changed; the round spot in the ring where the spring was pressed for the case to fly open and show the face with its Roman numerals; and then the ticking—that peculiar metallic sound like nothing else. Words will not describe the satisfaction we boys felt as we stood examining our presents.

"Why, they're both exactly alike," said Mercer at last. "I say, take care, or we shall get 'em mixed."

There was no fear of that after the first few minutes, for further examination showed that they were numbered, and those numbers were burned into our memories at once.

"Oh, I say," cried Mercer at last, "talk about watches! these are something like. Why, one of 'em's worth a dozen of old Eely's."

"Don't talk about it!" I said, with a shiver; and after carefully opening mine so as to gaze at the works, Mercer of course following suit, the watches were carefully returned to their cases and placed in our pockets.

"What shall we do now?" asked Mercer; "go and show them to the boys?"

"No; it will only make them disappointed. Let's go down at once to Bob Hopley's."

"What for?"

"To take this."

Mercer looked at the smaller packet I had for a few moments.

"What is it?" he said.

"A present from my mother for Polly."

"Oh! Why, it must be a watch."

"No," I said; "I think it's a brooch or a pair of earrings."

"Oh, won't she be pleased!"

We walked down to the lodge, where Polly met us at the door, eager to point to a tin of jam pigs which she had just drawn from the oven.

"I was wishing some of you young gentlemen would come," she said. "They're red currant and raspberry. You're just in time."

Polly's ideas of our visits to the cottage were always connected with tuck, and she looked at me wonderingly when I said we had not come for that.

"There aren't nothing more the matter, is there?" she cried, as she set down her tin.

I set her mind at rest by taking the packet from my breast.

"Is—is that for me?" she said, with her face flushing with excitement.

"Yes; open it."

I saw her little red, rough hands tremble as she untied the string, and after removing one or two papers, all of which she carefully smoothed out flat, she came upon a thin morocco case.

"Oh, it's earrings!" she cried; "and you two have bought 'em for me, because I—because I—because I—How do you open it? Oh my! It's a little watch."

"Yes," I said, "a watch."

"Yours, Master Burr junior?" she cried. "Oh, it was good of you to come and show it to me!"

"No, Polly," I cried, looking at it eagerly. "I told you. It's for you."

"But—but—it can't be."

"Yes," I said, pointing to a little three-cornered note. "Open that and see what it says."

Polly's trembling fingers hurriedly opened the paper, which she read, and then handed to me, Mercer looking over me as I held it out and read these simple words:—

"For Mary Hopley, with a mother's thanks."

I saw the tears start to the girl's eyes, and there was something very charming in her next act, which was to carefully fold the note and kiss it before placing it in her bosom.

"I shan't never part with that," she said softly; and then she stood gazing down at the watch, till a shadow darkened the door, and big Bob Hopley came striding in.

"Hullo, young gents!" he said; "how are you? Why Polly! What's—"

"A present, father, from Mr Burr junior's mar. Ought I to take it?"

"Yes," I cried eagerly, "of course. You don't know how happy you made me by what you said. She is to keep it, isn't she, Bob Hopley?"

"Well," said the big fellow, holding the little watch carefully and admiringly in his great brown hand, — "well, seeing, my lass, how it's give, and why it's give, and who give it, and so on, I almost think you might."

Chapter Thirty Two.

A man once said to me that our brains are very much like a bee's honeycomb, all neat little cells, in which all our old recollections are stored up ready for use when we want them. There lie all our adventures and the results of all our studies, everything we have acquired in our lives.

Perhaps he was right—I don't know—I never saw my brains; but, if he is, some of us have got the cells so tightly packed together, and in so disorderly a way, that when we want some special thing which we learned, we cannot find it; it is so covered up, so buried, that it is quite hopeless to try and get at it. This is generally the case with me, and, consequently, there are no end of school adventures during my long stay at "Old Browne's" that I cannot set down here, for the simple reason that I cannot get at them, or, if I do, I find that the cell is crushed and the memory mixed up all in a muddle with wax.

I suppose I did not pack them into the comb properly. Oddly enough, my recollections are clearest about the part of my days which preceded the trouble over the watch.

After that, life seemed to go on at such a rapid rate that there was not time to put all the events away so that they could be found when wanted for further use.

Still, I recall a few things which preceded my leaving the school for Woolwich.

There was that hot June day down by the river—little stream it really was—that ran through a copse about half a mile from the school. It was on Farmer Dawson's land, down in the hollow of the valley, up one side of which lay his big range of hop-gardens.

The Doctor paid him a certain rent for the right of the boys going down to this place, where a great dam had been built up of clay and clinkers. It was not all new, but done up afresh after lying a couple of hundred years or so untouched. All round it, Farmer Dawson used to send his men in the winter to cut down the coppice, trimming the ash and eating chestnut trees down to the stumps to make the young growth into hop-poles; but when the Doctor offered to take it and repair the dam, the hop-poles were left to grow and form a beautiful screen round this dell.

I remember what interest we boys took in it during one winter, when the Doctor had set a lot of men who were out of work to dig and wheel the clinkers and clay, a barrowful of one, and then a barrowful of the other, along the dam; and with old Lomax to give orders, we all marched and counter-marched in our thickest boots over the top of the dam, to trample it all down strong and firm.

You will think, perhaps, that it was easy enough to get clay, and so it was, for a thick bed lay only a few yards from the stream; but what about the clinkers?

I'll tell you. There was quite a mine of them, hard, shiny fragments, some of which had run just like so much black or brown glass.

How did they get there, looking like so much volcanic slag? Why, they were the refuse from a huge iron furnace that used to be in full blast in the days of Queen Elizabeth or King James, and the dam we were repairing, after it had been grown over with trees, and the water reduced to a little stream, belonged to one of the old hammer ponds whose waters were banked up to keep a sufficiency to turn the big wheel that worked the tilt-hammers and perhaps blew the iron furnace till it roared.

For that peaceful rural part of Sussex was in those days a big forest, whose wood was cut down and made into charcoal. The forest is gone, and only represented now by patches of copsewood saved for cutting down every ten years or so for poles; but the iron lies there still in great veins or beds, though it is no longer dug out, the iron of to-day being found and smelted north and west, where coal-pits are handy; and the ironmasters of Sussex, whose culverins and big guns were famous all the world round, have given place to farmers and hop-growers, where grimy men used to tend the glowing metal and send it running into form and mould.

I have mentioned before how there used to be a furnace by Sir Hawkhurst's penstock pond, where the embankment was still firm, but there had been a far more extensive one here, and the refuse went, as I have said, to repair the dam.

When this was done, the Doctor had a long low shed built and thatched and supplied with form-like seats, and a diving-board arranged, beside steps down in the shallow part for the younger boys, and the whole when finished made a glorious long pool of about an acre in extent, very deep by the dam, and sloping gradually up to a few inches only of water where the stream trickled in. And there, on the hot sunny afternoons, beautifully shut in by green waving trees, and with the water when we came to bathe so clear that you could see every stone on the gravelly bottom, we boys used to collect for a regular water frolic. But, as you may suppose, the water was not so clean when we had done, the paddling of the little fellows in the shallows discolouring it from end to end.

That special hot June afternoon cricket had been voted too tiring, and we had all gone down to the bathing-place, the non-swimmers having strict injunctions not to pass a couple of posts about half-way between the stream and the dam.

It was always Lomax's duty to come down with us at bathing times, and, with his walking cane under his arm, he used to stride to and fro along the bank, barking out orders to the lesser boys, who were constantly breaking the rules, and getting toward the deeper water.

By that time I was a pretty fair swimmer, and had got over my natural nervousness to the extent that I was ready to dive off the board into the deepest part, and go anywhere with ease. Mercer was better than I, and Hodson better still; Burr major, from being so long, bony, and thin, was anything, as Mercer used to say, but eely in the water,—puffing and working hard to keep himself afloat; while

Dicksee, though naturally able to swim easily from his plumpness, was, I think, the greatest coward we had there.

The water was delightfully warm that afternoon, but it soon got to be very thick, though that did not trouble us in the least, and we were in the full tide of our enjoyment, swimming races, diving, and playing one another tricks, while all the time, sharp and short from the bank, Lomax's orders would be snapped out.

"You, young Jenkins, what did I tell you? Phibbs, you're the wrong side of the posts. Mullins, if I have to speak to you again, I shall report you. Wilson, if you don't go up into the shallows, I shall fetch you out."

"Can't," cried the impudent young dog.

"Then I'll send a big boy to fetch you, sah. How dare you, sah! What do you mean, sah?"

Then there would be the pad, pad, pad, pad of naked feet, as a boy ran along the diving-board, sprang out, and then splash he would be into the water.

And so it went on, with some tiring, and going and sitting in the sun, which played the part of warm towel, till they would come in again, for it was declared to be the most delightful day we had had.

Then Mr Rebble and Mr Hasnip came down to see how we were getting on, and stood cheering and encouraging the timid ones, who were loth to get duckings by learning to swim.

I had been trying for some time, right out in the middle, to float without moving, while Mercer and Hodson in turn had their tries. Burr major was swimming from side to side, blowing like a grampus, and other boys were about us unnoticed, for we were too much occupied over our own efforts to heed them, when all at once, as I lay back with the water nearly all over my face, and my hands right down paddling softly, a wave turned me a little on one side; I raised my head, and a horrible yell sent a cold chill through me.

"What is it? the matter?" cried Mercer.

"Help! help!" shrieked Burr major, who was only a few yards away, splashing the water heavily as he swam with all his might for the side.

But he only shrieked out, "Help! help!" in a horror-stricken voice, and we all swam toward him as he made for the shore, all the lesser boys splashing out as fast as they could, to congregate shivering on the bank.

"What is it? What's the matter?" cried Mr Rebble, hurrying along the path, while Lomax came running round from the other side, for he had crossed the dam to act the part of water shepherd over some of his wet lambs.

But Burr major only kept on shrieking, "Help! help!"

"What's the matter, boys?" cried Mr Hasnip, who was now standing on the bank just where Burr major would land.

"Don't know, sir."

"He's frightened, sir."

"Got the cramp."

This, and half a dozen other replies, came in a confused chorus, as we swam on in a half circle behind Burr major ready to help him if he ceased to swim.

But he was striking out strongly, though his voice grew hoarser and more weak as he neared the edge, where, ghastly-looking and shivering, he snatched at Mr Rebble's hand, and allowed himself to be helped out.

"Don't make that noise, Burr major," cried the master. "What's the matter with you? Speak."

"Gone down—drowning! Oh—oh!"

He said this last in a husky whisper, and with white rings showing round his wide-open eyes, he turned and pointed toward the middle of the great pool.

"Who—who has?" cried Mr Hasnip frantically, and we looked eagerly from one to the other, but no one seemed to be missing.

"Speak, sir. Who is? Where?" cried Mr Rebble, seizing Burr major by his wet shoulders and shaking him. "Don't go on like that. Speak."

But Burr major made one gesticulation, and then his limbs seemed to double up beneath him, as he dropped fainting on the grass.

"What is it? cramp?" cried Lomax, coming up, and taking off his coat. "I'll soon put that right."

"No; he says some one is drowning."

"What?" roared Lomax wildly. "One of my lads! Here, who's missing?"

There was no answer, and the boys all gazed in a frightened way at each other.

"Here, Burr major, rouse up," cried Mr Rebble, shaking the long, thin lad, as he knelt down on one knee. "Who was it? Any one with you?"

The boy's eyes opened a little, he looked up wildly, and, trying to rise, pointed again to the middle of the pool.

"Was—by me," he moaned—"went down."

"Never mind who it is," roared Lomax, literally tearing off his clothes. "Now, boys—divers. In with you!"

His loudly-spoken command acted like magic upon us, and Mercer, Hodson, and I dashed into the water abreast, and swam for the middle of the pool, where in turn we began to dive down and try if we could find our luckless school-fellow, whoever he might be, but without result.

"That's right," cried Lomax, as I came up, for he had joined us in an incredibly short space of time. "Keep trying. This way."

He stretched out his arms, joined his hands as high as he could above his head, so that their weight should help to sink him, and he slowly went down out of sight, while, as fast as our efforts would allow, we boys went down and tried to search about, gradually extending the distance from each other in obedience to the orders shouted to us from the bank.

I suppose it was in ten feet water, about thirty yards from the great embankment, where we dived down most, but our attempts became more feeble, and I found myself at last swimming heavily close to Lomax, whose fierce-looking head suddenly rose close to my hand.

"Does nobody know anything about where the boy went down?" he roared; but there was no answer, and he panted out, —

"Take care of yourselves, boys. Don't overdo it. We must keep on, but it's unkind work."

We dived again and again, till I felt that I could do no more, and once more I was close up to Lomax, who had been down till he was almost completely exhausted.

"Oh, my lad! my lad!" he groaned, as he began to tread water slowly, "I'd have given anything sooner than this should have happened. Here, you, Burr junior, you're spent, boy. Swim ashore."

"I'm not," I said. "I'm going down again."

"I'm done," groaned Lomax. "I seem to have no more strength."

Shouts and orders came from the bank.

"They're saying we don't dive," said Mercer piteously.

"Not diving?" cried Lomax. "Well!"

As he spoke, he sank again, and the water closed in a swirl over his head, while, after taking a long breath, I dived under into the depths, with the water thundering in my ears, as, during what seemed to be a long space of time, though less than a minute, of course, I groped and swam about till a curious sensation of confusion came over me, and, frightened now, I touched something and clung to it wildly, believing in my startled state that it was Lomax.

The next instant I was at the surface, surprised to see the old sergeant making a rush at me, as he uttered a shout. Then he seized something by me, and I knew that I had brought one of my schoolfellows to the surface.

We swam ashore, to reach it soon after Lomax, who had borne the white, limp figure we had rescued into the dressing shed.

"Boys who can run!" shouted Mr Rebble. "Blankets, quick!"

A dozen boys dashed off, and Lomax panted,—

"You two—work him like this—gently. I'll relieve you directly."

He left the two masters rubbing and moving the boy's arms to their full extent, and pressing them to his sides, while he hurried on some clothes, and, shivering with horror and exhaustion, we followed his example, while, with my ears ringing, I heard Mercer gasp out,—

"Poor old Dicksee! Oh, Frank, I hope he ain't drowned."

But as, after our hurried dressing, we saw him lying there rigid and cold, it seemed as if the boy would never say another unkind word to a soul.

By this time Lomax had relieved the two masters, and with all the vigour of his strong arms he was trying to produce artificial respiration somewhat after the fashion that has of late been laid down as a surgical law, but apparently without avail.

The blankets had been brought, the boys, all but we few elder ones, sent back to the school, and a messenger had gone for the nearest medical man, so that nothing more could be done than was in progress.

"I'm afraid it's a hopeless case," said Mr Rebble, with a groan.

"Never say die, sir," cried Lomax. "I remember a lad of ours in my regiment was swept with his horse down the torrent below where we were fording a river away yonder in India. He seemed to be quite gone when we got him ashore half a mile lower down, but we rubbed and worked him about for quite three hours, taking it in turns, before he gave a sign of life. But he opened his eyes at last, and next day he was 'most as well as ever. What time do you expect Doctor Browne back, sir?"

"Not till quite late to-night. And what news for him! — what a shock for them both!"

"Shock!" said Lomax. "Here, you take a turn now, Mr Hasnip; we mustn't stop for a moment."

Mr Hasnip, whose coat was off and sleeves turned up, sprang to his side and went on.

"I'll relieve you again soon, sir," said Lomax, wiping his dripping forehead. "But how was it, Mr Burr major?"

"I—I don't know," said my school-fellow, starting. "I think he suddenly remembered it was so deep, and he turned frightened, for he went under all at once and right down, and then I cried for help."

"Better have lent him a hand," said Lomax gruffly. "Well, Mr Hasnip, sir, feel him coming to?"

"No, no," said the second master dolefully. "He is dead! he is dead!"

"Not he, sir," cried Lomax roughly. "We're going to bring him round; all we've been doing has helped him, and it's a long way off three hours. Here, let's have him out in the sunshine, please. I believe in the sun."

The poor fellow was carried out, the two masters each taking a corner of the blanket on which he lay, Lomax and I the others.

It was quickly done, and then Lomax recommenced rubbing, working the boy's chest so as to make it contract and expand, and all the time with perspiration dropping from his brow. Mr Rebble and Mr Hasnip both relieved him, and we boys did our best to help; but the afternoon glided on, no doctor arrived, and we felt chilled and hopeless, till all at once, after a rest, Lomax had begun again apparently as fresh as ever, and to our horror he suddenly began to whistle a merry tune.

"Lomax!" cried Mr Hasnip.

"What's the matter, sir?"

"For goodness' sake—at a time like this—it is too—"

"Why, haven't I got cause to whistle, sir?" cried the sergeant merrily. "What did I tell you? Only wanted time and plenty o' muscle."

"What! is he reviving?"

"No, sir, he's revived," said Lomax. "Look at the colour coming, and his eyelids quivering. He'll be sitting up directly. Here, you can feel his heart beating now."

Mr Rebble went down on one knee and laid his hand upon Dicksee's breast; then, jumping up again, he caught Lomax by the wrist.

"Heaven bless you for this!" he cried, and Mr Hasnip forgot his dignity as a master, and, taking off his hat, joined us boys in a hearty, "Hip! hip! hip! hooray!" which seemed to give the finishing impetus to our treatment, for Dicksee opened his eyes wide, struggled up into a sitting position, stared about him for a few moments, and then cried, in a harsh, unpleasant tone,—

"Where's my clothes?"

As he spoke, there was the sound of footsteps, and the medical man and the messenger who had been sent to bring him hurried up.

"I'm very sorry," he said. "I was right at the other end of the parish, and had to be fetched. Is this the patient?"

Dicksee had now huddled the blanket round him, and began in a whining, queer way, —

"What's been the matter? What are you all doing? Here, somebody, I want my clothes."

"No occasion to have fetched me," said the surgeon, smiling. "You've brought him round, I see. They're often like this when they've been nearly drowned. Come, squire, can you dress yourself?"

"Yes, if you'll all go away," cried Dicksee in a snarling tone. "Who's a-going to dress with you all a-staring like that?"

"Go into the shed, Dicksee," said Mr Rebble. "Can you walk?"

"Of course, I can, sir;" and he scrambled up.

"Had a long job of course," said the surgeon; and then— "He don't seem very grateful for being brought back to life. Well, gentlemen, there's little to do. Let him go to bed soon, and have a good night's rest. I don't suppose he will be much worse in the morning when I come."

So little seemed to be the matter, that, when he was dressed, Dicksee walked slowly back to the school, Mercer and I following him with Lomax.

"Rum thing," he said, "how crusty the being nearly drowned makes a lad. Hardly worth all the trouble we took over him, eh?"

"Oh, don't talk like that, Lom!" I cried.

"But he was precious disagreeable," cried Mercer; "and after the way in which you saved his life too!"

"I didn't," I said; "it was Lom here."

"Nay, lad, you got hold of him diving, first. If it hadn't been for you, I shouldn't have had anything to rub. But I was thinking."

"What of, Lom?"

"Of how strange it is, lads, that we somehow have to help and do good to them who've always been our enemies. That chap's always hated you, Mr Burr."

"Yes, I'm afraid so, Lomax," I said, with a sigh.

"And so you go into the water, and save his life."

"Yes, 'tis rum," said Mercer. "A nasty, disagreeable beggar. I hate him. But I am glad he wasn't drowned."

Chapter Thirty Three.

Dicksee only stayed till the following Christmas, and there was a general feeling of satisfaction in the school when it was known that he was not coming back after the holidays, Mr Hasnip forgetting himself so far as to say, —

"And a good job too."

It was a great relief to be rid of him, for, as I told Mercer, he was always ten times more sneaky and aggravating during the last half, and you couldn't stoop to hitting a fellow like that, especially when you knew how easily you could lick him.

"Oh, couldn't you?" said Mercer. "I could, and I would too, if he spoke to me as he does to you."

"Not you," I said.

"I would. I believe he never forgave you for saving his life."

It was during the autumn of the following year that Mercer and I, who had grown pretty big lads by that time, and had come to be looked up to by the others as captains of the cricket eleven and of the football, were standing at the window looking out over the woods talking, and watching the flickering of the lightning in the far east. We had all come up to our dormitories, but, instead of going at once to bed, we two were talking in a low voice about what a dark, soft night it was, when all at once there was a flash that was not lightning, apparently a short distance away, followed by the report of a gun.

"Oh, Tom!" I cried; "poachers!"

"Hush! Listen!" he said; and hardly had the words left his lips before there was another report, this time without the flash being seen.

"It is poachers," I said excitedly, "and they're in Long Spinney. Why, where's Bob Hopley? They're clearing off the pheasants."

We listened, and there was another report, and another, and I was certain that it was in Sir Hawkhurst's best preserve, where I had seen Bob Hopley feeding the beautiful birds only a week before, and Mercer had come away with me feeling miserable because he could not have one to stuff.

There was another report, and I grew more and more excited.

"Tom," I whispered, "let's go down and slip out of the schoolroom window."

"And go and see. But suppose we're caught?"

"We shan't be," I whispered; "let's go. I can't bear to stand still here and listen to those birds being shot. Sir Hawkhurst is so proud of them."

"I should like to go."

"Come on, then. Bob Hopley must be asleep."

"One moment," said Tom, hesitating. "Let's ask the Doctor to let us go."

"He wouldn't," I cried impatiently.

"No, he wouldn't," said Tom. "Come on."

We opened our door softly, stole down, and reached the schoolroom unseen, after listening at the masters' sitting-room door, and hearing them chatting together. One of the windows was open to ventilate the place after its crowded state all the evening, for, in that out-of-the-way part of the country, there was no fear felt of housebreakers, and, stepping up on the desk, I thrust out my legs, and dropped lightly into the playground, to be followed by Mercer, who was breathing hard with excitement. Then, making for the grounds in front, we saw a light shining out before us on to the closely-cut lawn.

The Doctor's window was open, and, as we crept by, sheltered by the shrubs, there was another report, and the Doctor came and looked out.

"I'm afraid it's poachers, my dears," he said. "Well, I'm not a gamekeeper."

We hurried along the lawn, leaving him looking out, ran lightly along the grassy marge of the carriage drive, and passed through the swing gate, but stopped short.

"Caught," I said to myself, as a tall, dark figure stepped out before us.

"Hallo! where are you young gents going?"

"Oh, Lom, don't tell," I panted. "There are poachers down in Long Spinney."

"I know," he said; "I heard 'em."

"And we're going down to tell Bob Hopley."

"On the sly?"

"Yes; the Doctor don't know. You won't get us into a scrape?"

"Well, you know, I ought to; but—"

"You won't, Lom?"

"Well, not this time. I was just going to bed when I heard them, and thought I'd run down and ask Bob Hopley if he wanted any help. Look here!"

He held up a big oaken stick, and, thoroughly in accord, we all started off at a trot, and in a very short time were in the lane where Bob Hopley's lodge stood.

"He's off somewhere at the other side of the estate," whispered Lomax, "and they've watched him go. I say, don't you boys come near if there's a row."

"Hist! Who's that?" said a familiar voice out of the darkness. "Father?"

"No, my dear, it isn't your father."

"Oh, Mr Lomax, what shall I do? Father's been over to Hastings to-day, and hasn't come back. There's a gang of poachers clearing the Long Spinney, and it will break his heart. I thought it was him come back. There—there they go again."

For there were several reports of guns not very far away.

"I don't know what to do," said Lomax; "I've got plenty of fight in me, and I'm ready to charge down on them, but they'll be too much for one."

"I'll come with you, and bring father's gun."

"But you mustn't use it, my girl. If we could frighten them somehow. Come on, and let's try. I know—we'll all go close up and shout."

"They won't mind that," said Polly; but we went on in the darkness so quickly and quietly, that we were soon alongside a black plantation of Scotch fir-trees, in time to hear two more shots, and the heavy thuds of falling bodies.

"Now, are you ready?" whispered Lomax.

"Yes," we said, but at that moment a figure darted by us, and entered the black wood.

"One of them," said Lomax. "Let's holloa, all the same."

But, before we had drawn breath for the shout, there was a yell, a dull sound as of a stick striking a gun-barrel, then a crashing of the lower branches, cries, blows, and a loud voice calling to the poachers to give in.

"Why, it's father got back," cried Polly Hopley. "Oh, Mr Lomax, go and help, or they'll kill him!"

The old sergeant's mettle was roused, and he dashed into the wood, while, with every pulse throbbing with excitement, we boys followed the direction taken, finding that the poachers were evidently retreating, from the sounds growing farther away.

Then all at once there was the sharp report of a gun, followed by a wild shriek.

"It's father! They've shot him!" cried Polly, who, unknown to us, was close behind. "Run, run!"

We pressed on. It was impossible to run in the darkness, and as we hurried along, a voice cried just in front, —

"You've shot my mate. Take that!"

At almost the same time came a sharp rap, a loud report, and then a heavy, dull blow.

"Father, father!" shrieked Polly, as we heard the rustling and breaking of branches, evidently caused by men in full retreat.

"All right, my lass. Quick: go back to the lodge for a lantern. Man shot."

She turned and ran back, while we kept on, and reached an opening in the wood, where we made out, dimly, two tall figures, and my blood turned cold at a piteous moaning from somewhere on the ground.

"Who's there?" cried Bob Hopley's voice.

"Only us, Bob," I said. "Are you hurt?"

"Nay, lad, not a bit. I should ha' been, though, if Mr Lomax hadn't knocked up the barrel with his stick and then downed the man."

"You've murdered my mate," came from close by our feet. "You've shot him."

"First time I ever did shoot anything without a gun," said the keeper. "One of you hit him, or he did it himself."

"You shot him—you murdered him," cried the man who had spoken, struggling to his knees, and then crouching among the pine needles, holding his head with his hands as if it were broken, and rocking himself to and fro.

"Oh, if that's it," said Bob Hopley, "I must have witnesses. Mr Lomax, I've just come from Hastings. I heard the shooting o' my fezzans, and I come on with this stick. You see I've no gun, and you, too, young gents?"

"Yah! you shot him," groaned the man, who was evidently in great pain; "and then you knocked me down with the bar'l o' the gun."

"Oh, come, that won't do, lad," cried Lomax; "that was a cut from the left. I gave you that, my lad, to keep you from shooting me."

"Pair o' big cowards, that's what you are."

"Cowards, eh?" cried Lomax. "Not much o' that, Hopley. Two men with sticks against a gang of you fellows with guns. How many were you?"

"Nine on us," groaned the man. "Oh, my yed, my yed!"

"Nine of you to two honest men. Serve you right. Should have stopped at home and earned an honest living, not come stealing game."

"What!" cried the man fiercely; "'taren't stealing; they're wild birds, and as much our'n as his'n."

"You're a donkey," said Lomax. "Why, there'd be no pheasants if they weren't reared like chickens."

"That's so," said Hopley. — "Why don't that gal bring a light?"

"Here she comes," cried Mercer, for he caught sight of the dim glow of the horn lantern among the trees, and as it came nearer, Bob Hopley said, —

"Hadn't you young gents better get back to bed? this here aren't no place for you."

"No, no, don't send us away, Bob," I said; "we want to see."

"Well, you will be witnesses," he growled, and the next minute he took the lantern from Polly, who was panting with excitement.

"Oh, father dear," she cried, "are you hurt?"

"Not a bit, my lass," he cried, stooping quickly and kissing her. "Will you stay or go? It's ugly."

"Stay, father."

"Right, my lass. Now, Mr Lomax, what about this chap you downed," he continued, holding the lantern so that the light fell upon the kneeling man, whose forehead was bleeding freely. "You give it him and no mistake," he chuckled. "Here, tie this hankychy round your head, and don't bellow there like a great calf. Master

Burr junior, pick up and take charge of that gun, will you? Stop! let's see if she's loaded. No. All right. I forgot. She went off herself, I suppose," he added grimly, "when he tried to shoot Mr Lomax or me."

"I didn't," whimpered the man.

"There, don't make wuss on it by telling lies, you skulking hound," cried Bob, who was as fierce now as could be. "Mr Lomax, will you see as he don't get away?"

"He'd better try to," said the old sergeant, making his stick whizz through the air.

"Now, where's t'other?" said Hopley. "Mind, keep back, you lads. He's got a gun too, and he's hurt, and may be savage."

"Oh, take care, father!" cried Polly. "Let me go first—he wouldn't shoot a woman."

"Want to make me ashamed of myself and get hiding behind a gal's petticutt!" cried Bob. "G'long with you."

He strode forward with the lantern for a few yards, and then held it down over the spot from which a low groaning had come, but which had ceased for some minutes now.

It was very horrible, but the weird scene beneath those heavy boughs, with the keeper's burly form thrown up by the yellow glow of the lantern and the shadowy aspect of the trees around, with the light faintly gleaming on their trunks, fascinated us so that we followed Hopley with his daughter to where he stood.

"Now, squire," he said, "where are you hurt?"

The man, who seemed to be lying all of a heap, uttered a groan, and Hopley held the light nearer.

"I'm fear'd he's got it badly, Polly," growled the keeper. "Hah!"

"Oh, father!"

"None o' my doing, my lass. Here, all on you. This is a madgistrit's business, and I don't want to get credit for what I never did. So just look."

He held the lantern down for us to see.

"He's got one o' them poaching guns, you see, with a short barrel as unscrews in the middle, and he must ha' been taking it to pieces when it was loaded, and shot hisself when running among the bushes."

"Why, it's Magglin!" I shouted excitedly.

"What!" cried the keeper, holding the lantern lower, and Polly uttered a cry. "Magglin it is!" he said, as the man opened his eyes, and gazed wildly up at the lantern.

"Where are you hurt, my lad?" said the keeper quietly.

"My arm! my arm!" groaned the man piteously.

The keeper took out his knife, and, giving Mercer the lantern to hold, deliberately slit up the sleeves of the injured man's jacket and shirt.

"Hah!" he ejaculated. "He's put the whole charge o' shot through his arm, above the elbow;" and, hurriedly taking a piece of cord from his jacket pocket, Hopley made a rough tourniquet, and stopped the bleeding as much as he could.

"You, Polly," he said as he worked, "go down to the house and see Sir Orkus. Tell him all about it, and ask him to send help, and some one off for the surgeon. One of the young gents'll go with you, I dessay."

"I'll go with her," said Mercer, and they hurried away.

"There," said Hopley, as he finished his rough dressing of the wound, "I can't do no more, and we can't carry him to my place. We must wait."

"Oh, Master 'Opley, sir," groaned the unfortunate man, "is it very bad?"

"Wait and hear what the doctor says, when he comes. I didn't do it, did I?"

"No, sir; I was taking the gun to pieces, and she— Oh!"

"Bear up, man, bear up."

"I'll—I'll never go poaching any more," groaned Magglin, and his head fell back.

"Never with two arms, my lad," said the keeper. "Poor fellow! my fezzans do tempt 'em. He's fainted. Could you take the lantern, sir, and find your way to my cottage?"

"Yes," I said eagerly; "what shall I do?"

"Open the corner cupboard, sir, and you'll find a small flask on the top shelf—flask with a cup on it. Bring it, please. It's brandy: drop'll bring him round."

I went off directly, saying a word to Lomax as I went, and returning pretty quickly with the spirit, which had the effect of reviving the sufferer.

Then we waited, till at the end of half an hour we heard voices, then saw lights, and the General, with Polly, the butler, two gardeners, and the groom, came up, the coachman having driven off to fetch the doctor; and the wounded man was carefully raised, placed on a rug, and carried off by four men, Hopley and the General following with the other prisoner, who could walk, while Lomax and we two boys went slowly back toward the school, talking about the exciting scene.

"I say, young gents," said Lomax suddenly, "it'll all come out about your breaking barracks."

"Yes, Lom," I said; "we shall be found out."

"Of course. You'll have to go with me as witnesses."

"Yes. What had we better do?"

"Go and make a clean breast of it to the colonel in the morning."

"To my uncle?"

"No, no; the Doctor. Good-night."

We slipped in as we had come out, reaching our room unheard, but it was a long time before excitement would let us sleep.

Chapter Thirty Four.

It required some strength of mind to go straight to the Doctor's study next morning, tell him the whole truth, and ask for his forgiveness. But we did it, and though he looked very serious, and pointed out our wrong-doing strongly, he forgave us, and became deeply interested in the affair, making us relate all we had seen.

"I heard of the encounter as soon as I came down," he said. "Lomax ought to have sent you both back to your room. So it was that labourer. Poor fellow! I gave him a fresh chance twice over, but I'm afraid he is a ne'er-do-weel. However, he is severely punished now."

The man Lomax knocked down went before the magistrates, and was packed off to prison, but Magglin had to go up to London, to one of the great hospitals, and some months after, the chief magistrate in our district, that is to say, General Sir Hawkhurst Rye, had him up before him in his library, and punished him.

Bob Hopley told me all about it, just after he had announced, with a good many grins and winks, that Polly was— "Going to be married to master's favourite groom, and they're to live at Number 2 lodge."

"And how did he punish him, Bob?" Mercer said eagerly.

"Punished him, sir? why, he's took him on as a watcher under me. Says poachers make the best keepers; but, o' course, he can't never be a keeper, with only one arm."

"Ah," I said thoughtfully, "you said he would lose his arm."

"Yes, sir, and they took it off pretty close. But there, I think he'll mend now."

My story, (or rather my random notes), of my old school-days is pretty well ended now, though I could rake out a good deal more from the dark corners of my memory. For, after that adventure in the wood, the time soon seemed to come when Tom Mercer had to leave, to begin his course of training for a surgeon, while I was bound for Woolwich, to become a cadet.

It was a sad day for me when I first went to "Old Browne's," but it was a sadder day when I left, for I felt very sore at heart, and it required all my strength of mind to keep up a brave show.

For every one was very kind, and it was like parting from old friends whom I might never see again. The boys were all out in the front drive, where the General's carriage stood waiting to take me and my mother to meet the London mail coach, and the two gentlemen were with us. For my mother and my uncle had come down to fetch me, and say a few kind words to the Doctor and Mrs Doctor, as well as to visit Sir Hawkhurst. I saw Lomax too, and Mr Rebble and Mr Hasnip, at the door, and it seemed as if there was always some one fresh to shake hands with, the old sergeant shaking mine with both his, and his voice sounded very husky as he said, —

"You won't forget your drill, sir, nor your balance in the saddle; heels well down, and ride your horse on the curb, mind—don't forget, and—and—"

The old fellow could get no further. The tears started to his eyes, and to hide his emotion, and to save me from breaking down, he drew himself up stiffly and saluted me.

Lastly, I found that the servants were all outside too, waiting to say good-bye, and I couldn't go without stepping aside to shake hands with Cook, who uttered a loud sob, snatched me to her, and gave me a sounding kiss.

Then I was back on the steps saying my farewells to the Doctor and his wife, and I felt that I had bade every one now good-bye but Tom Mercer, who was to leave the following day, but, to my intense disappointment, he was missing; and, time pressing, I was at last obliged to climb into the britzska, where my mother, my uncle, and the General were already seated, the word was given, the coachman touched his horses as soon as the groom had climbed to his side, and the boys nearly frightened them into a headlong gallop, as they burst out into a volley of cheers, mingled with, "Good-bye, Burr junior! Good luck to you, soldier!" and amidst the waving of caps from the lads, and handkerchiefs from the door, I stood up in the carriage and roared excitedly, —

"Where's old Senna?"

I faintly heard the words, "Don't know," and I stood looking about wildly, full of bitter disappointment at leaving without seeing him.

I was standing up at the back, where my mother had the other seat, the two old officers being before us, but there was no Tom Mercer, and I was about to sit down, feeling that the poor fellow could not face the farewell, when, at the turn of the road, there on the bank stood Polly Hopley, with a parcel in one hand and a bunch of flowers in the other, and beside her, Bob Hopley in his brown velveteens, his gun under his left arm and his hat in his hand.

As we trotted by, the parcel and bouquet fell into the carriage, and I waved my hand back to them till we were out of sight, when I found that my mother was holding the flowers, which had her name on a label like that used with a doctor's bottle, while the parcel was directed to me.

I couldn't help my face working as I looked from one to the other.

"Cheer up, my lad," cried the General, as my mother pressed my hand, for I had sunk down beside her on the seat.

"Of course he will," cried my uncle; "soldiers cheer up directly. I say, Frank, the Doctor gave you a splendid character, but it wasn't wanted. Your popularity staggers me."

"But I haven't seen poor old Senna," I cried.

"Seen whom?" said my uncle, laughing.

"Poor old Tom Mercer," I cried, when a hand from the back knocked my cap over my eyes, and a familiar voice shouted, —

"'Bye, Frankie. Hooray! 'ray! 'ray! 'ray!"

There was Tom Mercer's face looking at us over the hood at the back, for he had darted out from the hedge as the carriage passed the corner half a mile from the school, climbed up behind, and was holding on with one hand as he clutched at me with the other.

Then quickly—nay, more quickly than it has taken me to tell it—he let go and dropped down into the road, where I could see him standing waving his cap till a curve hid him from sight; and I once more sank into my place too low-spirited to think, for my happy school-days were at an end, and there before me in the dim distance, toward which I was being hurried fast as two good mares could trot, was the great gateway of a fresh life, through which lay the road to be followed in my progress to become a soldier and a man.

The End.